PUFFIN BOOKS

Back Home

Michelle Magorian's first ambition was to be an actress and, after three years' study at the Bruford College of Speech and Drama, she went to mime school in Paris. All this time she had been secretly scribbling stories, and in her mid-twenties she became interested in children's books and decided to write one herself. The result was *Goodnight Mister Tom* – a winner of the Guardian Award and the International Reading Association Award – which she has also adapted as a musical with the composer Gary Carpenter, and it has been adapted for the stage by playwright David Wood. Since then she has published several novels, including award-winning *Back Home* and *Just Henry* (published by Egmont), which won the Costa Book Award in 2008. She has also published poetry and short-story collections and picture books for young children.

Michelle lives in Petersfield, where she continues with both her acting and writing careers.

Michelle Magorian

Back Home

PUFFIN

For Kay, and in memory of her best friend, my mother

*My thanks to all the people in England and America who talked with me,
wrote letters, sent tapes, gave me access to archive material, showed me areas of
Devon and Connecticut, and generously put up with me*

PUFFIN BOOKS

Published by the Penguin Group
Penguin Books Ltd, 80 Strand, London WC2R 0RL, England
Penguin Group (USA) Inc., 375 Hudson Street, New York, New York 10014, USA
Penguin Group (Canada), 90 Eglinton Avenue East, Suite 700, Toronto, Ontario, Canada M4P 2Y3
(a division of Pearson Penguin Canada Inc.)
Penguin Ireland, 25 St Stephen's Green, Dublin 2, Ireland (a division of Penguin Books Ltd)
Penguin Group (Australia), 250 Camberwell Road, Camberwell, Victoria 3124, Australia
(a division of Pearson Australia Group Pty Ltd)
Penguin Books India Pvt Ltd, 11 Community Centre, Panchsheel Park, New Delhi – 110 017, India
Penguin Group (NZ), 67 Apollo Drive, Rosedale, Auckland 0632, New Zealand
(a division of Pearson New Zealand Ltd)
Penguin Books (South Africa) (Pty) Ltd, 24 Sturdee Avenue, Rosebank, Johannesburg 2196, South Africa

Penguin Books Ltd, Registered Offices: 80 Strand, London WC2R 0RL, England

puffinbooks.com

First published by Viking Kestrel 1985
Published in Puffin Books 1987
This edition published 2011

2

Text copyright © Michelle Magorian, 1985
All rights reserved

The moral right of the author has been asserted

Set in Baskerville
Printed in Great Britain by Clays Ltd, St Ives plc

British Library Cataloguing in Publication Data
A CIP catalogue record for this book is available from the British Library

ISBN: 978-0-141-33226-0

www.greenpenguin.co.uk

MIX
Paper from
responsible sources
FSC™ C018179
www.fsc.org

Penguin Books is committed to a sustainable
future for our business, our readers and our
planet. This book is made from paper certified
by the Forest Stewardship Council.

I

'Do they have movies in England?'

'Sure they do!' said the boy in the beige suit. He was sitting cross-legged on the cabin floor, attempting to draw a liner on a sketch-pad.

A small girl was curled up on the bottom bunk nearest him.

'Films,' she interrupted. 'They call 'em films.'

On the third bunk above, a plump sixteen-year-old girl was lying on her back. She gave a deep sigh. 'I wish we coulda come back a few months later,' she murmured.

The small girl leaned out to look at her.

'Aren't you pleased to be going back to England?'

'I guess,' she said unconvincingly. 'It's just that Frank Sinatra's going to be at the Paramount Theater in November and I won't be there.'

Rusty, who was lying on one of the bunks opposite glanced up in her direction.

Poor Susie, she thought. She had hardly said a word the entire crossing. Even when she had been sea-sick, she hadn't whined or made a fuss but had just gazed vacantly into the distance.

After the previous night's farewell concert, given by all the groups of children and teenagers to the crew and each other, Rusty had sat next to her. She had watched the others play party games and had felt herself growing more and more distant from them.

Just as we've made friends, she had thought, we have to say goodbye all over again. The sailors had given them ice-cream. All the kids had adopted their own special sailor. Rusty's was from Brooklyn. 'Irish' they called him.

Rusty had stared through the crowd of children to where he was sitting. He had spotted her and given her a friendly wink. She had forced herself to smile back and had then turned to Susie. Alarmed at the despair in her eyes, she had put her arm round her.

'Susie,' she whispered. 'It'll be O.K. You'll see.'

But Susie hadn't even looked at her.

'I was going steady with a boy at my school,' she said quietly. 'I miss him so much.' And she glanced hastily into the palm of her hands. 'I may never see him again.'

Rusty rolled over on to her side and tried to catch her attention, but Susie's face was now deep in the pillow. Below her, a small group of children continued to chat and play 'jacks' on the floor.

'You'll be able to hear him much better on a phonograph,' said the boy in the beige suit. 'If you went to his concert you wouldn't hear anything for all the squealing.'

'Gramophone,' said the small girl. 'They call 'em gramophones.'

'It's not the same as seeing him,' Susie muttered.

Rusty glanced down at her open suitcase. A few weeks ago, she had been staying at the Omsks' summer cottage right by the ocean. Now she was here, in a cabin that had thirty-six bunks squashed together in tiers of three.

As she gazed at the contents of her case she could hardly see them, so blurred were her eyes. She blinked her tears away and wiped her face hurriedly with a handkerchief.

'Now, remember,' Grandma Fitz had said, 'you have to think yourself into being a pioneer. I came out to America, a scrap of a thing with all I owned in a carpet-bag, and I didn't know what the heck I'd find. You show 'em that a bit of that old American pioneer spirit has rubbed off on you.'

And Grandpa had added, 'You don't want 'em to think you're an old misery-guts.'

2

Only a couple of weeks back, she had been standing on the New York docks saying goodbye to them all: Aunt Hannah, Uncle Bruno, her American sisters, Grandma Fitz and Gramps, Skeet and Janey, her best girlfriend. Janey hadn't seemed to realize what was happening. She had looked as excited as if Rusty was just making some kind of a weekend trip. They had both vowed eternal friendship and had promised to be pen-pals for ever.

If only Skeet was with her, then she wouldn't feel so lonely. She wondered what he was doing. Probably out in the rowing boat with the fishing tackle. For four years they had roomed together, and even in her fifth year their bedrooms had been next door to one another. She couldn't imagine life without Skeet close by. This summer he had turned fourteen and his voice had started getting all croaky. Now she'd never get to hear him sounding grown-up. Heck, she was crying again.

She slammed the case shut and blew her nose. Uncle Bruno had been crying, too, when he had said goodbye, and he was a man, so it couldn't be so bad that *she* was doing it. When he had given her a final hug, he had held her so tight that she had thought that perhaps he wasn't going to let her go after all. But then one of the escorts had touched them and they had broken apart, and Rusty had felt herself being pushed towards the gangway. She had felt so dazed walking up it, as if she had been winded by a fast-flying baseball – only instead of the sick feeling going away, it stayed there, deep and heavy in the pit of her stomach.

Suddenly the cabin door was flung open and a freckled teenage girl rushed in.

'Hey, you guys, come on up,' she said excitedly. 'Everyone else is up on deck. We can see the quayside!'

Rusty lay on her back and listened to the stampede of footsteps and the yells as the other children fled to join her. As soon as they had gone, she slipped out from her bunk, smoothed her flared green-and-white-check skirt out and pulled down her large lemon cardigan.

A small hand-mirror was propped against a book on one of the bunks. Rusty peered into it. It had taken her all morning to manoeuvre her dark-red hair into ringlets. Janey had taught her to do that before leaving, but the other girls on board had helped her along a bit. She straightened the green bows that held her hair back from a central parting. One of her ribbons looked crumpled through endless jiggering around with. She just couldn't seem to get each side level with the other.

She glanced down at the white toes of her brown-and-white saddle-shoes and wiped them along the backs of her legs.

At least her bobby socks didn't look so grubby, now that they were inside out and plumped out a bit. It had been so difficult keeping them clean on the ship.

She was about to join the others when she heard muffled sniffs from the far end of the cabin. She edged her way past the rows of bunks.

On a lower bunk in a corner sat a dark-haired girl in a plaid red-and-green dress. She was thirteen, a year older than Rusty. Like Rusty's had been, her case was open. Half the contents were strewn across the floor.

She looked up, startled. 'I was just checkin' I had everything,' she blurted out.

Rusty stared at all the bottles on her bed.

'Vitamins,' she explained anxiously. 'My Aunt Joan says you can't have too many.'

Wedged in among her clothes Rusty noticed Palmolive soap, nylons, linen and peanut butter.

'Aunt Joanie,' she said, 'she knows all about English rationing. Do you think our luggage will be all right?' she added, and a look of terror came into her eyes.

'Sure it will,' said Rusty.

The girl blew her nose.

4

'I guess I must have a cold.'

'Yeah,' said Rusty. 'Same as the one I got.'

They smiled guiltily at each other.

'Can I go up on deck with you?' asked the girl.

'Sure you can,' said Rusty.

The girl swept the bottles off her bunk into the suitcase and banged it shut.

Arm in arm, they squeezed their way down the narrow aisle between the bunks. At the doorway the girl hesitated.

'I've always known I'd be coming back to England,' she murmured. 'I guess I really didn't believe it.'

'Me neither,' confided Rusty.

The boy in the beige suit had saved them a place by the rail.

'How does my hair look?' asked Rusty. 'My ribbons don't look scrunched up, do they?'

He had a go at straightening the bows, but no sooner had he pushed one up higher than the other one looked too low.

'Oh,' he said, giving up, 'you look swell.'

'You really mean it?'

'Sure I do.' He looked puzzled for a moment. 'Do you know you have your cardigan on back of front?'

'Sure I do. It's the fashion.'

He grinned.

'Oh, you're just teasin'.'

He stepped back. 'How 'bout me? I brushed my hair.'

Rusty didn't have the heart to tell him that the knees of his suit looked as if he had been scrubbing the decks with them, and anyway, his hair did look tidier than usual.

'You look swell, too.'

Elbows on the rails, they gazed out at the approaching docks.

The ship moved heavily and slowly forward. It was a

dull sort of a day, thought Rusty, especially for summer, and the buildings around the docks seemed so ugly. She knew that they were still at war with Japan but somehow she had imagined that, because the war in Europe was over, everything would look bright and cheery.

A small group of people were clustered around the docks. Rusty grew aware that all the other children had stopped speaking and were just staring quietly at the great smoking funnels in the distance and the tugs in the nearby harbour.

Someone began waving. Rusty and the dark-haired girl joined in and soon all the other children and the waiting crowd were raising their arms. As the ship drew closer to land they could see that most of the group was made up of women.

'I guess those must be our mothers,' whispered the boy.

'Uh-huh.'

'Which one is yours?'

Rusty didn't recognize any of them. 'Uh. I don't think she's arrived yet. I guess she's waiting somewhere else.'

He nodded. 'Guess mine must be, too.'

They both began waving again.

'Do you think,' began the dark-haired girl hesitantly. 'Do you think they'll recognize us?'

'Sure they will,' he said. 'I know I've growed some, but my family, I mean,' he added, 'my American family, sent photographs of me.'

Mine too, thought Rusty, but not for nearly a year; and in the last ten months she had grown inches taller. She was big enough for some of Kathryn's clothes now, and Aunt Hannah had even bought her some brassieres.

She started waving vigorously again, aware that she was smiling and feeling very shy. Unusual for her.

Suddenly there was a great jostling of people around her. One of the escorts was ushering a group of children past her towards the cabins to collect their luggage. Her two companions turned to follow them.

Rusty remained on her own by the railing. A flock of seagulls dipped and soared around the dark grey buildings that surrounded the docks. So this is it, she thought. England.

2

Rusty was standing in the crowd on the quayside, when suddenly she found herself being hugged tightly by a woman in her thirties, dressed in green. After a few seconds Rusty realized that the woman was her mother. She was smaller and thinner than she had remembered, and her hair was now cut short. Rusty couldn't help staring at the woman's face. It was the first time in five years that she had seen it. For a moment it seemed as if they had never parted.

'Hi,' she said.

'Hello.'

Peggy Dickinson knew from last year's photographs that Virginia had grown up. When she had been evacuated from England in 1940, she had been small and quiet, with spindly legs and milk-teeth, a far cry from the twelve-year-old girl who now stood in front of her, tall, robust and tanned, with thick long hair and intense green eyes.

Peggy let go of her hurriedly. 'Did you have a good crossing?' she asked awkwardly.

'It was O.K.'

'Hey, Rusty!' yelled a voice from behind.

A boy in the crowd who was being led away by his mother was waving. 'So long,' he yelled.

Rusty smiled and waved back.

'Come on, Virginia,' her mother said stiffly. 'Let me take your suitcase.'

Rusty picked up her grip, duffel bag and coat, and followed.

She glanced aside at her. 'I like your green hat,' she

said, looking up at the small-brimmed felt hat her mother was wearing.

'Oh,' said her mother. 'Thank you.'

'Did you choose the wine-coloured trimmings to match the sweater?'

'Not exactly.'

Looking down at her mother's lace-up shoes, she noticed that her legs were bare.

'Hello there!' said a woman's voice.

By the entrance to the docks two women were serving tea and sandwiches from a mobile canteen. They waved. One of them was wearing green overalls with *W.V.S.* on it, the other an outfit identical to her mother's.

A long queue was forming in front of the canteen.

'I'd help if I could,' called Peggy. 'But I've just come to meet my daughter, and I've promised to pick up a furniture van at your headquarters.'

'You stop there, Peggy,' said the other woman. 'We're giving you a cup of tea before you start driving.' She leaned over the counter and smiled at Rusty. 'We have to watch your mother, you know. She's a terror. Once, after an air-raid, she went to sleep on a door balanced on two milk churns in amongst all the rubble, using her coat as a blanket. When the milkman came to take them away at dawn, she stood there in the debris making stoves out of old bricks and a dustbin, and started making soup.'

'Oh, go on with you,' said Peggy, reddening. 'We're all trained to do that.'

'Yes. But only a few are brave enough to stay out of their beds on a winter night.'

'What do you mean, trained?' said Rusty.

'In the W.V.S.,' said the woman.

'That's the Women's Voluntary Service,' added her mother. 'This is our uniform.'

'Oh, I get it,' said Rusty. 'The green outfit.'

Peggy Dickinson thrust a cup of hot liquid and a jam

9

sandwich into Rusty's hands. 'Welcome back to England,' she said.

Rusty sipped the weird brown liquid. It was no use. She was never going to get used to this stuff. It tasted awful.

'If you don't mind,' said Rusty politely, putting the tea back on the counter, 'I'm not too thirsty.'

'I suppose you're used to drinking coffee,' said Peggy.

'No. I drink milk, mostly.'

'Oh, dear,' said one of the women. 'You'll have to get used to our daily half-pint now.'

Rusty bit into the sandwich. The bread looked grey, as if someone had kicked it along the ground. It tasted grey, too.

'Thanks for the tea,' said Peggy, picking up Rusty's case.

As they walked along the streets, Rusty couldn't help being drawn to the empty spaces where buildings must have been. Old lamp-posts, the kind she'd seen in Sherlock Holmes movies, were twisted violently into odd shapes. Gaping holes with broken wire fences surrounding them appeared at random amid all the brick and rubble. A large building with *Odeon* on it stood by itself in the crippled landscape.

Peggy Dickinson strode on. Usually people would yell after her to slow down, but when she checked to see if she was leaving her daughter behind, she discovered that Rusty was walking firmly beside her.

'Why do they call you Rusty?'

'On account of my hair. Uncle Bruno started it, and it sort of stuck. Say,' she said suddenly, 'look at that house there. It's like a stage set.'

Peggy stopped to look.

It was a familiar sight. Half a house swept away, leaving the other half intact.

'It reminds me of an Andrew Wyeth painting I've seen,'

whispered Rusty, stepping off the kerb and running across the road. 'There's this painting, see,' she said, attempting to explain. 'And it's just a plate and a cup on a table, and out back of the window you can see someone's been sawing up wood. And it's the wallpaper, see, it's old and faded and peeling and the sun is shining through the window.'

Her mother looked puzzled.

'I don't see what there is to get excited about old faded wallpaper.'

'Well, in the painting it's a sort of parchment-yellow colour, and the sun makes it kind of alive and, oh, I don't know.' She swung around to look back at the building. One room on the upper floor, complete with floor, door-way, and a little staircase at the side, was suspended in mid-air. 'It could be a terrific open-air theatre,' she said. 'And it's raised, too. That means that the audience would be able to see what was going on. You could get chairs out here and . . .'

Virginia reminded Peggy so much of Harvey Lindon, it unnerved her. Suddenly she remembered him standing in Beatie's garden, a broad grin on his face, his G.I. cap askew.

'Impossible,' she had said the first time he had suggested taking a picnic out in a boat. 'You'll never find one, and even if you did, it'd be full of holes.'

'Difficult, yes; impossible, no,' he had remarked. And within twenty-four hours, there they were drifting lazily up the river in a hired dinghy.

Peggy had insisted they turn back after an hour.

'Your wish is my command,' he had said, standing up and bowing, and the boat had immediately capsized. Luckily it had been near a wooded bank, but it had meant that Peggy was forced to relax in the sun until their clothes had dried.

Listening to her daughter's voice brought it all back with disturbing clarity. Her accent sounded like a strange mixture of Katharine Hepburn and James Cagney. Peggy knew that Bruno Omsk was a New Yorker and that Hannah was a New Englander, but somehow she had not been prepared for her daughter to have picked up their accent.

'We have to be going,' she said abruptly.

'But,' said Rusty, running after her, 'don't you think it'd be a good idea?'

Her mother didn't answer.

They stepped into an alleyway that lay alongside an old church.

'Is that medieval?' asked Rusty.

'No.'

'It looks so old.'

'Don't you remember *anything* about England?'

Rusty looked at her mother's face. It was pale and taut.

'Some.'

Next to the church a large Ford van was standing in the road. Two young women in green overalls were carrying old furniture out of a red-brick house. An elderly woman stepped out smartly from the front door.

'So this is Virginia,' she remarked, eyeing Rusty's clothes. 'Quite the young American.'

Peggy Dickinson smiled politely.

Rusty stood by the chicken-wire netting that served as a fence. No one spoke.

'Nice day, isn't it?' she began.

It wasn't a nice day at all. It was dull and clammy.

'Yes. We're lucky it isn't raining,' said the woman.

'That would be too bad, with all the furniture and stuff. Can I help carry some?'

'I'm afraid some of it's rather dusty. You'd spoil your nice clothes.'

'Dusty Rusty, that's me!'

The woman looked blank. Her mother cleared her throat awkwardly.

'Rusty is my daughter's nickname.'

'Oh, I see.' She smiled. 'No need for you to help, dear,' she said. 'That's the last piece going in now.'

Her mother walked over to the van.

'Wait a minute,' said Rusty. 'Are you gonna drive that?'

Her mother nodded.

'But it's so big.'

'Your mother,' said the woman, 'can drive anything. She can also make a vehicle run on almost nothing but elastic bands. We're going to miss her dreadfully.'

'Well,' said Peggy briskly, 'let's climb in.'

Rusty moved towards the door.

'That's the driver's side.'

'Oh, I forgot, you drive on the wrong side.'

Her mother flinched.

'I mean,' Rusty added hastily, 'on a different side than we do.'

Rusty followed her around to the passenger side. Her mother made a cup with her hands.

'For you to step into,' she explained.

Rusty noticed how stubby and dirty her mother's nails were.

'I'm awfully heavy,' she protested.

'I'm used to it.'

'O.K. Here goes.'

She stepped on them gingerly and hauled herself up to the seat. Her mother ran to the other side and pulled herself effortlessly into the driver's seat. Rusty watched as she swiftly lowered her hand towards the three gear-levers. The van gave a shudder and her mother released the hand brake.

Rusty looked at her mother. She hadn't expected her to be so quiet. She thought she would have had a warmer welcome, that there would have been more people to greet her; but her mother was acting as if it was an ordinary day. She hadn't even dressed up for her. She could at least have worn some stockings. After all, Rusty had tried to look nice, and her mother hadn't even noticed.

She leaned back and hugged her L.L. Bean coat, her 'Beanie'. It was like wrapping a piece of home around herself. The van rumbled and hummed around her, and her mother kept her eyes fixed intently on the road. Rusty stared miserably out of the window and thought of the Omsks. Her eyes filled again. She closed them quickly and sank back into the seat.

Peggy Dickinson glanced at her daughter. For years she had imagined how this reunion would be, how they'd chatter away and how her daughter would slip her hand into hers and look up at her with a sweet smile, like she used to do. It had hurt her deeply when Virginia had stopped calling her *Mummy* in her letters and called her *Mother* instead. It sounded so formal. Now here they were, together at last. No more endless sea between them. And yet she couldn't seem to find anything to say. And Virginia looked far from happy to be home. It had never occurred to her that she would feel so tongue-tied.

She drove on in silence.

Several hours later, Peggy parked the van outside a large, drab hall.

'This is Exeter, where we're leaving the furniture,' she said.

She cupped her hands again.

'It's O.K. I can make it,' said Rusty.

'Hand me down your luggage first, then.'

After several more *So this is Virginia*'s from various other green-clad women, Rusty and her mother made their way to a railway station.

Rusty couldn't help comparing the small shabby train that chugged into the station with the ones back in America. The English train had none of the grace and power of a Pullman. It was pathetic in comparison.

'Why is there a First Class and a Third Class and no Second Class?' she asked.

'I don't know,' said her mother.

'Weird,' said Rusty.

They stepped into a compartment that consisted of two long seats and a door at either end.

'Isn't there an aisle?' said Rusty.

'No.'

'What happens if you want to go to the bathroom?'

'The bathroom? Oh, you mean the lavatory?'

'Uh-huh.'

'You get out at a station and ask the station-master to make the train wait.'

Inside the compartment were several men and women in uniform. They glanced at Rusty's ringlets and bright clothes.

The train drew out of Exeter station.

'When do I get to see Charles?' asked Rusty.

'When we get home.'

Charles was the four-year-old brother she had never met. He had been born a year after she had left for America.

'I thought maybe he'd be around to meet me.'

'It's a long journey for a little boy to make.'

'I guess so.'

Her mother gazed out of the window.

'And Father? When will he be back from the Far East?'

'I don't know. I'm keeping my fingers crossed for Christmas, but it depends how long this war with Japan goes on.'

The train had just drawn out of another station when suddenly the land on one side disappeared, and the train seemed to be running alongside water.

Rusty leapt to her feet and ran towards the door. 'How do I open this window?'

'I think it would be safer if you sat down.'

Rusty sat back down in her seat and stared at the soldiers in the carriage.

Eventually they drew into a small station called Totnes.

As Rusty hopped down on to the platform, she noticed another green-clad woman by the entrance. The woman, who was tall and lanky, visibly sighed with relief when she spotted her mother. Then she noticed Rusty, and her face fell.

Some welcome, thought Rusty.

'Hello, Mrs Robins,' said Peggy. 'Anything the matter?'

'Afraid so,' said the woman, still eyeing Rusty. 'The van's broken down. I saw the Bomb outside, and I just hoped you'd be arriving soon. I'm supposed to be picking up half a dozen Dutch children and bringing them back here.'

'I see.'

Peggy knew what a terrible state the children would be in. The W.V.S. had begun organizing holidays in Devon for war-torn children, in the hope that it would help them recuperate.

'The Bomb!' said Rusty, alarmed.

'That's your mother's car,' explained the woman.

'Where's the van?' said her mother suddenly.

'On this side of the bridge.'

'I'll pick up my tools and see what I can do.'

'Oh, you're an angel!'

Peggy moved swiftly out of the station and headed for her car, which was parked outside.

The Bomb was an old Morris, painted navy blue. 'It looks like a gangsters' car,' whispered Rusty. It was large and L-shaped, with a running-board on either side. Through the windows Rusty could make out a rolled-up blind at the back and an armrest in the middle of the back seat. Several chains kept the old black-leather seats upright.

Her mother patted the car fondly and swung open the front door.

'Put your things in the car, Virginia,' she said. 'If you like, you can wait here, but it'd be quite nice for you to see the town.'

As Rusty threw her belongings into the back, she noticed a grubby pair of overalls and a large toolbox. Her mother opened the car door opposite. For a moment they paused and looked at each other. Then her mother grabbed the overalls and toolbox and drew herself out.

This was about the meanest thing anyone could do, thought Rusty, just to go off and look at someone else's van on her first day back.

Meanwhile Peggy strode hurriedly on, anxious to get the job over and done with so that she could be with her daughter. As she clutched her overalls and toolkit, it suddenly occurred to her that her daughter wouldn't have seen this side of her. When Virginia had left for America, Peggy couldn't even drive.

As the three of them half ran, half briskly walked through the town, Rusty felt as though she was travelling through a picture book, so quaint and tiny were the buildings. Green hills and trees sloped gently behind it. Even the small streets wound upwards.

Ahead, her mother and Mrs Robins stopped by a rickety old W.V.S. van, painted that interminable green. To Rusty's amazement, her mother stepped deftly into the overalls, whisked a scarf from a pocket, and wound it into a turban around her head. Within seconds the engine was exposed to the clammy, overcast sky and her mother was bent over it, her fingers tracing the wires.

It had been like pulling teeth, trying to get her mother to talk to her. Now she was smiling and murmuring gently to the engine as if it was an invalid that needed comforting. 'Your mother says that if talking to plants helps them grow, talking to engines makes them run better,' Mrs Robins explained.

Oh, yeah, thought Rusty, angry tears welling up in her eyes. She can talk to a machine all right, but not to me.

Her mother glanced up at her.

'Virginia, why don't you go on up to the bridge?' She wanted to add, 'It's lovely there. One of my favourite spots.' But somehow the words felt too intimate, and they stuck in her throat.

Rusty, who thought she was merely being got rid of, nodded and ambled past them. She held her head up high, pretending she didn't care.

Peggy returned hastily to the engine.

As Rusty approached the bridge, a cluster of grey-blue clouds drifted behind the grey spire of a church. Even the darned churches were grey, she thought. She leaned over the wall of the bridge. Two boats bobbed against the muddy slope of the river. She looked out to where it wound and curved past an old mill. She longed to be able to turn to Skeet and say, 'Hey, let's go take the rowboats and see what's around that corner.' Skeet would have yelled, 'Sure thing. Let's go.'

A cloud of cigarette smoke came wafting across the bridge. She turned to find her mother approaching, her hands covered with oil. Rusty glanced at the cigarette. She didn't remember her mother smoking.

Peggy leaned on the wall beside her and gazed out at the river. She was about to ask her daughter what she thought of the town when she caught sight of the two dinghies. It reminded her of Harvey rowing her and some fishing tackle smoothly along the water. He loved the River Dart.

A sudden breeze shook the trees along the banks, and the sky grew darker.

'We'd best be moving,' she said hoarsely. 'The others will be waiting.'

Rusty soon discovered why her mother's car was called the Bomb. As it bumped, spluttered and banged its way along the narrow lanes with their high hedges, Rusty's seat leapt at every bump and hole in the road. Behind them smoke poured from the exhaust.

Rusty had just gripped the sides of her seat when the car swung up a dirt road leading to a sheltered and untidy garden.

They stopped in front of a dilapidated and rambling house. Underneath an arched porch the front door was flung wide open. An old tyre was hanging from the lowest branch of a tall, leafy tree. Behind the upper branches sat a five-year-old girl.

'Charlie!' she yelled. 'Hee, hee, hee. Can't find me.' And she hid quickly behind the leaves.

A freckled four-year-old boy, wearing nothing but grey flannel shorts held up by braces, came tumbling out of the doorway. His thick curly hair was a blonder version of Rusty's. He stopped when he saw the car, ran up to it, and leapt deftly on to the running-board, his bare feet firmly gripping the frayed rubber.

'Hello, darling,' said Peggy.

She leaned back as Charlie hauled himself up to the open windows to peer inside.

'Virginia,' she said, turning to Rusty, 'this is your brother.'

3

Charlie gazed for an instant at his sister and then frowned. He jumped off the running-board and headed in the direction of the tree.

'He doesn't really understand,' said Peggy gently. 'I'm afraid you'll have to give him a little time.'

'Sure.'

But her mother could see that Rusty was disappointed.

Just then, a short robust woman in her eighties came bounding out of the house. A young woman, dark-haired and lean, followed her. The old woman flung the car door open and grabbed Rusty's hand. She then proceeded to pump it up and down vigorously.

'Welcome to England, Virginia. My, you look fit.'

One look at the beaming face of this ruddy, white-haired woman, and Rusty instantly couldn't help liking her.

'You must be absolutely ravenous,' the woman exclaimed, and she released Rusty's hand, opened the back door and proceeded to drag out the luggage.

'Let me,' Rusty insisted.

'For the next hour you're a guest, and after that,' she added, throwing Rusty's coat untidily over her arms, 'you're part of the family.'

Rusty had had no idea her grandmother was like this. Grandma Fitz and Gramps would just adore her. She noticed the dark-haired woman smiling shyly.

'Afternoon,' said the woman.

'Hi!'

The woman laughed. 'Oh, you sound so American.'

The young woman had a strange accent. It reminded Rusty of Maine.

'I'm Ivy Woods. I'm billeted here, too. I'm from Plymouth. You'll have to tell me all about America. I'm going there next year.'

'Where to?'

'Chatham New Jersey. I'm marrying one of the G.I.s stationed near here.'

'Hasn't he told you about it?'

'Oh yes. But it sounds so wonderful, I don't know whether to believe him or not.'

'It *is* wonderful,' said Rusty. 'You better believe it.' She turned to her mother. 'I guess I'd better go inside. Grandmother will be wondering what's keeping us.'

Her mother looked alarmed.

'That's not your grandmother. She's still in Guildford. She doesn't like travelling long distances. That's the Honourable Mrs Langley –'

'*Beatie*, if you don't mind,' interrupted a loud voice from behind. 'If you call me by my full name you'll die of exhaustion.'

Rusty turned and grinned.

'You can call me Rusty if you like. Everyone back home does.'

There was a terrible silence. Out of the corner of her eye Rusty could see that her mother had become still. She hadn't meant to say 'back home'. It had just slipped out.

Beatie put her arm around her and gave her a squeeze.

'It shows what a kind family you stayed with, to make you feel so at home.'

She turned to the others.

'Time for tea, everybody!' and she dashed back into the house.

Charlie and the little girl scrambled barefoot down the branches to the old rope that was connected to the tyre.

They stood inside the tyre and swung backwards and forwards.

'Come on, you two,' said Peggy. 'Come inside and wash your hands.'

They giggled and rocked, ignoring her.

'Well,' she said, 'I suppose we'll have to eat those chocolate cakes ourselves.'

'Chocolate!' they screamed.

They leapt off the tyre and skipped wide of the vegetable patches.

'He's real husky,' said Rusty, trying to find some complimentary adjective for her brother.

'Husky?' said her mother, startled.

Ivy laughed. 'That's what Harvey Lindon used to say, wasn't it?'

Her mother nodded.

Charlie and the little girl ran towards them and stopped abruptly. They took one look at Rusty and started to giggle.

'Hi,' said Rusty.

They giggled again.

'Susan,' said Ivy, 'shake hands with Virginia. Oh,' she added, 'would you prefer to be called Rusty?'

'I don't care. I guess Rusty is what I'm used to.'

The little girl held out a grubby hand. Her straight brown hair hung untidily from a side parting. Her faded blue dress was tucked into a pair of heavy black knickers.

'How do you do?' she said politely.

'Pleased to meet you,' said Rusty, shaking her hand.

'Charlie?' said Rusty's mother.

Charlie had stuck his hands into his pockets and had been scrunching up the flannel in them. One hand appeared from underneath his shorts.

'Oh, not another hole, Charlie.'

He swung from side to side. 'Only a little one.' He looked up at Rusty. 'Hello,' he said.

'Hi,' said Rusty.

They stared awkwardly at each other.

Suddenly Beatie leaned out of the dining-room window. 'Come on, you slowcoaches,' she yelled.

It was obvious that a lot of effort had gone into the sparsely set table. Six small chocolate cakes stood on a plate next to two platefuls of buttered grey bread. A jar of jam and a saucer of whipped cream completed the picture. Next to each plate was a paper hat made out of painted newspapers. The white linen tablecloth was patched in several places.

'This looks swell,' said Rusty, trying to sound enthusiastic.

She eyed the bread as she sat down, hoping that the jam would drown the taste.

'The National Loaf,' said Beatie. 'There's a shortage of flour. It's not very nice, but it's better than nothing.'

'I've had some already. It's O.K.'

Beatie and Ivy sat at either end of the table. Facing Rusty sat Charlie and Susan. Rusty's mother seated herself beside her.

Charlie gazed silently across at Rusty, picked up his hat, and pulled it on.

'Now you're the King of the Castle,' said Peggy.

'And she's the dirty rascal,' he said, pointing to Rusty and pursing his lips.

'Charlie!'

He scowled and looked aside at Susan.

'When you two have finished eating,' said Peggy, feeling it was wiser to take Charlie's remark as lightly as possible, 'there's a surprise for you from Uncle Mitch.'

'Is it ice-cream?' exclaimed Susan.

'It's a secret.'

'Isn't there a present from Uncle Harvey?' said Charlie.

'No.'

Charlie fell silent and peered at Rusty out of the corner of his eye.

'Uncle Mitch is going to be my dad,' said Susan suddenly, 'and I'm going to be a bridesmaid, aren't I, Mum?'

'Am I going to be a bridesmaid too?' said Charlie.

'No,' said Peggy. 'You're going to be a page.'

'Like in a book?'

Peggy smiled. 'No. A page is like a boy bridesmaid.'

'Oh.' He paused. 'Will Uncle Harvey be my daddy too?'

Peggy blushed. 'No, Charlie, I've told you before. You already have one.'

'Why is Susan having another one, then?' he said crossly.

Rusty could feel the atmosphere tighten up. She didn't know for sure, but she guessed Susan's father had been killed.

'Susan,' she said, 'when you go to America you'll have *lots* of ice-cream.'

Ivy gave a relieved smile. 'So Mitch tells me.'

'Is it true,' interrupted Susan, 'that you can go to a special place and eat the ice-cream on a high chair?'

'Uh-huh. And you can get all kinds of ice-cream. You can have it with chocolate and crushed nuts on, or a malt ice-cream or with milk all whipped up and served in a tall glass with a long spoon.'

Charlie scowled. 'Mummy,' he said, 'she sounds like Uncle Harvey.'

'Yes,' said Peggy. 'I thought that, too.'

'I guess Uncle Harvey must have spent a lot of time here,' said Rusty.

'I've never seen a man adore children as much as that man,' said Beatie. 'He drew children to him like a magnet.'

'Mitch too,' added Ivy.

'They were quite a pair.'

'Where is Uncle Harvey?' said Charlie, insistent.

'I told you, he's had to go away.'

'Doesn't he like us any more?'

'Of course he does, but he has to go where he's sent.'

'Why?'

'Because he's a soldier, and soldiers have to do what they're told.'

'Why?'

'Because they do, that's all.'

Charlie glared at Rusty.

'Couldn't we swap her for Uncle Harvey?'

'Charlie!' said her mother. 'Virginia's come all the way from America, and she's been looking forward to meeting you, haven't you, Virginia?'

Rusty swallowed. 'Sure.'

After wading through the bread, jam and cream, Rusty bit into her chocolate cake. It tasted like sawdust. She gulped frantically at the milk in her glass in an attempt to rid herself of the sickly dry sensation in her mouth, but it was all she could do to keep herself from spitting that out, too.

'It's powdered, I'm afraid,' said her mother. 'Once I get your ration book, we'll be able to buy milk for you.'

'Now,' said Beatie, clapping her hands, 'for the ice-cream.'

'I knew it was ice-cream,' said Susan. 'I knew it was ice-cream.'

'Can we come and help you?' cried Charlie.

'As long as you don't eat it all up while you're carrying it.'

As soon as they had left the room, Peggy leaned towards Rusty.

'I'm sorry about Charlie,' she said quietly. 'He doesn't understand. You'll have to be rather patient with him, I'm afraid.'

Charlie and Susan entered, clutching old chipped bowls filled with ice-cream.

'You'll spill it!' shrieked Susan.

'No I won't,' said Charlie. 'I got it tight.'

As everyone tucked into the ice-cream, Rusty withdrew into herself. She was vaguely aware of her brother and Susan making jokes that no one else thought funny. It was only when she heard her name being mentioned that she began to listen.

'Oh, nonsense,' said Beatie. 'She'd settle down splendidly there. A lot of it is based on the work of an American educationalist.'

'That's what I'm afraid of,' said her mother. 'I think she'll concentrate far better in an all-girl environment.'

Beatie caught Rusty's eye.

'You were co-ed in your American school, weren't you? Boys and girls?'

'Sure. Isn't that how the schools are here?'

'Beatie,' said Peggy in a warning voice, 'I don't think this is the time and place to talk about it.'

Outside, suddenly it started to rain. Without warning Charlie and Susan gave a loud shriek and leapt from the table, followed hastily by Beatie, Ivy and Peggy.

'What . . .' began Rusty.

She followed them out into the hallway and watched as Beatie and the two children emerged from the kitchen carrying saucepans and a copper bowl. Ivy and her mother leapt up the first flight of stairs two at a time, and within seconds had dived into the bathroom and reappeared with tin buckets.

Rusty stood in the hallway as they thundered to the top of the house. She listened to the sound of their laughter, then turned hurriedly away and returned to the dining-room table alone.

Beatie was the first to stride back in. 'Oh dear,' she said breathlessly. 'One of these days we won't get there in time. I suppose,' she added, 'you'd better know what to do. We'll have to find you something to carry up. Leaks in the roof, you see. Can't afford to fix it yet. Fearful nuisance. Your mother managed to mend part of it, but she's been so busy.'

Rusty stared down at her empty ice-cream bowl. She wasn't really interested. If they weren't interested in her, why should she be interested in them?

When tea was over, Rusty began clearing the table. Beatie, noticing how quiet she had become, whisked the bowls out of her hands.

'No you don't,' she admonished. 'Not today. You've had a long journey. Charlie,' she said, 'show your sister the back garden and the river.'

Charlie gave a weary sigh. 'Can Susan come, too?'

'Of course she can,' said Rusty.

'I weren't talking to you,' he said crossly. 'I were talking to Beatie.'

'Now, Charlie,' said Beatie, 'don't be an old prune. These should fit you,' she added, handing Rusty a pair of large rubber boots. 'You don't want to spoil those marvellous socks and shoes.'

She had actually noticed them!

'They're all the rage back home.' She stopped. 'Sorry, it slipped out again.'

'Oh tosh,' said Beatie, waving her arms about. 'It's good to have lots of homes. Means you can make one anywhere.'

'That's what Grandma Fitz says. She says if you put your heart and hands and back into a place, then it'll be home.'

Beatie smiled.

She has such a beautiful face, thought Rusty. All the wrinkles around her eyes swooped upwards as though she'd laughed them all there.

'I've heard such a lot about you from your mother,' said Beatie warmly. 'She's been so looking forward to having you back.'

'I guess,' murmured Rusty.

'It won't be easy,' Beatie whispered. 'But if you follow your grandmother's advice – Oh, Lor'.' She laughed. 'Now *I've* started. I mean your *American* grandmother – you'll be fine. Now,' she said, 'go and explore.'

By the time Rusty had put the boots on and stepped outside, Charlie and Susan had run off by themselves. She could hear them giggling conspiratorially behind one of the large hedges.

Apart from a tiny crooked path of grey flat stones, the large back garden was made up of several vegetable patches. Surrounding the garden were numerous fruit bushes and apple trees. From a shed came the sound of clucking chickens. A smaller shed stood near a coal bunker. Rusty pushed open the door. Inside were logs and uncut branches. She was about to make her way down to the river when she heard her name. She ducked swiftly behind the woodshed and peered out.

By the open window, Beatie and her mother were doing the dishes. They were talking about school again, and obviously disagreeing.

'She'll be home every weekend,' her mother was saying.

'You'd be a fool not to stay here,' said Beatie.

'I'd love to, you know I would, but I can't possibly let her go to that school. It's out of the question. Roger would be horrified.'

'You don't mind Charlie going to the nursery part of it.'

'But that's just playing. I want Virginia to have a chance of catching up with her education and not leave school unqualified like I did. There's a competitive atmosphere at this school, and I think it'll help her to settle down.'

'But if she's coming home every weekend, why haven't you chosen a day school?'

'I don't want my mother-in-law and her friends getting

their hands on her. I know it's a terrible thing to say, but the War was one of the best things that happened to me. Look what a state I was in when I arrived in Devon. I'm so much happier and more confident since I've been here.'

'I know, Peggy, so why on earth go back?'

'Roger.'

There was a long silence.

Rusty was dying to peep out and see what their faces were saying, but she didn't dare risk it.

'He was born in that house.'

''Bout time he left it then, dear,' said Beatie jovially.

'Look, Beatie, he's looking forward to picking up the pieces there again. It's going to be hard enough as it is for both of us to adjust to each other after having been separated for nearly five years. I think it's important we start from a familiar base.'

'But you hate that house – you've told me a hundred times. I'm sure Roger could find a job near here.'

'Oh Beatie, don't,' said Peggy. 'It's going to break my heart enough as it is, to leave here. I . . .' She stopped.

'Come on, dear, let's go and have a sherry.'

As soon as they had left the kitchen, Rusty came out of hiding and headed for the river. A rowing boat was tied up alongside a tiny makeshift jetty. Rusty slid down a muddy bank and stood at the river's edge. As she gazed at the trees, leafy still with summer, she suddenly felt very cold.

4

Rusty was woken by the sound of a telephone ringing from downstairs. She sat up and glanced down at her narrow canvas bed. Beatie had called it a camp bed. Surrounding it were several boxes and pieces of broken furniture. She was in a tiny attic room, on the landing where the roof leaked. The windows were fixed into a sloping alcove in the ceiling, so Rusty had to stand on a chair to open them.

Rusty liked being tucked away at the top of the house. Already, as she sat cross-legged in her spotted pyjamas, she was mentally redecorating the room. The wallpaper was brown with fussy patterns on it. The wrong kind of paper for a room so small. 'Now,' she whispered, 'I could paint over it, or pull the paper off and paint the wall underneath.'

Aunt Hannah had helped her decorate several of the rooms in the Omsk house. Together they used to make cardboard models and paint them to see how they'd look, and then maybe add some stencils. They'd sit in Aunt Hannah's studio and mix colours, and then, when they thought they had hit on a nice idea, there would be a family discussion and everyone would chip in and say, 'Ugh! Not that colour. That'd drive me nuts,' or 'Say, I like this colour combination.' But when Rusty reached eleven years old and Alice took over Jinkie's room and Kathryn needed to have the room to herself so she could walk up and down and learn her lines in peace, Aunt Hannah and Uncle Bruno said, 'The spare room's all yours,' and, best of all, 'You can decorate it how you like.' She'd loved decorating that room!

Her suitcase was lying open on the floor. She leaned down and picked up a little box that was wedged in among her clothes. Inside was a special blunt knife, plus a little sharpening device and some stubby brushes. They were for her stencils. Grandma Fitz had given them to her.

Also in the box were some jars of paint – barn red, dark green, and a mustardy yellow, which Aunt Hannah called ochre.

Rusty closed the box and slipped it back under her penny loafers. The loafers were from Aunt Hannah. Aunt Hannah had begun to give her a monthly clothing allowance like the older girls when she'd reached twelve, even though her birthday had only been in the June.

'I know it's only a month before you go back,' she had said, 'but while you're still here, I'll treat you girls all the same.' And she had handed her the money and then turned her back to tidy up something on a shelf that didn't need tidying at all.

Downstairs, the front door slammed. Rusty sprang out of bed and climbed up on to the chair to look out through the window. Her mother was hurrying out in her green outfit, her overalls thrown over her shoulder. She climbed into the Bomb and backed it out of the front garden in a cloud of smoke.

Rusty turned and leaned against the wall, amazed. Her mother was just carrying on as if she wasn't even there! She might just as well have stayed with the Omsks. She leapt down, grabbed a pair of jeans, a T-shirt and sneakers out of her suitcase, and angrily flung open the door.

She noticed that the door to Beatie's bedroom was ajar. She tapped on it lightly, but there was no response. She slipped inside.

It was what Aunt Hannah would have called a south-facing room. One that got a lot of sun. That would mean that the room she had slept in must be north-facing. Perfect for a studio, since the light would stay pretty much the same. She took in the hideous mud-green wallpaper with its mottled purple and pale-green flowers. Over by the door where the ceiling sloped, it hung in damp lumps.

'That roof,' her mother had said, as they had sat down to a supper of imitation hamburgers and a tasteless blob called Spotted Dick, which was supposed to have been Rusty's favourite dish when she was aged seven, 'is my first priority before I leave.'

'Oh tosh,' Beatie had said. 'I can always sleep in a mackintosh with an umbrella over the bed.'

Rusty imagined what it would be like to decorate Beatie's bedroom. She looked at the drab brown chairs and bed, and the dark faded carpet. 'A few of Grandma Fitz's rag rugs on the floor would cheer it up.'

She let her fingers glide down the black curtains that hung raggedly at the sides of the bay window. A startled spider scuttled rapidly from the folds and along the window-seat.

'It's like someone just died,' she muttered.

She gave the curtains a deft flick and watched the dust rise up into the sunlight.

Her sneakers and clothes in her arms, she tiptoed out on to the landing, down the stairs, past the two bedrooms on the next landing, and down a smaller flight of stairs. She slid her hand along the sturdy wooden banister. Neat to slide down, she thought.

As soon as she had closed the bathroom door behind her, she noticed that the pants, bra and bobby socks she had washed the previous night had been removed from the towel rail. She stood naked on the bare wooden floor and washed at the sink with a bar of soap that smelled of nothing and refused to lather. After dressing, she brushed her hair well back from a central parting and slid two grips in at the sides to keep it back. No ringlets!

'This'll do, Janey,' she said to her face in the mirror. 'It's neat and off my face.'

Not good enough, said the imaginary Janey, *and* you're wearing your jeans again.

'It's no fun if you dress up every day. It doesn't make it special. And anyway,' she added, 'they didn't even notice.'

As she scooped up her pyjamas, she glanced at the bathtub. It was large and white, with claw-shaped feet. A line had been painted five inches from the base. Even the water was rationed! It was going to be difficult managing with only one bath a week, after having been used to showers every day. Lucky it was summer and she could take a sponge bath without freezing to death. Even so, she had broken out in goose-pimples.

She opened the door and moved swiftly out on to the landing.

The living room was almost bare but for a long sofa and an armchair by the fireplace. An old carpet covered the floor, and along the wall stood a large bookcase. Black curtains hung from the bay window which overlooked the front garden. Rusty went over to the bookcase and picked out the thickest book there. Hearing footsteps, she turned to find Beatie standing in the doorway. 'I thought I heard you up,' she said.

'How come you have black curtains everywhere?' asked Rusty.

'They're blackout curtains. We had to have them to keep the light from showing.'

'But you don't still have to have them, do you?'

'No, but I gave all my other curtains to the W.V.S. They *are* gloomy, I agree.'

'I didn't say they were gloomy.'

'But you think so, don't you?'

Rusty grinned and nodded.

'Unfortunately, it's either black curtains or nothing.'

'Why don't you dye them?'

'I don't think black takes to dyes.'

'You could bleach 'em first.'

'Good Lord,' exclaimed Beatie. 'Of course I could. That's a fearfully good idea. Absolutely splendid.'

Rusty laughed. 'I love your English accent.'

Beatie smiled.

'What accent is Ivy's?' asked Rusty. 'It sounds like a Maine accent. Charlie and Susan have it a little bit too, don't they?'

'Devonshire.'

'Are they awake yet?'

'Up long ago. I let you lie in. I thought you could do with the sleep. The others are all out finding clothes they can borrow for the wedding.'

'You mean,' said Rusty, 'Ivy'll be wearing someone else's wedding dress?'

'Yes. It's impossible to get hold of material. Even if you could, you couldn't afford to waste clothing coupons on it.' She paused. 'I'm afraid all yours and most of your mother's will be going towards some ridiculous school uniform.'

Beatie gave a loud 'Hmph!' and strode out through the door. Rusty followed.

The dining-room table had one place set. Breakfast, alas, did not consist of orange juice and rolled oats with hominy grits, or corncakes with butter, or waffles and pancakes with maple syrup. Hunger made Rusty able to eat the scrambled dried eggs on toast, but she made do with a glass of water rather than face the powdered milk again.

Beatie joined her at the table. 'That's a hefty-looking tome,' she remarked, indicating the book Rusty had chosen.

'It's not for reading,' Rusty explained. 'It's so I can have good posture. My friend Janey is always talking about it. Look, I'll show you.'

She sprang up from the table, placed the book on her head, and glided gracefully around the room.

'It's a dumb way of learning to walk right, though, 'cause you can still walk badly and balance the book on your head.'

She proceeded to walk with exaggerated bow-legs as if she had been born in a saddle, then stuck her behind out so that she was S-shaped. Beatie threw her head back and laughed.

'See what I mean?' said Rusty, sliding back into her chair.

'I do. Is Janey your best friend?'

'Best *girl* friend. I guess Skeet's my best friend. He's the youngest Omsk.'

'Tell me about the others in the family,' said Beatie.

Rusty cupped her chin in her hands and leaned towards her.

'Didn't Mother tell you about them?'

'A little, but you weren't exactly the most wonderful of letter writers, you know.'

'Yeah,' said Rusty. She twirled a piece of her hair into a hoop and stroked it. Aunt Hannah was always having to nag her to write those letters, but it was difficult, because her mother didn't seem real. Nor her father, and he never wrote to her except at birthdays.

'You were the youngest. I know that.'

'Uh-huh. Now I'm the oldest. I guess I'll have to be a little more grown-up.'

'How old are the others?'

'There's Jinkie, she's twenty-one. She got married last year. Ted, that's her husband, he's in the army. They got a little apartment downtown. She just had a baby. Then there's Alice. She's the smart one. She's been working all summer so she can pay for her wardrobe and books for college. She's just about good at everything. She'll be a freshman in the fall.'

'A freshman? That's a first-year student?'

'Uh-huh.'

'How old is she?'

'Eighteen. She's the tops. She's even good at softball and basketball, ice hockey, tennis, you name it. So's her steady.'

'Her "steady"?'

'Uh-huh. We call him Bo the Beau.'

Beatie looked blank.

'Get it?'

Beatie shook her head.

'His name is Bo and he's her Beau. Bo the Beau.'

'I see.'

'Oh well, I guess it's not that funny. They're nuts about each other. They saved up for an old car together, and sometimes they take it for weekends up by one of the lakes.'

Beatie looked surprised. 'On their own?'

'Sure.'

'What do Mr and Mrs Omsk think about that?'

'They think it's great. They worked hard to buy that car.'

'I meant about them not having an adult with them.'

'But they're in love!' said Rusty, amazed. 'They gotta be able to spend some time alone.'

Beatie cleared her throat. 'I think you'll find it different here.'

'Oh, it's different back home, too! Not everyone likes the Omsks. They call us "that Bohemian crowd".'

Just then Rusty thought of Aunt Hannah sitting in her old shirt, in the studio, scraping away at a piece of wood or chipping pieces out of stone. Rusty would be sitting in a corner with paint and charcoal, and Uncle Bruno would come in with cookies and milk, and whisper, 'We gotta keep these artists from starvin'.'

'Penny for them,' said Beatie.

'What?' said Rusty, startled.

'Penny for your thoughts.'

'Oh, I was just thinking of Uncle Bruno. Wondering if he was coming into the studio with cookies for Aunt Hannah.'

'He sounds very kind.'

'Oh, he's about the kindest person I know. He's like a big bear.' She paused. 'Sometimes he's awful mean, though. Sometimes when Aunt Hannah has her hands full of clay, he'll try and pinch her rear, and she goes leaping around the studio telling him to look out for the statues. So then she runs outside and he chases her around the lawn, but if he catches her she covers his face with clay. Sometimes if she does that, he picks her up and carries her into the sprinkler.' She began to giggle. 'Only then he gets wet, too. If they do it at night when it's hot and me and Skeet are in bed, we peek through the screens and watch. But if it's daytime we try and get hold of the hose so we can aim it at Uncle Bruno, but we have to be quick, 'cause he'll just sneak around a corner and grab it first and chase *us*. Once he hosed Aunt Hannah through the kitchen window. She'd just made her hair nice because the Hodgkinses were coming over for drinks. She yelled and yelled and called him everything. She went storming upstairs, and Uncle Bruno sat in the kitchen and got real quiet and said it was kind of a dumb thing to do and we all sat in the kitchen with him. Then he said, 'S'pose I'd better go apologize.' So he got up and was just heading for the door when there was this loud shriek.'

'What happened?' said Beatie.

'Aunt Hannah saw herself in the mirror all wet and angry and just started laughing like a hyena. Uncle Bruno said sorry and she said no *she* was sorry for not being a good sport and Uncle Bruno said no it was *his* fault for being so inconsiderate, and then Aunt Hannah started getting angry again and saying it was *her* fault. And then we all groaned and they looked at us and started laughing.'

Beatie picked up Rusty's plate.

'Oh no,' she said. 'Let me help with the chores. Makes me feel more at home.'

Beatie watched Rusty as she bustled around the dining-room table. She appreciated the effort the girl had made at the supper table the previous evening, trying to keep the conversation going. Rusty had asked Ivy questions about her wedding arrangements, attempted to be kind to Charlie who obviously resented her presence, and all the while her own mother had seemed tongue-tied.

Beatie had been surprised by Rusty, too. Peggy's description of her daughter bore no relation to the lively young girl who had arrived. If only she could find something that mother and daughter could do together to help break the ice.

'What about the others in the family?' asked Beatie.

Rusty pushed the plates through the hatchway.

'There's Kathryn,' she said, leaning against the wall. 'She's fifteen. I think she's going to be an actress. She got offered a part in two of the plays in our University Little Theatre Stock Company, so she's been rehearsing and performing most of the summer. She's awfully quiet, but when she's onstage, it's like someone turned the lights on. And she makes the best ice-cream ever, with chocolate and melted peppermints added.'

'And Skeet?'

'Oh, Skeet – he makes me laugh. I make him laugh too. We go everywhere together.'

They made their way to the kitchen, Beatie washing the dishes at the sink, Rusty drying. As Rusty stared out of the window, she remembered the conversation she had heard between Beatie and her mother.

'That school,' she blurted out. 'The one near here, what's it like?'

'Marvellous, but terribly disapproved of.'

'How come?'

'The children are too happy there, I suppose. Children in English schools are supposed to suffer in order to develop good characters.' Beatie beamed at her. 'I have a feeling that you'll survive, though.'

'I guess it'll be fun at boarding school, won't it?' said Rusty, wondering why she felt that lump in her throat again. 'I've read stories about them. Living in dormitories and finding secret passages and having midnight feasts.' She looked anxiously at Beatie. 'I mean, do you think Mother is sending me away again because she thinks I'll have a good time there?'

'Why don't you ask her?'

'Because when you started talking about it yesterday in front of me, she didn't want to talk about it.'

'Is that why you eavesdropped from behind the wood-shed?'

Rusty reddened. 'How d'you mean?'

'I saw your shadow.'

Rusty slapped her forehead with her hand. 'After all I learned about stalking, I go do a dumb thing like that! What a goop! Did Mother notice?'

'No, but I think if you want to know something, it's better to ask.'

'I didn't mean to listen, but I heard my name mentioned so I figured it was O.K.'

'I see.'

'I heard you say I'd be miserable at boarding school and that Mother doesn't want to leave here.'

'You don't miss much, do you?'

Rusty laughed. 'I guess not.'

'Want to help me feed the chickens?'

'You bet.'

They stepped over the clutter of tools and boots in the conservatory and headed for the chicken coop. Hanging from a line between two trees were Rusty's socks, bra and pants.

'Who put my laundry on the line?' she asked. 'Was it you?'

'No,' said Beatie, who was crouching down in her tweed skirt, stroking a chicken's neck. 'Your mother thought they would dry more quickly outside.'

Rusty squatted down beside her.

'Don't you feel terrible eating the chickens if you make friends with them?'

'I just keep them for eggs. There's a woman who lives near here who also keeps chickens, and whenever we're desperate for a bit of poultry, say at Christmas, we exchange a couple.'

'How come I had *dried* egg this morning, then?'

'They don't always lay.'

They strolled over to the jetty and sat at the edge. Rusty asked about the War, chatted aimlessly about her American family, and lay on her stomach so that she could look underneath the jetty at all the plants under the water. And all the while, Beatie listened and observed her, for every now and then she heard Peggy's voice when she was at her happiest.

It was almost teatime when Peggy, accompanied by Ivy, Charlie and Susan, drove into the front garden. The exhaust gave a loud bang before the Bomb steamed to a halt. Peggy and Ivy leaned out of the windows, while Charlie and Susan stood on the back seat to get a better view.

'What's 'appened to the curtains?' said Ivy.

'They're gone,' said Charlie.

Everyone clambered hastily out of the car. The dining-room windows were flung open. Rusty was up a stepladder, which was being steadied by Beatie.

'It's all Rusty's idea,' said Beatie. 'We're going to bleach and dye the curtains.'

To Rusty's surprise her mother hauled herself up to the window and swung her legs inside. She was still in her overalls and turban.

'What a marvellous idea,' she said. 'Anything's better than black.'

'Only snag is,' said Rusty, grinning, 'that some of them are falling to pieces.'

Charlie and Susan peered inside.

'Doesn't it make a difference,' said Peggy, 'just having them down? It's so light and cheery without them. I never want to see black again.'

Charlie, who was watching Rusty, scowled.

'She's stupid,' he said. And he stepped back from the window and headed for the tree with the tyre. Susan ran after him.

Ivy hitched herself up on to the windowsill to have a look. Beatie had asked Peggy to hold the stepladder while she went and prepared tea. As they exchanged places, Beatie gave Ivy a wink.

Crafty old Beatie, Ivy thought, throwing them together. Oh, how she'd miss her.

5

'Every spider in the neighbourhood must be living in here,' said Rusty, throwing down the last curtain. As it landed on the floor, a large cloud of dust burst into the air. 'See what I mean?' she spluttered.

'Yes,' said Peggy. 'They're going to need an awful lot of washing.'

Rusty rested her elbows on her knees, thinking. 'I got it!' she yelled. 'The river! We can wash 'em in the river.'

'Well, we could certainly try.' Peggy glanced at Rusty's grubby T-shirt and jeans. 'You haven't any older clothes to work in, I suppose?'

'Oh, these wash easy. Thanks for hanging my stuff out on the line.'

Peggy looked up awkwardly. 'That's all right.'

She didn't mention how surprised and disturbed she had been to discover that her daughter wore a brassiere.

'I looked in the bathroom closet and the john for sanitary pads,' said Rusty. 'but I couldn't find them anywhere. Where do you keep them?'

Peggy blushed. 'You haven't started, have you?' she began.

'Oh, no,' said Rusty cheerily. 'But I'd like to know where they are when I do.'

'Well,' said her mother, relieved, 'you can always tell me, and then I'll give you some.'

'Oh sure, I will,' said Rusty, scrambling down the ladder. 'I don't want to miss the celebration.'

'Celebration?'

'You know,' said Rusty. 'The celebration dinner for

when you start your period. I missed Jinkie's, but I was there for Alice's and Kathryn's.'

'And do all American girls have this?' said Peggy slowly.

Rusty shrugged. 'They do at the Omsks'.' She looked down at her jeans. 'Boy, I'm just a dust pile. I better go wash.'

As they reached the door, Peggy found herself reaching out for her daughter's shoulder.

'This celebration dinner,' she said hurriedly. 'Was it just you girls and Aunt Hannah?'

'Oh no,' said Rusty. 'Uncle Bruno and Skeet get invited, too. Skeet says it's not fair that girls get to have periods and he doesn't, so he's going to have a celebration dinner either when his voice breaks or he grows a hair on his face, whichever comes first.' She looked down at her hands and brushed them hastily against each other. 'I guess I'll miss that one.'

There was an awkward silence. Rusty could feel the tears in her eyes. Peggy couldn't speak. She felt hurt that she hadn't been able to tell her own daughter about periods, and yet she knew from her upbringing that she would have found it impossible to broach the subject.

Rusty faked a smile. 'I guess they'll write and tell me, though.'

'Of course they will,' said Peggy. 'Come on. It's time for tea.'

For the next few days it rained. Rusty stayed in the house and watched it through the curtainless windows. The telephone rang constantly for her mother, who was always out fixing someone's car. Sometimes when Beatie had one of her bouts of 'ruddy indigestion' and had gone upstairs to rest, and Ivy, Charlie and Susan were out getting fitted up for the wedding, Rusty was left alone to answer the phone and take messages.

The curtains lay unwashed on the floor, and Rusty's

loneliness grew more acute as no mail arrived from the States, and the rain continued to fall.

Every evening her mother would return, oil-stained in her overalls and turban, disappear into the bathroom to wash, and re-emerge in an old pair of slacks, blouse and much-darned cardigan. Rusty soon realized that the green uniform of the W.V.S. was one of her better outfits.

One day Beatie came into the dining room and discovered Rusty staring out of the window crying. Rusty wiped her cheeks hurriedly.

'Boy, does it rain a lot here.' She sniffed.

'Yes,' said Beatie. 'In fact I've come to ask if you'd help me empty out the buckets on the top landing. They're starting to overflow.'

'Sure.'

They had hardly reached the door when the telephone rang.

'Darn that phone,' snapped Rusty. 'Why don't they go fix their own darned cars?'

Beatie ambled over to the phone and picked it up. Rusty gazed guiltily at her for a moment and then left the room.

She met Beatie as she came out of the bathroom from emptying the copper bowl.

'Sorry,' she muttered. 'I just get sick of it ringing.'

'You need company,' said Beatie. 'Everyone knows that your mother is leaving here soon, so they're all panicking and asking her to mend their cars, and she hasn't the heart to refuse.'

'Is she really such a hotshot with engines?'

Beatie nodded. 'The best.'

Rusty gave a sigh.

'Come on,' said Beatie, 'before those buckets overflow.'

Rusty darted up the stairs with the copper bowl.

'I'll get in touch with Ruth Hatherley. She's the woman with the chickens. Her children go to that school I was telling you about. I would have contacted her sooner, but her children have all been helping out there, and also I thought you and your mother would be spending more time together.'

'So did I,' said Rusty, and she turned sharply and carried a slopping bucket down the stairs.

The following morning it had stopped raining. Rusty slipped out of her pyjamas in the bathroom and peered at her face in the mirror. There was such a lot of goo in her eyes, and her eyelids were awfully puffy. 'I guess it's from crying,' she thought.

She wasn't usually a cry-baby. Except for odd moments during the day, she seemed O.K., but as soon as night-time came and she went to bed, she'd find her face squeezing hard into the pillow and the tears just flowing out like a waterfall.

'You're sure to feel a little lonely at first,' Aunt Hannah had said, 'but once you make a few friends, it'll work out just fine.'

She turned on the tap and flung cold water over her eyes.

Once she had got dressed, she didn't feel so slowed up. She gave her hair a vigorous brush and gripped it back firmly from her face.

Her mother was in the dining room, reading the thinnest newspaper Rusty had ever seen.

'Hi,' Rusty said, surprised.

Her mother lowered the newspaper and smiled. 'Morning.' She looked at Rusty's shorts, check blouse and sandals. 'You look very summery.'

'As soon as I saw it wasn't raining, I thought it'd be kinda neat to put them on. I hate wearing a lot of clothes.' She stood hesitantly at the door. 'I'll go make myself some toast.'

'There's milk in the larder for you. I have your ration book now, so you can have butter on your toast as well.'

As she poured the milk, she could feel her salivary glands tingling. She'd never have dreamed she could get so excited about a glass of milk. She'd taken it so much for granted in Connecticut. There she just used to open the refrigerator door and help herself.

Her mother walked into the kitchen.

'Aren't you going to work today?' asked Rusty.

'I've told Beatie that I'll only take emergencies.'

'It sounds like you're running a doctor's office.'

'Well, it does seem like that sometimes.'

'Do they pay you for it?'

'It depends who I'm doing it for. If it's W.V.S. work, no. But if it's private work, yes, I'm paid for it.'

Rusty sipped the milk.

'It tastes different from back home.' She blushed. 'I mean, back in the States. More creamy.'

'Do you like it?'

'Uh-huh.'

'I thought we could tackle those curtains this morning. It'd be nice if we could dye them for Beatie before leaving.'

'Where is she?'

'Lying down in her room. That indigestion's playing her up again.'

'Has she seen a doctor?'

'It would take wild horses to persuade Beatie to see one.'

'Couldn't you get one to visit?'

'I have done, but as soon as he arrives, she starts leaping around saying she's as fit as a fiddle, that he's wasting his time being here, and he's only come round because he's after her sherry.'

'Doesn't he get mad?'

'Oh no. He likes calling. They've known each other for years. I think he has quite a soft spot for Beatie.'

Rusty lowered her voice. 'Did Beatie ever get married?'

'Yes, but her husband died, twenty years ago.'

'So how come she didn't marry again?'

'There aren't many men of her age around.'

'So couldn't she go with someone younger? How old's this doctor?'

'Ooh,' said Peggy, attempting to suppress her laughter. 'I think he's in his seventies.'

'Too old,' said Rusty. 'Couldn't we find somebody younger?'

'Stop playing matchmaker and drink your milk.'

'We could invite someone over for a meal, couldn't we?' said Rusty, taking a sip.

Her mother pushed some buttered toast towards her. 'Beatie is quite happy without a husband.'

'Oh I know, but it's more fun when you can share good times with someone else, isn't it?'

'If you want to catch this butter before it's melted entirely into the bread, you'd better eat it up quick.'

They decided to do the dining-room curtains first, and carried them in shifts out into the garden. Ivy was cutting back a hedge with some shears.

'Are you sure they won't fall apart?' she asked.

'No, I'm not,' said Peggy. 'But Beatie's all for it.'

Charlie and Susan suddenly appeared from behind the shrubbery. Charlie took one look at Rusty and then haughtily turned his back on her and ran off with Susan. Peggy gave a sigh.

'He's just very jealous,' she said.

They walked down towards the river. Well, I'm jealous of him, too, thought Rusty. After all, *he* hadn't been sent away.

When they reached the jetty, they knelt down and lowered the ends of the curtains into the water.

'Look at it come out!' exclaimed Rusty, as black liquid trailed out of the material.

They gathered up the ends and began squeezing and wringing them.

Peggy was elated. Her daughter's accent and exuberance still disturbed her, but she knew that in time the accent would disappear, and that a year in an English school would calm her down. Virginia would return to the quiet, gentle little English girl who had left her five years ago. She squeezed the curtains firmly. This was a marvellous idea of Beatie's to bleach and dye the curtains, and how kind of her to pretend that her daughter had thought of it.

Rusty twisted and turned the material. It was so satisfying to see the black oozing out.

'Say, my water's turning grey. That's a good sign. I just hope when I start squeezing the next part, it won't run into the end that I just did.'

'That I've just done,' said her mother.

'Pardon?'

'It's *that I've just done*, not *that I just did*.'

Rusty looked blankly at her.

'I was correcting your grammar.'

'Oh, I see.'

No one had corrected her grammar before. English was one of her best subjects.

They went on dipping and squeezing.

When they had each completed a curtain, they draped the sodden black material over the sides of the jetty and began a second batch. They were just beginning the dipping process again when the sound of a car pulling into the front garden caused Peggy to sit up, startled.

A tall man in his forties with broad shoulders and thick, dark hair came striding around the corner. He was wearing the uniform of an American army captain.

'Hi there!' he yelled.

Ivy, who had sprung to her feet at the sound of the jeep, was now frantically tearing off her apron and smoothing her hair.

'Oh, Mitch,' she said. 'You should have warned me. I'm such a mess.'

Charlie and Susan ran crazily up to him. He scooped Charlie up in his arms.

'Hiya, Charlie boy,' he yelled. 'How ya doin'?'

'I'm doin' O.K.,' yelled Charlie, dropping into American.

Mitch whirled him round and round.

Rusty swallowed. That was what Uncle Bruno used to do with her. He was like the centre of a merry-go-round and he'd just lift her up and whip her around high in the air. She remembered how shy and scared she had been when she had first arrived at the Omsks', and how noisy she had thought the family. Uncle Bruno had just winked at her quietly and they had walked out to his workshop, and for months after that she had clung to him like a shadow. That's how she had come to learn some carpentry. He said she was his trusty assistant. He was always complimenting her like that. And when he used to whirl her around, he'd throw her back in the grass and the earth would rock and spin around her.

She watched as Mitch swung Susan round too, but instead of putting her back on the ground like he had Charlie, he held her tightly to him. Then Charlie began to play what looked like hide and seek, only it seemed he was playing it by himself.

'Uncle Harvey,' he giggled. 'Where are you? Can't catch me.' And he fled up to the end of the conservatory and peeked around. 'Uncle Harvee!' he yelled. 'Hee, hee, hee. Can't find me.'

Peggy looked hastily down at the curtain and began squeezing it again.

'Uncle Harveee,' went on Charlie.

Rusty was mesmerized by the scene. She knew something awful was going on, but she didn't know what it was.

Mitch lowered Susan and ruffled her hair.

'Hey, Chuck,' he said. 'Uncle Harvey isn't here. You know that.'

'Yes he is. Yes he is,' said Charlie, dancing around. 'He's hiding, isn't he?'

'No, boy. He went away. You know that. He said goodbye. Don't you remember? He told you to take good care of your mom.'

Charlie looked puzzled for a moment and then broke into a grin.

'I did look after her. I did.' He turned to look in the direction of the jetty and then swiftly back to Mitch. 'Is he in the jeep?'

Mitch shook his head slowly, and picked him up.

'When's he coming back, Uncle Mitch?'

Rusty watched as Mitch carried him towards the shrubbery. He muttered something gently in his ear. Charlie let out a piercing scream and began to hit him violently.

'Come on, Susan,' said Ivy, taking her hand. 'Let's go and get changed. Uncle Mitch is going to take us out.'

From behind the shrubbery came the sounds of sobbing. Rusty glanced at her mother. Peggy's face looked like a pale mask.

'Is the man called Harvey dead?' she whispered.

'No, it's just that he won't be coming back, and Charlie's finding that difficult to accept.'

Rusty wanted to say something that would comfort her mother, but she couldn't think of anything. I guess, thought Rusty, this man called Harvey was a good buddy of my mother's, too.

After a while the sobbing subsided and Mitch emerged

from the bushes with Charlie still in his arms. He was holding a large handkerchief to Charlie's nose.

'Hey, Charlie boy,' he protested. 'Don't blow it away!'

'I'm not blowing it away.'

Charlie gave a short sniffle into the handkerchief. Mitch staggered backwards.

'Hey, watch it, you're blowing *me* away!'

Charlie fell exhausted against Mitch's chest and laughed.

Mitch walked down to the river and gave a nod to Peggy.

'Thank you,' she said quietly.

'And who is this young lady?' he exclaimed.

Rusty leapt to her feet.

'Hi,' she said.

'You must be Virginia. Peggy, you didn't tell me she was such a redhead.' He winked at Rusty. 'I bet you have all the boys after you!'

Peggy flinched. 'She's a bit young for that,' she remarked stiffly.

'How are you finding England?' he said.

Before Rusty could answer, her mother said, 'She did live here before, you know.'

'Sure you did, but how does it compare with the good ole U.S. of A.?'

Now Rusty was stymied. If she said she preferred America, her mother would get all stiff. If she said she liked England, he'd get mad.

'Difficult to choose, eh?' said Mitch, rescuing her.

'Uh-huh. There's good things in both.'

'My sentiments exactly.' He lowered Charlie to the ground. 'I thought it'd be nice to take a trip down to the beach. You coming?'

'No,' said Peggy.

'I was talking about Virginia,' he said.

Rusty longed to go to the beach. She loved swimming,

and this Mitch looked like so much fun, and it was so wonderful to hear an American voice again, but since her mother was staying to do the curtains, she'd better refuse.

'No, thanks,' she said, and she lifted the curtains. 'We got a project going. Better do it while it doesn't rain.'

Mitch nodded with understanding.

'Be seeing you then,' he said, and he bent down, deftly picked up Charlie, and threw him on to his shoulders.

Peggy and Rusty watched him for a moment before returning to the curtains. For a while they didn't speak. Rusty glanced at her mother.

'How's your curtain coming along?' she began.

'Pardon?'

'Your curtain, how are you doing?'

Peggy gazed blankly down at it.

'Oh, fine,' she said suddenly. 'It was a good idea of Beatie's to dip them in the river.'

Rusty was astounded. 'It was *my* idea,' she said. 'Don't you remember? I was sitting on the ladder in the dining room.'

'Oh, yes.'

They pushed their hands into the material.

'Are you sure Beatie hadn't suggested it to you in the first place?'

Rusty felt bewildered. 'No,' she said firmly. 'It was all my own idea. Actually,' she added, 'when it comes to interior decoration, I have some very good ideas.' Leastways the Omsks think I do, but she left that part out.

Peggy sat up abruptly.

'Boasting doesn't go down too well in this country,' she said.

Before Rusty could say anything, there was a shout from Beatie, from the kitchen window.

'Peggy,' she yelled, 'there's a phone-call for you. One of the ambulances has broken down in Newton Abbot, and they can't find a mechanic anywhere.'

'I'll just go and see how urgent it is,' said Peggy hurriedly.

She sprang to her feet and sprinted across the garden. Rusty returned to the curtains. She couldn't go now, could she? Not after Rusty had turned down the beach trip?

As Rusty squeezed and twisted the black curtain, a painful ache lodged itself in her chest, and her arms seemed almost as if they didn't belong to her body any longer. A fog rose into her eyes. She knew her mother was going to leave, and it hurt so much she could hardly breathe. As she heard her mother calling to her, she turned as if in a dream.

'I'm awfully sorry, Virginia!' she said. 'It really is an emergency.'

'That's O.K.,' Rusty heard herself say, and she moved slowly back to the curtains.

It wasn't until she heard the Bomb spluttering out of the front garden that her hurt exploded into anger.

'Damn you!' she yelled angrily, and she slapped the curtains against the jetty. 'I'm not going to hang around for you any more. I'm going to do what *I* want to do! I don't need you, anyway.'

It was then, as her eyes cleared, that she saw the boat tied up by the jetty. She slid swiftly into it and untied it.

Gripping the oars, she dipped them firmly into the water and with all her strength drew the wooden craft away from the jetty, her anger rising with each stroke.

Beatie stood on the jetty and gazed down at the abandoned curtains. She had come down to tell Rusty that the eldest of the Hatherley children, a girl of thirteen, was sitting in the dining room waiting to meet her. Beatie thought it would be nice for them to have lunch together.

Now she was not only going to have to tell her that

Rusty had disappeared, but she was also going to have to break the news that Rusty had gone off in the girl's boat.

6

Rusty rowed until she had exhausted herself. She glided into a small inlet in the bank and attached the rope to the branch of an overhanging tree. Sliding into the centre of the boat, she leaned back. The palms of her hands burned, but she didn't care. It was such a relief to be doing something she liked. For the first time since her return to England, she didn't feel lonely. She raised herself up on her elbow and peered over the side of the boat. There wasn't another boat to be seen, and the banks of the river were too overgrown with trees and bushes for anyone to walk with ease through them.

Within seconds she had peeled off her clothes and had plunged into the river. There was nothing to beat skinny-dipping, she thought, as she glided and turned and somersaulted in the water.

Oblivious of time, she swam and dived, gazing at the fish and plants as she let herself sink under the surface or lie face down in a dead man's float. After a while she hauled herself back into the boat and lay there, dripping.

Above her the leaves flickered. She stretched her arm out and brushed them with her fingers. This river was so pretty, she thought. Gradually the gentle plash of the water and the mild rocking of the boat soothed her into an exhausted sleep.

It wasn't till she turned over to adjust her pillow that she realized that she didn't have one, and neither was she in her bedroom at the Omsks'. She was lying in a boat on a river somewhere in Devon, and the reason she was lying there was because she was angry with her mother. She thought back to how her mother had bounded across the garden to answer that emergency call, and she realized that it was dumb to be so mad at her. After all, if her mother fixed the ambulance, it might save someone's life. She gave a sigh. Why couldn't she save someone's life in a more hygienic way, though, like being a nurse or something?

She sat up. A slight breeze was moving through the leaves, and it was beginning to grow cool. Her anger had subsided, and the swim and the sleep had refreshed her. She felt ravenous. What she wouldn't have given for a plateful of baked beans and hamburgers, followed by an ice-cream soda! But then, she thought, pioneers didn't have hamburgers and ice-cream soda. And pioneers also didn't have showers when they wanted, or refrigerators or washing-machines. They had to be inventive. If she was lonely and she wanted a buddy, she'd have to go out and find one. Forget about her mother and Charlie. Boy, he got up her nose. She was on her own, in the wilderness.

'Think pioneer,' she muttered.

She slipped back into her clothes, untied the rope and pushed one oar against the bank to ease the dinghy into the deeper part of the river. Even as the oars scraped against her sore hands, she thought 'pioneer' and that made her feel proud.

> *'Row, row, row your boat*
> *Gently down the stream,'*

she sang,

> *'Merrily, merrily, merrily, merrily,*
> *Life is but a dream.'*

When she got back to Beatie's, she'd write lots of letters. Here she'd been waiting for letters from America, and she hadn't sent any off herself.

She'd write to Janey, and the Fitzes, and to Aunt

Hannah and Uncle Bruno and the girls, and a private one to Skeet, and one to her Girl Scout captain to read to the troop, and one to Miss Jenkins, her art teacher.

Just the thought of them all made her feel good. Too bad she didn't have a fishing rod – then she could have caught some fish and brought them back to the house for tea. For tea! That sounded so English. Like she was in a movie.

She realized that she must have rowed a good distance in her temper, for the journey back seemed much longer. She had no idea what time it was. It was difficult to tell in England. The night crept up so slow. She let the oars rest against the sides and drifted for a moment. The palms of her hands were pink and blistered.

'They'll toughen up,' she said in her pioneer voice, and she grabbed the oars firmly and began whisking the boat swiftly past the banks.

As the trees began to clear, she knew that she would soon see the jetty. She pulled a little more slowly on the oars. Even though it wasn't yet dark, the sky had grown dull, and there were lights on in the house. Hanging from a clothes-line were the two pairs of blackout curtains. Rusty stared guiltily at them. Beatie must have hung them up herself. She glanced back at the jetty and began rowing towards it.

As the boat slid alongside it, she grabbed one of the wooden posts and flung the rope around it, knotting it quickly. She was about to clamber out when she noticed a girl striding briskly across the garden. Her short wavy hair fell untidily from a side parting. Below a shabby blouse, a pair of worn blue corduroy slacks was rolled up to her knees.

Rusty guessed from the size of the girl that she must be about eleven. She waved. 'Hi!'

The girl frowned and strode very firmly in her direction. Rusty could see that she was angry.

She stopped abruptly on the jetty, her bare feet apart, her hands on her hips. 'I must say,' she yelled, 'you've got a bloody nerve!'

7

'*Your* boat!' said Rusty, astounded. 'I thought it belonged to the house.'

'Well, it doesn't. It belongs to me. Beatie lets me keep it here.'

'I didn't know.'

'Well, you know now.'

Rusty scrambled up to the jetty. She was almost a head taller than the girl.

'I'm sorry,' she said. 'I had no idea.'

The girl scowled and turned on her heel.

Rusty ran after her. 'Hey, what more can I say? It's a swell boat.' The girl attempted to shrug off a smile. 'I'd be mad too if someone just went off in it,' Rusty said.

'Yes. Well,' said the girl. She caught sight of Rusty's hands, took hold of one and turned it palm upwards. 'Ouch!' she said.

'Yeah. I haven't been rowing for a while. They'll harden up again with more practice.' She paused. 'I guess I won't be getting that practice now, though.'

The girl began walking towards the house. 'We'll see,' she said.

'That'd be great if you'd let me,' said Rusty.

The girl swung round. 'Not on your own, though.'

'The two of us, you mean?'

'Perhaps.'

'That'd be even better.'

'I said perhaps.'

'Sure.'

The girl looked steadily into Rusty's eyes and then took

in her brightly coloured blouse, shorts, and sandals. When Rusty stopped at the conservatory door, she went on walking.

'Say,' said Rusty, 'won't you come in?'

'I've been waiting "in" since lunchtime.'

'I didn't know. No one told me.'

'Anyway, I think you have a reception committee waiting for you.'

'A reception committee?'

'You're in for a bollocking.'

Rusty wasn't too sure what a bollocking was, but she guessed that it wasn't too pleasant. As the girl turned away, Rusty caught her arm.

'My name's Rusty. What's yours?'

'Elizabeth, but most people call me Beth.'

'Sure is nice to meet you. Sorry I made you mad.'

Beth shrugged.

'Be seeing you,' said Rusty.

She watched Beth pick up her bicycle. Although it was an old one, it seemed much lighter than the ones in the States. Beth hopped on to the machine and pedalled swiftly around the corner.

It was deathly quiet in the house. Rusty felt as though she should tiptoe. As she stepped into the hallway, she saw that the living-room door was ajar. She walked up to it and eased it open.

Her mother was standing by the empty fireplace. Beatie was seated in the armchair. No one spoke.

'Hi,' said Rusty quietly.

Rusty's mother looked pale.

'I hope you have an explanation, Virginia,' she said tightly.

Beatie gazed sympathetically at Rusty.

'Uh-huh,' said Rusty. 'I had no idea the boat belonged to someone else. I've apologized to her.'

'Who did you think it belonged to?'

Rusty glanced at Beatie. 'I thought it was yours.'

'I see,' said Peggy. 'And are you in the habit of borrowing people's belongings without asking?'

'Uh-uh,' said Rusty, shaking her head. 'I just didn't think. I just . . .' She wanted to say, 'I was just so mad that you went away,' but the words stayed at the back of her throat. 'I'm sorry.'

'Are you also in the habit of going off on your own without asking permission?'

Rusty was puzzled. 'Sure I am. I can take care of myself. Sometimes I tell people where I'm going. But no one was around.'

'What about Beatie?'

Rusty looked at Beatie. 'I guess I should have told you.'

Before Beatie could speak, Rusty's mother stepped forward.

'Virginia, in future you don't *tell* either Beatie or myself where you are going. You ask permission.'

'Ask permission?'

'Yes. Do you understand?'

Rusty swallowed. 'Uh-huh.'

'Have you any idea the worry you've caused?'

'There's no need to worry. I can handle a boat just fine.'

'Don't answer back.'

As another silence sucked the air out of the room, Beatie took in Rusty's dishevelled, damp red hair and penetrating green eyes. Her face was flushed with anger. She stood upright, uncowed. Peggy stared at her and lit a cigarette.

'I think bed without supper is in order,' she said quietly.

'But Peggy,' said Beatie, 'the girl hasn't had any lunch.'

'She would have had lunch if she hadn't decided to go off on her own.'

'I coulda gone to the beach and I didn't because I said

I'd work on the curtains,' yelled Rusty. 'And so did you and you broke your word!'

'Virginia,' said her mother. 'That is enough. You will go to your room.'

'That's not fair. You haven't heard my side of it.'

'You obviously think yourself more important than people who need medical help.'

'I never said that.'

'I told you it was an emergency. There has been a war on here, you know.' She drew in sharply on her cigarette. 'There still is in Japan.' She turned hurriedly away. 'Just be grateful you're alive.'

Rusty caught Beatie's glance. Beatie gave her a nod. The nod seemed to say, 'Leave it for now.'

Rusty headed for the door. She refused to be beaten. If she let herself collapse in the middle, she'd just howl. She'd walk tall. Chest and chin raised, she made her way up the stairs to the bathroom. Even in the privacy of the washroom, she held her head high. She filled the sink with water and lowered her blistered hands into it. 'Boy, does that hurt,' she muttered, gritting her teeth.

Washing her hair made them sting even more. She was glad she'd taken the boat down the river. As soon as she was in bed, she'd lie back and think about it and pretend she was still there.

For a moment she thought of all the letters she had planned to write. She couldn't write any tonight. It would upset the Omsks too much to know how unhappy she felt, and she couldn't lie to them. She'd been handling rowing boats since she was eight years old. What was wrong with her going off in one?

'I guess I should have asked first, though,' she murmured.

She wrapped a towel round herself and slipped out on to the landing.

She had no sooner put her pyjamas on than the window

rattled and it began raining. Suddenly, in her narrow bed, she felt as though she was in prison. She buried her head in her hands and thought 'pioneer' as hard as she could.

Footsteps came hurrying up the stairs, followed by whispers. It was Beatie, Ivy and her mother. She heard the clang of the buckets and bowls out on the landing and sat up, defiant, waiting for them to enter, but the door never opened and the footsteps continued downstairs.

Outside, a car drew up. Rusty got out of bed and stood on the chair by the window. It was Mitch. In two days he and Ivy would be married.

She slid down on to the chair. The wedding preparations seemed awfully dull. There had been no shower, where everyone brought gifts for the future bride. Rusty drew her knees up and hugged them. Jinkie's shower had been the best. Aunt Hannah had made beautiful dresses for them all. Hers was a pale-yellow organdie. It flared and flounced out from the waist. Rusty liked to dress up, although she had to admit that it was always a relief when she could peel a dress off and get back into her jeans. Maybe she was two people: Virginia and Rusty. The Virginia part would float around in long gowns like Scarlett O'Hara in *Gone With The Wind*, and the Rusty side would disappear into the woods with Skeet. She closed her eyes tightly. She could see Jinkie with her blonde hair and tall willowy figure, sitting in the rocker on the back porch. It was summer. Aunt Hannah had made little lanterns, which she had placed on tiny tables. White moths had fluttered and bumped themselves against the screen. She remembered asking, 'Why is it called a shower?' 'I guess,' Aunt Hannah had said, 'it's because people shower you with gifts.'

Jinkie had looked so happy. All the time up to the wedding, the house had vibrated with excited voices. And then Jinkie would sometimes get all pink and flustered and burst into tears and say, 'I don't want to get married after all,' and Aunt Hannah would put her arm around her and they would disappear into Jinkie's room, and Rusty would sit on the stairs outside, not eavesdropping exactly, but just because she knew something important was going on in there, and that it had to do with growing up.

Sometimes, after Rusty had her own room, Aunt Hannah would sit on the bed and they would talk about all kinds of things. How Rusty was worried that her maths teacher didn't like her, or about a quarrel she'd had with Janey, or what she was going to do when she grew up. When they talked about that, Aunt Hannah would sometimes look sad and start stroking her hair. Now she knew why. It was because Aunt Hannah knew she wouldn't see her grown up.

'Gee whiz,' she said, feeling the tears roaring into her nose and throat. She pressed her forehead into the wall in an effort to control herself.

From the garden came the sound of Ivy's laughter. Rusty climbed back on the chair and peered out. Mitch, who was holding an enormous piece of canvas tarpaulin over her head, was escorting her to the jeep.

Downstairs, the telephone rang. She jumped down and tiptoed out of the room on to the landing. Within minutes the dining-room door had opened, and Beatie and her mother were in the hallway.

'At least take an umbrella,' Beatie said.

'I won't be able to hold it.'

'Yes, but someone else will, and it'll keep your head and the engine dry.'

'Yes, that's true. It's a fearful nuisance, really. Still, at least it'll take my mind off everything.'

'Of course it will, dear. It's a horrifying business, I know, but it'll mean there'll soon be peace.'

'Oh, I wish I could believe you, but now that they've

invented a bomb like this, it'll mean lots of other countries will want to have one, too.' She sounded awfully sad. 'And what if they invent one that's worse?'

'Go and attend to that car,' said Beatie. 'I'll have a nice hot bath ready for you when you come back.'

'Now, don't go waiting up for me.'

'Oh, go on with you.'

Avoiding the drips from the ceiling, Rusty found a dry spot on the floorboards and sat and listened to the front door opening and closing.

'Bread and cheese do you?' said Beatie up the stairs. Rusty froze. 'It's all right,' Beatie continued. 'I know you're eavesdropping. I'm afraid it'll have to be powdered milk. You've had your ration for today, but I'll flavour it with a bit of cocoa-powder and saccharin. All right?'

Rusty leaned over the banister and grinned sheepishly. Beatie was standing at the foot of the hallway stairs, looking up.

'That'd be swell. Shall I come get it?'

'No. Your mother said I wasn't to let you out of bed as soon as her back was turned. She didn't say anything about not feeding you, though.'

As soon as Rusty heard Beatie's step on the landing, she flung open the door and took the tray from her hands. On it was a plate with two pieces of toast with melted cheese, a large pear, and a tin mug with hot brown liquid in it.

She sat on the bed and put the tray on her knees. 'Thanks,' she said.

'May I come in?' said Beatie.

'Take a seat,' said Rusty, moving up.

She was about to take a bite from the toast, but stopped.

'I'm sorry about making everyone upset. I'm used to going off by myself, or with friends, exploring and everything, but I shoulda asked about the boat, I know that.'

Beatie placed a hand on hers.

'Your mother doesn't know that you can look after yourself. Remember, you left her at the age of seven. And you did come back rather late.'

'I know it. I just couldn't tell how late it was. I didn't have my watch. In Connecticut when it gets to be night, it gets dark. Going to bed when it's still light here is weird.'

Beatie nodded. 'You wait till the winter. It gets dark more quickly then.' She paused. 'Your mother was also upset by today's news. Another of those atom bombs has been dropped in Japan on a city called Nagasaki. They say the last one killed eighty thousand people.'

'Eighty thousand!' Rusty gave a low whistle.

'And even the survivors are suffering because of the radiation from the bomb.'

'But we're at war with Japan. Doesn't she want us to win?'

'Of course she does, but this is the most devastating bomb that's ever been used. Your mother saw what the V2s did to the people in London and the South. That's why it's shaken her so badly.'

'I didn't know she was in London.'

'Yes. She was one of the W.V.S. volunteers who went up last year.'

'I guess I had it lucky in the States,' said Rusty guiltily.

'Anyone who's alive is damned lucky,' Beatie said, ruffling her hair. 'And your hair is soaking! Hand me that towel.'

She pressed Rusty's head down.

'What are you doing?'

'Making you a turban.'

'That's what Jinkie used to do when she washed her hair. Alice's and Kathryn's hair is short, so they just let it dry by itself.'

Beatie placed the towel over her head and twisted it. 'Lift your head up, chatterbox.'

66

As Rusty did so, she folded the towel back. 'There, you look like the Queen of Sheba.'

Rusty grinned.

'Now eat!'

The following two days were filled with preparations for the wedding. Ivy was the centre of attention, and it was obvious from the faces of the women who visited Beatie's house with their home-made food and presents that everyone was pleased for her. However, Rusty was quick to pick up, from odd remarks, that although G.I.s were made welcome in England, marrying one of them was a very different matter.

'I don't usually tolerate G.I. marriages,' one woman had muttered to her friend on leaving, 'but Ivy Woods deserves to be happy.'

'I quite agree,' said her friend. 'She's had enough tragedy in her life. If that American makes her happy, then I approve.'

'Approve?' whispered Rusty angrily to herself. Any-one'd think American soldiers were the pits. They'd been in the War too and got killed!

Since Rusty was restricted to the house and garden, she attempted to help out with the visitors but, as soon as she opened her mouth, they gazed at her in astonishment. Rusty did her best, offering to make them some of that horrible tea they all liked, with powdered milk. But they just nodded politely and said, 'That's very kind of you, dear, but no thank you.'

Beatie saved her. Just when Rusty was at her loneliest, she'd say, 'Come on, let's go down to the jetty for a while.'

Then they'd both sit there and chat, and Rusty would picture herself rowing and fishing on the river and Beatie would savour each ripple and colour.

Rusty and her mother hardly spoke to one another. It was all Rusty could do not to disobey her and just disappear, but she knew that, if she did, it would spoil the wedding.

Keeping her temper under control took so much energy and concentration that it was difficult to speak. At least with Aunt Hannah they could yell away until they'd sorted it all out, but answering back seemed like a crime to her mother.

The wedding was a simple affair at a small church near the Estate. Although Rusty wore her best outfit with her bobby socks and saddle shoes, her mother seemed embarrassed instead of pleased, and even asked her to wear her cardigan with the buttons in front.

The reception was held in Beatie's back garden. Friends lent their white tablecloths so that they could be spread out along trestle tables. A tiered cardboard wedding cake rose above a concealed fruit cake. Rusty avoided eating it. She had seen what had gone into it . . . or, rather, what hadn't. It was sugarless and almost eggless. Ugh!

Beth was among the guests. Beatie sat them together, although Rusty could see by her mother's face that she disapproved. Beth's dress was a dowdy pale-blue affair with a muslin collar and muslin cuffs. There seemed to be no darts in it at all, so it billowed outward above the waistband and appeared rather sack-like.

'I love your clothes,' Beth said.

'Thanks.'

'Don't bother telling me about mine. This dress is ancient and it's been fiddled around with so many bloody times, it's a wonder it hasn't fallen apart.'

Rusty grinned.

Beth caught sight of Peggy at the end of the table.

'Oops,' said Beth. 'I forgot. I have to watch my language here. Your mother doesn't like it.'

Rusty shrugged. Her mother could go drown herself.

'Everyone's saying that the Japanese are going to surrender,' said Beth. 'We're going to build a bonfire to celebrate. Do you want to help us?'

'I'd love to,' said Rusty earnestly, 'but I have to get my mother's permission first.'

'Permission?'

'Uh-huh.'

'Why?'

'Search me. I guess she's afraid of losing me. I don't know why. She doesn't see me much, anyway. She's always fixing someone's car.'

'Oh dear. I'm afraid my mother's car is one of the cars she's always putting back on the road.'

'It's O.K. I'm getting used to it.'

'Listen,' said Beth. 'It's so hot, how about us taking my boat down the river after the reception?'

'Great!' said Rusty.

'Bring a towel – then we can go swimming.'

As soon as the reception had ended, Rusty approached her mother. 'Mother,' she began quickly. 'Beth would like me to go in the boat with her, and for us to go swimming. Is it O.K.?'

'I'll think about it.'

'Uh-huh. When will you let me know?'

She looked awkward. 'Tomorrow.'

'Tomorrow! But I mean for us to go in the boat this afternoon.'

'Virginia! That's out of the question. It's Ivy's wedding day.'

'She wouldn't mind, would she?'

'That's hardly the point.'

'O.K. So I can't go today,' said Rusty, still determined. 'How about tomorrow, then?'

'Tomorrow is Sunday.'

'I know it,' said Rusty. 'What's that got to do with me going in the boat?'

'Look, Virginia, I'd rather you didn't.'

'Why?'

'Because you could drown. If there was an adult with you, it would be different.'

'But Uncle Bruno taught me to swim, my first summer. I'm a good swimmer.'

'So you say, but I'd prefer it if an adult was with you.'

'O.K.,' said Rusty. 'S'pose I just go in the boat and I don't swim?'

Peggy felt confused. She wanted Virginia to have company, but it would be awful if she had an accident after five years of being away. Beth, who had been listening, stepped forward.

'I can lifesave,' she said firmly. 'It's hardly bloody likely that the boat will capsize, but if it does I can always plunge in and save her.'

That did it, thought Rusty. Why on earth Beth swore so much, she couldn't understand. She spoke such good English, just like they did in the movies, but she took the cake when it came to swearing!

'I'll think about it.'

Disappointed, Rusty turned away. Beth walked beside her.

'I see what you mean,' she said sympathetically.

They had just about reached the shrubbery when Rusty heard her mother call out to her. She swung round.

'You may go in Beth's boat tomorrow, but no swimming, mind,' she said.

'I promise,' said Rusty, her fingers crossed behind her back.

She walked on behind the shrubbery, controlling her victory exhilaration.

'Thanks, Beth. It must have been your lifesaving experience that changed her mind.'

'Balls,' muttered Beth. 'I don't know anything about lifesaving.'

8

On Sunday it rained, and the boat trip was cancelled. Rusty was bitterly disappointed. Her mother left the house with the only decent umbrella.

'It's O.K.,' Rusty had said, when permission had been refused for her to take a walk. 'I don't mind getting wet.'

'I do,' her mother had said politely. 'We don't want you catching a cold, do we?'

'I don't mind catching a cold.' But her mother had simply shaken her head.

Ivy Woods, now Ivy Flannagan, was no longer in the house. She and Mitch Flannagan were spending a brief honeymoon at a nearby cottage. Charlie and Susan played in the living room.

If it hadn't been for Beatie's suggestion that they attempt to bleach the curtains, Rusty would have rampaged around the house all day, but Beatie had looked so cheered at the thought of not having black curtains any more that after a while Rusty became infected by her enthusiasm.

They soaked one curtain in the kitchen sink, sprinted quickly up the stairs and threw it into the bathtub, where the bleach solution was made up. Once both pairs of curtains were immersed, they began stirring them around with wooden spoons.

For the next hour, the two of them sat on chairs by the tub and stirred continuously as the rain pelted down outside. Occasionally they glanced down to check that the material hadn't disintegrated, then went on staring out of the window and drifting in and out of conversation.

'I thought they said on the radio that this was going to be a heat wave,' said Rusty.

'It's only a shower.'

Downstairs there was a loud knocking, followed by a yell. 'Anyone at home?'

'It's Beth,' said Rusty excitedly. 'I'll go ask her in.'

Before Rusty could reach the bathroom door, it was flung open. Beth stood in the little alcoved landing, her canvas cape dripping all over the floor.

Rusty glanced down at her feet. 'Oh,' she said. 'You have rubbers here, too.'

'You mean my galoshes?'

Beth peeled off the rubber shoes, revealing her sandals underneath.

'Bloody hell,' said Beth, eyeing the bathtub. 'Your material's losing its colour.'

Rusty swung around.

'It's working!' she yelled.

They all leaned over the bath, mesmerized.

'It's like magic,' exclaimed Rusty.

Within minutes Beth had thrown off her cape and had joined in the stirring. The three of them whooped and yelled as the material slowly turned white.

Charlie and Susan, who had become attracted by the noise, came flying up the stairs, and were soon swept up in the excitement.

'Now,' said Beatie. 'We have to take it all out and rinse it thoroughly until the smell of the bleach is out of it.'

Beth took her shorts and shirt off and stood barefoot in a faded pair of grey knickers.

'That's a good idea,' said Rusty, and she stripped down to her white bra and pants.

'Oh, envy, envy,' said Beth, gazing at her. 'I thought only rich models wore that kind of underwear.'

Soon Susan and Charlie were down to their underpants too.

They hauled the dripping curtains down to the large stone kitchen sink and rinsed and squeezed the voluminous curtains over and over.

Rusty drew up two chairs for Charlie and Susan. She had never seen her brother look so cheerful in her presence. Sometimes she had watched him in hiding, and he had often made her laugh, but as soon as he caught sight of her he would frown and close up. Now he was as happy as a clam.

'Squeeze, squeeze,' he said, pushing his small hands into the material.

Susan jumped up and down on the chair, laughing.

Rusty lifted up a great clump of the material and held it towards them.

'Take another sniff,' she said. 'Smell anything?'

They all sniffed the material, and then Rusty pretended that Charlie was the material, and started sniffing him.

'Say, this curtain's got freckles on it. Guess we'll have to put it back in the bathtub.'

'I'm not a curtain,' protested Charlie, giggling.

'Hey, it talks too.'

She scooped him up in her arms. Charlie began squealing.

'And wriggles.'

Susan leapt on to Rusty's shoulders in a bid to save him.

'A curtain just jumped on me!' Rusty yelled.

'You're all bloody mad,' said Beth.

Rusty strode around the kitchen, jigging Charlie up and down, while Susan hung wildly on to her.

'Ever get the feeling you're being strangled?' she gasped as Susan's arms tugged on her neck.

Beatie was leaning through the hatchway, watching. 'I still have some of that powdered lemonade left,' she said. 'Anyone interested?'

Susan let go of Rusty and landed in a heap on the floor. 'Oh, yes!' she shrieked.

'Yes, please,' said Charlie.

'Curtains don't drink lemonade,' said Rusty firmly.

'I'm *not* a curtain,' said Charlie, pressing his nose against Rusty's. 'I'm a boy.'

'So you are!' said Rusty, feigning shock. And she put him back on the chair.

'You know,' she said, as they sat at the table sipping lemonade, 'a ginger snap with this would make it just perfect.'

'You could have a try at making them,' said Beatie. 'Only you'll have to make them without sugar, I'm afraid.'

'Don't you just die for something sweet?'

Everyone nodded.

'Say, you could melt candy down, and use that.'

Charlie buried his face in his glass, taking another sip of lemonade. He took a deep breath. 'Got any gum, chum?' And he and Susan burst into giggles.

'Why are they cracking up?' said Rusty.

'Cracking up!' repeated Susan, and again they collapsed with mirth over the table.

'I'm afraid,' said Beatie, 'that sweets are rationed, too.'

'So what do you do when you're dying for something sweet?'

'Bite into a bloody carrot,' said Beth.

When they had finished the lemonade, they stared out of the kitchen window at the rain.

'You know,' said Beth, 'we might as well hang them up in it. After all, it would give them the final rinse.'

'That's a swell idea,' said Rusty.

'Swell idea,' repeated Charlie.

'Swell idea,' added Susan.

'You're nuts,' said Rusty to the little echoes.

'Nuts! Nuts! Nuts!'

chanted Charlie.

'Here we go gathering nuts in May,'

sang Susan,

> *'Nuts in May, nuts in May,*
> *Here we go gathering nuts in May,*
> *On a cold and frosty morning.'*

'It's August, dumbo.'

'Here we go gathering nuts in August,' sang Charlie, 'nuts in August, nuts in . . .'

Beth grabbed hold of him and squeezed her hand over his mouth.

'Come on,' she said, 'before these two have me up the wall and tickling the bricks.'

At this Rusty threw back her head and collapsed into a chair.

'Tickling the bricks!' she shrieked.

Beth shrugged, released Charlie, picked up one of the curtains and threw it at her.

'Ugh!' cried Rusty as it landed in her lap.

'Come on,' said Beth. 'Let's take it outside. We can wring it out there.'

Within minutes of being out in the garden, they were soaked.

'What's the point of wringing it out here,' asked Rusty, laughing. 'when it's raining?'

Beth grinned and looked down at her drenched knickers, dropped the curtain in the grass, and peeled them off.

'Oh boy, this is fun!' said Rusty, and she undid her bra, took it off with her pants, and started to dance around.

> *'I'm swimming in the rain,*
> *Just swimming in the rain.*
> *What a glorious feeling . . .'*

Charlie and Susan, who were watching from the kitchen, leapt off the chairs and fled out through the conservatory, leaving their underpants on the tiled floor.

Beatie, who was up in the bathroom emptying out the bleach, looked out of the back window to see what all the noise was about. She leaned out and smiled. It was so grand to have children around.

Downstairs, the front door opened. Beatie slipped back into the bathroom and on to the landing. Peggy was shaking a wet umbrella in the porch.

'Quickly,' urged Beatie from the top of the stairs. 'Come up and see the children. Rusty and Charlie are actually playing together.'

'What!'

'Oh hurry up. Don't bother about taking off those overalls.'

Peggy leapt up the stairs. Beatie drew up a chair by the bathroom window and leaned out, laughing. Peggy stood and rested her shoulder against the window frame. Unlike Beatie, she didn't even smile. She was too shocked. It was only too clear that her daughter, like the Hatherley girl, was used to being naked. There were none of the patches of pale skin caused by a swimsuit. Nor did her daughter have the body of a little girl. Below her tiny breasts, her hips had already started to round, and fair traces of ginger pubic hair grew in a light triangle.

'Aren't they marvellous!' said Beatie. 'So full of life!'

Peggy whispered a yes.

She thought so much of Beatie, yet Beatie had such strange ideas about bringing up children. Looking down at the four of them shrieking and dragging each other towards the slopping bleached curtains, she couldn't blame Beth for this naked display. She suspected it was Virginia's fault. Still, she should never have allowed her to mix with the Hatherley girl. She was far too free and easy.

She turned hurriedly away from the sight of her naked daughter dancing, strong-limbed and totally lacking in self-consciousness.

'My overalls,' she muttered, 'are rather wet. I'll go and change.'

'Double, double dare you to jump off the jetty,' yelled Rusty.

They sprinted across the grass and over the vegetable patches.

'Last one in's a donkey,' panted Beth.

With one yell they tore along the rough wooden planks of the jetty, leapt high in the air and tumbled, splashing, into the river.

Charlie and Susan stumbled after them and stood at the edge.

'Oh boy,' said Rusty, surfacing, 'this is the tops.'

Peggy, umbrella in tow, marched up to the jetty. Charlie and Susan looked up and grinned.

'Go indoors at once,' she said. 'You'll catch your deaths of cold.'

'Can't we go in the water, Mummy?' said Charlie. 'Can't we?'

'Certainly not. Now go indoors.'

'Don't want to,' said Charlie.

'Don't want to,' repeated Susan.

Peggy glared fiercely down at them. 'You'll get a smacked bottom if you don't do as you're told.'

Susan took hold of Charlie's hand and pulled him sulking back along the jetty.

Rusty and Beth glanced at each other, treading water.

'I think,' said Peggy quietly, 'you had both better get out.'

She held out two towels. The girls hauled themselves up.

'We were only having a little fun,' said Rusty.

'You have deliberately disobeyed me. I told you not to go out in the rain.'

'You did not. You said I couldn't go out *walking* in the

rain. You didn't say anything about *dancing* in the rain, or *swimming* in the rain, or hanging up curtains ...'

'That will do. Now cover yourself up with this towel before the neighbours see you.'

'There aren't any neighbours except Beth, and she's seen me already.'

'If I hear any more from you, you will go to bed without lunch.'

Rusty snatched the towel from her and flung it on to the jetty. 'You know what you are?' she yelled. 'A party pooper!'

Beth suppressed a smile.

'Virginia, if you don't put that towel round yourself, you won't be attending any bonfire night.'

'O.K.,' Rusty said, snatching it back up.

She dropped her head and placed the towel round her head, twisting it in front as Beatie had done so that she had a Queen of Sheba turban.

With that she walked haughtily past her mother and strode back across the garden, never once looking down.

Beth began to shiver. 'I think I'd better go home now,' she said.

Peggy, who was still holding the umbrella over her head, nodded. Together they walked back in silence towards the house.

9

'She's an independent, free-spirited young girl,' said Beatie, pouring away the washing-up water. 'Quite able to look after herself. If you're worried about her safety, why don't you take a boat out with her?'

'I'm not a strong enough swimmer.'

'But she is. And after all you did say she could go with Beth, didn't you?'

'Beatie, she won't be able to go wandering off on her own in Guildford or at school. It wouldn't be fair to allow her to begin doing that here.'

'Then stay.'

'Please, Beatie, don't start that again.'

'She could go to Beth's school and run and explore to her heart's content.'

'I've told you, it's totally out of the question, so there's no use discussing it.'

Beatie and Rusty's mother were standing in the kitchen looking out of the window. Rusty was sitting on the jetty. Since the rain incident, the river was out of bounds until such time as her mother wished. The jetty was the nearest she could get to it.

'Charlie and Susan have more freedom to go off on their own than she does.'

'They know the area better, and anyway,' she murmured, 'they haven't been away for five years.'

The telephone rang. She turned away stiffly and left to answer it.

Beatie couldn't bear to see Rusty sitting on her own. She decided to wander down and have a chat.

She had hardly reached the conservatory when Beth appeared around the corner with a wheelbarrow.

'Hello, Beatie,' she said brightly. 'Got anything I can take for the bonfire?'

'Oh, I'm sure I have. Look in the woodshed and help yourself.'

Beth glanced around briefly and lowered her voice. 'Is Rusty allowed out of bounds yet?'

Beatie shook her head. 'Her mother won't give her permission to go on the river until she's apologized. Rusty apologized and then apologized for apologizing.'

'What!'

'She said that she wasn't really sorry. That she was only apologizing because she wanted to go on the river. So her second apology was for the lie she told when she apologized.'

'Bloody hell.'

'So it's stalemate. Rusty doesn't believe she's in the wrong. Her mother believes she is.'

'I suppose,' said Beth, whispering, 'it's all right us being together, is it? I mean I'm not supposed to contaminate her or anything, am I?'

'No,' said Beatie, laughing. 'Why don't you go and join her? She's down by the jetty.'

Beth put down the wheelbarrow and sprang off in the direction of the back garden. 'Hey!' she yelled. 'Hey!'

Rusty turned and gave a light wave. 'Hi.'

Beth ran up to the jetty and flung herself down beside Rusty.

'You look bloody miserable,' she commented.

Rusty gave a shrug.

'It's shitty of her to be so strict,' said Beth. 'I never knew she'd be like this.'

'Me neither,' murmured Rusty. 'She even got mad when I moved the furniture around in my room. She said it wasn't my room, they weren't my possessions, and I had no right to touch them. I only wanted to make it homey. But I suppose she's right. It isn't my room, or my home, or my anything. As soon as we leave here, I'll be going to boarding school.'

'I wish you could stay here, don't you?'

'Oh, I don't care any more. I'll be glad to go away. Anything's gotta be better than this. At least I'll have company. I get so lonesome here.'

'Thanks,' said Beth.

Rusty swung around.

'Oh, I don't mean with you. It's just that I'm not allowed to do anything with you, that's all. When I'm at boarding school, I won't have her breathing down my neck any more. I'll have more freedom.'

'Hm,' said Beth. 'I don't know about that. We've had people come to our school from boarding schools, and they've been so surprised at the difference that they've just gone berserk.'

'Why?'

'Oh, because at my school there aren't so many rules, and you don't have to go to the classes if you don't want to, and –'

'You don't have to go to classes?'

'No.'

'You mean, you can just play around all day?'

'If you want to.'

'But isn't your school a private school? I mean, you have to pay to go to it, right?'

'Yes. My parents don't, because they work on the Estate. Anyone who works on the Estate, their children can go there free.'

'But the ones that pay, don't they get mad, paying for their children to play around all day?'

'Sometimes they get a bit funny when they're older, and then they take them away when it gets near School

Certificate exams, but most people who stay and take the exams usually pass them.'

'But you said no one goes to any classes.'

'No, I didn't. I said you don't *have* to if you don't want to. But some of the classes are really good.'

'I wish I was grown up,' said Rusty. 'Then I could go wherever I wanted instead of having someone else tell me where I was going to and where I had to live.'

'Where would you go?'

'America.'

'Do you think you'll go back when you're older?'

'You bet. I hate this dump of a place.'

'It is not a dump,' said Beth hotly. 'You've only seen a little patch of it.'

'Don't I know it!'

'Listen,' said Beth, 'do you want to help me collect wood for the bonfire?'

'You bet.' She frowned for an instant. 'I hope I get to go to it.'

Beth put an arm round her. 'I'll tie some sheets together and throw them up to your window so you can climb down.'

Rusty smiled. 'So where can we find dead wood? I mean, the river is still out of bounds for me.'

'Beatie says there's some wood in the shed.'

Once inside the woodshed Beth let out a loud groan. Leaning up against the walls were several thick branches.

'We'll never get those into the wheelbarrow,' she said. 'I suppose I could drag a couple home and ask my father to cut them up.'

Rusty spotted two axes leaning in the corner, one large and one small.

'That's O.K.,' she said, 'I'll cut them up.'

'With what? Your magic wand?'

'With the axe, dumbo.'

'Listen, I don't fancy telling your mother that you're

lying in the woodshed with amputated hands or feet, thank you very much.'

Rusty waved her aside.

'Uncle Bruno taught us all to chop wood. So did the Fitzes. I sometimes earned money doing it.'

Beth stared at her in disbelief as she took hold of the smaller axe.

'Now wait a minute,' she said, backing towards the door.

'Don't worry, it's a cinch.'

She cleared the top of a huge log, propped a branch on top, and held it firmly. As the axe swung upwards and whistled diagonally downwards, Beth placed her hands over her eyes and peered through her fingers.

'Bloody hell!' she exclaimed, when the first branch had been sliced into a pile of clean fragments. 'You really can do it!'

'I'll keep them a little long. You don't want them too short for the fire. Doesn't it have a great smell?' she said, holding a freshly cut branch. 'Reminds me of cookouts, back home.' She turned eagerly to Beth, who was now sitting in the wheelbarrow. 'We used to cook over a big wood fire: hamburgers, pickles, olives, potatoes baked in the hot ashes, stuff like that. And Uncle Bruno would throw some butter in the fudge pan and start making up fudge. And we'd play games and music, and people would bring their latest swing records for the music box. Last summer we used to play Frank Sinatra records over and over and over. And when the guests had gone home, we'd all huddle around the fire and have hot chocolate and cinnamon toast or dip cinnamon sticks in hot milk. Did it taste good!'

'Oh don't,' groaned Beth. 'You're making me hungry.'

'I'm making me hungry too.'

She lifted up the axe and started chopping again. Last summer? she thought. It wasn't last summer. It was this one. Only it seemed so far back. Was it only a few weeks ago that she was in America, and Janey and her American sisters were nuts over Frank Sinatra? She began humming.

'What's that tune?' said Beth.

'"This Is A Lovely Way To Spend An Evening". It's one of the songs Frank Sinatra sings. Don't you know it?'

'No. I've never even heard of him. Is he popular in America?'

'Popular? He's the tops. Everyone's crazy about him. Girls just line up for hours so they can get to see him perform. Phew!' she added, putting the axe down. 'This is hot work.' She gazed at two large branches leaning up against the wall. 'I guess I better cut those up outside. Work up a good swing.'

'You're not going to use the big axe, are you?' asked Beth, alarmed.

'Sure I am. If you get a good swing, it's O.K. I'll probably have to yell some to get the strength.' She picked up the axe. 'It's heavier than I thought.' She glanced at the branches again. 'You know, I think a saw would be better. Then you could hold it steady for me.'

Beth tipped herself out of the wheelbarrow.

Between them they dragged out the two branches and rolled out the large chopping log. In the conservatory they found an old saw. At first they took turns, one holding the branch steady while the other pressed her knee on one side of the log and began sawing; but Beth didn't seem to have the same strength as Rusty.

'Did you do body-building exercises in America?' she exclaimed as Rusty eased the saw through the wood.

'No. It's just you gotta let the saw do the work for you.'

'Why do you sometimes close one eye?'

'To keep the line straight. It helps some. You don't have to press so hard.' She looked at Beth, who was steadying the branch. 'What you gotta do is pull the saw toward you to make the first groove, then keep your head over the saw so you can keep it straight. If you can keep it straight, it's not hard.'

Rusty had almost finished a third branch when she became aware of someone striding briskly towards them. It was her mother.

'Uh-oh,' she muttered. 'What have I done wrong this time?'

She pretended not to have seen her, and continued sawing. Her mother stopped and stood beside her. Rusty slowly raised her head.

'Hi,' she said.

Peggy glanced at Beth. 'I think you had better go home,' she said.

'We're nearly finished,' said Rusty. 'I'd like to give Beth a hand loading up the wood.'

'Very well.'

Peggy followed them into the woodshed and held open the door for them as they pushed the wheelbarrow out. She caught sight of the small axe lying beside some newly cut branches.

'Virginia,' she said quietly, 'have you been using that axe?'

'Uh-huh. The branches were too long, so I cut them down a little. Oh,' she said, catching the repressed wrath in her mother's face. 'I should have asked permission, right?'

Her mother nodded slowly.

'Sorry. I didn't think.'

'She was only helping me out, Peggy,' said Beth.

Peggy flinched. She was used to Beth, and her brothers and sister calling her by her first name, as they did most adults, but now suddenly, in front of her daughter, it made her feel strangely uncomfortable.

'Do you realize you could have had a serious accident?'

'Uncle Bruno taught me how to do it a safe way,' Rusty explained.

'Well, in this country we don't expect young girls to chop up wood. That's a boy's job.'

Rusty could feel herself getting riled.

'O.K. Next time I'll ask Charlie to do it, seeing as he's the only boy around here.'

'That's enough,' retorted her mother. 'Hurry up and finish helping Beth. I want to have a word with you.'

Rusty continued picking up the branches. 'Party pooper,' she muttered.

Once the wheelbarrow was loaded, it was obvious that Beth would need help wheeling it.

'I think I ought to give Beth a hand pushing it,' said Rusty. Clenching her fists behind her back, she asked permission. 'May I?'

'I want a word with you first.'

Rusty followed her mother through the conservatory. As she passed the kitchen window, she glanced aside, hoping to catch a glimpse of Beth, but all she could see was the forbidden river gurgling at the bottom of the garden.

Her mother remained silent until they had reached the living room.

'Now,' she said, whirling around, 'I don't want you helping yourself to other people's property without asking. I thought I had made that quite clear after you borrowed the boat.'

'I was only helping out.'

'Don't answer back.'

'Why not? I have a right to have my say, same as you.'

'You're a child and you'll do as you're told.'

Rusty gave a loud sigh.

'I don't know why you're so insolent all the time,' Peggy began. 'I thought you'd be glad to be back here in England with your brother and me and –'

'You're both out doing things,' said Rusty. 'Charlie's with Susan and you're always helping people out.'

'Don't answer me back!'

'I might as well leave, then,' said Rusty, 'since I'm not supposed to say anything or do anything. Maybe I ought to just go back to the Omsks. They don't think I'm such a nuisance.'

'Virginia!'

Her mother's face reddened. Rusty watched her light a cigarette. That was another thing Rusty didn't like about her mother: her smoking. If she smoked long cigarettes in an elegant holder, maybe, just maybe she would have approved, but her cigarettes were always such cheap, stubby-looking things, and often she'd only smoke half of one, stub it out, and then put it back into the cigarette packet for later.

Her mother was staring down at the carpet.

'Sit down,' she said quietly.

Rusty wandered over to the sofa.

Her mother sat down beside her. 'Virginia,' she began, 'when in Rome, one does as the Romans do. Do you understand?'

'Uh-huh, I think so. You mean toe the line, that it?'

'Not exactly,' Peggy said slowly. 'But you'll have to learn to adapt to the English way of life and, of course,' she added, 'to living with us again.'

'Uh-huh, but I don't know when I'm doing anything wrong until after I've done it, and even then it doesn't seem so bad. I mean, what's wrong with chopping up wood?'

'Nothing. It's just that' – Peggy hesitated – 'well, it's not very lady-like.'

'Grandma Fitz does it. She's all for us girls learning to fend for ourselves. I mean, it isn't as if I cut down a tree'

'But it'd be considered a bit odd here if you chopped up wood.'

'The Omsks didn't think I was odd.' She paused.

'Sometimes other people thought we were a little odd, but they were usually pantywaists.'

'Panty what?'

'Pantywaists. You know. Cowards. People who are too cowardly to do *anything*.'

'Well,' said Peggy, 'you're not with the Omsks now. I expect when you were with them, you had to make adjustments to their way of life.'

'Yeah. I guess.'

There was a brief silence.

'Well, I'm glad we've had this little talk, Virginia,' said Peggy, and she stood up awkwardly. 'I suppose you'd better hurry up and join Beth.'

'You mean I can go?'

'Yes.'

Rusty sprang to her feet. 'Zowee!'

Peggy found it impossible to restrain a smile.

Rusty ran for the door, and then stopped.

'I guess,' she said, 'you'll want me back for tea.'

'If you're hungry. Otherwise you don't need to be back until six.'

'See you later, then. So long.'

As Rusty dived out through the door, Peggy found herself saying 'So long' back. She gave a groan and stared out of the bay window.

The door swung open. It was Beatie.

'What's going on?' she said excitedly. 'I heard a lot of whooping down here.'

'Oh dear. I hope it didn't wake you up.'

Just then Rusty and Beth pushed the wheelbarrow past the window.

'Hello' said Beatie curiously. 'What's changed your mind?'

Peggy drew on her cigarette. 'Oh, I don't know. I'm at my wits' ends to know what to do with her. I mean, honestly, do you know what I found her doing in the back garden? Sawing wood! Before that, she'd been chopping it up!'

'Oh good,' said Beatie. 'It'd be splendid if she could tackle some of that pile.'

'Oh Beatie, don't be silly. She's a girl. I can't have her breaking up wood.'

'I see. So it's all right for you to fix car engines, but not for your daughter to saw wood.'

'That's different. I did it because there was a war on. And I have to do it now because, well, there's no one else to do it.'

'Tosh! You love it.'

10

As soon as they reached the road, Rusty let go of the wheelbarrow and did a crazy dance, throwing her head back and beating her chest with her fists.

Beth lifted the wheelbarrow up again and Rusty joined her. Together they pushed it along the bumpy road. No sooner had they heaved it up one hill than they were leaning back and skidding on their heels to prevent the barrow from careering down the other side.

When they reached the foot of the final hill, they hauled the wheelbarrow up to a hedge, leapt up on to the bars of a gate, and sat straddled across the top. Rusty turned herself around so that she could see the fields.

'You know, I can't get over how green it is here.'

'Isn't it green in America?' asked Beth.

'It's green in Connecticut, but not like this. I mean, this is greener than green.'

They sat silently, drinking in the view: the yellow stubble of cut cornfields, the pinky-brown soil of a ploughed field, the rows of green leaves in vegetable patches, the hedgerows interspersed with low walls made of small grey rocks.

'It sure is pretty,' murmured Rusty. 'Everything's so small here, though. Even the trees seem small.'

'Are you ready for a hard one?' asked Beth.

Rusty leapt to the ground. 'Sure I am. Let's go.'

Beth spat on the insides of her hands and rubbed them together.

'This is more like going up a wall, not a hill,' said Rusty, as they began to push.

Halfway up, they stopped and leaned heavily against the wheelbarrow for a rest.

They took a deep breath and with grinding slowness eased the wheelbarrow further upward. A handful of branches rolled off it down the hill.

'Maybe if we yell, like the Indians, that'll give us more strength.'

Beth nodded, red-faced.

'Ready,' said Rusty, 'set, go!' And with that they whooped and howled and screamed their way up the rest of the hill. As soon as they had tipped it over the top, they pushed it off the road, flung their arms around each other and danced in circles.

'Yahoo!' yelled Rusty.

In the distance there was a pyramid of wood, branches and rubbish. Several boys and a girl were attempting to drag an enormous branch towards the mound. As Rusty and Beth pulled the wheelbarrow through the gate, two of the boys looked in their direction and waved.

'My brothers,' explained Beth.

The taller of the two ran over to help them.

'Where did you find all this?' he exclaimed.

'At Beatie's. Rusty chopped and sawed it up.'

The boy gazed at her in admiration.

'Hi,' she said.

'Pleased to meet you.' And he held out his hand.

He was a skinny boy with untidy auburn hair that stuck out at weird angles and hung across his forehead. His large ears protruded like a pair of jug-handles. He was slightly smaller than Beth. As he shook her hand vigorously, she noticed that he had the same blue eyes.

'Harry's the name.'

He let go of her hand, flung his arms around the pile of wood as if embracing it, and dragged up a huge pile of branches.

'By the way,' he said, through the spaces in the wood, 'any news about the Japs?'

'Not a sausage,' said Beth. They began walking. 'You don't think that after all this they'll change their minds, do you?'

'No,' said Harry. 'Those awful bombs the Americans dropped will make them agree to anything.'

Rusty felt embarrassed.

'But if it stops the War, won't the Americans have saved lots of lives?' she said.

Harry shrugged. 'All I know is that they dropped them on women and children. Makes you sick.'

'Harry's a pacifist,' said Beth.

'What's a pacifist?'

'Someone who doesn't believe in war.'

'But wouldn't you fight if there was a war?'

'I'd be a conscientious objector,' he said.

'What's that?'

'I'd refuse call-up.'

'Is that the same as being drafted?'

'Yes.'

Rusty gave a low whistle. Back home, no boy she knew would ever refuse the draft. Even Skeet was just dying to fight for his country. Anybody who refused was a coward. Rusty didn't know what to say.

They had almost reached the bonfire when a younger boy joined them. He had straight mousy hair, a snub nose, and freckles. He nodded to Rusty and gathered an armful of wood from the barrow.

'This is Ivor,' said Beth. 'He's my youngest brother.'

'Hi.' He gave another nod and went back to the bonfire.

'How old is everybody?' said Rusty.

Beth lifted up the handles of the wheelbarrow and spilled the wood out.

'Harry's twelve, Ivor's ten, and my sister Anne, who you haven't met yet, is seven.'

After they had placed all the branches against the pile, Rusty and Beth stood back for a moment.

'What now?' asked Rusty.

'Come home with me. We'll go for a cycle ride.' Beth turned swiftly. 'Harry,' she said, 'can Rusty borrow your bike?'

He nodded. 'The front tyre needs pumping up, though.'

'Thanks,' said Rusty, but Harry had his back to her and was absorbed in dragging another piece of wood towards the bonfire.

Rusty had imagined that Beth's house would be bigger. Instead, it was grey and small and tacked on to another house. Back in Connecticut, no one's house was joined to anyone else's; each one stood on its own patch of land. A tall thin woman in her thirties waved to them through an open window at the back. 'You must be Rusty,' she said in the same sort of accent that Ivy had.

'We's takin' the bikes,' said Beth, and she chatted to her mother about the big bonfire they were making.

At the back of a small vegetable garden beyond a dilapidated shed, Rusty noticed a small girl peering at her over a swinging hammock.

'Hi,' she said.

The girl smiled. 'Hello. You Rusty?'

'Uh-huh. How'd you guess?'

'Beth told us about you. Your clothes look American, too. Nice colours.'

'You must be Anne.'

She was about to walk over and chat with her when she felt Beth touch her shoulder. 'Let's pump Harry's tyre up.'

'Are you staying for tea?' asked Anne.

'I'd like to, but ...' She shrugged.

Beth's mother leaned out of the window.

'You're welcome to,' she said. 'I can phone Beatie's and ask yer mother.'

'That'd be swell.'

'I'll tell you what she says when you gits back.'

As Rusty cycled, barefoot, she felt like an eagle released from its cage. Having been used to wide, smooth roads and riding on the right-hand side, she had felt a little uneasy at first, but with Beth leading she soon grew used to the hilly, high-hedged lanes and ringing the bicycle bell each time they approached a corner. Once, they had to press themselves back against the hedges to allow a lorry to pass.

In spite of the battered state of Harry's bicycle, it was much better than the one she had back home. Not only was it lighter, but she was able to free-wheel on it.

She loved the feel of it beneath her as it shuddered over loose stones and sailed past fields. She even liked pushing it up steep hills, and having to suddenly leap off it and fling herself into a hedge every time she and Beth heard the beep of an approaching car.

They had been cycling for some time when she noticed a tiny railway line.

'Say,' she yelled, 'is that for little kids?'

Beth stopped and waited for her to catch up. Rusty eased herself up alongside.

'It leads to Staverton Bridge station,' said Beth.

'You mean regular trains run along here?'

'Yes. Come on, I'll show you.' And she pushed the bicycle forward.

Sure enough, a small building came into view. Rusty gaped at it, astonished. They cycled up to it and hopped off their bikes.

'You mean this is a regular station?' asked Rusty, amazed.

'Yes. Want to have a look?'

'You bet.'

Little lamp-posts stood on the platform. Across the tiny track was a small signal-box. A field and a clump of trees stretched out beyond it. There was a railway station with a small garden in front of it. Beth and Rusty stood barefoot on the scorching platform, the sun beating hotly down on them.

Rusty's thick hair clung damply to her T-shirt. She let her bike rest against her legs and scooped her hair up on top of her head to allow some air to cool her neck.

'Where does that river go?' she murmured.

'Past our school. The railway lines run alongside it.'

'Oh, I wish I could go for a ride on it.'

Beth began to wheel her bike out. 'The school actually gets complaints from the people around here who take that ride.'

'What about?' said Rusty. She allowed her hair to fall in a hot heap around her shoulders.

'Sometimes they see us swimming.'

'What's wrong with that?'

'We aren't wearing swimsuits.'

'They shouldn't look, then.'

'Exactly.'

They mounted their bicycles and began cycling steadily. It wasn't too hilly now.

'Do your parents complain, too?'

'No. They think the school's a bit strange, and so do the villagers, but we love it. They both hated school, so they're pleased we like it so much.'

'Why don't they send you to a regular school, instead of a private one?'

'Because we'd have to leave at fourteen. At *my* school, if we want to go to university or college or whatever, at least there's a chance. I mean, it's up to us.'

They dawdled past a bridge and high hedges and grey stone houses.

'Does that mean that if you want to take exams for college, you have to go to a private school?' asked Rusty.

'Yes. Unless you can get a scholarship into a grammar or a public school. And,' she continued, 'at most other schools the boys are separated from the girls. At least at this school me and my brothers can all stay together.'

'Do you want to go to college?'

'No. I want to be a farmer.'

'But,' said Rusty, 'if you don't want to go to college, you might as well go to a regular school.'

'My school has its own farm, so I can help out. Next term I move into the senior part of the school. They have stables there.'

'You're kidding!'

She turned and smiled. 'I'm bloody lucky. I know that. If my parents weren't working on the Estate, I wouldn't be able to go there at all.'

That afternoon they cycled all through the lanes, stopping every now and then to laze in the grass or lean over a gate and talk. Rusty still felt like a visitor on holiday in a foreign country. She found herself automatically reminding herself to tell Skeet about this, or Janey about that, or Uncle Bruno and Grandma Fitz about something that Beth had said, or Aunt Hannah about a little stone church she had seen, or Gramps about English bicycles.

It was as they drew nearer Beth's home that Rusty's spirits began to sink. It'd soon be time to return to Beatie's place. But as they pushed open the large wooden gate into the garden, Anne appeared from the back doorway.

'You's stayin' for tea,' she announced.

A few old mats were thrown on to the scrubbed wooden table, and soon home-made brown bread, butter, plum jam, cheese, tomatoes, boiled eggs, lettuce, and dark carrot cake were spread out on them.

It was such a chatterbox family. For a while they talked

about the bonfire, so Rusty was able to join in, but then they started to talk about other things and to use words that she didn't understand. Every now and then they would drop into a Devonshire accent, which made it even more difficult.

It was Beth's mother who drew her back into the conversation. 'Come on, you lot,' she said. 'Rusty don't know what yer on about.'

Beth, who was sitting beside Rusty, looked apologetically at her. 'Sorry, I forgot.'

'Tell us about America,' said Mrs Hatherley.

So Rusty told them about blueberry pie, and milkshakes with walnut syrup, and how she had seen a wonderful film called *The Wizard of Oz* and it was in colour.

'Is it true,' said Beth's mother, 'that you can actually 'ave yer hair permed by a hairdresser and that it stays?'

'Sure,' said Rusty. 'You must mean having a permanent wave put in your hair. Aunt Hannah sometimes has that done.'

And she told them how they made Valentines and how she went through crazes of collecting things like coins and dud bullets and arrowheads.

'Real Indian arrowheads?' asked Ivor, the quietest of the four.

'Uh-huh.'

And she told them how they sometimes had corn muffins for breakfast, and how one afternoon they'd been taken to see a brand-new musical called *Oklahoma* and there were cowboys dancing and singing and leaping all over the place. And how they'd make fudge and listen to phonograph records.

Rusty was absolutely the centre of attention. Everyone was listening, wide-eyed, to her. She left out the fact that she had to save up all her allowance and do odd jobs so that she could go to the cinema and buy milk-shakes and roller-skates.

Eventually the talk returned to the bonfire.

'Roast corn on a stick is nice,' suggested Rusty.

They shook their heads and started on about the school and the work being done on it, now that all the evacuees had left. Rusty was beginning to grow sick of the sound of their school, especially since she wouldn't be going to it. She had expected to feel different with a big family again, not so lonely. Instead, she felt even lonelier.

At six o'clock the radio was turned on, only they called it a wireless. It was a huge, brown, wooden affair that sent out lights when it was switched on. A man with a voice like something out of an English film was reading the news. Back home, she wouldn't have bothered listening to the news at all, so she was surprised when everyone fell silent, even seven-year-old Anne.

The news was disappointing. There was still no news of a Japanese surrender.

'Cheer up, my loves,' said Mrs Hatherley. 'They might announce something on the Nine O'clock News.'

After tea, Rusty had to return to Beatie's house. Beth was going off to give some more help with the bonfire, so Rusty walked back by herself. She found that she was walking deliberately slowly. She couldn't understand why she felt so miserable. What was wrong with her? She imagined that she was in bed and Aunt Hannah was sitting at the end of it, and they were talking.

'Aunt Hannah,' she whispered, 'why don't I fit in? I just can't figure it out.' And she tried to guess what kind of answer Aunt Hannah would have given.

'Wait till you go to school' came the words in her head. 'It'll get better.'

Of course, thought Rusty, all the Hatherleys went to the same school. Once she started at her own school, *then* she'd make friends. Grandma Fitz had warned her that the first few months might be lonely. She stopped and leaned against a hedge. The first few months! She saw the long years without the Omsks and the Fitzes and her friends stretching out before her.

'Walk tall,' she muttered, thinking of Gramps.

She straightened herself up, swung her sandals carelessly in her fingers, and continued walking.

11

There was a loud hooting from the front garden and someone was yelling. As Rusty tipped herself hastily out of the camp bed, it fell over. She stepped on to the chair by the window and peered down.

Mitch Flannagan was sitting in a jeep with Ivy. 'Wake up, everyone,' he yelled. 'Wake up!'

Rusty heard Beatie move on the landing and voices coming from downstairs. She leapt off the chair and flung open the door.

Beatie was halfway down the stairs, followed by a bewildered and sleepy Charlie and Susan. Rusty met her mother on the first-floor landing. She was wearing the oldest-looking pair of pyjamas Rusty had ever seen. They were faded pink with patches on them.

Rusty jumped down to the bathroom landing and slid down the banisters. By the time she reached the hall, Beatie had disappeared into the garden.

'What is it?' Rusty cried. 'What is it?' She ran through the hallway and collided with Beatie coming back.

'It's the Japs,' Beatie cried ecstatically. 'They've surrendered.'

'Oh thank God,' whispered a voice behind her.

Rusty turned.

Her mother was standing, with her green W.V.S. coat around her shoulders.

Just then came the faint sound of church bells ringing. Peggy, startled, grabbed Beatie by the arm.

'It's the invasion,' she gasped.

Beatie laughed. 'Oh, Peggy,' she chuckled. 'No, it's not. No more invasions. No more war.'

Peggy smiled at her own foolishness.

Charlie and Susan came rushing in from the garden, squealing with excitement, followed by Mitch.

'Hurry up!' he said. 'You're missing all the fun. They've lit bonfires in Plymouth. You can just about see the light from them up the hill. And people are letting off fireworks in town. Come on, you kids, just put sweaters on over your pyjamas,' he said. 'Move.'

'I bet they're lighting the big bonfire here,' said Rusty.

'There'll be nothing left to celebrate with tomorrow,' said Peggy.

'Oh, who cares!' yelled Mitch. 'It's over. All over. I can go home.' He flung his arms round Beatie and twirled her around. 'O.K., baby, let's cut a rug.' And he proceeded to manoeuvre her all over the hall.

A hooting from the jeep interrupted this strange display.

'That's Ivy,' he said, 'telling you to hurry up.'

Charlie and Susan, Beatie and Rusty tore up and down the stairs, throwing on the nearest clothes at hand.

It wasn't until they had run out into the garden and clambered into the jeep that Rusty realized her mother wasn't with them. For a moment the sinking feeling returned. Surely she didn't have to ask permission to celebrate, did she?

It was Beatie who commented. She saw Peggy standing in the porch, smoking a cigarette. 'Come along, Peggy,' she said.

Peggy shook her head. 'No. You all go on.'

'Aw, come on Peg,' insisted Mitch.

'I'd rather stay, if you don't mind. I suddenly feel terribly tired.'

Ivy touched Mitch's arm. He turned and smiled. Gee, thought Rusty, they really love one another. You could see it in their eyes.

'O.K., honey,' he whispered. 'I guess everyone's gotta celebrate in their own way.'

He gave a nod to Peggy. 'So long,' he said.

She waved, and watched the jeep hoot and rumble its way towards the dirt road.

Staring out at the night sky, Peggy listened to the faint chimes of the church bells still ringing. So it was all over, she thought. Now her husband could be sent home. She had lived for this moment. Now that it had come, she felt absolutely nothing.

Rusty folded her blue sweater and placed it neatly in her suitcase. She slid her sandals in alongside. Her best skirt and cardigan were lying over the chair with a pair of washed white bobby socks. Beatie had even managed to find some Meltonian so that she had been able to whiten up the toes and heels of her saddle shoes. She wanted to look the tops for her grandmother. The following day she would be meeting her for the first time in five years.

She knelt by the bed and spread out all the letters that had suddenly avalanched on to the house in the past two weeks.

There was only one letter from Skeet – he had never been the greatest letter-writer – three from Janey, two from Grandma Fitz and Gramps, and a bumper one from Aunt Hannah and Uncle Bruno with all little bits written in by Kathryn and Alice and Jinkie.

She rested her head against the bed. It was September. Soon it would be Labor Day. Everyone would be leaving their summer cottages and heading back home. People would be selling pumpkins and squashes and apples and goat-milk candy on the roadside. The ice-cream parlours would start closing and the shutters would go up for the winter. She closed her eyes. For an instant she could see schoolbooks in the Omsks' hall and hear the sound of kids playing ball in the driveway, and someone yelling because the door of the hall cupboard had burst open and a whole stream of baseball bats, tennis racquets, roller skates and boots had come tumbling out on to the floor.

She wondered who had taken over her newspaper

delivery. She just hoped that Mr Harpstein had kept the signs that she had painted for him. She'd made the stencil designs herself.

Soon Skeet and Janey would be playing Chinese chequers and pick-up-sticks down in the romper room, and lots of other games like Five Hundred, Tripoli and Monopoly, and there'd be Sunday-night suppers for the gang. And the house would be full of students again. Kids would be dropping in from school and Jinkie would be forever baking brownies. No, she wouldn't. She'd be busy taking care of the baby, and looking foward to Ted coming home.

'I bet they'll have a swell homecoming for him,' she whispered.

She remembered Jinkie and Ted's little flat. She liked paying visits there. Jinkie would make beautiful huge light New England-style biscuits.

She glanced at the Fitzes' letters. They had been spending time at their summer cottage on Lake Champlain. She loved it there, no matter what time of the year it was. Sometimes, even in the winter, she and Skeet would go and stay with them and camp out in the cottage, and they'd go ice-boating and skating on the frozen lake.

Oh, she missed them. And Janey.

Poor Janey. Her mother had dragged her off to some place and got her to record her voice on a disc so that she could hear how screechy and monotonous it was. Sometimes her mother was the end. Janey had worked for a whole week on her voice, softening it and making it go up and down as she spoke. Skeet had met her down at the drugstore, and, when she had started talking in her new way, he had just cracked up and fallen off the stool. He said she sounded like a drunk on a roller-coaster.

She heard her mother calling to her from downstairs.

'Yeah?' she yelled back.

'We'll be leaving in ten minutes.'

'O.K.!'

For their last afternoon, her mother thought it would be nice if they could go out for a drive in the Bomb. Rusty was just folding the Fitzes' letters when she caught sight of a postscript at the bottom of one of them. It was in Gramps' handwriting.

'Remember the Fitz motto,' it ran. ' "Believe in yourself, believe in others, and work like hell." '

She laughed, grabbed her Beanie, and ran downstairs.

Charlie was standing in the hallway, his freckled face so scrubbed that it had a shine to it. He scowled briefly at her. Rusty was not looking forward to spending an afternoon with him. He'd been so darned grouchy lately. It had been a week since Susan and her mother had left for Southampton; they had moved there so that they would be ready to leave for America as soon as all their papers were in order. Charlie seemed to blame Rusty for their going.

He stuffed his hands into the pockets of his grey frayed shorts and walked slowly out to the porch. She looked at his thick, curly red hair, his old white shirt sticking out between his braces, and his little bare legs, and wanted to hug him. She knew how much his heart was breaking.

Her mother was standing outside in an old sweater and slacks, smiling brightly. Too brightly, thought Rusty.

'Hop in the front, you two,' she said.

Beatie was sitting on the sill of the dining-room window.

'Aren't you coming?' asked Rusty.

'And have all my innards thrown around in that thing?' she retorted. 'The real reason,' she whispered quickly, 'is that I'm preparing an extra-special tea. I want it to be a surprise for Charlie. So keep mum, won't you?'

Charlie refused to sit in the front with Rusty. Instead, he insisted on having the back seat all to himself.

Rusty gripped the side of her seat as the car jerked violently into life.

'Atta girl!' her mother whispered to the throbbing engine. She pushed the large gear lever across and down with a grinding creak. The car leapt forward and then relaxed into a humming rumble.

'For gosh sakes,' commented Rusty, 'aren't you afraid it'll explode?'

'That's why she's called the Bomb,' explained her mother. 'But don't worry. She won't explode.'

Once they had backed down the dirt track and were out on the road, Rusty sat back.

'I've never seen earth such a sort of pinky-brown colour,' Rusty remarked.

'They call it red,' said her mother. 'In some parts of Devon, even the bricks of the houses look pink!'

She had hardly finished speaking when a large tractor came whirring round the corner. Her mother wheeled the window down and leaned out. 'Hello, George!'

'Can't back, I'm afraid, Peggy,' he yelled in a broad Devonshire accent. 'I's got a trailer fixed at the back.'

'Hang on,' she said. 'I'll reverse.'

Rusty was amazed to see her mother pat the dashboard affectionately.

'Come on, old girl,' she whispered, 'don't go letting the side down.'

Within minutes the car was groaning backwards. Charlie stood up to watch.

'Look out the side-window, Charlie, will you?' said Peggy. 'Tell me how far I am from the hedge.'

Rusty leaned out of the window. Charlie gazed briefly at her, stuck out his tongue, and turned away.

Little monster, she thought.

Deftly her mother manoeuvred the ancient bit of metal and rubber back along the lanes and squeezed it into a tiny gap in the hedge. The tractor rumbled by. The trailer was a large wooden box on wheels.

'*That's* a trailer?' gasped Rusty. 'Our trailers are six times the size of that, and you can live in them.'

Her mother frowned.

'Yes, well,' she began. 'The Americans tend to use our words to mean different things.' And with that she backed the Bomb out of the gap and on to the road.

They stopped at a stretch of deserted beach.

Charlie threw open the door and ran down to the sea, his sandals discarded on the running-board.

Rusty shivered. She couldn't understand how her mother and brother could bear not having a coat on.

Beth didn't think it was cold at all, either. 'It's only September,' she had said that morning. 'It gets far colder than this. I thought you'd be used to it. Don't they have snow in Connecticut?'

'Sure they do,' Rusty had replied. 'But we have this thing called central heating. Ever heard of it?'

Rusty and Beth had said their goodbyes just before lunch. She would miss Beth, too.

Rusty wandered up to where her brother was playing in the sand. His legs were a little blue from the wind that was blowing in from the sea, and his nose had started to run, but that didn't seem to bother him.

'Need any help?' she said.

'No, thank you,' he replied icily.

Her mother drew Rusty away, and they strolled in the direction of the sea.

Charlie looked on, furious, and threw a handful of cold sand back into the pit he had begun digging.

'I know,' said Rusty, when they were out of earshot. 'Be patient.'

'He's missing Susan.'

'I know that,' said Rusty angrily. 'And I'm missing

Aunt Hannah, and Uncle Bruno and my American brother and sisters, and Grandma Fitz and Gramps, and Janey, and my school-friends.'

Peggy turned away and stared into the distance. 'Aren't you pleased to be back?' she said shakily.

Rusty was shocked at how pale her mother had become. She hadn't meant to hurt her.

'Of course I am,' she lied.

They had a small picnic, which consisted of jam sandwiches, and tea from a thermos flask. The tea tasted as lousy as usual, but Rusty was so cold that she just poured it down her throat.

Later, while Charlie and her mother built a sand-castle, Rusty sat on the running-board and felt sick. Somehow things were going to get better, she told herself fiercely. Come hell or high water, she was going to make it so.

When they clambered back into the car, Rusty noticed that it was spluttering more than usual.

'Now come on,' murmured her mother. 'It's a long way home.'

It sure as hell is, thought Rusty soberly.

'What's the matter, Mummy?' said Charlie. 'Have the sparks gone wrong?''

'I hope not.'

She turned the engine off, climbed out of the car and rolled up her sleeves.

Charlie gave a dramatic sigh and threw himself wearily back on the seat.

Rusty hopped out. Her mother unfolded the bonnet of the car sideways and peered inside.

'Can I help?' said Rusty.

Her mother, who was staring at a tangle of cables, looked up briefly.

'I don't know yet.'

Rusty stood beside her as her mother stood on tiptoe and leaned over the large wing of the car.

'Would you get me a spanner from the boot?' she said over her shoulder.

'Sure thing,' said Rusty.

She made for the door, and then she stopped.

'Oh dear,' she murmured. 'What's a spanner?'

She didn't want to ask her mother. Whatever a spanner was, it was in the boot. First thing to do was to locate the boot.

She knelt on the front seat and looked into the back, where Charlie was sitting with a picture book. And then she saw them: two large rubber boots standing upright on the floor. All she needed to do now was to find out which one her mother needed.

She leaned over and thrust her hand into one.

Charlie looked up sharply. 'What are you doing?' he said grumpily.

'I'm looking for a spanner.'

Charlie watched her, puzzled. Rusty pushed her hand deeper into the boot.

'Why are you looking in there?' he said.

'Because' – and she was dying to add 'dummy', but she didn't – 'Mother says it's in the boot.'

At that, Charlie took one look at her and began to laugh hysterically.

'O.K.,' said Rusty, 'what's so funny?'

'In the boot!' he spluttered.

'Charlie,' she said, irritated, 'did you hide it?'

He shook his head and laughed even louder.

Her mother, hearing the shrieks, took her head out from under the bonnet. 'What's going on?' she said. She smiled at Charlie. It was the happiest she had seen him all week.

He pointed wildly at the floor. 'She's looking in the Wellingtons!' he yelled. 'She's looking for a spanner in the Wellington boots!'

Rusty was baffled.

'Oh,' said her mother, smiling, and she squeezed Rusty's

shoulder. 'I'm sorry, it's what you call the trunk. We call it the boot.'

'I see,' said Rusty.

'And a spanner is what you call a wrench. That much I learned from . . .' She paused. 'From the G.I.s. And this,' she added, pointing to the bonnet of the car, 'is what we call a bonnet, not a hood.'

'Sorry,' Rusty said, feeling like a fool.

Her mother strode briskly around to the back of the car, fixed it so that it stayed open, and rummaged around inside. Within minutes she was back by the engine, one leg up on the wing of the car. Seconds later, she was lying full length across it.

Charlie by now was outside, peering through the long vertical bars of the radiator, attempting to see the upside-down head of his mother inside.

'Hurrah,' she yelled suddenly. 'I've got a spark!'

She pulled her head out and sat gleefully on the wing.

'Is that good?' said Rusty.

'Marvellous. It means that I don't have to check lots of other things, like the coil or the distributor or the H/T leads or the condenser or the . . .' She stopped. 'It means that it shouldn't take too long to mend.'

She rolled full length on top of the wing again and disappeared inside, mumbling something about the mixture.

'Aha!' she yelled.

'What is it?' said Rusty.

Her mother raised her head. 'There's water in the juice.'

'Juice?'

'Pool.'

'What's that?'

'Petrol. Very cheap, awful petrol,' she said. 'And they have the nerve to ration it, too.' She paused. 'Petrol is what you call gasoline.'

'Yeah, I sorta guessed that. So does that mean we're stuck here?'

'No. It just means that I have to clean it out. There's probably some dirt in there, too. You see, there's a small pipe that comes from the tank at the back of the car and leads up to the engine. The petrol is sucked up by the lift pump down here,' she said, pointing down into the engine.

Rusty peered in, but there was so much to look at that she didn't know which was which. Before she could ask, her mother had begun talking again.

'Then when it's sucked up, it goes into this filter,' she said, indicating a small glass bowl, 'which has this under it. Then the petrol goes into the carb. The carburettor, I mean. Now, the only snag is ...'

To Rusty's amazement, Peggy began to wave her arms about excitedly.

'... if any water or dirt gets through to the jets.' She stopped. 'Jets are these tiny fine nozzles that spray. They're thinner than a needle.' Rusty nodded. 'If these jets get blocked up, that means that no petrol will get sucked into these cylinders,' she said, indicating several of them over her shoulder, 'just lots of air. And, much as I wish we could drive on air, we can't. If there's no petrol coming through, the car won't fire.'

Just as she was about to do her slow dive into the interior of the car, she glanced at Rusty. 'Do you still want to help?'

'Sure.'

'I'm going to unscrew things, and when I'm sure they're clean, I'll put them back together again,' said her mother. 'The important thing is to unscrew the filter bowl, swill out the element, and then ...'

Rusty sat on the running-board to wait for her mother's instructions. She had no idea what she was talking about. While her mother rambled on about how she was going to pump petrol up by priming with some lever under the lift pump, Rusty watched out of the corner of her eye as Charlie came slowly nearer and sat nonchalantly on the running-board.

'Virginia!' called her mother.

She sprang to her feet.

'Now,' Peggy said, 'if you'll just turn the engine over on the self-starter, I'll cover the air intake with my hand. That way the suction in the engine will unstick any bits out of the jets, and,' she added, crossing her fingers, 'it may start.'

'I have to turn the engine over?' said Rusty.

'Yes, that's right, on the self-starter. You turn the key, and when the light goes on, you press the button beside it.'

'O.K.!' And she threw open the door and slid in behind the wheel.

After much key turning and instructions of 'Now push' and 'Stop!' from her mother, the engine suddenly rumbled into life.

'It's firing!' yelled Peggy.

'It's firing,' repeated Charlie. 'Bang! Bang!'

Rusty laughed, and this time when she looked at Charlie, he didn't scowl at her.

On the journey home, Rusty began to sing. She persuaded her mother to help her make up verses about fixing the car engine to 'Ee aye the addio'. They took turns. Her mother began first.

> *'There's water in the juice, there's water in the juice,*
> *Ee aye the addio, there's water in the juice.'*

And Rusty sang,

> *'There's dirt inside the gas, there's dirt inside the gas,*
> *Ee aye the addio, there's dirt inside the gas.'*
> *'It's in the filter bowl,'*

added her mother,

> *'It's in the filter bowl,*
> *Ee aye the addio, it's in the filter bowl.'*

Then Rusty made up the next two.

> *'The jets are all fouled up, the jets are all fouled up,*
> *Ee aye the addio, the jets are all fouled up.*
> *Unscrew the whole darned thing, unscrew the whole*
>   *darned thing,*
> *Ee aye the addio, unscrew the whole darned thing.'*
> *'And then we'll swill 'em out,'*

sang her mother,

> *'And then we'll swill 'em out,*
> *Ee aye the addio, and then we'll swill 'em out.'*

To their surprise, Charlie suddenly joined in with:

> *'And then it'll all go broom! Then it'll all go broom!*
> *Ee aye the addio, and then it'll all go broom!'*

By the time they reached Beatie's, they were all feeling quite happy. Beatie had prepared an enormous spread of food. Somehow she had managed to obtain a tin of condensed milk for Charlie and Rusty. It was gloriously sweet. Rusty drank hers slowly in one long gulp.

'That's the equivalent of diamonds,' remarked her mother.

'Wait till I tell the Omsks,' Rusty spluttered, 'that I swallowed diamonds!'

When Rusty was in bed and her mother was taking a bath, she heard strange whisperings coming from the hall. She sneaked out on to the landing in her pyjamas. Down in the hallway she could see four women, dressed in the green outfits that she recognized as being the Women's Voluntary Service uniform. Beatie was beckoning them in with lots of hand-waving. She glanced up. Immediately she tapped her mouth with her finger.

Rusty crept back into her room.

She was about to get back into bed when she heard the sound of tyres crawling slowly up the dirt track to the garden. She climbed up on to a chair and peered down. Squashed into three old cars were women of all ages and shapes. The ones who weren't pushing the cars piled slowly and quietly out of them. For a moment Rusty felt sad that she had been left out of the surprise – but then Charlie had, too. She jumped off the chair and eased the door ajar so she could eavesdrop. At last her mother emerged from the bathroom. She was wearing her green outfit. Rusty remembered now. She was supposed to be driving to a W.V.S. headquarters that night.

Rusty held her breath and listened to her mother's footsteps going down the stairs. Suddenly there were several loud whoops, followed by a muffled chorus of 'For she's a jolly good fellow, for she's a jolly good fellow'. Rusty slipped out on to the landing, but she couldn't see a thing. They must all have gone into the living room.

It was fun, lying in bed listening to the sounds of a party going on downstairs. It reminded her of the Omsks' place. She intended to stay awake till everyone had started leaving but, when she next awoke, the house was quiet. She put on her Beanie and sneakers and made her way downstairs. She was so thirsty. She crept into the kitchen and filled a jam jar with water, draining it several times. Before returning to bed, she decided to take a last look at the blackout curtains she and Beatie had dyed. She had hardly crossed the room when she sensed that someone was in the front garden. She dropped quickly to her knees, crawled under the bay window, and rose up slowly behind the curtain.

She could see nothing unusual. Just the Bomb standing by one of the trees. She was about to walk away when she saw the glow of a cigarette coming from the driver's seat. She turned away hurriedly and leaned back against the curtain. In that brief moment, the light had exposed her mother sitting alone behind the wheel, and Rusty had seen only too clearly that she was crying.

13

The train pulled into the station at nine o'clock, five hours after it was due. Charlie was exhausted, his face smudged with dark streaks where his grubby fingers had pushed away the tears.

It had been a miserable journey. Rusty and her mother had attempted to act cheerfully for Charlie's sake, but after he had realized that they wouldn't be returning to Beatie's that night, and nor would he be seeing Susan, he collapsed into a corner and wept for hours.

As they stepped off the train with their luggage, a slow drizzle began to fall. They clambered into a taxi. Rusty stared out of the taxi window. The houses, which were made of dark bricks, were all joined up. There were no wide, sweeping lawns leading up to them, only tiny walled gardens.

'Where have all the trees gone, Mummy?' said Charlie.

'Oh,' she said brightly, 'I expect we'll see some in a minute.'

The driver slid down the glass window behind him.

'What number is it, madam?'

'Eighty-three.'

Rusty grew excited. They were almost there. 'When was the last time Charlie saw Grandmother?' she asked.

'A long time ago,' murmured her mother. 'She doesn't like travelling much, and it's a long way for a little boy.'

The taxi drew up at a tall, dark-bricked house. As Rusty pulled out the luggage, she noticed an elderly grey-haired woman standing behind the curtains watching them.

'Is that her?' she whispered.

Her mother nodded.

The door was opened by a tiny, wizened old lady, who stood back and waited for them to enter.

'Hi,' said Rusty.

The old lady bowed. 'I'm Mrs Grace,' she whispered.

A sing-songy voice came tinkling from a room at the side. 'This way, dears.'

How weird, thought Rusty, that her grandmother hadn't come out to meet them. Maybe she had leg trouble. Rusty dragged the luggage into the hallway. Her mother glanced gratefully at her. The old woman showed them into a drawing room, where tea was laid on two low tables.

Mrs Dickinson Senior was sitting upright, on an old-fashioned stuffed chair. She smiled regally at them. Her grey hair was scooped neatly back into a bun, and fastened at the throat of her beige silk dress was a pale cameo brooch.

'Now, now,' she said sweetly to Charlie, who was half asleep in his mother's arms. 'Big boys don't need to be carried, do they?'

'That one does,' said Rusty. 'He's pooped.'

Her grandmother glanced quickly at her.

'Hi,' said Rusty. 'I'm Rusty. I mean, Virginia.'

There was a silence.

'Your granddaughter.'

Her grandmother stared at Rusty's shoes and slowly worked her way up to her head. Though her mouth was smiling, her eyes were not.

'I gathered that,' she said.

'Pleased to meet you,' added Rusty, stretching out her hand.

Her grandmother ignored this action and looked up at Peggy, who had begun whispering in Charlie's ear.

'Tea *is* waiting,' she said firmly.

Peggy lowered Charlie gently into an armchair. He gave a murmur and then opened his eyes.

'That's better,' said Mrs Dickinson Senior. 'Now sit up straight like a proper gentleman.'

Then, to Rusty's utter amazement, she leaned forward and said, 'Where did she pick up that frightful accent?' and she gave a short laugh. 'Well, I suppose school will knock it out of her, and the sooner the better, eh!' And she gave a conspiratorial little smile and leaned back.

'What's wrong with the way I talk?' demanded Rusty.

'It seems,' said her grandmother, 'that you didn't learn any manners while you were in America.'

'It *seems*,' said Rusty, emphasizing the word, 'that you never learned them here. In America we treat our guests with good grace.' If the old bag was going to be pompous, she'd darned well be pompous back.

Her grandmother's eyes blazed for a fraction and her voice became even quieter. 'We?' she repeated. 'You are English, my dear, though unfortunately one would never think it.'

'Mother,' interrupted Peggy, 'we're all terribly tired. It's been a long day.'

'It has for me, too. I've been waiting since four o'clock for you to arrive.'

'I explained that we'd probably be late. You know how the trains are. They're full of demobbing troops.'

At that Mrs Dickinson Senior smiled. 'Yes. You're right. I'm sorry, dear. I suppose I was just a little anxious.' And she waved to Mrs Grace, who had been hovering by her armchair. 'I think we'll have that tea now, Mrs Grace,' she said lightly.

Tea was a miserable affair. Because they hadn't yet been able to change to the shops that would accept their ration books, there was little butter or milk to go around, and Rusty's grandmother did little to conceal her annoyance that they hadn't brought some with them.

'But then you always have been a little helpless,' said Mrs Dickinson Senior, in jest.

If Rusty hadn't caught her mother's eye, she would have exploded again. She really tried to be friendly to her grandmother, but every time Rusty opened her mouth she could see the older woman visibly flinch.

'My dear,' she said at one point, 'you don't have to speak so penetratingly loud.' And sweetly, 'We have a saying here. It's "Don't speak until you are spoken to".'

Rusty glanced at her mother, who was gazing stupefied at the antique furniture and ornaments, and at the large floral curtains at the high windows.

'How on earth did the army manage to keep this all in such good condition?' she exclaimed.

'After the house was requisitioned, I had the furnishings stored away. I left the army to find their own furniture. Good Lord,' she added, 'it was enough that they were allowed to take over the house.'

'But all that curtain material,' Peggy murmured, 'lying somewhere unused.'

'I'm not a charity!' exclaimed Mrs Dickinson Senior.

Peggy could not help thinking of Beatie, who bit by bit had given away all her curtains to the W.V.S. so that clothes could be made from them for bombed-out families.

'Good job I did,' continued her mother-in-law. 'They're impossible to obtain now. Roger can come home and find the place just as he left it.'

Peggy blanched.

Eventually, Rusty carried up the cases behind her mother who, ignoring her mother-in-law's protests, had picked Charlie up again. Her grandmother didn't help at all. She just stood at the foot of the stairs, suggesting that 'Charles' should walk up them.

Rusty had a bedroom all to herself. It had been her bedroom when she was seven, but she didn't remember it at all. It was a dark, cold room with furniture to match.

'It's a bit bleak up here,' said her mother, 'but I'll

decorate it for you while you're at school, once we're settled.'

'Can't I do it myself? I could paint the walls and then put some stencils in the corners, and –'

'Of course you can't,' said her mother.

'Why not?'

'That's enough, Virginia.'

Rusty climbed into bed. The sheets were freezing. 'Mother,' she said hesitantly, 'is Grandmother going to be living with us?'

'Yes.'

'Oh.' She paused. 'Doesn't she have anywhere else to go?'

'No.'

They looked at one another.

'Why is she so mean?'

'Virginia! That's a terrible thing to say!'

'But she doesn't like me, does she?'

'Nonsense. Of course she does. She's just old, that's all, and –'

'So's Gramps and Grandma Fitz, but they aren't mean.'

'Things are bound to be a little difficult at first. Your grandmother's not used to having children around. She's still a little Victorian, you know – "Children should be seen and not heard," that sort of thing.'

And sometimes, thought Rusty, they shouldn't even be seen. She wished so much that Aunt Hannah was with her. She would have at least sat on the end of the bed and listened. All her mother ever said to her was 'Nonsense' or 'Do as the Romans do'.

'Cheer up,' said her mother awkwardly. 'Tomorrow we'll be buying your uniform. I did order some from last year's measurements, but I'll have to get you a larger size now.'

Rusty studied her mother's face. She looked exhausted.

'Why do I have to go away to school?' she persisted. 'Why can't I go to a regular one? With boys?'

'There'll be quite enough time for all that when you're older,' Peggy said tautly. She opened the door.

'But why are you sending me away again? I just got back.'

Peggy whirled around, irritated. 'So that you can catch up on your education. You're far luckier than most young girls. At least you'll be coming back here every weekend.'

'But –'

'I don't wish to discuss it any further. Now you'd better get some sleep. We've a busy day ahead of us.' And she closed the door firmly behind her.

Rusty stared at the panels of the door, her eyes blurred. 'You just don't want me around, that's all,' she muttered.

Her grandmother didn't have breakfast with them. Rusty thought it was weird, but was secretly relieved. Down in the kitchen, Charlie's sheets were soaking in a large bucket. He had wet his bed. Poor kid, thought Rusty.

They sat at the dining-room table. Charlie pushed aside his toast and slumped his head on his arms. The toast was dry, but for a scraping of margarine, and the milk was powdered, but Rusty was so hungry that she forced it down.

'I'll have our ration books sorted out as soon as I can,' her mother said. 'I'm afraid I'll have to hand yours over to Benwood House. That's your school. Never mind. From next week, everything will be a bit more settled.'

Charlie raised his head.

'When am I going back to nursery school?' he said.

'In a couple of weeks' time,' said Peggy brightly. 'It'll be a different one.'

'What kind of animals have they got?'

'It isn't like your other school. They don't have animals at this one.'

'They don't have them?' he said, amazed. 'Not any?'

'No, I told you. It's different. It's more grown-up.'

'Why don't they have any animals?'

'Because it's a town school and, well, it's unusual to have animals in a school.'

'What's "unusual"?'

'Different.'

'But you said *this* school's different.'

'Oh boy,' said Rusty, and she ruffled his hair. 'You're the end.'

'Now, Charlie,' said her mother hastily. 'I want you to look after Grandma today while I go and buy Virginia's uniform.'

'Don't want to,' he said, and he thrust a finger in Rusty's direction. 'She can stay with Granmer.'

'I have to go with Mother,' said Rusty, 'so I can try the clothes on.'

'Go away,' he said grumpily.

As Charlie ran out of the dining room, he collided into his grandmother. 'Walk, don't run,' she said gently.

He thrust his fists into his pockets and scowled at her.

'What a baby,' she said sweetly to him. 'Mrs Grace tells me you wet the bed last night. That was very naughty, wasn't it?'

'Mother,' said Peggy, 'it's his first night here.'

'Well,' she said brightly, 'that's no excuse, is it?' She leaned down towards him and smiled. 'Big boys don't wet the bed, do they?'

Charlie swung round. 'Where's Beatie?' he said.

'She's in Devon,' said Peggy.

'Is she coming here?'

'No, darling. Devon's her home.'

He looked puzzled. 'Is this our holiday?'

'No. This is our home now.'

'No it isn't,' he stated. He took a brief glance at his

grandmother. 'Don't like you,' he said, and he stalked out of the room.

The saleswoman, who was a well-spoken woman in her fifties, knelt down and checked that the hem of Rusty's gymslip fell to the centre of her knees. 'Perfect,' said the woman.

Rusty liked her.

As Rusty turned to look in the full-length mirror, she heard the woman whispering discreetly to her mother. 'By the way, madam,' she said, 'I'd just like to remind you that the Headmistress has obtained a licence from the Board of Trade allowing us to sell second-hand school garments without taking coupons.'

'Oh, that's marvellous,' said Peggy. 'She's such a sensible woman. She's already said that if my daughter has an overcoat we needn't buy the school cape.'

Rusty gazed into the mirror. The gymslip was dark green and an awful shape. It fell in wide box-pleats from the bust, around which she had to wear the coloured girdle of the House she was in. Hers was red.

Underneath the gymslip she wore a beige blouse. Around her neck was a green tie with a beige-and-red stripe running through it, the red again indicating the colour of the House.

'That's providing that it isn't above eightpence for stockings or woollen socks, or undergarments, a shilling for footwear, and two shillings for anything else.'

Rusty watched in horror as the woman proceeded to lay out the most archaic underwear she had ever seen. Pairs of long green bloomers were held up against her.

'You don't mean I have to wear those?' she said.

Her mother nodded. 'All the girls do. It's part of the uniform.' She picked up what looked like a pair of ordinary heavy white underpants. 'These are called linings. You wear them underneath the knickers.'

'Ugh!' Rusty picked up a long woolly garment with short sleeves. 'And this?' she asked. 'Is this an undershirt?'

'Yes. It's what we call a vest. They should keep you warm.'

The woman straightened Rusty's tie and pinned a tiepin on to it. 'And now,' she said, glancing at Rusty's long hair, 'I'd better find some ribbons.'

Her mother sighed.

'Yes, madam,' said the saleswoman, 'it never ends, does it?'

'I can wear it like this,' suggested Rusty.

Her mother shook her head. 'If you have long hair, you have to wear it away from your forehead in plaits. The ribbons have to be the regulation colour and width.'

'You're kidding!'

While the woman began to unravel and measure some dark-green ribbon, Rusty glanced at the coupon books on the counter. All the clothing coupons inside had tinted backgrounds with different letters and numbers on them. Her mother had explained that some of them were worth three points while others were worth only one, and that each person was only allowed so many points a year. There was a General book, a Child book and a Junior book. It all looked very complicated.

'Here,' said her mother. 'Try this on.'

It was a square green jacket with a beige-gold braid around the edges of the lapels and pockets. A shield was embroidered on the single breast pocket, with some Latin wording around it.

'This is your school blazer,' she said.

Rusty slipped it on. The woman wrapped a striped green-and-beige scarf around her neck and placed a green round-brimmed hat on Rusty's head.

Rusty wondered what the Omsks would say if they could see her. Aunt Hannah always said that green suited her, but then so did blue, and yellow and cream and . . .

She thought of Skeet and couldn't help smiling. He would just crack up. And Janey? She'd either gasp and say how it didn't do anything for her figure, or she'd swoon and go all 'Anglophile' and say how wild it must be to go to a real English girls' boarding school. Suddenly, Rusty longed to be with Uncle Bruno and have him wrap his big arms around her, and hug her tight.

But they weren't finished. Her mother bought brown lace-up shoes, galoshes, sandals, a pair of black canvas shoes with rubber soles that looked a little like sneakers, but were called *plimsolls*, lacrosse boots, stockings, a Greek dance tunic, two pairs of flannel pyjamas, and a plaid woollen dressing gown.

When Rusty and her mother left the shop, laden with large bags and boxes, it was pouring with rain. They stumbled into a J. Lyons teashop nearby. Rusty's mother told her the names of the four School Houses. They were Nightingale, Curie, Fry and Butt.

'Butt!' exclaimed Rusty.

'Yes. That's your House, the red one.'

Rusty doubled over, laughing.

'I don't see what's so funny,' said Peggy. 'Nightingale House is after Florence Nightingale, Curie after Marie Curie, Fry after Elizabeth Fry, and Butt after Dame Clara Butt.'

Rusty almost choked.

'Virginia!' whispered her mother. 'Please. Behave yourself.'

'Butt House!' she repeated.

Peggy Dickinson cleared her throat. 'Dame Clara Butt was a famous classical singer,' she explained, but her words were having no effect on Rusty. 'Now come on, Virginia,' she said, 'you're getting hysterical.'

Rusty leaned over the table. 'Don't you know what your butt is?'

Her mother looked blankly at her.

'It's your ass!'

By the time they had walked up the steps of Number 83, wet and dripping, the bags had begun to fall apart. Her mother knocked at the door.

'We'll begin sewing on name-tapes as soon as possible. I'd like to send off the trunk tomorrow.'

Mrs Grace opened the door. 'Mrs Dickinson Senior is in the drawing room,' she whispered. She appeared very grave.

'Is anything the matter?' said Peggy.

Mrs Grace opened her mouth for a moment and then closed it again.

'I think I'd better let Mrs Dickinson Senior tell you herself.'

'It's not Beatie, is it?'

'Beatie?'

'Obviously not,' said Peggy, relieved.

'It's Charles.'

'Oh, my goodness!' she said, dropping the bags immediately on the hall floor. 'What's happened to him? Is he all right? Has there been an accident? Where is he?'

Mrs Grace opened the drawing-room door. Peggy ran in, quickly followed by Rusty.

Seated on the sofa next to Rusty's grandmother sat a tall elderly woman with a huge aquiline nose and heavy-lidded eyes. She wore a suit, hat and gloves.

'Where's Charlie?' began Peggy.

'Charles is in bed,' said Mrs Dickinson Senior. She indicated her guest.

'Oh, excuse me,' said Peggy hurriedly.

Rusty saw her grandmother gaze disapprovingly at her mother's old grey gabardine coat and darned lisle stockings. Her guest was transfixed by Rusty's saddle shoes.

'Hi,' she said, reminding her that there was a body attached to them.

The woman opened her mouth in dismay and glanced at her grandmother, who nodded in an I-told-you-so manner.

'Will you have some tea, Margaret?' she said.

Rusty's mother was growing frantic. 'For goodness' sake,' she panted, 'what's happened to Charlie?'

'Charles has misbehaved.'

Poor kid, thought Rusty, he's probably wet his pants again.

'Misbehaved?'

'I'd rather you sat down and we talked about it calmly over a cup of tea. Mrs Grace,' she said, 'another cup for Margaret.'

To Rusty's surprise, her mother removed her gabardine coat and sat down in one of the stuffed chairs.

The guest looked awkwardly at Rusty.

'I'm Rusty,' she said, throwing her Beanie over the back of her mother's chair.

'Virginia is her real name,' said her grandmother, smiling. 'Why she was given that silly nickname I can't imagine.'

'Because of my hair.'

'I suppose,' said her guest, 'Americans do find anything longer than two syllables a trial to pronounce.'

And they both laughed.

Before Rusty could answer back, her mother interrupted.

'I'd like to know what Charlie's done.'

'Now, now, now.'

Boy, thought Rusty, she was treating her mother as if she was a kid!

Mrs Grace hobbled in with a cup and saucer. All was quiet as she poured out some tea.

Mrs Dickinson Senior took a deep breath. 'Charles was

playing in the back garden. Unfortunately the fences dividing these gardens are somewhat inadequate. In fact, in some places there aren't any fences at all. I told Charles not to go farther than a certain point. While Mrs Grace's back was turned, he deliberately disobeyed me. He wandered off and *picked flowers from other people's gardens*! At first I had no idea that this had happened until Mrs Smythe-Williams' – and here she indicated her guest – 'came to the door. Apparently all her Michaelmas daisies and peonies had disappeared. Charles was nowhere to be seen. We discovered a small trail of water going up the stairs to your room. He had filled a vase, one of my *best* vases, with her flowers and put them by your bed. I found him lying asleep there. When I told him off and asked him to apologize to Mrs Smythe-Williams, he was not only extremely rude to her, but he ordered her to go away. And he told her that she had a big nose. I've locked him in his room without any supper.'

Peggy rose slowly. 'You've what?' she said.

Boy, thought Rusty, here comes the showdown.

'The boy's wild. He needs a firm hand.'

Peggy turned swiftly to Mrs Smythe-Williams.

'I'm sorry about your flowers. My son is used to living in the country, where the flowers don't belong to anyone. It's only his second day here and he doesn't understand. I will pay for any damage that has been done. Now,' she said, facing her mother-in-law, 'I'd like the key to that room.'

'Margaret,' she exclaimed. 'He must learn!'

'I want that key.'

Mrs Smythe-Williams gave a small gasp.

'And if she doesn't give it to you,' added Rusty, 'I'll help you break the door down.'

Alone in her bedroom, Rusty drew the dull chintz curtains across the window. Anything to keep the draughts at bay. Her uniform was spread across her bed. Along the landing, she heard her mother go into Charlie's room.

As she unpacked her suitcase, grip and duffel bag, she had an odd feeling that someone had been prying into her belongings. She opened a letter from Aunt Hannah and Uncle Bruno and realized, to her horror, that the letter had been read. It was folded differently. She scrabbled through all the others to make sure that none of them was missing.

After a while she heard her mother walking along the landing, past her own room, and down the stairs. Rusty peered out. Her mother was carrying Charlie in her arms down to the bathroom. Soon she could hear the sound of running water and Charlie giggling over something. She envied him.

After half an hour her mother looked in. 'You can come downstairs now,' she said. 'Mrs Smythe-Williams has left.' She paused. 'I think you owe your grandmother an apology.'

'What for?'

'Well, it wasn't necessary to threaten to break down the door.'

'Is Charlie O.K.?'

'He's asleep.'

Rusty gave a shiver.

'There's a fire in the drawing room. Come on.'

'Is *she* down there?'

'Yes.'

Boy, was it cold. She looked down at her hands. They were mauve.

'I'll stay here, then,' she said.

14

Rusty and her mother sat on a wooden bench on the station platform. It was a dark, grubby station with jagged gaps in the roof where bombs had shattered the glass.

'You look quite the young English girl,' said her mother brightly.

Rusty nodded numbly. She felt angry that her mother was sending her away again, and she felt helpless to do anything about it.

The previous evening she had been tempted to say, 'I'm not going and that's that!' But she couldn't bear being at her grandmother's place either. Her life there consisted of making sure Charlie didn't pick any more flowers in the back garden. Poor kid, he was so miserable. Since leaving Devon, he'd wet his bed every night.

Just then, a woman and a young girl wearing the Benwood House uniform appeared on the platform. The girl had short straight brown hair and a round face. Rusty sat up sharply and nodded to them as they walked past. The girl glanced briefly at her out of the corner of her eye and then looked away.

'Of course,' said her mother suddenly, 'it'll be a bit different from your American school.'

'I know it,' mumbled Rusty. 'I told you before, the principal said it might be a little tough at first, but that I had a good head on my shoulders and I'd catch up soon.'

She stared down at her brown lace-up shoes. She hurt so much inside, she could hardly breathe.

A year ago she had begun her first semester at the junior high. She'd been so proud. She had had her own locker with its own combination. No more satchels. She had walked down the corridors in her sweater and plaid woollen skirt, from classroom to classroom, the new books in her arms, just as if she was in high school.

That was when Aunt Hannah and Uncle Bruno had let her have her own bedroom, with a real worktable of her own to do her homework on, and a corner in the studio and the workshop.

She pulled a handkerchief out of her pocket. It had a name-tape on it. It read 'V. E. Dickinson'. Her grand-mother had said that her mother ought to have had all the name-tapes marked 'V. C. Dickinson' so that when Charlie went to boarding school, she'd just have to cut the V off.

Charlie had got into a terrible state. 'Are you sending me away, Mummy?' he had asked frantically. Her mother had had to hold him on her lap for hours, comforting him. And her grandmother had said, 'Well, really, he shouldn't have been listening, should he?'

She blew her nose furiously and put the handkerchief back in her blazer pocket.

'You'll soon make lots of new friends,' her mother said.

'I guess so.'

'Look, here come some more girls.'

But they passed with hardly a glance.

As the train pulled in, several schoolgirls were hanging out of the windows, waving to those on the platform.

'Bag me a seat!' yelled the straight-haired girl.

'Already bagged,' answered one of them.

Rusty picked up her Beanie and satchel and stood up. Her mother gave her an awkward peck on the cheek and ushered her to a door. As it swung closed behind her, she pushed down the window. 'Don't worry,' Peggy said. 'There'll be someone to show you around.'

'It's O.K.,' said Rusty dismally. 'I can ask.'

The whistle blew and the train pulled slowly out of the station.

'I'll see you on Friday,' said her mother.

Rusty nodded and hastily drew herself away from the window.

From a nearby compartment came the sound of shrieks and laughter. Rusty moved along the narrow corridor and slid the door aside.

'Only Upper Fives,' yelled the girls inside. 'Scram!'

'I'm sorry,' began Rusty. 'I'm new. I don't know what an Upper Five is.'

At that, they all laughed. Rusty grinned. 'What's so funny?'

A tall girl with light-blonde hair and a long face leaned forward.

'Upper *Fifth*,' she explained curtly. 'And what's funny is your accent.'

'Hardly *funny*,' interrupted her friend opposite. '*Frightful* would be a better word.'

They all started laughing again and making comments. Rusty stood, perplexed, for she could hardly understand a word they were saying.

Eventually the blonde girl turned to her abruptly. 'Didn't you learn English at your school?' she said. 'Scram. This is our patch.'

'Perhaps they haven't got as far as having schools in America,' added her friend.

Rusty flushed, slid the door shut, and opened the door of the next compartment. Four girls were seated on the edges of their seats, looking at holiday snapshots. They looked up and frowned.

'Hi,' said Rusty. 'I see you have a spare seat. Mind if I join you?' And with that she walked in and sat down.

The girls stared at her in disbelief.

'This compartment is bagged,' said the straight-haired one she had seen on the platform.

'What?'

'Bagged,' repeated the girl. 'Taken.'

'But you have empty seats,' said Rusty.

The girl sighed wearily. 'Go and find somewhere else,' she said. 'We're having a private conversation.'

'Do you own this train?'

'What a cheek!' said one of the other girls. 'Are you deaf or something? We don't want you here. Or perhaps you can't understand good English when you hear it.'

'Don't,' said a girl in the corner, gently. 'She's a new girl.'

'Bit cheeky for a new one, don't you think? I'd never have dared answer back.'

Rusty snatched up her Beanie and satchel from the seat.

'Ah, go stuff yourself,' she snapped, and she flew back out into the corridor.

There was a section in the train where the carriages were joined. Through the gaps Rusty could see the earth and the rails moving underneath her. Even though it seemed dangerous standing there, it felt like her own territory. The rest of the train seemed to be claimed.

'Now what?' she whispered fiercely to herself.

As she stood there she remembered Uncle Bruno saying that when you started something new, like a business, and no one knew you, you were bound to have a lot of rejections at first, but that for every thirteen no's, the fourteenth was sure to be a yes. So every time someone said no, it meant that you'd be getting nearer a yes. 'I got twelve to go, Uncle Bruno,' she muttered.

Rusty walked down the corridor, opening compartment doors. Every time she was told to go away, she smiled more broadly, for she knew she was getting closer to a yes. The yes came at the twelfth compartment.

Two small girls were seated by a window. One of them, a skinny, dark-haired girl with plaits, looked as though she had been crying.

'Hi,' said Rusty, sliding back the door. 'You new?'

They nodded.

'Mind if I join you?'

'No. Of course not,' they said eagerly.

'Are you a prefect?' said the dark-haired one.

'A prefect?' Rusty shook her head. 'Uh-uh.'

'You're American, aren't you?' said the other one, who was plump and fair-haired.

'Uh-uh. I don't feel so English, though.'

They giggled.

'I lived in the States for five years. I only got back this summer. I was evacuated there.'

'So you're new, too?'

'You said it.'

They all looked at one another and gave nervous laughs. The dark-haired girl looked away for a moment and then forced a smile.

'There's going to be someone to show us around when we get there,' she said, 'isn't there? Mummy said there'd be someone.'

'I guess so,' said Rusty, 'but we got each other. We can just follow everyone else or ask the way.'

The plump girl looked relieved. She leaned towards the dark-haired girl. 'Do you know what form you're in?' she said.

'Upper Third.'

'A or B?'

'I'm not sure. I'm hoping it's A.'

'Me too.'

'What's all this A and B stuff?' said Rusty.

The girls looked pleased that they could impart information to someone.

'Each year has two forms,' said the dark-haired girl. 'The As are for the bright ones. Bs are for the duds.'

'Hey, watch it,' said Rusty. 'One of us might be in a B.'

They giggled.

The fair-haired girl looked expectantly at Rusty's tie. 'Oh,' she said disappointedly. 'You must be in Butt House. I'm in Curie.'

'Well, let's stick together anyway till we meet someone from our houses.' Rusty grinned. 'My name's Rusty, by the way – what's yours?'

'Charlotte,' said the fair-haired one.

'Rosalind,' said the other.

'So listen,' said Rusty. 'About this class business. I'm in what you call the *Fourth*. I'm not too sure what that means. We have grades back home. I mean, back in the States.'

'Which Fourth?' said Charlotte. 'Upper or Lower? A or B?'

'I don't know.'

Just then the train jerked to a halt, sending them flying.

'These English trains sure keep you on your toes,' Rusty remarked. 'Or maybe I should say, your knees.' She peered out at the station.

'Only one more to go,' said Rosalind quietly.

Rusty leaned with her back against the window for a moment. She suddenly felt sick. Maybe it was those tiny tasteless little cabbages she had been given at lunchtime. Brussels sprouts.

The train began moving. The two Third-formers were staring at her.

'Scary, isn't it?' she said, straightening up.

They both nodded.

At the next station they hung round one another like glue while hordes of chattering girls pushed past them.

Outside the station stood two double-decker buses. Rusty grabbed Charlotte's and Rosalind's hands and dragged them towards the front one. 'Let's go find a seat!'

As they scrambled on board, a commanding voice shouted, 'No holding hands!'

Rusty glanced over her shoulder.

A tall girl of about sixteen indicated their joined hands

with a disapproving shake of her finger. 'No holding hands,' she repeated.

'Who says?'

The girl looked astonished. 'I do,' she said angrily.

'Big deal.' And she dragged the two small girls up the stairs so that they could sit at the front. It was a three-seater. Perfect. A solitary one-seater stood next to them on the other side of a tiny aisle. Rusty threw her Beanie on it and nudged Charlotte and Rosalind. 'For another new girl,' she explained.

They stared uncomfortably back at her, already sensing that they were breaking some unseen rule. At that moment a small, mousy girl, drowned in a voluminous blazer and felt hat, emerged from the stairway. She looked petrified.

'Hey,' yelled Rusty. 'You a new girl?'

She nodded.

'I saved a seat for you.'

The girl scuttled hurriedly towards them and sank gratefully into the seat.

'I'm Rusty. This is Rosalind and Charlotte. What's your name?'

'Fiona,' she whispered. 'Are you the person who's looking after us?'

'Uh-uh. I'm new, too.' Fiona had a purple stripe on her tie, which meant Nightingale House.

Just then two older girls came striding up to the front.

'What a nerve!' exclaimed one. 'New girls bagging the front seats.'

'Excuse me,' said the other one, icily, 'but front seats are a Fourth priority.' It was the girl with the straight hair.

'Well, how about that?' said Rusty, enjoying herself.

The other new girls began to rise nervously. Rusty pulled them firmly down again.

'As a matter of fact, I happen to be in the Fourth.'

The girl noticed the red stripe in Rusty's tie. 'Oh no,' she said.

Her friend had the red stripe, too.

'I guess we're all in Butt House,' said Rusty, and she broke into a fit of the giggles. Boy, she'd never keep a straight face saying that.

The two girls turned sharply away, muttering angrily.

Within minutes of the bus moving, Rusty began to relax. They passed hedgerows, fields and trees.

'I have to remember every bit of this,' thought Rusty. 'I'll take a snapshot inside my head so's I can describe it to everyone when I write.'

Rosalind tugged at her arm. 'Look,' she cried.

Through the trees, across a field, they could see a large brick building.

The bus stopped and all the girls leapt down, still chattering noisily. They followed the crowd past a towering brick wall and up to a pair of high wrought-iron gates.

Ahead of them, a long drive led to the school. It was a little like a castle, Rusty thought, without the turrets. At the corners of the building were four wings. Rusty decided they must be the Houses. An arched entrance stood in the centre. Encompassing the entire building from top to bottom were rows of scaffolding and planks.

As they walked up the long drive, Rusty felt someone jostle against her. Immediately three other girls followed suit, sniggering. They were the four who had been looking at the snapshots in the railway compartment.

Rusty pretended not to notice.

'You're awfully brave,' whispered Rosalind. 'I'd die if anyone did that to me.'

They reached the archway and stepped into a vast hall. Rusty was transfixed by the wood-panelled walls, the large glass cabinets with trophies and shields in them, the oak staircase that swept up and curved around. She breathed in the smell of beeswax.

Charlotte and Rosalind tugged at her arm. 'The new girls have to go and meet Miss Bembridge. She's the Headmistress,' whispered Rosalind.

A group of girls was huddled together at the foot of the stairs. Rusty was conspicuous by her height.

'How old is everyone?'

'I'm eleven,' said Charlotte.

'Me too,' said Rosalind.

'Eleven!' gulped Rusty. 'You're only a year younger than me.'

Rusty looked around, baffled. She knew that her mother had been surprised by her height and that thirteen-year-old Beth was not as tall as most girls back in the States, but she thought that that was just Beth. Maybe all those oranges and sunshine everyone in England kept talking about missing had made her taller for her age.

A Fifth-former stood on the stairs.

'Quiet, please,' she said. 'I'm going to call out your names, and I want you to form into pairs.'

'Can't we stay with who we want?' said Rusty.

'No.'

'Why not?'

'Those are the rules.'

She was about to comment, but Rosalind squeezed her hand. She looked so frightened that Rusty remained silent. When everyone had paired up, Rusty found herself alone at the end of the line.

On a landing upstairs, twenty-one chairs were placed against the wall. Rusty was put at the end, since all the other girls were Third-formers. They were told to sit down and remain silent.

The wait seemed endless. Somewhere along a corridor a clock ticked loudly. Along a passageway, sunlight poured through the windows, sending oblong patches of light on to the dark wooden floor.

'Mind if I take a look out the windows?' said Rusty, rising.

She strolled down the passage. There was a lovely window-ledge, wide enough for sitting on. She hitched herself up and gazed out over the grounds.

'What do you think you're doing?' whispered the Fifth-former angrily. 'Get back to your chair.'

'I'm sorry,' said Rusty. 'I thought it was O.K. You didn't say not to.'

'And you're not allowed to use slang here,' she added.

'What *are* you allowed to do here?'

There was a gasp from the new girls who had been watching. Rusty sat down again. Gradually, several Fifth- and Sixth-formers drifted up the stairs to meet the new girls as they came out of the Headmistress's study. When Charlotte, Rosalind and Fiona had disappeared with their escorts, Rusty took a writing pad out of her satchel. She had hardly written 'Dear Skeet' when she felt the girl in charge tap her on the shoulder.

'Letter-writing day is Sunday,' she said.

'What?' said Rusty.

'You're not allowed to write letters except on Sunday.'

'You're kidding!'

The girl sighed. 'It's one of the rules.'

'Well, it's a dumb rule.'

'That's an order mark.'

'Huh?'

'For slang.'

The door opened and another girl came out. Including Rusty, there were now only three girls left. Rusty pushed her writing pad back into her satchel, and when the girl in charge had turned her back she made a rude face at her, sending the other two girls into fits of giggles. The Fifth-former whirled round, only to find an innocent-faced Rusty and two red-faced girls looking hastily down at the floor.

Up the stairs came three more older girls. Rusty noticed that one of them was wearing a red cord around her gymslip and had a red stripe in her tie. The girl was tall and lean, with short, black, wavy hair. She had a smooth pink-and-white complexion. She glanced at Rusty.

'Hi!' said Rusty.

'Quiet,' said the girl in charge.

At last it was Rusty's turn. Although her heart was beating, she opened the door with a firm hand.

The Headmistress was a grey-haired woman in her sixties. A pair of glasses hung on a black tape around her neck. She gave a nod and indicated the chair in front of her desk.

'Hi,' said Rusty. 'I'm Virginia Dickinson.'

The Headmistress raised her eyebrows. 'Sit down, please,' she said.

Rusty did so and gazed about the room. It was just like an English movie. The windows, which were made up of diamond-shaped pieces of glass, were flung open. Old faded curtains with a horses-and-hounds design hung heavily beside them. Lining the walls were framed photographs of women wearing mortarboards and black gowns like the one the Headmistress was wearing.

'Now,' said Miss Bembridge. 'I have your school report from your principal in Connecticut. She seems to think very highly of you. You were in what's called junior high, I believe.'

'Uh-huh. I mean, yes, Miss Bembridge. I was in seventh grade. I should have been in sixth, but they put me a year ahead.'

'I see, by this, that you have done no French or Latin. Don't they teach languages in American schools?'

'Oh, sure. But we don't start till high school.'

'I see. Well, I'm afraid you'll be a little behind here. I was thinking of putting you in a B form.'

Rusty felt herself grow hot. The Bs! That's what Charlotte and Rosalind called the duds.

'The B forms don't do Latin and French. They tend not to take the School Certificate either, but your mother seems keen for you to be in an A stream so that you can eventually go on to take Higher and Matriculation.'

'What's Matriculation?' said Rusty.

'They don't have matriculation examinations in America, I take it,' she said slowly and somewhat wryly.

'No, but they have other exams and tests. They're nuts about 'em.'

Miss Bembridge frowned. 'Before I continue, it is a rule here that no slang is allowed.' Before Rusty could say anything, she held her hand up. 'The Matriculation Examination is what is required for entrance into university or college. If you wish to attain a university place, you will also be required to have Latin. To matriculate, you must pass a certain number of subjects which must include a language, like French or Latin, and mathematics.'

'Oh,' said Rusty. 'It's the same as the Regents exams. Alice took those. She graduated last semester. You should have seen her! She wore a gown, like yours only it was maroon and grey, and a mortarboard like in those photographs you have on your walls.'

Miss Bembridge cleared her throat. 'Don't interrupt,' she said firmly. 'Now, your mother has some idea of you going to university. A little on the ambitious side, I feel, but we'll see what we can do.'

Rusty was surprised. Her mother had never mentioned anything about wanting her to go to a university. Rusty had always assumed she would do something more artistic.

'This means,' said Miss Bembridge, 'that you are to be in an A form. I know that you're used to being a year ahead, but I'm putting you into a form with girls of your own age. That will be Lower Four A. We'll see how you progress this week and go on from there. Your mother also seems to think that you might need elocution lessons to eradicate your accent.'

Rusty rose from her chair, blushing.

'Sit down,' said Miss Bembridge. 'I have dissuaded her. I think your accent will disappear of its own accord. But we'll have to watch the slang, my girl,' she said, smiling.

'Yes, ma'am,' whispered Rusty.

'It's always a little difficult for a new girl at first, but once you join in the school activities, I'm sure you'll be very happy. All our girls are. You'll also learn that we have a system here of marks and points, which are based on the rules and regulations of the school. The rules are for your own protection, for the smooth running of the school, and are a way of learning to be a valuable and useful member of the community.'

She indicated the door. 'And by the way,' she added, 'we don't say *semester* here. We call them *terms*.'

'Terms,' repeated Rusty, and she backed out of the room and closed the door behind her.

'Virginia Dickinson?'

It was the tall girl from her House.

'I'm here to show you around.'

Rusty swallowed nervously. 'O.K.,' she said. 'Let's go.'

The girl frowned, swung on her heel, and headed for the stairs.

15

Rusty followed the girl down numerous corridors and staircases. 'Don't you ever get lost here?' she asked.

'You get used to it,' said her escort, looking ahead.

'How many kids are in this school?'

Still the girl avoided turning round. It was almost as if she wanted to give the appearance that she wasn't with Rusty at all.

'About a hundred and fifty.'

'Is that all? Back in the States there were over four hundred in my elementary school, and in junior high there ...'

They turned a corner into a wide corridor outside an assembly hall. A group of girls were peering up at several notices on the walls.

'I knew she'd be Head Girl!' exclaimed one.

'Oh no,' groaned her friend. 'It's Ciggy Cuthbertson for Games Captain.'

'I say, what beastly luck!' exclaimed another.

'What's everyone getting so excited about?' said Rusty. As she spoke, five of the girls turned round quickly and stared at her.

'Hi,' said Rusty. There was no response. 'I'm just trying to find my way around,' she added. 'I'm new.'

To her amazement, they turned their backs on her and burst out laughing.

'Come on,' said her escort, embarrassed.

As Rusty began to follow her again, she overheard one of the girls say, 'Thank heavens she's not in our House!'

Rusty stopped, completely stunned. Surely they

couldn't mean her? Before she had time to think any more about it, her escort was hurrying her on.

'What's going on there?' said Rusty bravely.

'They're finding out who's Head Girl and Games Captain, and who the prefects are.' She turned slightly. 'They're selected from the Sixth Form. They're the girls who wear skirts and blouses instead of gymslips. There's also a list of rules on one of the noticeboards, which you'd better look at. We have an order and points system here. I expect Miss Bembridge explained it to you.'

'Well, not much,' said Rusty, trying desperately to look the other girl in the eye.

'Oh.' The girl fell silent for a moment. She gave a sigh.

'Each year, a Good Conduct Shield is presented to the House with the *least* amount of marks. There's another shield, too, which includes conduct, achievement in games, good works, and so on. We nearly won it last year. We came second.'

'So tell me about these marks,' said Rusty, puzzled. 'I have a feeling I've already gotten one.'

The girl glanced at her out of the corner of her eye. 'Yes. So I've been told.' She stared ahead again. 'There are bad marks, order marks, punctuality marks, and' – she paused – 'the worst kind. Discipline marks.' She then went on to explain that each House had a House Prefect, a Games Captain, and various dormitory monitors who saw to it that everyone kept to the rules. The House which already had *the* Head Girl or *the* Games Captain didn't usually elect another one. Then, one by one, she began to reel off the rules.

No talking or running in the corridors. No talking in class. No talking after Lights Out. No holding hands or physical contact of any kind. Those old enough to go for walks without the supervision of a mistress must go in a foursome ...

Here Rusty touched her arm. 'Hey, wait a sec. You

mean if I want to go take a walk, I have to be with three other girls?'

'That's right.'

'So I have to find three other girls to go with me?'

'Yes.'

'You mean I can't ever go out alone?'

'Of course not,' said the girl, amazed.

'But,' stammered Rusty, 'what if I can't find three girls to go with me? Does that mean that I can't even take a walk?'

'No. It means that you'd have to go with the Juniors. They're the Third-formers. They go in crocodile with one of the mistresses.'

'In crocodile?'

'In pairs. Two by two. Anyway, you don't have to worry about that. Miss Bembridge has told me that you're going home every weekend.'

'So?'

The girl gave an exasperated sigh. 'We're only allowed out during the weekends.'

Rusty couldn't believe it. 'You're not kidding me?' she asked. 'How come nobody's complained about not being able to go out except weekends?'

The girl whirled round, furious. 'Complained! You're jolly lucky to be in a school as free and easy as this one. In most other boarding schools, one isn't even allowed out of the school during the weekends. And also, *you're* jolly lucky to be allowed to go home for them!'

At that she turned and strode angrily away.

Neither she nor Rusty spoke again until they reached the end of an extremely noisy corridor.

'I'll wait for you here,' said the girl abruptly. 'You have to go down to Matron to get your linen, sheets, that sort of thing. Your trunk with all your other clothes will be waiting for you in your dormitory.'

'O.K.,' said Rusty.

No sooner had she turned than her escort called her back. For a moment Rusty didn't recognize her own name.

'Virginia Dickinson!' repeated the girl.

'Oh, sorry, that's me. I'm so used to being called Rusty that I –'

'Virginia Dickinson, "O.K." is considered slang.'

'It is?'

'I shan't report it as you're new, but from now on I'll have to give you an order mark if you say it again.'

'O.K. Oh boy, that did it!' she exclaimed, and she burst out laughing.

'That's an order mark.'

Big deal, thought Rusty. She shrugged, and headed on down the corridor. Behind her, her escort stood open-mouthed, horrified that this ghastly girl should be put into her House and amazed that, being new, she hadn't crumpled on being given an order mark.

Rusty, who was struggling between a desire to weep and to walk angrily out of the building straight for the nearest train, swaggered as nonchalantly as she was able towards a line of chattering girls.

The Matron was a tall, bony woman with a grim face. She handed Rusty a pile of clean sheets and towels, and a laundry bag.

Rusty rejoined her escort, and they descended a flight of stairs that led to a tiny hall and a porch with an arched doorway.

'This is Butt House,' muttered the girl.

'How many are in this House?'

'Thirty-seven, but the Juniors all sleep in a different section. Their dormitories are bigger.'

'Oh,' said Rusty, disappointed. 'I met a couple of neat kids from the Third Form on the way here, and I was hoping, maybe ...'

'Mixing with different forms isn't really encouraged here,' interrupted her escort.

'Why not?'

'It's obvious, isn't it?' she said, icily.

'Uh-uh.'

The girl looked confused. 'Does that mean yes or no?'

'It's obvious, isn't it?' said Rusty.

The girl began climbing another flight of stairs. Rusty was determined not to give up. 'So why isn't it encouraged? I mean, you're older than me and we're together.'

'It's so that the younger girls *respect* the older ones,' said her escort, glaring.

'I don't see how keeping people separate makes them respect one another. Doesn't make sense.'

'No, well it wouldn't to you, would it?' the girl muttered. She took a deep breath. 'What dormitory are you in, by the way?'

'Number three. I guess those are all Lower Four As. Right?'

'No. It'll be a mixture of Lower Four As and Upper Four As.'

'But I thought you said there was no mixing of the forms.'

'Oh Lor'! Wait until I explain before asking so many questions.'

Eventually they arrived at the end of a long landing, outside a door marked '3'.

'I'll wait downstairs for you,' said the girl. 'Baths for this dormitory are Wednesdays. When you've made your bed and unpacked your trunk, bring your coat, hat and shoe bag down with you, and I'll show you the Fourth Form cloakroom. Then I'll bring you back here so that you can change into mufti for supper.'

'Mufti?'

'Ordinary clothes. Out of your uniform,' she added slowly, as if speaking to a mental defective.

'O.K.,' said Rusty.

'Order mark,' growled the girl.

Rusty shrugged and opened the door.

The four girls in the dormitory were sitting on their beds talking. Rusty closed the door quietly behind her. 'Hi!' she said.

They fell silent and turned to look at her. Slowly two of them stood up. They were the girls who had come up to her in the bus.

'You?!' they spluttered.

'I hope so. I sure wouldn't wanna be anyone else.'

But nobody smiled.

Rusty cleared her throat. 'My name's Virginia but everybody calls me Rusty. What's yours?'

The four of them gazed at her in horror.

'I'm in Lower Four A,' she continued.

At that the straight-haired girl smirked. 'Well, we're both in *Upper* Four A.'

Rusty turned to the other two girls. They seemed awfully small, but then she'd been used to being with girls a year older than herself. One of them had waist-length long blonde braids, a round nose and a broad mouth. Her eyelashes were so white that they were almost invisible. Her friend had cropped, dark hair. Her round face and freckles gave her the appearance of a lost nine-year-old schoolboy.

'Are you Lower Four A?'

They nodded.

'Pleased to meet you,' said Rusty, manoeuvring her belongings to the other arm.

They shook hands.

Suddenly the girl with the straight hair tossed her head to one side. 'For a new girl you talk too much,' she remarked. 'And considering the way you talk, it's a wonder you dare open your mouth at all.'

Her friend moved in beside her. 'Come on, Judith,' she

said to the straight-haired girl. 'It's like being in a G.I. camp in here.' And with that, they both flounced out.

Rusty was astounded by their rudeness.

'I was only trying to be friendly,' she murmured.

The two girls in her form blushed.

'Filly,' said the one with the boy's haircut, 'fancy having a dekko at the stables?'

Rusty faked a smile. 'What's a dekko?' she said lightly.

'A look at.'

'Oh,' said Rusty. 'That's what we call a look-see.'

At that they burst into giggles and fled out of the door.

Rusty stood motionless in the large room with its brown scrubbed walls. On the dark wooden floor stood five black iron bedsteads. She could see instantly that the far bed had to be hers. It was the only one that was unmade. At the foot of each bed stood a trunk and a laundry bag. There wasn't a rug on the floor, not a picture on the walls, no curtains and, worst of all, no sign of any kind of heating.

Rusty dumped the sheets on her mattress. After making the bed, she opened up her trunk. There was nowhere to hang anything, not even a chair. She gave a sigh, slowly folded everything carefully into her three dresser drawers, tucked her pyjamas under the pillow, and slung her dressing gown across the end of the bed. At the side of the bottom drawer she squeezed in her green-and-white sneakers. She was just putting her loafers in on the other side when she lifted up the fringed tongue of one of them and felt the little slit underneath. Carefully, she drew out an American penny. She twisted it fondly over and over between her fingers before sliding it back in again. She didn't know why she was putting her shoes in a drawer. It had something to do with them being American shoes. It sort of protected them, being hidden away.

Finally, she opened her satchel and pulled out her photographs of the Omsks, the Fitzes, Janey and the gang, and one of Skeet by himself, and placed them on the chest of drawers. She pushed her plimsolls, sandals and lacrosse boots into her black shoe bag and was just picking up her Beanie and hat when her escort stormed in.

'Oh, do get a move on,' she said. 'You've probably missed the tea and bun.'

'That's O.K.,' said Rusty. 'I don't go much for tea anyways.'

'Look,' said the girl angrily, 'are you deliberately trying to break the rules?'

'You mean there's a rule I have to drink tea?' she exclaimed.

'No! You said "O.K." again.'

'I'm sorry. I didn't even notice.'

'Well, you'd better *start* noticing, otherwise you're going to be jolly unpopular. The more bad marks our House receives, the less chance we have of winning the Shield. Now hurry up.'

'Oh –' She stopped midstream. '– Kee-dokey,' she added hurriedly.

The girl pressed her lips together.

Oh boy, thought Rusty, as she followed her out of the door.

As the day progressed, not one girl made her feel welcome. They all seemed to have their own friends or cliques, and each time she attempted to join in a conversation, she was made to feel as though she was butting in.

When she was back in the dormitory, changing for supper, she stared hard at her photographs of the Omsks and pretended that they were all keeping her company. Inside her head they were laughing and cracking jokes. It took her all her concentration to keep them there, but every time she felt them fading away, and the dormitory coming into view, she'd take another glance at them.

She put on her slip, her cream-coloured blouse, her

plaid tan-green-and-yellow skirt, and her emerald-green sweater. With great care she folded down a pair of white cotton bobby socks and put her sneakers on. She could hear the others whispering and giggling behind her. She sat on the bed and unplaited her hair, giving it some firm brush-strokes. From a central parting she brushed it to two sides and held it in place with hair-grips.

When she turned round she found herself staring into four very hostile faces. Rusty gulped, for their jerseys and skirts were faded and darned. The two older girls were wearing shapeless grey suits.

'What *do* you think you look like?' commented the straight-haired girl called Judith.

'I was told to bring sweaters and skirts,' said Rusty.

'Did you have to choose traffic-light colours?' And she and her friend turned their backs on her.

'You know,' said Rusty quietly, 'at my school in the States we made a point of making new kids welcome. So far the only people who've been nice to me have been the new kids. How come? Is it one of your rules to be nasty?'

'Oh,' said Judith. 'Did they have schools in the States, then? I thought they all rode around on horses and chewed gum.'

At that they all giggled.

'What a bunch of stupid kids you are!' said Rusty angrily.

Judith whirled round. 'You watch what you're saying, New Girl. I'm in the Upper Fourth, so you'd better show a bit of respect.'

'Respect? For you? You gotta be kidding!'

Judith glowered back. 'You'll pay for that!'

'Come on, Judith,' said her friend. 'I don't like the company in here.'

As they left, Rusty looked at the two girls in her form.

'Mind if I follow you?' she said. 'I'll walk a long way behind you, so you can pretend I'm not with you.'

They reddened.

'Look here,' said the girl called Filly. 'You can't expect everyone to drop their friends and surround you just because you've got an American accent and new clothes.'

'So what am I supposed to do? Walk round naked and keep my mouth shut?'

'Don't be silly,' said the boyish-looking one. 'You'll learn that there are more important things here in England than dressing up. It's bad form not to look shabby. There's been a war on here, you know.'

'I know it. But I'm not dressed up. This is just a sweater and skirt.'

'Oh, come on, Cecil,' said Filly, grabbing her friend's arm.

Rusty followed them at a distance.

Eventually they arrived at the Refectory, a vast room with four long wooden tables. A mistress sat at each table end. Rusty noted which table Filly and Cecil sat at, and slid into an empty chair.

After grace, Rusty attempted to eat the meal, which consisted of Spam, turnips and a plentiful supply of potatoes. She didn't know what they'd done to the turnips, but they tasted so foul that she nearly retched. There was no fruit to be seen, no ginger ale or milk or seltzer to rid herself of the dry sensation in her mouth, only a cup of lukewarm water.

No one spoke until dessert, which they called pudding. It was that heavy white mixture with currants in it that her mother had made for her, Spotted Dick. Everyone went nuts about it, as if it was a special treat. The speckled blob was covered with a hot, tasteless yellow mixture that was supposed to be custard. At the end of the meal they stood up for grace and pushed back their chairs. As everyone left with their friends, Rusty realized that she had been the only new girl in the Refectory. She was about to leave when she heard someone call her name. It was one of the mistresses.

'Good evening,' she said, smiling. 'I'm your House Mistress.'

She was a little taller than Rusty and about fifty-five years old. Her thin brown hair was flecked with grey, and she wore a simple brown tweed skirt, blouse and cardigan. 'I'm Miss Paxton.'

'Oh,' said Rusty, relieved almost to tears. 'Hi! I sure am pleased to meet you.'

'That's quite an accent you have there.'

'So everyone keeps telling me. I keep thinking it's everyone else who has got an accent.'

'I thought we could go somewhere for a chat. You've never been to boarding school before?'

'Uh-uh. I'm used to public school.'

The teacher looked puzzled for a moment.

'Oh yes,' she said. 'Of course. Your public schools are like our elementary schools. And our public ones are private. It's a little confusing.'

'I guess,' said Rusty, smiling.

'Come with me,' Miss Paxton said, 'and we can talk in private.'

She led Rusty through several corridors and into an empty classroom full of old wooden desks. 'Sit down,' she said, indicating one of the desks. Rusty hitched herself on to it and swung her legs. 'On a chair,' she added.

'Oh, sorry,' said Rusty, jumping off and pulling one out.

What followed was a lecture about the history of the school, its achievements and its aims, which were to produce courteous, good citizens, young women who would make good wives and mothers, who would serve their King and Country to the best of their ability, and who could be dependable in any place and at any time.

Then came a list of the rules that had been handed

down from year to year, to help form the tradition of the school. These had produced girls worthy of the school, some of whom had not only played an active part in the armed services during the War, but had also been officers and leaders.

'Sometimes it can take as long as two years for a new girl to settle down and become a Benwood girl,' she said, 'but courage, hard work and goodwill are what count. Now I know already that you've been in a bit of trouble over the use of slang' – and here she smiled – 'but this rule applies to everyone. Miss Bembridge also thinks that the sooner you can lose that accent, the sooner you'll fit into the school community. Now, if you have any problems, you just come and see me. That's what I'm here for.'

Rusty nodded, dumbfounded. King and Country? She believed in Democracy and Freedom. Everything she'd learnt in history was how the kings had lived off the hard-working Americans. Now that she'd tasted the lousy tea, she understood why they'd dumped boxes of it into the harbour in Boston.

'And now,' said Miss Paxton, 'I'll take you to the Fourth Form sitting room.'

'I'd like to go to my room, if you don't mind.'

'I'm sorry, that's not allowed until bedtime.' Miss Paxton smiled again. 'You'll never make friends if you go off on your own, will you?'

'I guess not.'

For the remainder of the evening Rusty sat at a table in the Fourth Form sitting room and pretended to read a book. Occasionally, when she heard snippets of a conversation that aroused her interest, she attempted to join in, but her remarks were ignored. Several of the girls talked about a Harvest Camp they had worked at in June.

In June, thought Rusty, she had gone on a camp trip, too, with Janey. She remembered the campfires at night; she and Janey sitting with all the others, singing every single song they could think of, and roasting marshmallows. Their favourites were s'mores. Janey and she made theirs up with a slice of apple, a melted marshmallow, chocolate chips and another slice of apple, so that it ended up like a weird kind of sandwich. And everyone kept on saying, 'Oh gimme some more s'mores.' It was all so corny. But out there in the dusk, with the sunburn on their faces and the different smells coming from the wood all mixed up with the sweet smell of the marshmallows, it was just beautiful. Janey even forgot to squeeze vanishing cream on her freckles. Away from her mother, she said, it was a relief not having to be dressed smart and act grown up all the time. It was such a strain being sophisticated. And Rusty had laughed till she was almost sick. She laughed so much, she didn't even know what she was laughing about, only that everything seemed so funny.

It was a heck of a long time since she'd laughed like that.

Just then a bell rang, and everyone started leaving the room.

In the dormitory Rusty lay in bed, freezing. The sheets were starchy and cold. There was no chance of her breaking the rule of talking after Lights Out, for there was no one she could talk to. She heard the girls whispering to one another, and then it was silent. Gradually, as her eyes became accustomed to the darkness, she looked over at her photographs.

'Good-night, Skeet,' she whispered. 'Good-night, Kathryn; good-night, Aunt Hannah.' But when she tried to say good-night to Uncle Bruno, she started to cry. She didn't want the others to hear her, but every breath she took only seemed to hasten the flow of tears. She drew her knees up and put her hands around her feet in an attempt to warm them.

16

Rusty had just put her gymslip on over her blouse when a bell started ringing.

She flung on her cardigan, threw her tie around her neck, and ran with her pyjamas and dressing gown back to the dormitory. When she opened the door, a strange sight greeted her. The four girls were standing by her bed, peering at her photographs. They looked up, startled.

'You're not supposed to leave your bed until the bell rings,' said Judith.

'What if I have to go to the bathroom?' said Rusty, striding towards them.

'Bath nights are Wednesdays,' said Judith's friend Reggie.

Rusty threw her pyjamas on the bed. 'I know that. I meant the john.'

Filly and Cecil shifted hastily towards their wash bags. The other two followed.

'By the way,' said Judith, turning at the door, 'are those photographs of relatives?'

'They're my American family.'

'And the boy?'

'That's Skeet,' she began. 'He's my –' but she got no further.

'I see,' said Judith meaningfully, and she and her friend gave each other a knowing look and disappeared.

Rusty soon learned that there were bells for waking up, bells for breakfast, bells for assembly, bells for each lesson, bells for recess – which they called *break* – bells for everything.

It was certainly different from her school in the States. In Lower Four A there were only twelve pupils. Each girl had a wooden desk with a lid, underneath which was a deep well for her books and stationery. Their class teacher, who was a tall, crisp, fast-talking woman in her sixties called Miss Everton-Harris, told each girl where to sit. As she rose to leave, they all had to rise and say in unison, 'Good-morning, Miss Everton-Harris. Thank you, Miss Everton-Harris.' And they rose all over again when the next teacher walked in for math, only they added an *s* and called it *maths*.

The mathematics class consisted of algebra, which the others had all been doing for a year. Rusty hadn't even begun. She was given arithmetic problems to sort out on her own. The following lesson was French, and she was no wiser.

At recess, she stood shivering at the back of the school grounds and watched the other girls running around or strolling together talking. Some of them weren't even wearing cardigans, yet she had put on her Beanie over her blazer and still found the cold unbearable. Occasionally a girl would run up to her and ask her a question, just to hear the way she spoke, and would instantly scuttle away with 'What a scream!' or 'How frightfully funny!'

By the end of that first break, Rusty had begun to detest the ways of the English. As far as she was concerned, they were a bunch of limey pantywaists.

After break came English. Here, at least, thought Rusty, was a subject she would be able to cope with. But she was wrong.

Upright and smartly dressed, with her hair twisted into a French roll, Miss Webster looked at the girls with an air of disdain, and in Rusty her sarcasm found a ripe target.

'This term we shall be reading *A Tale of Two Cities*. By Charles Dickens,' she added, looking pointedly at Rusty.

'I don't suppose they've ever heard of him from where you've just come.'

Rusty flushed.

In turn, each girl began to read from the first chapters. Never once raising their head from the page, they mumbled monotonously into the textbook, and sometimes so quietly that Rusty had to strain her ears to hear. At last she had found something she could do better. Eventually her name was called. It was a neat dialogue section, too.

'"Wo-ho!" said the coachman. "So, then! One more pull and you're at the top and be damned to you, for I have had trouble enough to get you to it! – Joe!"

'"Halloa!" the guard replied.

'"What o'clock do you make it, Joe?"

'"Ten minutes, good, past eleven."

'"My blood!" ejaculated the vexed coachman, "and not atop Shooter's yet! Tst! Yah!"' Rusty yelled. '"Get on with you!"

'The emphatic horse, cut short by the whip in a most decided negative, made a decided scramble for it, and the three other horses followed suit.'

Rusty continued to read with gusto, not noticing that Miss Webster and the girls were exchanging wry looks.

'That will be enough,' the teacher said, but Rusty did not hear. 'That will be enough,' she repeated.

Rusty looked up. 'But I just started.'

'It's a pity you did,' the teacher said.

A round of giggles.

'And I think until you stop talking in that affected manner, you'd best not read again.' She turned to the girl next to her. 'Gladys Crawley, continue.'

Gladys Crawley continued in the monotonous tone of the other girls.

Rusty clenched both her hands into fists and stared at the blurred pages of her book, swallowing down tears of rage.

When enough of *A Tale of Two Cities* had been read, Miss Webster rose and began writing on the blackboard from a book. 'This is your homework,' she said. 'Copy it into your jotters.'

At the top of the board she wrote, '"To a Skylark" by Percy Bysshe Shelley.'

As Rusty stared up at the words, she remembered that 'Skylark' was one of Skeet's favourite records. Dinah Shore sang the song. They used to go down to the romper room and he'd play it over and over. The others were busy scribbling down the first verse.

> *Hail to thee, blithe Spirit!*
> *Bird thou never wert,*
> *That from Heaven, or near it,*
> *Pourest thy full heart*
> *In profuse strains of unpremeditated art.*

What did that mean? thought Rusty. But the next verse she liked.

> *Higher still and higher*
> *From the earth thou springest*
> *Like a cloud of fire;*
> *The blue deep thou wingest,*
> *And singing still dost soar, and soaring ever singest.*

When the mistress had finished writing out six verses, she began walking around the desks, looking over the girls' shoulders as they hurriedly went on writing. When she reached Rusty's desk, Rusty looked up at her.

'Those are pretty lines, aren't they?' she said.

> *'From one lonely cloud*
> *The moon rains out her beams, and heaven*
> *is over-flowed.'*

'Did I ask you to speak?' Miss Webster snapped.

'No, ma'am,' said Rusty, startled.

'No, Miss Webster,' the teacher corrected. She picked

up Rusty's jotter, took one look at it and flung it down on the desk. 'And this writing will not do. Didn't you learn anything at your American school?'

'Not if her maths and French are anything to go by,' muttered one of the girls.

More smothered giggles.

'What's wrong with my writing?' said Rusty.

'Have I asked you to speak?'

'Uh-huh,' said Rusty firmly. 'You just asked me a question, which some smart-aleck over there,' she added, glaring at the girl, 'gave a dumb answer to.'

'Virginia Dickinson, when you have completed one hundred lines of "I will not be insolent", you will begin some simple writing exercises.' She stalked up to her desk. 'Come up here,' she said.

Rusty left her desk, seething.

'This,' Miss Webster said, indicating an exercise book, 'is for improving your writing. You will write within these red lines. And this book here,' she said, throwing a slim textbook on top, 'is the style of writing we require. Now please take it with you.'

As Rusty walked back to her desk, the class rose to their feet.

'You have a week to learn those six verses. Ample time. I expect you to be word-perfect. You will receive your essay on Wednesday.'

'Yes, Miss Webster,' they all chorused. 'Thank you, Miss Webster. Good-morning, Miss Webster.'

As she left, everyone began talking until Miss Paxton, Rusty's House Mistress, entered the classroom. She had come to teach Latin.

After the humiliation of the English lesson, Rusty kept silent for the duration of the class, as Miss Paxton went through a new declension on the blackboard. The homework she gave was a revision exercise and a small piece of translation from Latin into English.

After a dismal lunch of a rubbery kind of fish that sounded like *snook*, together with overcooked vegetables and prunes, Rusty attempted to cope with the longer, half-hour lunch-break that followed. Her hands became so cold that after the bell had rung for them to go indoors, it took her longer than usual to untie her shoelaces. When she had finished buckling up her sandals, the others had already left the cloakroom.

By the time she reached her form room, one order mark in tow for being seen running in the corridor, she was late for class. She flung open the door and was greeted by a loud bellowing from a large, stout woman in her sixties whom she had heard referred to as 'the Bull'.

'What time do you call this?' she roared.

'I'm sorry, Miss Bullivant,' Rusty said. 'I got lost. I'm new.'

'Newness is not an excuse for unpunctuality. Take a punctuality mark. Now go and sit down.'

Rusty moved swiftly to her desk.

'Now we will commence the lesson proper.' Miss Bullivant peered at Rusty over the half-moon spectacles that were balanced precariously on the ridge of her broad nose. 'I was just informing the rest of the class that we shall be following the events of the Civil War. I know little of your previous schooling. Have you covered this period at all?'

Rusty beamed. 'Uh-huh. We covered it last year.'

Miss Bullivant smiled. 'Is history a subject that interests you?'

'Oh yes, I love it. I just love finding out how people lived. I guess if I didn't want to go to some kind of art school, I'd like to be an archaeologist. You know, find out how people lived from the stuff they left behind. But the Civil War is real interesting because –'

'Well,' Miss Bullivant interrupted, 'perhaps you could tell the class a little of what you know. Stand up.'

Oh boy, thought Rusty, I'm saved!

She cleared her throat and took in the rest of the class boldly.

'It all started,' she began, 'when the slavery of the Negroes had spread so much that it had gotten as far as Kansas, and the Northerners, they didn't agree with it, so they tried to stop it. That's when the Republican party started. They were all people in the Northern states then. So anyway, they started putting taxes on all the stuff that was coming out of the Southern states. The Southerners came to be called the Confederates, and the Northerners the Union Army.'

Miss Bullivant slapped her hand hard on the desk. Rusty jumped.

'What are you talking about, my girl?'

'The Civil War,' said Rusty, astonished. 'You asked me if I –'

'I'm talking about the *English* Civil War,' the woman spluttered.

'The *English* Civil War?'

'Sit down!'

Miss Bullivant was about to speak to one of the other girls when her face suddenly froze. 'Virginia Dickinson,' she said, her voice trembling, 'I take it you have covered *some* aspects of English history?'

Rusty stood up. 'Uh, a little.'

'Indeed. What would that be?'

'The War of Independence. When we stopped the king living off the Americans' hard work.'

'You consider yourself an American, do you?'

'No, I meant –'

'And is that all the English history you've covered?'

'Yes, Miss Bullivant.'

At this the entire class broke into gasps.

'What *did* you learn in your school, then?'

'Why, American history.'

'American history would hardly cover a term, my girl.'

She gave a sigh. 'Oh, sit down. Cecilia Rogers, hand her a history textbook.'

The lesson continued in lecture form. There were no discussions, no projects given, just a list of dates and events to be memorized.

Rusty was still determined not to be beaten. She'd had a lot of no's that day – she had to be close to a yes.

The following lesson was art. It was taught by Miss Collins, the gym mistress, a pleasant middle-aged woman who knew nothing about art. Art to the other girls was what they called 'a bit of larking around'. When Miss Collins asked if anyone had been to an exhibition during the holidays, Rusty was the only one who had raised her arm. Miss Collins seemed delighted by her response.

'Tell us about it,' she said.

'My American father took me to an exhibition of Winslow Homer,' she said.

'Winslow Homer,' repeated Miss Collins slowly.

'Uh-huh, and it was just beautiful.'

She could hear someone giggling. Miss Collins frowned at the girl and returned to Rusty. 'I'd be interested to hear why you thought it so beautiful.'

'Well, I guess I like paintings that make you *feel* something, and it's his sea and river and outdoor pictures I like. Sometimes the sea is so *wild*, and sometimes when he paints someone on a lake, it's so calm and peaceful ... makes me break out in goose bumps.'

'Goose bumps?' repeated Miss Collins. 'We call those goose-pimples. That's interesting.'

Rusty was so thrilled at not being criticized that a great stream of words came tumbling out of her mouth. When she had finished, the teacher was still smiling.

'And this Winslow Homer,' she said, 'is this someone you know? Does he live in the town where you lived?'

'Oh no,' said Rusty. 'We had to go to New York City' – and then it dawned on her that the teacher had never even heard of him. 'He's a very famous American artist,' she added.

'I see. Well, we all have a lot to learn, haven't we?'

'Especially Virginia Dickinson,' muttered one of the girls.

As the first week dragged on, Rusty not only felt more of a 'dud', but in many of the classes she became increasingly bored. Even in the singing lesson, the songs had none of the verve and power of the American songs. As they sang 'Cherry Ripe' in the shabby Music Room, Rusty longed to sing out lustily:

> *'Oh, Shenandoah, I long to hear you,*
> *Away, you rollin' river!'*

or:

> *'Thus spoke the Lord, bold Moses said,*
> *Let my people go,*
> *If not, I'll smite your firstborn dead,*
> *Let my people go.'*

or:

> *'Oh bury me not on the lone prairie*
> *Where the wild ki-yotes will howl o'er me;*
> *Where the rattlesnakes hiss and the winds blow free,*
> *Oh, bury me not on the lone prairie.'*

In gymnastics the girls resented the way she grabbed a rope and hauled herself effortlessly up to the ceiling, and, though she had never leapt over a gym horse, she rapidly picked it up.

'Virginia Dickinson, you have springs in your heels!' said Miss Collins.

Miss Collins also taught Greek dancing, and even in her first lesson Rusty did well. Her flying skips and Mercury steps were a little wayward, but she was complimented on the way she flung herself into it.

'A lesson to you all,' commented Miss Collins, and Rusty could see that the others hated her for it.

But in subjects like geography and biology she was hopeless. Nor could she cope with lacrosse. She was used to basketball and softball. She loathed the hysterical life-and-death approach to the game, and hated standing around in a small gymslip on a cold lacrosse pitch.

She longed to put on her roller-skates and go flying along the pavement, or hop on to a bicycle and go somewhere with the gang – maybe to the movies, or out for a soda – or even just play a game of jacks.

The height of her misery came within twenty-four hours of Judith Poole being made Dormitory Monitor, when Rusty was summoned to report to the House Mistress. She was met in the downstairs hallway and taken to the same classroom where she and Miss Paxton had had their earlier little 'chat'. Rusty sat in the chair, her blazer done up tightly. It wasn't that it was cold, exactly; it was more damp, and it seemed to be soaking into her very bones.

Miss Paxton looked serious. She sat at the teacher's desk and clasped her hands.

'This morning,' she said, 'one of the Sixth Form prefects told me that you were found talking to two of the workmen at the back of the school, and that when she asked you to come away, first of all you ignored her, and then were insolent.'

'Oh, that,' said Rusty, thinking that that encounter was over and done with.

'If it happens again, I will have no alternative but to give you a discipline mark.'

Rusty attempted to make light of it. 'I have so many marks already, it won't ...' She stopped. 'A discipline mark is the worst kind? Right?'

'That is correct. It is given publicly in assembly, and if any girl receives three, she is automatically expelled.'

'Expelled! You mean I could get kicked out for talking to the workmen?'

Miss Paxton nodded.

'But why?' she stammered. 'I mean, I was just asking them what they were doing and they were explaining about pointing. You know, filling in the spaces between the bricks where it's got worn away.'

She could see that Miss Paxton was not interested.

'The prefect who reported you said that you were smiling; that you were behaving in a manner not suitable for a girl from this school; and that you were extremely rude to her.'

'*I* was rude! *She* was the one who was rude. She interrupted me in the middle of a conversation. I said I'd like to finish my sentence, please, but she just went on.'

'Virginia Dickinson, when a prefect speaks to you, you treat her with respect, and you answer her immediately. For one thing, she's a few years older than you.'

'Well, the workmen were even older. You wouldn't want me to be disrespectful to them, would you?'

Miss Paxton gave the impression that she was about to explode. 'While you are under the school's jurisdiction, you will speak to no males, unless it be your father or brothers.'

'You're kidding,' said Rusty.

'Which brings me to my next matter.'

She opened her bag and placed all Rusty's photographs on the desk.

Rusty gasped. 'Where did you get those?' she cried. 'They were on my chest of drawers.'

'From where I took them.'

'But why? I mean, I thought we were allowed to have photographs.'

'Of relatives.'

'But,' spluttered Rusty, 'they're as good as my relatives. I'm one of the family.'

Miss Paxton lifted the picture of Skeet and placed it in front of the others. 'I am informed that this happens to be ...' She stopped, barely able to form the words. '... Your boyfriend.'

'My what!' said Rusty. 'Well, you're *informed* wrong. That's Skeet. He's my American brother.'

'I'm sorry, but it's against the rules for girls to have photographs of boys.'

Rusty stood up, furious. 'Well, your rules are cruel. I don't care if I do get expelled. I hate this school, and the sooner I get kicked out, the better!'

Miss Paxton blanched. 'Do you know what it means to be expelled, my girl? Aside from the shame it would bring to the House and the school, it will mean that no other school will ever take you on as a pupil. You and your family will be disgraced. No institution or college will even consider you.'

Rusty sat down slowly. If only she could talk to someone. If only there was someone who would take her side.

'So you see,' said Miss Paxton quietly, 'we're only trying to help you.'

Rusty stared back numbly at her.

'I believe your mother is collecting you outside the gates tomorrow afternoon,' she said. 'I suggest you take the photographs with you then. After all,' she added gently, 'you will be able to see them at weekends.'

As Rusty walked down the drab corridors, hugging the photographs, she felt as though she had stumbled into some ghastly nightmare; all the time she kept asking herself, why was she being punished like this? What had she done that was so terrible?

Thursday was dance night in the gymnasium. Rusty sat on one of the long wooden benches as the girls walked up to the mistresses and asked to be put on their list of prospective partners, and the Sixth-formers asked the younger girls to dance. It was all so formal and so dead.

The girls danced as if they had been frozen from the neck downwards.

Rusty thought back to the square-dancing evenings in Connecticut where all the boys and girls whirled around each other, hollering. She remembered how in junior high a nickelodeon had been rented for the end-of-semester school dance; a real nickelodeon with the latest hit records.

She heard Miss Collins say to her, 'Come along, Virginia, I'm sure you could show us a thing or two. You'll probably put us all to shame.'

Rusty just faked a smile, because in fact it was true. She could dance better than any single girl or mistress in that gymnasium, but then she reckoned even Skeet could, and he had two left feet.

That night, in the dormitory, she avoided looking at the four other girls. She had a feeling that if she caught Judith's eye or heard her make one snide remark, she might just grab hold of her and throw her out through the window.

The following day she drifted through the lessons in a stupor, but as each one ended she knew that she was closer to leaving. When the final bell rang, she had to use every ounce of concentration to keep herself from running away from the place there and then.

Even so there was prep, in which she had to sit struggling through her homework.

At last she was accompanied by one of the prefects down the school drive. As soon as she saw her mother waiting for her, she broke into a run. Once through the gates, she felt so happy she could have danced.

Peggy Dickinson took Rusty's grip and smiled. Seeing her daughter's cheerful face, she realized that she had made the right decision. Now she could ring Beatie and tell her that her worries had been unfounded. Virginia, if her expression was anything to go by, was loving Benwood House.

told her that her grandmother had reached retirement. Anyway, pressure was mounting up to be watching three hours.

17

Her mother raised the knocker.

'Haven't you gotten a key yet?' asked Rusty.

'Your grandmother doesn't like to have more than one key to the house. It makes her nervous. She's afraid I might lose it.'

Rusty was amazed. 'Couldn't you just get another one made secretly? I mean, what if there was an emergency or something?'

'I've thought of that, but you need to take the key in order to have another one made, and your grandmother keeps a firm grip on it.'

Just then the door opened. Mrs Grace looked older than ever. She hung on to the doorknob as if it stood between her and life itself.

Before Rusty could say anything, a small figure rushed up to her mother and hung on to her, sobbing. It was Charlie.

'There, there,' said his mother as she picked him up. 'I told you I'd be back.'

Rusty had never seen such a change in a person. He was behaving just like a baby. As he sank his head into the nape of her neck, he jammed one thumb tightly into his mouth. In his other hand he clutched a piece of well-sucked material.

From the drawing room came the sickly-sweet sound of her grandmother. 'I'm in here, dear,' she sang out.

Rusty was tempted to sing back, 'And we're out here, dear.' Instead, she hung her Beanie, hat and scarf on the hall-stand and followed her mother and Charlie into the drawing room.

Seated in her own winged armchair sat her grandmother. Her friend, Mrs Smythe-Williams, was sitting on the sofa. Her grandmother looked disapprovingly at Rusty's mother as she sat down with Charlie on her lap. 'Now, now, now,' she said sweetly. 'Big boys don't cry, do they?'

I wonder, thought Rusty, if they have the electric-chair for murder in England. She shoved her clenched fists into her blazer pocket.

Her grandmother turned to Mrs Smythe-Williams.

'Looks just like a little English girl now, doesn't she?'

'So much nicer,' her friend crooned.

'And so how are you liking school?'

Rusty shrugged. 'It's O.K.'

Her grandmother cleared her throat awkwardly. The girl looked fine as long as she didn't open her mouth.

After tea, Rusty's mother started looking very mysterious. 'Virginia, I've a little surprise for you,' she said.

'What is it?'

'It won't be a surprise if I tell you.'

'So when do I get to see it?'

'In a minute. Go on into the dining room.'

Rusty and Charlie, accompanied by their grandmother, walked into the dining room. Charlie had dispensed with the piece of cloth and was now clinging to an old teddy-bear.

'Leave that in the hall, Charles,' said their grandmother.

'Where's Mummy gone?' he said, startled.

'She's just going to get a surprise for you. Now you just sit up at the table properly and leave the teddy-bear in the hall.'

'I want to keep him with me. Then he can have a surprise, too.'

'Don't be silly. A big boy like you . . .'

Rusty could see the tears welling up in his eyes. 'I'll go get Teddy a chair,' she said swiftly.

'You will do no such thing,' said her grandmother, but Rusty had an acute attack of deafness and placed a chair beside Charlie.

He sat the bear on it and then, realizing that it was Rusty who had brought the chair, scowled at her. Oh boy, she thought. Nothing's changed.

Just then her mother entered, carrying two steaming plates.

'Baked beans on toast!' yelled Rusty.

'Aunt Hannah told me it was one of your favourite dishes. She said you used to have it on Saturday nights, but I thought you might like it sooner.'

'Oh, this is the tops!'

As her mother sat down, she took a letter out of her pocket.

'That reminds me, Beatie sent on this letter from America. It's for you.'

'Margaret,' said Mrs Dickinson Senior, 'you really must inform the Omsks that you've moved. You can't expect this woman to keep forwarding Virginia's mail!'

Peggy nodded wearily.

Rusty looked at the writing on the envelope. It was Skeet's. She was about to open it when on second thoughts she put it into her blazer pocket.

'Aren't you going to open it?' said her grandmother.

'Sure. Later.'

'Well, I expect we'd all like to hear the news, too.'

I *expect* you would, thought Rusty.

'Unless, of course, you have something to hide.'

Ever heard of privacy? thought Rusty.

'Children shouldn't have secrets from grown-ups. Margaret, what do you say?'

Rusty glanced at her mother. She looked as if she could do with a week's sleep.

'Why don't you want us to know what's in the letter?' she said.

'I was taught it was bad manners to read at the table,' said Rusty.

Her mother smiled and turned to her mother-in-law. 'She's quite right, you know.'

Rusty hastily began eating her beans. She could see that her grandmother was furious.

She rattled her teacup rather loudly and gave a short laugh. 'It's a pity, Virginia, that when Mr and Mrs Omsk were teaching you table manners, they didn't deem it fit to teach you how to use a knife and fork correctly.'

O.K., thought Rusty, you asked for it.

She flung down her fork. 'Why the hell don't you just get off my back!' she yelled.

'Virginia!' said her mother.

'You're always bitching about something or other in that sugary voice of yours. I've never heard you say a nice word about anybody.'

'Margaret,' gasped her grandmother. 'Are you going to let her get away with this?'

'I certainly am not.'

'I'm warning you,' went on Rusty, growing more heated, 'that if you say one nasty thing about the Omsks, I'm going to give it to you!'

Charlie began beating the table delightedly with his fists. He didn't know quite what was happening; all he knew was that his grandmother was upset, and he hated her more than he hated his sister.

'Virginia!' said Peggy. 'You will go up to your room immediately!'

Rusty flung back her chair and stood up. 'It's a pleasure.'

'That's the gratitude you get for sending her to a good

school!' said her grandmother. 'I told you it was unwise to have her home for the weekends.'

Upstairs, Rusty slammed her bedroom door shut behind her.

She propped up a chair under the doorknob to keep out interruptions and sat on the bed, wrapping the eiderdown around her. Then she tore open the letter.

'Hi!' it said:

I am writing this on your bed. Makes me think of you easier. Tonight we had a big celebration dinner. I have two hairs on my upper lip! I'm real glad I got hairs before school starts. I wish you'd been there.

Janey's mother gave one of her 'sophisticated' parties for her. I was invited. We had to wear formals! Bow-ties and all! Janey was wearing lipstick. She even had high heels on.

I hear it always rains in England. Want me to send you your rubbers?

This is the longest letter I ever wrote. Hurry up and write.

Love,
Skeet

P.S. It's awfully quiet in your room.

Rusty read it through slowly again. She wished Skeet had told her what the dinner was like. She folded the letter up neatly and opened the drawer where she had put her other American letters. They were nowhere to be seen.

She took a deep breath. She felt as though she was about to throw up. She scrabbled desperately amid her clothing and whipped open each drawer, but there was no sign of them. Finally, she found them on top of the wardrobe. She couldn't tell whether they had been read or not, but she wasn't going to take any more chances. This time, she'd hide them.

She lifted up the rugs on the floor and started feeling her way around the floorboards. In books, people could always find a handy piece of wood that would lift up, revealing a neat little cavity underneath, where you could store secret documents. Unfortunately, in her room there was no loose plank.

She was just feeling her way around the sides of the wardrobe when she heard footsteps. She flung the letters into a corner, threw herself on the bed, and opened a book. The footsteps stopped on the landing below.

'Virginia!'

It was her mother.

I suppose this is the apology routine again, thought Rusty.

She leapt off the bed, threw open the door and strolled on to the landing. Her mother was standing on the stairs. 'Beatie's on the phone,' she said abruptly.

'Beatie!'

Rusty jumped down the stairs, two steps at a time.

'Yes,' said her mother, following her. 'But you don't deserve to talk to her.'

The phone was lying on a small table in the hall. Rusty grabbed it. 'Hi!' she said.

'Hello there,' came a bright voice at the other end.

'How you doin'?'

'I'm doing splendidly.'

'How's your ruddy indigestion?'

'Oh good gracious, I'm not ringing you all up to talk about the state of my innards.'

'It's good to hear your voice.'

'How's school?'

'Terrible.'

'Your mother seems to think you're loving it.'

'What?'

'She said you looked very cheerful when she met you.'

'That's because I was glad to get out.'

Rusty suddenly remembered that her mother was standing behind her.

'Mother says all girls grumble about boarding school,

and that as soon as I make a few friends, I'll be fine.' She sighed. 'So I guess I'll just have to stick it out.'

There was a pause. 'When's your half-term?'

'November.'

'Why don't you spend it here?'

'Oh, Beatie,' she cried, 'I'd just love to!'

'Put your mother on and I'll ask her.'

Trembling, Rusty handed the receiver to her, then sat at the bottom of the stairs and crossed her fingers.

'Yes,' said her mother. 'Well, that's awfully kind, but ... Oh, Beatie I'd love to, you know I would. Are you sure? Yes. Yes, I promise.' She turned and looked at Rusty out of the corner of her eye. 'Yes, all right, even if she's naughty I'll bring her. Yes.'

Rusty sprang up. 'Oh boy,' she whispered. 'Oh boy!'

Her mother handed the receiver back.

'Hi again!'

'It's all arranged. Your mother's going to tell me the dates.'

'Oh, Beatie!'

'Whatever happens,' said Beatie slowly, 'will you promise me that you'll travel to Devon with your mother?'

'You bet.'

'Even if you've quarrelled?'

'Yeah. Sure I will.'

'And even if I can't manage to be there?'

Rusty was puzzled. 'Are you going away somewhere?'

'Yes.'

'Oh, I hope you'll be there,' said Rusty.

'I'll do my best.'

'Don't stay on too long,' said her mother. 'It's a long-distance call.'

'I have to go now, Beatie,' said Rusty hurriedly. 'Will you be phoning again?'

'Next weekend. Rusty?'

'Uh-huh?'

'Don't let them get you down. Chin up, eh?'

'Yeah. Walk tall.'

'Absolutely.'

'So long.'

'Goodbye.'

Rusty handed the receiver back and leapt up the stairs.

She wished she could have told Beatie about not being able to have her American photographs at school. She couldn't let her mother know about it, because she would have felt hurt at discovering that her photograph wasn't among them.

She undressed quickly and hopped into bed. For what seemed like hours, she lay there in the dark, too uncomfortable to sleep and too cold to get out and put more clothes on.

The window rattled, and the rain outside grew heavier. She heard Charlie crying, a door opening, and footsteps. Her mother, probably.

Within minutes, she heard her grandmother muttering on the landing. 'I told you you shouldn't have let him speak to that woman!'

No sirree, thought Rusty. She certainly wasn't going to apologize.

18

Rusty stood outside the Headmistress's study. It was Monday and she had been summoned to report to Miss Bembridge during the lunch-break. She knocked at the door.

'Enter.'

Rusty pushed it open. Miss Bembridge was sitting at her desk. 'Sit down,' she said, indicating a chair.

Rusty did so.

'Now,' Miss Bembridge said. 'I have just been having a long talk with your mother on the telephone. It's about your schoolwork.'

'I'm a little behind, but I'll –'

'Did I ask you to speak?'

'No, Miss Bembridge.'

'Then kindly remain silent.' Miss Bembridge picked up several pieces of paper.

'According to the mistresses, you are more than "a little behind". As well as having done no Latin or French, you have also done no algebra, geometry, English history, or geography.'

Rusty opened her mouth to speak, and then closed it again.

'I have therefore decided that this year you will give up the lighter, more peripheral subjects, and instead take extra Latin, French and mathematics. Some of those lessons will take place with the Juniors, the rest will be private in your break-times and after supper. For the remainder of this term there will be no art, singing, gymnastics or Greek dancing.'

'But,' stammered Rusty, 'art and gymnastics are two of my favourite subjects. Couldn't I give up lacrosse instead?'

'Certainly not. There is no better place to learn team spirit than on the lacrosse pitch. I hope that when the school holds Saturday matches, you will stay and support the teams,' said Miss Bembridge. 'Of course, that will be entirely voluntary, but you could do with some good points to cancel out several of the marks that you have collected in the course of the last week.'

Rusty wondered if they were going to do something different to her each week to make her more miserable.

'Now,' said Miss Bembridge kindly, 'are there any problems you'd like to discuss with me?'

'Is it possible for me to have a hot-water bottle? I'm awful cold at night.'

'I'm afraid not. There's a shortage of rubber in this country. There's been a war on here, you know. Hot-water bottles are difficult to come by.'

'Uh, then could I have the window by my bed shut?'

'I'm afraid not. We believe that girls will have a fresher and deeper sleep with the windows open.'

'But I get so cold, I can't sleep. Maybe if I had an extra blanket.'

'If you washed less frequently, you'd stay much warmer.'

'Excuse me?' said Rusty.

'I hear that you wash all over at least once if not twice a day. You realize that, by doing that, you're removing all the natural oils from your skin?'

I don't believe I'm hearing this, thought Rusty. 'So I don't get to have a blanket, is that it?'

Miss Bembridge pulled herself up sharply. 'Don't you dare speak to me in that manner, young lady!'

'It feels like everyone here is trying to make me as unhappy as they possibly can.'

'Nonsense. We can't change the way the school is run

just for one pupil, simply because she's been a little softened by luxury.'

Luxury! thought Rusty. Oh, what's the point? She doesn't want to listen. She fell silent.

'Well, Virginia Dickinson, is that all?'

'Wha, yes ma-a-am,' drawled Rusty in an American accent so broad that it bordered on Deep South. She saw immediately that it had infuriated the Headmistress. Feeling exhilarated, she stood up.

'Ah guess ah'd best be moseying on back to class, Missy Bembridge. Ah sure as heck don't wanna be late!'

Miss Bembridge got to her feet, red-faced with anger.

'Thank you. That will be all.'

'Whah, thank you, Miss Bembridge. Good-day to you, Miss Bembridge.' And with that she walked out, head raised, triumphant.

That night, after lights out, as she stared across at the empty top of her chest of drawers, she vowed that from now on she'd be more American than an American.

When she awoke, she was standing barefoot in her pyjamas in one of the school corridors. She had no idea where she was or how she had got there. Once she had recovered from the shock, she began to feel her way slowly along the walls. She raised her pyjama collar up high around her neck. Under unseen doors, cold draughts of air blew across her feet. Fumbling and shivering in the dark, she seemed to pad around the icy floor for hours, till she began to believe that she'd never find her way back to Butt wing.

Eventually she found the stairway and climbed swiftly up it, her hand resting on the banister to guide her.

The next night, she woke up at the bottom of the stairs.

As the weeks went by, the sleepwalking continued. Sometimes nothing would happen for two or three nights.

Mondays were the worst. She always seemed to travel further on Mondays.

September crawled slowly into October. The branches of the trees surrounding the high walls of the school dripped with rain. The skies and mornings grew darker and colder, and the leaves from the woods began to drift across the sodden lacrosse pitches. Flowers died, the dawn chorus grew quieter through lack of member birds, and the wind found new openings in the doors and windows.

Because of her difficulties in sleeping at night and her sleepwalking expeditions when she did sleep, Rusty grew constantly more tired.

She loathed Latin, and since it was Miss Paxton who gave her extra Latin coaching, Miss Paxton loathed her. Each evening, when the girls shook hands formally with the mistress before going up to the dormitories, Rusty was last in line, for in Butt House they lined up in order of popularity. Every Monday evening Miss Paxton read out the new order, and every Monday Rusty was last. The girl who was always in front of her sweated visibly when the list was read out, and such was her joy when she heard it wasn't her who was last that Rusty felt she was doing her a favour, and all with no effort.

She was reported to Matron for spending too much time in the lavatory. She had hoped that there, at least, she could be alone with her thoughts, but someone must have noticed ... Judith Poole, she suspected. Rusty had to quickly make up her mind to say whether she had constipation or Montezuma's Revenge. She chose the former.

Matron gave her something called 'Number 9', and within a short space of time she was clutching her stomach and spending even more time in the lavatory.

One Saturday, for a treat, her mother took her and Charlie to the cinema. It was an American film with Mickey Rooney in it. Rusty had seen it before, one summer in Vermont, and she started to cry. She was so worried that her mother would take her out that she buried her head in her handkerchief and pretended to have a cold.

Sometimes, alone in her room, she would sing every American song she could remember, ending off with 'The Star-Spangled Banner'. One afternoon she heard Charlie creeping up the stairs, and she knew that he was listening, so she chose one that Uncle Bruno used to sing to her when she was little.

> '*A horsie and a flea and three blind mice*
> *Sat on a kerbstone shooting dice.*
> *The horsie sneezed and fell on the flea,*
> "*Whoops*", *said the flea*, "*there's horsie on me!*"
>
> '*Boom-boom, ain't it great to be crazy!*
> *Boom-boom, ain't it great to be nuts!*
> *Silly and foolish all day long,*
> *Boom-boom, ain't it great to be crazy!*'

And Charlie laughed.

Rusty slowly opened the door and found him sitting on the floor with his teddy-bear.

'Like that one?' she said.

'No,' he said crossly. 'It's silly.'

'So who was doing all that laughing?'

He thrust the teddy-bear forward. 'Teddy,' he said, and he picked himself up and stalked off.

She tried to tell her mother she didn't want to go to college, but she was never able to get very far.

'You're far too young to know what you want to do when you leave school,' her mother said. 'You'll go to university.' And that was that.

Each morning, back at school, when the bell rang, a sense of doom sank deep into the pit of Rusty's stomach and, as she hauled herself out of bed, she wondered how she was going to survive another day.

She began to notice that her breasts were getting smaller

and that her clothes were loose. In fact, it wasn't just her breasts that were shrinking, but her whole body. Sometimes she had the feeling that she was disappearing altogether. Often, when she hadn't spoken to anyone for days, nor they to her, she had to pinch herself to make sure she was still there.

She felt as though she was being shrunk to fit the school, her grandmother, and England itself.

Her accent and her L. L. Bean coat were the only things she possessed that reminded her of America. She hung on grimly to both.

19

It was a Wednesday night in October, and Rusty was sitting with her French teacher in one of the empty classrooms. She would really have enjoyed French if it hadn't been for Mademoiselle, who was short and fat and reeked of stale cabbage-water and mildew. As Rusty was gazing at the thin moustache on her upper lip and the unwashed vest sticking out over her greasy suit, there was a knock at the door. It was a prefect from her House.

'Excuse me, Mademoiselle,' she began. 'There's a message from Miss Bembridge for Virginia Dickinson.' She handed Mademoiselle a piece of paper.

She glanced at it and looked up. 'You are to remain at the school for the weekend,' she said. 'Your mother is to visit a friend in Devon who is seriously ill.'

'In Devon? Does she say who it is?'

Mademoiselle looked down again. '*Oui*. The Honourable Mrs Langley –'

'Beatie,' she whispered. 'It's Beatie and her ruddy indigestion.'

'Insolence!' shouted Mademoiselle, but Rusty hardly heard her.

The prefect left and Mademoiselle tapped her desk. '*Attention, s'il vous plaît. Rapportez-vous à la page vingt-trois, numéro huit.*'

'*Numéro huit*,' repeated Rusty, dazed. She gazed down at her French reader. Mademoiselle tapped the desk again.

'*Dans un petit village de Normandie*,' Rusty began, '*il y a deux meuniers.*' She stopped. 'Please, Mademoiselle, may I go to the john?'

'*Qu'est-ce que c'est, ce* john?*'

'I mean,' said Rusty, remembering the procedure and raising her hand, 'please may I be excused?'

Mademoiselle gave a loud grunt and slammed the book shut.

'*Très bien,*' she said. 'But you will translate this exercise for me.'

'*Oui, Mademoiselle,*' whispered Rusty.

As soon as the French mistress had left the classroom, Rusty hurried out into the corridor, her head down. There was a large broom-closet at the end of the next passage. She moved swiftly towards it and flung open the door. Once safely inside, she stood in the darkness and leaned against the wall.

On Saturday morning, no one would have her in their group, so she had to go with the Juniors into town. She was put at the back and paired up with the other unpopular girl in her House, a small slight girl with a pasty complexion, from the Lower Fifth. Recognizing a fellow sufferer, Rusty gave her a friendly wink, but the girl turned miserably away.

Rusty spotted Rosalind and the other two girls at the front of the 'crocodile'. They were paired with girls from their respective Houses. She waved to them. They waved shyly back. The 'Bull' marched up and down, checking to see that they all were wearing their outdoor shoes and stockings, their capes, gloves and hats. She paused at Rusty and glared at her L. L. Bean coat.

'Virginia Dickinson, the sooner your mother obtains a proper uniform, the better.'

'I have permission –' she began.

'If you answer me back, young lady, you will remain at school.'

'Yes, Miss Bullivant.'

As soon as her back was turned, Rusty shook her fist at her.

The girl next to her blushed. 'Please don't,' she begged. 'If you have to stay in, I won't have a partner and she might not let me out either.'

'O.K.,' Rusty whispered.

They walked briskly down the school drive, through the gates and towards the bus-stop.

'Say,' said Rusty to the girl, 'how come you aren't winning the popularity contest either?'

'I'm a Scholarship girl,' she mumbled.

'You mean you won a scholarship?'

She nodded.

Rusty gave a low whistle. 'That means you must be pretty smart.'

The girl shrugged.

'Come on. Don't be so modest.'

'I suppose I am a bit. I mean, I do well in exams.'

'So the others are jealous, is that it?'

The girl looked astounded. 'Jealous!'

'No talking in the ranks!' shouted Miss Bullivant over her shoulder.

In the distance they could see a bus approaching.

'No,' said the girl quietly. 'They look down on me because my father doesn't have to pay any fees. They call me "Charity Girl".'

'You're kidding!' whispered Rusty.

The bus slowed down and the girls in front stepped on to it. It wasn't until they had reached the town that Rusty felt it was safe to talk to the girl again. Miss Bullivant was leading them towards a crossing. She stopped at the kerb, looked right and left, and then led them all firmly across the street.

'Say,' Rusty whispered out of the side of her mouth, 'why don't we be friends? At least we got something in common. Nobody likes us.'

The girl stared ahead. 'I can't. I'm sorry, but I just can't. You see, if I make friends with you I'll be even more unpopular. If I can just stick it out until the Upper Fifth, things will be different.'

'How long have you been here?'

'This is my fourth year.'

Oh boy, thought Rusty.

They halted outside a newsagent's and sweet shop.

'You have ten minutes,' said Miss Bullivant, 'and remember, you are all to stay with your partners.'

'Yes, Miss Bullivant,' chorused the girls. 'Thank you, Miss Bullivant.'

The full-time boarders had been given their week's quota of money from their term's allowance by Matron. Since Rusty went home at weekends, Matron had nothing to give her. Even so, Rusty would still have liked to wander in and out the shops.

What made the trip into town harder for Rusty to bear was that occasionally she saw girls from her own form walking freely about in fours; and some were sitting in a little Tudor teahouse with a plate of buns between them.

In spite of the quaintness of the town, everything looked grubby and run-down, as if the whole place needed a coat of paint; and Rusty still couldn't get used to seeing so many windows without shutters. They seemed unfinished, somehow, like faces with no eyelids.

Bare-legged girls in faded coats and lace-up shoes, old ladies in trousers, and younger women with scarves tied in turban fashion stood outside the shops in long queues. Everyone looked so tired and worn down. There were no bright colours anywhere, only khaki and grey and a muddy sort of green. An old faded poster with *We can take it* on it was peeling off a wall. Beside it a new poster read: EXTRA EFFORT NOW MEANS BETTER LIVING SOONER. Rusty was just glancing down a street where there was a large pile of rubble, when she heard a boy yell out, 'Hey, Yank, get a move on!' She whirled around.

Across the street three uniformed boys were waiting for a fourth to catch up with them. Above knee-length grey shorts they wore scarlet blazers and caps with black stripes.

Rusty was aware that the crocodile of girls was moving away. If she didn't take her chance now, it would be too late.

'Hey, Yank!' she yelled. The fourth boy, who was scowling, turned and looked across the road, puzzled. 'Are you from the States?' Rusty yelled.

He stood at the edge of the pavement and grinned. He had cropped brown hair and dark eyes. She guessed he was about thirteen or fourteen. He had a classical, regular sort of face. Nothing stuck out or looked squashed.

'I was evacuated there,' he said.

'Me too. Where'd they send you?'

'Vermont. Burlington.'

'Oh boy, I don't believe it! Say, do you know the Fitzgibbons?'

He shook his head. 'Sorry, can't say I do. Is that where you stayed?'

'No, but my American grandparents live there. We call 'em the Fitzes for short. Ever go ice-skating on the lake before it got snowed under?'

'Millions of times.'

'We coulda skated right past one another!' she cried.

He smiled.

He doesn't sound at all American, thought Rusty. I wonder why they called him Yank. 'Ever make snow candy?' she said.

'Snow candy?'

'Uh-huh. My grandparents taught me. You have to do it after a snowfall, so's it's clean or soft, I guess. Then you pour boiling-hot maple syrup on the snow, and shazzam! – snow candy!'

'You know what I miss?' he said. 'Hot chocolate.'

'Me too. And Coca-Cola.'

Rusty and the boy were totally unaware that the two groups of boys and girls had stopped walking and were staring, transfixed, as Rusty and the boy yelled across to each other.

The boy spoke of buying a nickel's worth of hot cocoa on the lake, and of going to an old movie theatre, where the most beautiful stars and planets were lit up on the ceiling just like a planetarium, and during the movie you could just tip your head back every now and then and take a peek at them.

The drab grey town faded, and Rusty was suddenly back on the frozen lake in Vermont with Gramps and Uncle Bruno and Skeet.

But her journey was short-lived. Within minutes, she felt a hand grip her arm; it was the Bull. Below her steamed-up spectacles her thin lips were pressed into a single line. Outraged, she dragged Rusty away from the kerb.

'How dare you!' she spluttered. 'How dare you!'

'He was sent to Vermont,' Rusty began. 'Burlington, where my American grandparents –'

'That will do,' the Bull snapped. 'Do you realize the disgrace you've brought on the school? Do you?'

'What did I do?'

'Go and stand next to your partner immediately!'

'Yes, Miss Bullivant.'

As she approached the line of girls, Rusty caught sight of the look of horror on their faces. Her partner was staring down at the ground. Rusty noticed that she was blushing. 'He was a sea-vacuee like me,' she whispered.

'Silence,' said Miss Bullivant fiercely. 'One more word out of you and I'll see that you're expelled, my girl. Benwood House doesn't need *your* type.'

As the crocodile of girls trooped back in the direction

of the bus-stop, the silence was electric. None of the girls dared even look at one another, let alone speak.

Rusty was completely bewildered. Didn't they realize how lonely she'd been ever since she had come to this school? Didn't they realize what it meant to meet someone who knew something about where she had come from? Whenever she had tried to talk about America, she was always stepped on. 'Oh, America this, America that,' they'd say. 'Can't you talk about anything else?' But what? That's all she'd known for the past five years. And then she'd hear them talking about the War, and that made her feel left out. Especially when Judith Poole said one night, 'Of course, *some* people have never known what it was like to be *really* at war. *Some* people have never even heard one single bomb. *Some* people ran away to other countries.' But Rusty hadn't run away. She'd been sent to America, whether she had wanted to go or not, in just the same way as she'd been sent to this horrible school.

For the rest of the day and on Sunday she was put into an empty classroom to sit in disgrace and to eat her meals there alone. On Monday morning, a public announcement was made in assembly concerning her crime – talking to a boy – and she was given a discipline mark. As the others sat, Rusty was made to stand up in front of everyone to add to her humiliation.

Throughout the day she was greeted with open hostility, not only by the girls who felt that the honour of the school had been soiled, but especially by members of her own House. She had only to walk down a corridor or into a classroom, and immediately the girls would stop talking. At supper she found gravel and stones in her food, and when she slipped into bed, her sheets had been drenched in water.

The following morning she was summoned to the Headmistress's study, to be told that she would have to remain at school the following weekend. Her mother was still in Devon. Beatie, she was informed, had died.

20

Rusty lay in bed, wide awake. She screwed up her eyes to see her wrist-watch in the dark. It was nearly midnight. She had it all worked out. All she had to do was climb out of the window on to the scaffolding, and then jump off, just like those people who had jumped out of skyscraper windows after the Wall Street Crash.

As the hands of her watch reached twelve, she slipped out of bed and crouched on the floor. She'd kept her underwear on under her pyjamas, together with two pairs of woolly socks. After all, if she was going to die, she might as well die warm. She put on her cardigan and dressing gown, tying the cord firmly round her waist.

Kneeling by the bed, she pulled the sheets and blankets up to the pillow, opened a drawer, and took out her sneakers. Her sneakers should grip well enough, she thought. She didn't want to fall till she'd reached the edge. She put them on, crept towards the open window, climbed over the sill, and grabbed hold of one of the iron bars that formed the scaffolding. She pulled hard on the bar and raised herself to her feet, so that she was standing alone, high above the grounds. The sense of freedom was intoxicating. As she slowly worked her way towards the outermost bars, she felt no fear, only a growing calmness. She sat for a moment on one bar, holding another that was in front of her face.

A crescent moon hung high above the woods beyond the wall. The air was crisp. Rusty took a deep breath. Boy, it was going to be such a relief to die. No more people hating her. No more rotten meals. No more sleepwalking. No more cold.

She poked her head out from behind the bar in front of her and pulled herself up. 'Here goes,' she muttered. She bent her knees, ready to take a good hard leap. 'I hope I get to see Beatie.'

Then she remembered her promise. Only two weeks earlier, Beatie had said yet again, 'Promise me that whatever happen, you'll stay at my house during your half-term.'

And Rusty had said, 'I told you a million times, that's a promise that's a cinch for me to keep.'

'Even if I can't be there?'

'Sure.'

Rusty whipped her head back under the bar and sat down sharply.

'She knew,' she whispered. 'She knew!'

She gripped the bar hard and began to shake.

'Why didn't she say?'

She leaned against the cold scaffolding and started to sob, her head buried between her arms. All her grief at Beatie's death, all her loneliness and misery at being torn away from Aunt Hannah and Uncle Bruno, overwhelmed her.

As she wept, she remembered how, one night, she had crept downstairs to the back porch in her pyjamas and discovered Aunt Hannah sitting on Uncle Bruno's lap on the rocker. Aunt Hannah had pulled her gently on to her knee, and the three of them had rocked there together. Rusty longed desperately to be hugged that warmly again. She missed them both so much. And Beatie!

After some time she stopped sobbing and opened her eyes.

She fumbled around inside her pocket for a handkerchief. Beside it was her small torch. She had put it there in case it had been too dark to see the scaffolding. As she wiped her nose and face, she realized how funny she must look, sitting out there, high above the ground, in her dressing gown and pyjamas.

'You win, Beatie,' she whispered. 'I'll be there.'

She was about to move back towards the dormitory when suddenly she looked at the scaffolding. What a goop! she thought. This has been here all the time, and I never even thought of it. She blew some warmth into her hands, rubbed them briskly together, and manoeuvred herself down to the bar below.

She grabbed the next pole, wrapped her legs around it, and slid like a fireman until she reached a wooden platform. It gave a light clunk as her foot hit it. She froze for an instant and stared up at the windows, but no light appeared. Stealthily she carried on, sliding and groping, swinging and pulling herself across to other bars, until finally she was standing on the stony ground that surrounded the building. She turned and moved swiftly towards the high wall, like a crazed prisoner just liberated from Alcatraz. She leapt over the lacrosse pitches, the smell of damp earth underneath her feet. It was all she could do not to sing, or scream, or yell out.

Impatiently, she felt along the old wall for any crevices where she might put her hands and feet, and began scrabbling frantically up the brickwork. She hauled herself up to the top, swung herself over, and dropped down on the other side. She pulled out her torch and turned it on, protecting it with her hand, and made an arrow with three twigs on the ground. She had never thought the trail signs she had learnt in the Girl Scouts would be so useful. For the first time, she was beginning to feel just a little like a real pioneer. Torch at the ready, she stepped into the woods and found herself ankle-deep in leaves. She picked up a great handful and threw it high in the air so that it cascaded in an autumnal heap on top of her. Slowly, she walked into the woods, stopping now and then to gaze up at the trees. After a while she came to a small clearing. In the centre stood a broad-trunked tree. Its huge branches grew up and outward so that, from below, it seemed like a great, sheltered hut. Rusty laid down another sign at the edge of the clearing, walked over to the tree, and squeezed herself into a sitting position between two enormous exposed roots.

Leaning back, she drank in all the smells and strange scuffling sounds from the surrounding woods. As she sat there, a wave of fatigue swept over her. If it had been warm, she could easily have fallen asleep. There and then she decided that she would run away, back to America. She didn't know how or when, but somehow she had to get hold of enough money to get her to a port.

'Plymouth!' she exclaimed. That was where the first pilgrims had set sail from England to America. One day she'd go to Plymouth and stow away on a ship. That settled, she rose and headed for the edge of her protected circle and began following her trail signs back.

At the foot of the scaffolding she realized that it was going to be more difficult climbing up than it had been slithering down. She glanced at her sneakers. They were filthy.

'Too bad,' she muttered. 'Pioneers do not worry about Matrons.' And with that she began climbing.

With all her strength, she shinned up the scaffolding like a monkey, gripping the long vertical poles with her knees and feet. At last she reached the right level. All she had to do now was find the right window. When she had found it, she noted that there was a large crack in the brickwork underneath it. Looking down, she also noted that one of the cloakroom windows was almost perfectly in line with it. If she could make a small mark beside each, that would save time the next night.

She clambered through the window into the dormitory,

pushed her sneakers off, and began wiping off the dirt on them with her handkerchief. By the time she had undressed and climbed back into bed, it was already growing light. She had no sooner closed her eyes than the bell rang.

The sound made her heart sink. For a moment she wondered if she had dreamt her escapade. While the other girls groaned and roused themselves out of bed, Rusty leaned over and pulled open her bottom drawer. There was still a slight trace of dirt on the toe of one of her sneakers, and on the floor by the window was one tiny russet leaf.

The following night, as she clambered out, she marked the window with a stub of chalk she had taken from the class wastepaper basket.

In the woods her track signs remained untouched, and within a short time she had reached the sheltered copse. She rested for a moment at the foot of the tree, and then began exploring the woods on the other side, laying down a fresh set of signs.

Because of her explorations, it took a little longer for her to reach the school wall again. She hoped that her chalk marks would make up for the time lost. When she climbed back through her dormitory window, the other girls were still fast asleep. No one, it seemed, suspected a thing.

The next day, school seemed just as dreary as before, but the knowledge that the scaffolding surrounded the building made the tedious hours more bearable. That night, however, it rained. Rusty lay awake for hours, hoping and praying that it would subside, before finally giving up and closing her eyes.

When she awoke, she was shocked to find that she was standing yet again in a dark corridor. Once she had stopped shaking, she began to feel her way along the damp walls. Even as she worked her way along the passageways, she could hear the rain falling outside.

The next day was clear and windy. Rusty nearly dropped off to sleep in history.

At break time, Rusty eyed the scaffolding, willing the wind to dry it. During the last two lessons in the afternoon, a clump of dark clouds had come lowering across the sky, so that the lights had to be turned on.

Rusty couldn't even eat her supper, so anxious was she for the clouds to pass. The mistress in charge of her table, seeing how pale she looked, gave her permission to leave it.

She had been in the Fourth Form sitting room for only five minutes when a prefect summoned her to see Miss Paxton. As Rusty walked past the other Fourth-formers, Judith Poole scowled at her.

'If you've another order mark, Virginia Creeper, you'll pay for it,' she sneered.

Rusty ignored her.

To her surprise she was taken, not to an empty classroom, but to Miss Paxton's own sitting room. The mistress was seated in an armchair by a log fire. She beckoned Rusty in and indicated the armchair opposite.

'Shut the door and sit down,' she said.

'Yes, Miss Paxton. Thank you, Miss Paxton.'

Miss Paxton gazed at Rusty's ashen face. It was her pallid complexion, coupled with the report from Miss Bullivant, that concerned her. Although she disliked the girl, she was, after all, her responsibility.

'Is there anything troubling you, Virginia?'

Rusty felt safer keeping her mouth shut, so she glanced away and stared quickly at the fire. Boy, she hadn't seen a fire since summer camp, except for the big bonfire, the night of the Japanese surrender.

'Are you sleeping all right?'

Rusty looked up sharply. 'I get a little cold. That keeps me awake some.'

'I'll see if Matron can give you an extra blanket.'

'Thank you.'

Rusty longed to tell her about the sleepwalking. How it sometimes frightened her so much that she was afraid to close her eyes, and how lost and cold she felt when she woke up somewhere strange. But she couldn't now. If she mentioned it, Miss Paxton would keep an eye out for her at night, and that would mean goodbye to her midnight expeditions.

Miss Paxton looked awkward for a moment. She picked up a poker and pushed over one of the logs so that the flames rose up around it.

'This friend of your mother's,' she began. 'Did you know her?'

Rusty nodded. She tried to swallow back the tears, but her general tiredness, coupled with a wisp of smoke that made her eyes smart, prevented her. She brushed the tears swiftly aside with her fingers.

'I see,' said Miss Paxton.

'Sorry,' said Rusty, pulling out an already damp handkerchief. 'I guess I'm not used to the smoke.'

Miss Paxton nodded. It was admirable of the girl to blame her lack of control on the smoke. Still, she was worried.

'Well, in view of your circumstances, I will have a word with Miss Bembridge and see if she will grant permission for you to go into town this weekend. And now you'd better return to the sitting room with the others.'

Rusty stood up. 'Yes, Miss Paxton. Thank you, Miss Paxton.'

As soon as Rusty reached the empty corridor, she leaned back against the wall.

The town! She was going to get to see the town again, and maybe the boy from Vermont. Somehow she had to find a way of getting in touch with him without anyone else knowing.

When she returned to the sitting room, everyone stared at her.

'It's O.K.,' she said. 'I haven't gotten a bad mark.'

The girls groaned.

'Order mark,' snapped Judith Poole.

'What for?'

'You said O.K.'

Rusty sighed and went over to the window. Outside, the sky was dark and very, very still. She crossed her fingers.

He was standing by the Town Hall with the same three boys. Rusty kept her head bowed and glanced sideways at him. She knew that everyone in the crocodile would be keeping their eyes on her. He turned, a frown on his face, and then he spotted her. Immediately, he grinned. It was all Rusty could do not to break free from the line of girls and yell out, 'Hi!'

Without looking in his direction, she raised her fingers in a surreptitious wave, at the side of her leg, hoping that he would see it and not think she was snubbing him. She made a pointing gesture and waved it in the direction of the girls, hoping that he would follow them. She shoved her hands into the pockets of her Beanie, but swiftly took them out again, remembering that it was against the rules, and she didn't want to attract attention to herself.

Miss Bullivant stopped at the crossing, marched them across it, and led them towards the newsagent's and sweet shop. Once inside, Rusty moved to the comics section by the window, while the Bull paced up and down outside. Across the street Rusty could see the four boys. Three of them were studying a small booklet. The one from Vermont was standing by himself, looking towards the shop. As soon as the Bull's back was turned, Rusty lifted up a copy of the *Dandy* and slipped a note inside. Even as she held it, she wasn't sure if the boy had seen what she had done, since the Bull was on her return stalk back.

She felt a tap on her shoulder. It was Mary, the Scholarship girl.

'That's not approved of,' she whispered.

'What do you mean?' said Rusty hastily.

'The *Dandy*.'

Rusty stared at the comic. There was a thin-looking cat character on the front called Korky.

'It's considered frightfully *infra dig*.'

'Infra what?'

'Just put it down before the Bull sees you.'

'Oh, yeah, sure,' said Rusty, and she replaced it hurriedly.

Within seconds, the Bull was at the doorway. 'Back into line,' she commanded.

The girls who were crowding around the counter hastily pulled out their money and coupon books, while the harassed saleswoman attempted frantically to serve them all at once. Rusty slipped outside.

As soon as Miss Bullivant had turned to see that the Juniors were getting into line, Rusty looked across the road and pointed to the window. The Bull whirled around. 'Virginia Dickinson, get into ranks.'

'Yes, Miss Bullivant.'

In that short split-second, Rusty had no idea whether the boy had seen her signal or not. The Bull turned and headed in the direction of the bus-stop.

As they passed a corner teashop, while the Third-formers looked enviously in at the older girls having their buns, Rusty glanced across the street. There he was! The three other boys were close at his side. It seemed as though they were keeping an eye on him, too. Suddenly he knelt down to tie up his shoe-lace. His right hand was hidden from the other boys by his left knee. Just before he rose,

200

he gave a thumbs-up signal. Then he stood up and joined the others.

Rusty clasped her hands tightly together. It was the only way she could control her joy. Now all she needed was another clear night, for in the note she had scribbled: MIDNIGHT. BACK WALL OF MY SCHOOL. WHISTLE STAR-SPANGLED BANNER.

'Please, please, please,' she whispered, 'don't let it rain.'

Rusty pressed herself into the dark shadows of the corner and waited. On the other side of the wall a twig broke. She bit into her knuckles. There was a swishing sound of leaves being disturbed. Quietly she began whistling 'The Star-Spangled Banner'. Immediately, she heard it being whistled back. She scrambled up the wall, hauled herself over, and dropped in a heap on the other side. As she gazed up at the boy's surprised face, she grinned.

'Hi,' she said.

He burst out laughing and helped her up. 'Hi.'

They stared at each other's dressing-gowns. They were almost identical. He was fully dressed underneath his, while she had two pairs of long woolly socks pulled up over her pyjama trousers. Without his school cap, Rusty could see that his cropped hair fell neatly from a side parting.

They smiled foolishly at each other in the dark.

'Come on,' said Rusty, 'follow me. We might be heard out here.'

She brushed past him and ran into the woods, her torch pointing downward.

'Hey, where are you going?' he whispered. 'We'll get lost if we go too far in.'

'It's O.K. I've laid a trail. See.' She pointed to a small stone on a large stone. Beside it on the right lay another stone. 'That means "turn right".'

She led him through the woods and into the sheltered copse.

'Gosh!' he exclaimed. 'This is dandy.'

She smiled. 'Isn't *Dandy* supposed to be infra something?' she remarked.

He looked at her blankly.

'The comic,' she said.

'Oh. You mean infra *dig*. Oh, sure. That means it's not good enough for the likes of us.' He pushed his nose up with his fingers. 'It's far too common.'

They walked through damp leaves and rotting twigs towards the large tree.

'Are all the English snobs?' said Rusty.

'You're English, aren't you?'

'I guess so, but I don't feel like it.'

As he sat beside her, his bare knees stuck out from underneath his shorts.

'Aren't you cold?'

'I'm always cold,' he said.

'Uh-huh. Me too! Doesn't it *ever* get warm here?'

'I don't think so. It wouldn't be so bad if it was a dry cold, but it's so damp that –'

'Say, listen to us. We're doing what the English do. We're talking about the weather.' She paused. 'You've hardly got an accent at all,' she said. 'You sound almost English to me.'

'I came back early this year. My parents sent me to a crammer so I could be ready for the entrance exam to public school. I suppose I must have lost it a bit then.'

'What's a crammer?'

'It's a place where you get stuffed with as much knowledge as possible. I was way behind when I got back. I had to do heaps of Latin and Greek and French and mathematics and history. I'm still trying to catch up.'

'Me too!' said Rusty mournfully. 'I was a year ahead, back in the States, *and* I got good grades.'

'It was the same for me.'

She glanced hesitantly at him. 'Do you think the American schools are really so awful?'

'I don't think so,' he said slowly. 'It's just that in England they get to learn a lot of subjects earlier. In America they catch up later. I think that's what happens. Also, did you have a lot of immigrants in your class?'

'Sure. Nearly half the class were immigrants. We had to spend forever on English like it was a foreign language, and we had American history till it was coming out of our ears.'

'It was the same at my school. In fact, English grammar is one of the few subjects I'm halfway decent at. Last term, at the crammer, I was held up as a good example.'

'Did you still speak with an American accent then?'

'Yes.'

'All I have to do is open my mouth at my school, and anything I say *has* to be dumb.'

'I have that at my school now, but it was nice at the crammer. There were only thirty of us in the whole school, and they really made us feel like a big family. There was another boy who'd been evacuated too. He'd been sent to Australia, so at least I had someone to talk with. It's horrid at this school. I don't seem to fit in at all. I can't be a wet bob and I'm useless as a dry bob.'

'A what?'

'If you're a wet bob, then you get to row. I can't be a wet bob because I can't swim. That means I have to be a dry bob. A dry bob means you play cricket. I've never played cricket, which at my school is almost as blasphemous as saying you don't believe in God.' He looked at her earnestly. 'If I could just get into the reserves for one of the rugger teams, then I'd have a chance of making friends. I've played American football, and I was on the school team in Vermont. It looks similar to rugger.' He gave a sigh.

Rusty stood up. 'Wanna explore some? I've set another trail on the other side.'

'Sure.'

They scuffed their way through the leaves. Rusty felt lighter than she'd felt for weeks. She breathed in deeply. 'By the way,' she said, pushing a branch aside, 'my name's Rusty. What's yours.'

'Lance,' he said awkwardly.

'Lance? Is that short for something else?'

'Lancelot.'

'You're kidding!'

'I'm not. If I'd been a girl, my parents would have called me Guinevere.'

'Oh boy, Guinevere!'

She swung the torch down on to the ground. Two stones were placed on a large one. She stopped.

'That's a warning sign. I remember that one. I couldn't get through.' She waved her torch on ahead and turned to her left. 'Ah,' she cried. 'This is the way.'

'How can you tell?'

She pointed to a freshly broken twig. 'I broke that.'

They went on past a tall clump of bracken.

'But,' continued Rusty, 'don't they tease you about being called Lancelot?'

'No. They don't call us by our Christian names. Only our surnames. I'm called Brownlow.'

'With me it's "Virginia Dickinson, walk, don't run in the corridor. Virginia Dickinson, if you wish to speak, kindly lower your voice. Virginia Dickinson, do you have to move your hands when you talk? Virginia Dickinson, stop speaking in that affected manner. Virginia Dickinson, don't you know there's been a war on?"!'

At this, Lance burst out laughing. 'I thought you said your name was Rusty.'

'It has been for five years. Boy, it's so weird being called by another name.'

'It's the same for me. Back in Vermont I was taught it was rude to call someone by his surname. You always had to put *Mister* in front of it, and you never said you were going to talk *to* someone. That was rude, too. It was always *with*. Here it's different. "Brownlow,"' he said sternly, '"I'm talking to you!" and having a "talking-to" usually means a beating.' He paused. 'Rusty, what am I supposed to be looking for?'

'A large arrow made with three branches. Ah,' she said, pointing, 'there it is.'

They made their way towards it.

'I did try another route, but this way looked more interesting.' She looked sideways at him in the half-light. He had such an earnest, sober sort of face.

'Do they really beat you?'

He nodded. 'It's mostly the prefects who do it. Especially to the new boys. We all have to fag for one of them, too.'

'Fag?'

'It's like be a servant to them. Clean their shoes, run errands for them, light the fires in their studies. And if you don't do it well, they're not only allowed to beat you, but they can stop you going into the town.'

They came to a clearing. A broken fence separated them from a field. They stopped.

'Doesn't anyone complain about it?'

'You'd end up getting even more of a beating then, *and* you'd probably be sent to Coventry.'

'What's that?'

'It means no one speaks to you.'

'I guess that's what everyone's been doing to me.'

He looked surprised. 'Why?'

'For talking to you.'

'Gosh.'

'Didn't *you* get punished for talking to me?'

'Not like that. They just jeered at me. A boy who likes girls is rather looked down on. Everyone hates their sisters and is embarrassed by their mothers. I'm odd because I don't hate mine.'

'Do you have any brothers?'

'No, just one sister. She's eight. She's at a girls' boarding school. I don't know her, really. She was too young to come to the States with me.'

'Eight years old? And at boarding school?'

He nodded.

They left the fence and made their way back to the copse.

'Do you think the English hate children and that's why they send them away?' Rusty wondered.

'I don't know,' he said miserably. 'Sometimes I think maybe they just don't like me.' He attempted to force a smile, but Rusty could see how unhappy he was. She slipped her arm through his and gave him a squeeze.

'That's nuts!'

He shrugged. 'Maybe, but then, why haven't I any friends?'

'Say, don't I count?'

He grinned.

Suddenly Rusty broke away. 'Let's run,' she exclaimed. 'Like as if we're being chased.'

'O.K.,' he said eagerly.

'When I say Chickie-the-Cop we –'

'Cut and run for it,' finished Lance.

They sank down behind some bushes and pretended to be on the lookout. Rusty gave a sudden gasp. 'Chickie-the-Cop,' she whispered urgently, and with that they tore through the woods, colliding into branches, leaping over clumps of bracken and bumping into each other. As soon as they reached the edge of the wood, they ran towards the school wall and sank down on to the ground, puffing and giggling.

'Oh boy,' said Rusty, gasping. 'I haven't had so much fun in ages.'

'Me neither.'

They leaned back and gazed up at the stars.

'I suppose,' said Lance, 'we'd better get back before someone misses us.'

'I guess so,' said Rusty. They stood up. 'You've got a good ways to go.'

'It only takes fifteen minutes. I know a short cut.'

'How did you get out?'

'Some of the doors are unlocked. How did you get out?'

She stepped back and pointed to the school building. 'See the scaffolding? That's how.'

Lance stared aghast at it. 'Is that the truth?'

'Cross my heart and hope to die.'

He gazed at her with admiration. 'You're awfully plucky.'

'Desperate, more like.'

'Do you think,' he said hesitantly, 'we could see each other again?'

'You bet. How about Monday?'

He grinned. 'O.K. Monday it is.'

Rusty hauled herself up the wall. As she reached the top, she glanced quickly down at him.

'So long!' she whispered.

'Be seeing you,' he whispered back.

On Monday it rained so heavily that it turned into hailstones. Rusty found herself thinking of Lance's remark, about how perhaps he had been sent away because his parents didn't like him. Maybe, way back when she was small, she had done something really terrible and this was her punishment. She could hardly breathe for the weight on her chest. Her only source of relief was to return to daydreaming. She would stow away on a liner to New York and then bus up to Connecticut, and Aunt Hannah and Uncle Bruno would be standing on the lawn, and they'd both run up to her and hug her, and she'd go up to her room and it would be just like she'd left it. White walls with stencil designs on them in russets and green, a canary-yellow windowsill and frame, with yellow-and-white-check curtains, and a canary-yellow wicker chair. And over the bed there'd be the big log-cabin patchwork quilt that Grandma Fitz made for her eleventh birthday, and on the floor the rag rug that Rusty had made one winter.

Back in America people used to laugh at her stamina. 'Doesn't this kid ever get tired?' Uncle Bruno would say when she and Skeet came hurtling back into the house from ice-skating, and Skeet would turn on the radio and flop into a chair, while Rusty would be badgering Uncle Bruno to let her use his carpentry tools.

They'd never believe she was the same person now. Her fatigue was sometimes so acute that she could hardly move at all. With the fatigue came the intense cold feeling, and as she grew colder so her tiredness grew. The only times she had any energy was when she was climbing down the scaffolding.

Tuesday night was clear and, as she had hoped, Lance was waiting by the wall at midnight. They dived straight into the woods. As soon as they reached the sheltered copse, Rusty sat at the foot of the large tree.

'Kinda homey, isn't it?' she murmured, taking in the sheltered circle. She looked up at him. 'Why don't you sit down and make yourself comfy?'

'Because if I sat down, I wouldn't be.'

'Did they beat you again?'

'The prefect I fag for did. I couldn't get his fire to draw. I'm not very good at fires.'

'Didn't you ever have cookouts in Vermont?'

'Sure, but the servants always used to make them up.'

'Servants!' She gave a whistle. 'Does it hurt real bad?'

He nodded. 'We have rugger practice tomorrow afternoon, too. If someone tackles me, it's going to be agony.'

'But that's just plain darned bullying,' said Rusty.

'They can't get away with that. Can't you tell your parents?'

'My father went to the same school. He said he hated it, but he thought that it did him good.'

'Jeepers! But if everyone hates it, why don't they stop it?'

'Everyone doesn't hate it,' said Lance, squatting on the ground, being careful not to touch it with his bottom. 'The prefects love it. I think they're pleased to get their own back on the young ones.'

'But that's dumb. I mean, the ones they oughta get their own back on are the *older* ones.'

Lance shrugged. 'I suppose so. Anyway,' he added with resignation, 'it's tradition.'

'Oh, *tradition*!' exclaimed Rusty sarcastically. 'Then it's gotta be O.K.' She shook her head. 'Boy, do I hate that word. Tradition this. Tradition that. Any suggestion you make for doing something in a different way has to be lousy or everyone looks at you like you're being a traitor to the school or the darned King.' She paused. 'I tell you, as soon as I get hold of some money, I'm going to leave this place and go back to America.'

He looked at her intently. 'You really mean that, don't you?'

'Sure I mean it.'

'But isn't your family here?'

'Uh-huh, but I miss my American family. Don't you?'

'Not really. I didn't see much of them. It was all a bit formal where I lived. I stayed with an old couple on a hill in a huge white house with pillars all the way up the front. I even had my own private suite and a butler. They were awfully kind to me but, well, it was a bit lonely. It's my buddies I miss most, and the forests and lakes and . . .'

He turned away. Then he stood up, pulled a handful of leaves from a nearby branch, and threw them to the ground.

'I just *have* to get into the rugger team, even if it's only in the reserves.' He looked soberly at her. 'You see, I don't have a home anywhere. One of my parents' houses was bombed, the other's been requisitioned. My mother's renting a tiny flat in London at the moment, and my father's in Scotland. I've been staying with aunts most of the time. I *have* to make school my home now.'

Rusty sprang to her feet. 'Listen,' she said, 'my American parents would love to have you stay. You could come with me.'

He gave a shrug. 'Maybe.'

They walked on through the woods, laying down fresh trails. Lance told Rusty about the compulsory cold baths the boys had to have first thing in the morning, and that in the winter they would have to break the ice before getting in. In spite of the baths, he said, the cloakrooms reeked of mildew and dirty socks.

As they broached the subject of teachers, Rusty found herself telling Lance about some of *her* most painful incidents, in such a way that she had Lance choking with laughter. Acting the clown seemed to be a good cure for her miseries.

It was on Thursday that they discovered what Rusty nicknamed the Cabin in the Woods.

They met as usual by the back wall and headed into the woods. Lance seemed more downcast then ever. He was still smarting from an afternoon of rugger.

'It's so damned annoying,' he said angrily at one point. 'I get the ball. I'm running like the wind. No one can touch me. Then someone yells out, "Hey, Yank!" and I just collapse in the middle, and the next thing I know everyone's piled on top of me. Today someone said, "What's the matter, Yank, don't they teach games in America?" If they're prefects I can't tell them to shut up, otherwise I have another beating. I'm still sore from the last one.'

Instead of stopping at the copse, they continued through to the trees on the other side.

'Sometimes when they speak, it's so quick that I just can't understand them. And they say, "What's the matter, Yank, can't you understand the King's English?" '

'Yeah,' said Rusty sympathetically. 'They talk like they got a bunch of marbles in their mouths, and they sort of half smile and speak like they're working a ventriloquist's dummy.' She stopped to give him a demonstration. 'I seh, Belindah, hah frahtfli decent.'

'That's it!' yelled Lance. 'That's it exactly!'

'And that's not all. They sound the opposite of what they're saying, too, like this: How awfully, terribly exciting,' she said in a dull monotone.

'It's perfect!' spluttered Lance, doubled over with laughter.

Rusty smiled. She'd never seen anyone change so much when he laughed.

'Say, you'd better keep the noise down. You'll wake the racoons.'

'They don't have racoons in England.'

'Well, chipmunks.'

'They don't have chipmunks.'

'That figures. They don't have anything interesting here.'

'Now who's being a snob?' commented Lance.

'O.K., O.K.'

They came to a sign indicating that they should turn left.

'Let's go take a right, Yank,' suggested Rusty.

Lance whirled round angrily. 'That was a nasty thing to do!'

'Look,' she said, 'I'm going to call you Yank when you're least expecting it, so's you can get used to someone else calling you it. At least you know I like you. Then maybe it won't hurt so much.'

Lance turned his back on her and began walking away.

'Say, Lance,' she said running after him. 'Come on.'

He spun around, his eyes full of tears. 'I'm just so sick of it all,' he said. 'Day in, day out.'

'Look, it's only a name. I'd be proud to be called Yank. I'd be pleased to have *any* nickname.' She paused. 'Come to think of it, I have one and I'm not so pleased.'

'Oh,' said Lance. 'What is it?'

Rusty turned away.

'It's only a name, surely,' said Lance, getting his own back.

She looked at him over her shoulder. 'O.K. I'll tell you if you don't go away.'

'If you call me by my nickname,' he said, 'you have to let me call you by yours.'

'Say, that's not fair.' Lance turned to go. 'O.K., O.K., it's fair. Yank,' she added, with extra emphasis. 'It's the Creeper, or Creepie for short.'

'What! How did you get that one?'

They started walking again.

'When I first came, no one would talk with me, so I used to go up to people and try and join in a conversation, but they didn't like it. One day some girl says to me, "Go away, Virginia Creeper." After that, every time I tried to be friendly, one of them would say, "Look who's just crept up on us. It's the Virginia Creeper."'

As Rusty drew aside an enormous overhanging branch, she caught sight of a small wooden gate almost hidden by tall trees.

They passed the trees and slid down a small slope towards it.

'Oh!' whispered Rusty. 'Will you just look at that!'

On the other side of the gate, through a large garden

of overgrown grass, stood the remains of a bombed house amid the debris of bricks, plaster and timber. Exposed to the sky were a small hall, a stairway, and a ceilingless room on top of the only whole one that remained.

Rusty pushed aside the gate, and together she and Lance ran through the grass. Rusty turned on her torch and swooped it around the building.

'Come on, let's take a look-see,' she whispered.

The roofless hallway was covered with dust and small gritty pieces of plaster. Rusty grabbed hold of two pieces of timber that lay near the doorway to the remaining room. The door opened easily. They stepped inside.

The room had been stripped of furniture. The wooden floor was bare. A wide fireplace with a grey raised stone platform in front of it stood between two alcoves. Hanging beside the two front windows that looked out on to the garden were long dark curtains.

Rusty looked up the chimney. 'Darn it! I can't see whether it's blocked up or not.' She turned. 'Tell you what – I'll go upstairs and you shine my flashlight up the chimney. If the light shows, that means it's O.K.'

'It's *torch*, not flashlight.'

'Don't *you* start on me, Yank,' she said warningly.

'O.K., Creeper.'

Rusty shook her fist at him and went outside into the hall and up the staircase. The tiniest speck of light was showing. It was so tiny that Rusty didn't know if she was imagining it or not. By the time she had hopped down the stairs and walked back into the room, she had made up her mind that she had seen it.

'I think it'll be O.K.,' she said. 'I guess we could light a fire there.'

Lance groaned. 'I've had enough of lighting fires,' he said. 'Anyway, I told you, I'm hopeless at it.'

Rusty gazed thoughtfully at him. 'Listen,' she said, 'I'm

good at fires. How's about I teach you? Then maybe that prefect won't beat you so much.'

He beamed. 'It's a deal. And I tell you what, I'll help you with your Latin.'

'Don't talk to me about Latin. It's one of the dumbest languages ever invented.'

'No it isn't. It's the root of lots of other languages.'

'Yeah, but nobody speaks it any more. I mean, the only people Latin's any use for is a bunch of dead Romans!'

They sat on the raised stone platform in front of the fireplace and gazed at the deserted, dust-laden room. 'What a find!' She turned excitedly to Lance. 'We can pretend we're in the middle of nowhere. We can make it like a real pioneer cabin.'

Just then there was a crash outside the door. Rusty and Lance sprang to their feet.

'They don't have bears in England, do they?' she whispered.

They moved slowly towards the closed door and stared, horrified, at it until Rusty, unable to stand the suspense any longer, whipped it open.

'Hands up,' she snarled, pushing the torch in her pocket forward as if it was a gun. Lance gave a startled jump. 'It's O.K.,' she said. 'There's no one there. Just a lot of junk. I guess I must have disturbed something walking up the stairs.' She turned her torch on again and pointed it at a large mound of rubble.

'You know,' said Lance, following her, 'I bet there's a lot of useful stuff in there.'

'Just what I was thinking, Yank.'

He stiffened and then relaxed.

'Nearly got me there, Creeper.'

She swung her torch over to the staircase and spotted a small door underneath. She tried to open it, but the hinges were too rusty. She and Lance gave it an almighty push. After a loud creak it opened stiffly. Rusty shone her torch inside and let out a loud whoop.

'A cellar!' she yelled. 'Now it really is like a Cabin in the Woods.'

'It looks as if it was used as an air-raid shelter,' said Lance.

They walked down the stairs to a tiny room.

'Oh boy,' whispered Rusty. 'They left two oil-lamps.' She picked one up and shook it gently. 'It's full of oil. Enough to last for ever!'

There were also the remains of three candles, some damp blankets draped over a couple of canvas camp-beds, and a fragile-looking card table. As Rusty sat down on one of the beds, it gave an ominous creak. Lance picked up a damp pillow, placed it on the other bed, and lowered himself gently on to it.

'Say,' said Rusty, 'I have half-term this weekend. I'll see what I can bring back. My mother's meeting me tomorrow at the school gates and then we're going straight to Devon.'

'Lucky you!'

'Not really. See, this friend of my mother's just died. I gave my word I'd go to her place for the mid-term vacation whether she was there or not. I think it's going to be pretty awful.'

'Still, Devon is nice, isn't it?'

She shrugged. 'It's O.K. What I've seen of it. And there's a neat girl called Beth there, that I met over the summer.'

'Maybe you'll get to see her.'

'I might. Anyway, it'll be nice to have this to come back to.'

'Our own den,' he said.

'Our own Cabin in the Woods.'

Just then Lance's bed collapsed in the middle. At first, Rusty let out a loud hoot of laughter, but when she saw the pain on his face she hastily helped him up. 'Sorry,' she said. 'I forgot your ass.'

'I wish I could,' he moaned. He rolled himself over on all fours before standing up. 'Do you know, he drew blood?'

'You're kidding!'

Rusty's eyes caught something white sticking out from under the collapsed bed. 'What's that?' she asked.

Lance pulled the bed back. On the floor was a large can. Several smaller ones were in the corner behind it.

'Paint!' she yelled. 'Cans of it!' I wonder if it's all frozen up.' She picked up the large one. 'Help me shake it,' she said.

Lance grabbed it, and between them they jumped up and down, swayed and rocked, and gave it a vigorous shaking. Eventually a gurgling sound emanated from inside.

'It's O.K.,' she breathed. They put it back on the ground. 'Oh, I hope no one gets to find this place. We must never let on to anyone. Do you swear? I swear.'

'I swear, too.'

They shook hands and fled up the steps, then ran through the open hallway and into the grass. Rusty stopped to take a last look at the house. 'So long, Cabin,' she whispered.

22

Her mother was waiting for her at the school gates, a battered leather suitcase in her hand. She gave Rusty an awkward wave.

Rusty stood on the pavement holding her grip.

'We're staying at Exeter tonight with one of the W.V.S. ladies,' said Peggy. 'There's a train in half an hour. Let's hope we don't have to wait too long for a bus.'

They crossed over the road and stood by the bus-stop.

'Did you come straight from Devon?' asked Rusty quietly.

'No, I went back to Guildford after the funeral.'

'Does Charlie know about . . .?' She stopped.

Peggy nodded. 'I had to tell him in stages.'

'What did he say?'

Peggy remembered only too clearly. 'Has she gone away like Uncle Harvey?' he had asked. Peggy had attempted to explain, but how could she tell him that Beatie could never come back, whereas Uncle Harvey still could but that he wouldn't.

Peggy had believed that once Harvey had gone, she would be able to shut him out of her mind and pick up the strands of her marriage. She should have realized that Charlie would always remind her of him. Perhaps if she had allowed Harvey to write to them, it would have made it easier for Charlie. And for her.

'I guess he took it badly,' said Rusty.

Peggy nodded again.

After five minutes a double-decker came crawling over

the hill. They hopped on to it and sat in the long seats near the door.

'Does the train go all the way to Exeter?' asked Rusty.

'No. We have to change at another station first. Then tomorrow we'll catch the Plymouth train from there to Totnes.'

Rusty nearly fell off the seat. Plymouth!

Later, when they had squeezed into a seat in one of the crowded compartments of the train, her mother commented on her appearance. 'Are you eating properly?' she asked.

'Uh-huh.'

'You've probably grown a little. I expect that's what it is.'

Rusty wanted to ask her mother about Beatie.

'So we're staying with the W.V.S.?' she asked instead.

'With one of their helpers. Yes.'

'Don't you miss helping them out?'

'Yes. I've been thinking about contacting the local headquarters, but Charlie is still so unsettled, I don't think it would be fair to him. And also, your father will be home soon.' She smiled bleakly. 'Then we'll be a proper family again.'

Rusty attempted to smile back, but the sadness in her mother's eyes made it impossible.

When it was time for them to change trains, they pushed their way through the crowded corridor and stepped on to the platform.

'We have a bit of time before the Exeter train,' said Peggy. 'Do you fancy tea and buns?'

To Rusty's surprise, the currant buns were wonderful. When the taste of the tea was too awful, Rusty just drowned it in another bite of bun.

After they had finished eating, Rusty couldn't remain silent about Beatie any longer. 'Mother,' she blurted out, 'I think Beatie knew she was going to die. Don't you?'

Her mother paled. 'Yes. She'd known for some time.'

'So why do you think she kept telling everyone it was indigestion?'

'Because she didn't want us tiptoeing around her and fussing. You know how much she loved excitement and noise.'

Rusty nodded. 'Are we . . .' She hesitated. 'Are we going to be staying at her house?'

'I'm not too certain we can now. I'm sure no one will raise any objections to us staying at least the one night.'

'Does that mean we'll be going back to Grandmother's on Sunday?'

'I think we'd better leave that decision till we get there.' Her mother looked intently at her for a moment. 'I suppose,' she said, 'you were hoping to see Beth.'

'Uh-huh.'

'Have you still not made any friends?'

There was Lance, but she couldn't mention him. 'Not yet. They hate my accent.'

'Perhaps if you made an effort to lose it, they'd be more friendly.'

'But I'd still be the same person, so what's the difference?'

'Well, as a matter of fact, Beth's mother has very kindly invited us round to their house for supper tomorrow.'

'Oh boy!'

'But before that, we have to go to Totnes,' said her mother, looking sad again. 'Beatie arranged to have the reading of the will there.'

'Were you with her when she died?'

Peggy nodded and took out a crumpled cigarette packet. Rusty noticed her fingers were shaking as she lit a match. She had hardly inhaled her cigarette when a voice from the loudspeaker announced the Exeter train. Her mother hurriedly stubbed out the cigarette and automatically put it back into the packet.

It was a slow journey to Exeter. The train seemed to stop at every tiny station. Rusty leaned back and drifted into a headachy sort of sleep, but was jolted violently out of it every time the train screeched into a station. She could hardly see out, for the dust on the windows was so thick that it created a filter over the glass.

'Don't they ever clean these trains?' she commented. 'Looks like it hasn't had a good cleaning in years.'

'That's probably because it hasn't,' snapped her mother.

Boy, thought Rusty, I knew it was too good to last. She felt hurt by her mother's sudden irritation. 'I guess,' she said smugly, 'I'm used to a higher standard of cleanliness.'

Her mother, aware of the other people in the compartment, was acutely embarrassed.

'I'd like to remind you that there's been a war on.'

'So everyone keeps telling me,' said Rusty grumpily.

'And keeping trains clean,' continued her mother, 'was not considered as important as building aeroplanes, working in munitions, and repairing bombed docks.'

'But that's all over now,' Rusty protested.

'There are still,' her mother emphasized, 'more important jobs than spring cleaning. Just be grateful that there are trains running at all.'

At that, her mother sank wearily back into her seat and closed her eyes. How she had longed for the war to be over, and how she, like her daughter, would love to return to no rationing, plenty of food and clothing, and pretty surroundings. The constant grime and drabness got her down, too, and what with her mother-in-law's continual carping, Charlie's distress, a complaining daughter, and now Beatie's death, she felt as shocked and uprooted as she had four years ago, when she had first evacuated herself to Devon to have Charlie. She realized now that her daughter must be feeling the same, and she felt guilty for snapping at her. She opened her eyes. Rusty was staring sulkily out of the window.

'I'm sorry if I sounded a little harsh,' she said. 'I'm just tired.'

'Yeah,' answered Rusty. 'I guess I'm a little pooped, too.'

At Exeter Station a young woman was waiting to greet them on the platform. 'Good Lord,' she said. 'You both look done in!'

They smiled gratefully as she snatched the suitcase and grip from them. 'There's a nice hot meal waiting for you. Come on.'

The following morning Rusty was shaken awake by her mother. As she drew aside the curtains, sunlight poured into the room.

'It's a beautiful day,' Peggy commented. Not the sort of day, she thought, for hearing a will read out. She turned. 'Come on, sleepy-head. We've another train to catch.'

Rusty watched her leave the room. She pushed herself up slowly to a sitting position. She knew that if she didn't, she could easily fall asleep again. She crawled out of bed and shuffled over to the window. In the distance she could see a beautiful old cathedral with its windows smashed in.

She rubbed her eyes vigorously with her fingers. They would be catching the Plymouth train that morning. It was vital that she remain alert so that when she ran away she'd know what to do.

The train she and her mother caught was a local one. Her mother was right about the weather. In spite of its being November, the sun seemed to light up everything. Rusty gazed intently out of the window. In the distance she could see pink-sided cliffs. On the other side green hills sloped upward to a clear sky.

'Virginia,' said her mother, 'look.'

Rusty turned to her mother's window. 'Oh,' she murmured.

Beside the railway lines was a long stretch of water where several small boats lay anchored. On the other side of the water, houses stood higgledy-piggledy on a hill. The water was so still, it was like a pale-blue mirror. Seabirds sat motionless on the surface.

'Do you remember this?'

Rusty nodded. 'But it seems prettier now,' she said. 'We'll be coming out to the sea soon, won't we?'

'That's right.'

They dipped into a tunnel in the cliffs, came out briefly, caught a glimpse of the sea, dipped into another, out, in, and then the train remained out in the open. It was breath-taking to be able to lean out of the window and look out at a great expanse of sea and sky, and the cliffs stretching like craggy fingers into the water.

'I'm afraid it's all land from now on,' said her mother.

When the train drew in at Totnes, Mrs Hatherley was waiting for them on the platform.

'I'm sorry Ivy couldn't be 'ere to meet youse,' she said, as they walked out of the station. 'I 'ad a message from her early this morning. She's feeling a bit on the rough side.' She paused. 'Actually, she's asked me to tell you her good news.'

'Has she managed to get an early posting to America?'

'Oh no. She's still gotta wait a bit yet. No. She's going to 'ave a baby.'

'Oh,' cried Peggy. 'That's wonderful! Oh, I'm so pleased for her.'

They began walking.

'Where's Beth?' asked Rusty suddenly.

'She's up at the school farm, helpin' out.'

'Does she have to go to school Saturdays?'

'No, but you try and keep her away, my love. Once term starts, I hardly see any of 'em, what with rehearsals for this, and choir practices for that, and making scenery, and then there's Pets' Corner and the farm, and country dancing, and helping out and, you see,' she added, 'some of their friends are boarders.' Mrs Hatherley could see that Rusty was disappointed. 'You'll see her this evening, though.'

Beatie had arranged for the will to be read in the sitting room of a friend's flat, above one of the shops in the main street. At the back of the room on a low table were a dozen assorted glasses and several bottles of sherry.

'Where on earth . . .?' began Peggy, astounded.

'Beatie's secret supply,' explained Mrs Hatherley.

At the end of the table stood a bottle of Coca-Cola. A small label was hanging round its neck. It read, FOR RUSTY.

Aside from Mrs Hatherley, the doctor and a couple of other people, it was almost like a W.V.S. reunion. As soon as Peggy entered the room, there were wild whoops of joy. 'I suppose this isn't quite the way to behave at the reading of a will,' commented one of the women.

'I don't know,' said Peggy wryly. 'I rather think Beatie planned it this way.'

The lawyer – a gaunt, elderly man with thinning white hair – had to clear his throat several times before anyone paid any attention to him. Eventually, everyone sat down on the sofa, in the armchairs or on cushions on the floor. The lawyer stood awkwardly by the mantelpiece. Behind him a log fire burned in the grate.

'This will, I must inform you,' he began, 'is rather unorthodox.' He looked down at the papers in his hand. 'Dear everyone,' he read. 'First of all, please have a good time. I didn't save all this good sherry so that you could blub over me.'

He cleared his throat again and then proceeded to read out what had been left to whom.

Mrs Hatherley had the chickens. Someone else had the Singer sewing-machine; Ivy, a set of suitcases and trunks; the doctor, the decanters; someone else, the table and chairs and beds; Charlie, some picture books and other books for when he was older, and so on. Then to Rusty's surprise she heard her name being called out.

'That's me!' she exclaimed.

The lawyer frowned and cleared his throat again.

'To Rusty Dickinson,' he read, 'I leave my husband's carpentry tools. These include a handsaw, a tenon saw, a hammer, plane, three chisels, file, screwdriver, mallet square, gimlets, vice, brace and bits, cramp, nail punch ...'

Rusty gazed open-mouthed at him as he continued reading the list.

'Are you sure?' she said when he had finished reading.

The man frowned again. 'Quite sure.'

'But,' stammered her mother, 'perhaps she meant them for Charlie.'

'No, madam,' said the man firmly. 'She meant them for a girl called Rusty.'

'I see.' She glanced aside. Rusty's face was flushed with excitement. How on earth could a daughter of hers look so ecstatic at being left carpentry tools? Really, it was too awful of Beatie.

'And finally' – and the lawyer looked visibly relieved that it would soon be all over – 'I leave my dilapidated house to Mrs Peggy Dickinson.'

There was an astounded silence.

'Mother!' whispered Rusty.

'Are you sure?' stammered Peggy.

The man raised his eyes. 'Quite sure.'

Suddenly someone said, 'Well, Peggy, you jolly well deserve it.'

'I wouldn't say that,' added one of the women wryly. 'Have you seen the roof?'

'I haven't quite finished yet,' said the lawyer loudly. 'With the ownership of this house, there are certain conditions. One: That the owner cannot sell the house until seventeen years have passed. Two: After seventeen years, if Mrs Dickinson then wishes to sell, she must only sell it to a woman. And three: If she dies before the seventeen years are up, the property must be passed on to a younger female of her own choosing.' He lowered his sheaf of papers and looked at her.

'I can't quite take it in,' she said. 'I ...' She shook her head. How could she explain? The Bomb was the first thing she had ever owned. As a young woman she had never been allowed to work, and she had lived under her parents' roof until she married. When her parents died, their house was sold to pay off debts, and the house in Guildford was solely in her husband's name. And now she owned her own house! She just couldn't believe it. And to own one with such wonderful memories in it ...

Just then a voice came thundering from the back of the room.

'What about this sherry then?' It was the doctor.

Whereupon everyone started talking and moving towards the table.

'I'd like to walk back,' said Peggy, when it was all over and they were standing in the main street.

'It's a long walk,' said Mrs Hatherley. 'Are you sure I can't give you a lift somewhere first? I'll take your suitcase, anyway.'

'Perhaps just up to the entrance of the Estate.'

'Is that where Beth's school is?' asked Rusty, suddenly alert.

'Yes.'

'Can I come with you?'

'You can't go and see her there,' said her mother.

'Why not?'

'Because it's just not done.'

Rusty took a deep breath. 'O.K.,' she muttered. 'But can I take a walk with you anyways?'

'All right.'

Mrs Hatherley drove them in her spluttering Morris past the railway station and dairy, and down the road to a tiny dirt-track. By the time they stopped, Rusty's mother had already offered to take a look at the Morris's insides before leaving.

Mrs Hatherley was delighted. 'I drive this car on a hope and a prayer these days.' She smiled. 'I'll see you this evening,' she said.

Peggy and Rusty headed down the track past a small lodge house and along a tiny road. At the foot of a steep, grassy slope to their right ran a river. The road sloped upwards. For a long time they followed its twists and curves, passing vegetable allotments and strawberry patches. They stopped briefly at a group of grey stone buildings so that Rusty could peer through an archway and take a look at the rows of arched doors and small-paned windows.

They hurried on silently past more buildings, till eventually the road narrowed and they found themselves staring at an open field. Beyond it were a small grey church, a farm, fields and woods.

Just then, Rusty heard some children laughing. They were roller-skating on a small dirt-track. From a clump of bushes two others were blowing tiny orange balls out of peashooters made of reeds.

'You little beasts!' yelled one of the roller-skaters, grinning. 'I'll have your guts for bloody garters!' And she began speeding towards them on her roller-skates, waving her arms wildly. The children in the bushes shrieked with laughter and then started running. Rusty noticed that they were all wearing rough old clothes.

'I expect they're boarders,' said her mother.

'Boarders!' said Rusty, amazed. 'But they ...' She stopped. But they all seem to be having such a good time, she wanted to say. She stared at the rectangle of buildings up on the slope. So that was Beth's school. Suddenly she felt very jealous. She looked up to find that her mother had gone ahead. She ran to join her.

They were just walking beside a grassy mound when the sun appeared. It must have been there before, thought Rusty, but it was as if it had been hiding somewhere and had sneaked out while her back was turned. Tinged with a fiery red fringe, it hung low, sending vast shadows across the grass.

Suddenly Rusty's mother said, 'Let's turn back and go through the woods.'

They crossed over the field in front of the school, up the muddy lane beside the farm, and veered right. Rusty gazed stupefied at the ploughed fields. They really were the most extraordinary ruddy colour, and the earth was so moist that it was almost as if someone had oiled the long, curved furrows.

They climbed over a wooden fence and up a sloping field towards the woods. They had hardly reached the trees when Rusty heard the faint sound of a river.

The more beautiful she found the wood, the more it hurt, and the more she hated its beauty. It was too tame, she told herself, too sickly pretty. But as she and her mother walked like tightrope walkers along dead branches to avoid the mud, she couldn't help but enjoy it a little.

Presently they stepped out on to a road and came to a stone bridge. As they crossed, Rusty glanced down and saw bright yellow and russet leaves floating along the water. They walked on a little before turning left, past the small railway station where she and Beth had stood with the bicycles.

She was so wrapped up in her thoughts that she hardly

noticed her mother's silence. Gradually the dusk closed in around them.

'We really need torches,' her mother muttered. 'I'd forgotten how dark Devon lanes can be.'

By the time they reached the Hatherleys', they were both exhausted. Mrs Hatherley was sitting with Anne on her lap, listening to the wireless.

'I've dropped your luggage and that at Beatie's place,' she said. 'Oh. I s'pose I should say *your* place, now.' She turned to Rusty. 'I wish I'd known you was comin' here sooner. I went and sent on some of them American letters for you last week.'

''Ello, Rusty,' said Anne. She stared, fascinated, at her green gymslip and striped tie.

'Looks a proper little schoolgirl, don't she?' remarked her mother.

'Do you have to wear those clothes all the time?' said Anne.

Rusty slid on to the bench by the table. 'Uh-huh.'

'Even when you play?'

'We don't play much.'

'Oh, come on now, Virginia,' said her mother. 'You have lacrosse, don't you?'

Rusty raised her eyes. 'Lacrosse!' she muttered.

'I thought you'd like the game. After all, it originated from the North American Indians, didn't it?'

'I hate it. It's a lousy game.'

'Virginia!' said her mother. 'Don't use such language. You're a guest here.'

'Oh, don't worry 'bout that,' said Mrs Hatherley. 'My children use much worse words. I've given up with 'em.' And she laughed. 'Sit down, Peggy. Put yer feet up.'

From outside came the sound of bicycles whirring up to the house. Within minutes Beth's brothers, Ivor and Harry, ran in, red-faced.

The quiet one smiled at Rusty and gave a nod before

sitting at the table. Harry, his ears as big as ever, stood and gaped at her.

'Bloody hell!' he exclaimed. He slid in beside her. 'You look as though you've walked out of a girls' storybook!' And he burst out laughing.

'See what I mean,' remarked Mrs Hatherley to Peggy.

Rusty didn't find his remark funny. She turned aside, wishing she was a million miles away. Harry didn't seem to notice. He began talking about some incident at choir practice. Occasionally Ivor added the odd remark. He was really smart, thought Rusty. He didn't say much, but when he did he managed to make everyone laugh.

'Is dinner going to be long?' said Harry.

'I bet you two 'ave bin eatin' with the boarders,' said Mrs Hatherley suspiciously.

'Well,' said Harry, attempting to look innocent, 'we felt we ought to help them out a bit.'

Anne hopped off her mother's lap and snuggled next to Ivor on the bench.

Rusty could feel a pain at the back of her throat. She longed to be part of a noisy family again. The room began to go out of focus as she resorted to what she had started doing back at Benwood House. She made her eyes go backwards into her head until all her surroundings became blurred, and the blur was like a soft wall that wrapped itself around her.

She was vaguely aware of the clatter of knives and forks and chattering voices, but it wasn't until the kitchen door was flung open that the wall was broken. As she looked up she saw Beth stride in, her cheeks flushed from cycling, her short straight hair in a tangle. She was wearing an old blue hand-knitted jersey and faded navy-blue serge trousers tucked into a pair of Wellington boots. She slid the boots off by the door and walked over to the table in her stockinged feet. One of her big toes stuck out through a hole.

'Move out of the way, Harry,' she said bossily, and she wedged herself in between Rusty and her brother. 'Sorry I couldn't be here sooner,' she said breathlessly, 'but there's so much work to do. How's your new school? You look as if they've worn you down. Is it wretched?'

'Didn't you know I was going to be here today?' Rusty said stiffly.

'Yes, but I'd already promised to help out. I couldn't just say, "Sorry, I've changed my mind, I've a friend coming down." Anyway,' she added, 'I'm here now, aren't I?'

Rusty nodded.

'So what's the woodwork like there?'

'We don't have it.'

'What, not at all?'

'Or art. I'm taking extra Latin and French and math instead, so that I can go to university.'

'Oh,' said Beth, puzzled. 'I didn't know you wanted to go to university. I thought you wanted to do something with wood or art.'

'Well, actually, I've changed my mind,' said Rusty haughtily.

Beth gazed at her outfit. 'Do you have to wear those gymslips all the time?'

'We can wear mufti in the evenings. I think a uniform is a good idea. It makes everyone the same.'

Beth looked astounded. 'Who wants to be the same as everyone else?'

'It's – it's,' went on Rusty relentlessly, 'useful for community spirit and all that stuff, working as a team.'

'They don't wave Union Jacks all over the place, do they?' said Harry, joining in. 'And have those awful assemblies with endless hymns and all that rot, do they?'

Rusty could feel herself growing angry. 'Some of the hymns are pretty neat!' she exclaimed heatedly.

Harry smote his chest melodramatically. 'King and Country, let me die and kill for thee!'

'Oh, stop teasin' the girl,' said Mrs Hatherley. 'It's nice to think she likes her school. The ones from America in your school aren't settling in so easy.'

Rusty turned, surprised. 'Are there kids from the States in your school?'

He nodded. 'Yes. They're the ones that are always grumbling, or going on about the food or the cold.'

'They're not used to rationing and the English climate yet,' said Mrs Hatherley. 'Give the poor things a chance.'

Rusty could feel herself blushing. Even as everyone returned to chattering, she kept hearing Harry's comments in her head about flag-waving 'and all that rot', for every day for the last few weeks she had been silently pledging allegiance to the flag of the United States.

She turned to Beth. 'What are you doing tomorrow?'

'I've promised to help out with the pigs. I'm sorry,' Beth said. 'I didn't know that you were coming down here until a few days ago. I can't let them down now, not after I said I would.'

See if I care, thought Rusty. 'Oh well,' she said, giving a shrug. 'I think we're going back tomorrow anyway.'

After everyone had started on the vegetable pie, followed by a rare treat of dried bananas and junket, Rusty was introduced to another 'delicacy'. The Hatherley children were still hungry, so they proceeded to spread margarine on slices of bread and sprinkle sugar on top.

It was growing late and her mother wanted to leave.

'I'm sorry I can't see you much,' said Beth.

'Oh, that's O.K.,' said Rusty blithely. 'I have *such* a lot to do tomorrow. Beatie left me a bunch of carpentry tools, and I want to sort them out. Maybe sharpen them up a little, too.'

'You'll be doing no such sharpening,' interrupted her mother.

Rusty scowled. Trust her mother to open her mouth and spoil everything. She climbed over the back of the bench and picked up her Beanie from one of the hooks on the wall. As she put it on, she could hardly bear to look at anyone in the room. She turned briefly, muttered a goodbye, and followed her mother out through the door into the black Devon night.

23

They stood in the front garden and stared at Beatie's rambling house. Peggy moved slowly towards the Bomb and gave the roof an affectionate pat.

'Hello, old girl,' she whispered.

They made their way to the tiny sheltered porch and Peggy unlocked the door. 'I'm afraid there's no electricity,' she said. 'It was switched off about a week ago.'

Rusty followed her into the living room. On the mantelpiece above a laid fire stood several candles and an oil-lamp. Two camp beds were made up in front of it.

'Oh,' exclaimed Peggy, 'Mrs Hatherley is kind.'

As she lit the candles and lamp, Rusty sat on one of the cushions that were spread out on the floor in front of the fireplace.

'Can I light the fire?' she asked.

But her mother had struck the match, and the flames were already spreading up from the newspaper through the wood.

Peggy sat next to her daughter on a cushion, and together they stared silently at the flames. 'You don't miss America too much, do you?' her mother asked suddenly.

Rusty glanced at her. She wanted to say, 'I think of America every day. And every day here in England away from my American family and friends feels like I'm slowly drowning in a dark pool. And it's not that I'm fussy about the cold and the food, it's just that they remind me of all the other things that I'm missing.'

But as she looked at her mother's face, she couldn't bring herself to tell her.

'I guess I'll get used to it.'

Her mother looked hurt.

For what seemed like an eternity neither of them spoke, until there was a sudden pattering sound that very quickly grew in intensity.

'What's that?' said Peggy.

'Rain,' said Rusty. 'Lots of it.'

They looked at each other, startled.

'Rain?' they chorused.

'The ceiling!' yelled Peggy, leaping to her feet.

'Jumping Jehoshaphat!' shouted Rusty, scrambling to join her.

They ran to the kitchen. Rusty grabbed an old tin bucket and the copper bowl from under the sink, while her mother picked up some baking tins. Together they tore back into the hallway and leapt up the stairs.

They placed the tins, bowl and bucket on the floor, and then, to Rusty's amazement, as soon as they had jumped down to the next floor, her mother slid down the banisters. Rusty followed suit.

Like demented creatures they ran round the kitchen and the conservatory, searching for anything they could lay their hands on, and then sprinted frantically up the stairs again. They spread all the battered objects under the remaining drips, then sank breathlessly to the floor.

'I really must do something about that roof,' said Peggy. She gazed at the strange collection of tins and bowls, took one look at her daughter, and burst out laughing.

Rusty leaned back against the small wooden railings and started laughing too.

'You know,' choked out her mother, 'I've been saying I must mend that roof for almost two years now! If I leave it any longer, it'll collapse altogether!'

Rusty had never seen her mother laugh so openly. As they pointed wildly at each other sitting on the floor under the leaking ceiling, they started howling all over again.

When they had finally calmed down, they smiled at each other.

Rusty listened to the drips as they fell.

'Sounds almost like an orchestra,' she murmured.

'Do you remember,' began her mother hesitantly, 'do you remember me filling up milk bottles with water at different levels and trying to play tunes on them? We always used to sing "Ten Green Bottles".'

'I'm not sure,' said Rusty. 'I remember way back teaching something like that to Skeet, but he said I had it all wrong. And when we sang it in Girl Scouts, they sang it different too.

> *'Ninety-nine bottles of beer on the wall,'*

she sang,

> *'Ninety-nine bottles of beer,*
> *If one of those bottles should happen to fall,*
> *Ninety-eight bottles of beer on the wall.'*

'It went on for ever!' she leaned forward. 'How does the English version go?'

> *'Ten green bottles,'*

her mother sang softly,

> *'Hanging on the wall,*
> *Ten green bottles hanging on the wall.*
> *And if one green bottle,'*

Rusty joined in,

> *'Should accident'ly fall,*
> *There'd be nine green bottles hanging on the wall!'*

They stopped and laughed shyly.

'I knew I had it right,' said Rusty. 'Well, sort of.'

They sat quietly in the dark. It was quite magical, listening to all the different sounds.

'Pretty, isn't it?' whispered Rusty.

'Yes. I never noticed it before. I suppose we always rushed quickly downstairs again as soon as we'd carried everything up. You know,' she said, 'Charlie would love this.'

'Are you going to tell him about owning the house?'

'Yes. But for the moment I'll say it's a holiday place. Good Lord!' she said, standing up quickly, 'we'll be missing the fire.'

The fire was roaring up the chimney from a generous pile of logs. They sat cross-legged in front of it, soaking up its warmth.

'Reminds me of cookouts,' said Rusty.

'When the summer comes,' said her mother, 'you'll have to show me what a cookout is like.' She was about to add, 'Harvey often talked about them.' But she swallowed the words.

'Mother,' said Rusty, 'how come you like fixing cars? I mean, how come you got to do it, anyway?'

'A lot of women had to take over the jobs normally done by men so that the men could join up. Didn't they do that in America?'

'Sure. I heard of women building ships in the New York docks, but I guess I didn't see much of it where we lived.' She paused. 'Couldn't you have done another kind of job?'

'You disapprove, don't you?'

Rusty squirmed. 'No,' she said slowly.

'Yes, you do.'

'We-e-ell. It's kinda weird, that's all. I never heard of a woman mechanic before. I guess I just can't figure out why you like it so much. I mean, how did it all happen?'

Peggy threw some more wood on the fire.

'Well, I'd been driving for the W.V.S. for over a year, and, like all the other drivers, we had to go through a daily routine of checking and caring for the vehicle and filling in charts recording mileage and fuel, that sort of thing. And I rather enjoyed it. The cars we had to drive were a bit of a menace, though, so I thought it would be useful if I started training to be a mechanic. I volunteered for a course. And I loved it.'

'What happens when you join the W.V.S.?'

'Oh, you're trained in how to cope with an air-raid. You do some first-aid, learn about fire-fighting, emergency cooking, that sort of thing. One of our biggest jobs here was evacuating about three thousand people from their homes in the South Hams.'

'Why? Was it bombed?'

'No. The whole area had to be cleared because the G.I.s were going to use it as a training ground for the D-Day landings.'

Rusty listened as her mother talked about how difficult it had been moving people and their belongings away from the villages, of heartbroken people torn from their homes, of bewildered young G.I.s thrown into a foreign country, of the necessity of finding new homes for the evacuated people.

'Is that how you met Mitch Flannagan and the man Charlie calls Uncle Harvey?'

She nodded. 'There were clubs set up for the American forces. We wanted to make the Americans feel at home.'

'Mother,' said Rusty slowly, 'what was he like?'

'Who?'

'Harvey.'

Peggy reddened.

'Oh. Tall. Brown wavy hair. Blue eyes.'

'But what was he like as a person?'

'Why do you want to know?'

Rusty shrugged. 'When Charlie talks about him, I s'pose I feel a little left out, not knowing anything about him.'

Peggy gazed into the fire.

'I remember the day Charlie first met him. It was just after his second birthday, and Harvey had come to tea.' She turned. 'You know how jealous Charlie can get. He just stood there in the hall and scowled. Harvey scowled back, and the next thing I knew Charlie was laughing! From that day on, Charlie worshipped him.'

'Go on,' urged Rusty. 'Tell me some more about him.'

Peggy looked thoughtful for a moment.

'Harvey had the most extraordinary energy. He was never afraid of making a fool of himself, either. He'd join in the most peculiar games with Charlie, even going as far as dressing up and painting his face.' She paused. 'At the same time he never made fun of him, or brushed Charlie aside when he was upset. He took what he said seriously.' She smiled wryly. 'He was also extremely determined.'

'How do you mean?'

'Well, I often tended to overdo working with the W.V.S., and because there was always such a lot to do, I'm afraid I was a bit stubborn about not taking time off. I knew I was being silly, but sometimes I seemed to be on a treadmill and I couldn't find a way of getting off it. I remember one of the women in charge telling me off. "An exhausted volunteer is no use to anyone," she said. "You're not being fair to the others." So I'd take a day off and then rush out to mend someone else's car.'

'What's this got to do with Uncle Harvey?' said Rusty, puzzled.

'He was the only person who could pull me off the treadmill. Once, when I was so tired I could hardly think, he said, "Say, let's find a nice sunny spot by the river and have us a picnic." And I said, "Why?" and he said, "For the fun of it." "But I *can't*." "There's no such word as can't," he said. "I, Harvey Lindon, have just assassinated the word and removed it from Webster's Dictionary. *And* the Oxford." I just laughed. After that I had to give in.'

'Do you think he'll ever come back here?'

Peggy reddened again.

'No. I don't think so.'

'Why?'

'Things are different in wartime. You're separated from your family, and so you make friends with other people to make up for that. Once a war is over, everyone goes back to their families.'

'Does he have a family?'

'Yes.'

'Does he have children too?'

'No, but he has seven brothers and sisters.'

'Does he have a wife?'

'A fiancée.'

Peggy gave the fire a poke and turned one of the logs over.

'Mother,' said Rusty a little later, 'I know you don't like to talk about it, but why do you want me to go to college?'

'Because I want you to have the chance of being more independent when you're older.'

Rusty was puzzled. Independence was not what her mother or school encouraged. 'You see,' she blurted out, 'I guess I just always figured I'd take some kind of practical or art course. I like fooling around with wood and paints, and drawing designs, and helping out with scenery and boats and stuff like that.'

'Well, you can still do that after you've finished your degree course. You can do those things in your spare time, as a hobby.'

Rusty nodded. It sounded sensible, so why did she feel so broken up inside? Way back, when she and Aunt Hannah had talked about it, Aunt Hannah had suggested that she take some kind of pre-art school course so that she could learn lots of things like drawing, sculpture, printing, pottery, woodcarving, and that way discover what she wanted to do most of all.

For a while Rusty chatted about the Weekeepeemee – the river where she and the gang used to play – and Alice's graduation day, and Jinkie's wedding and Kathryn's acting debut as a maid in summer stock. And, in turn, her mother talked about Charlie and the W.V.S. and occasionally, when Rusty pushed her, about Harvey.

Gradually, as the embers died down, they changed into their pyjamas and slipped, exhausted, into the camp beds.

Rusty was seated at the bar in their drugstore back home, reading a comic book and eating a chocolate ice-cream soda, when she heard a strange tinkling sound. She turned. Her friend Janey had walked in with a girl friend. She was wearing a flared red-and-white-check skirt below a white peasant blouse. Rusty could see from her wavy hair that she'd got a permanent. There were traces of lipstick on her mouth, and to Rusty's amazement both she and her friend were wearing nylons. The tinkling sound came from a bracelet on Janey's wrist, which had a row of charms hanging from it.

Janey sauntered over to the bar with her new friend and casually placed her schoolbooks on the counter.

'Two cherry Cokes,' she said.

Rusty leaned towards her. 'Janey!' she said, but her friend seemed not to have heard her. 'Janey. It's Rusty. Your best friend.'

But there was no response.

As Janey sat proudly up by the bar, Rusty noticed the points of her brassiere jutting underneath the peasant blouse. She turned hastily away and glanced down at her own breasts. To her horror, she discovered that they had disappeared entirely.

Rusty woke up with a jolt. Her mother's bed was empty. At the end of it lay jeans, a shirt and a sweater. On the pillow was a slip of paper. She leaned across and picked it up.

'Dear Virginia,' she read,

I thought I'd let you lie in. I'll be at Mrs Hatherley's. She's very kindly offered us breakfast. As you can see, I've put out clothes to change into.

I hope you had a good sleep.

Love,
Mother.

Rusty pulled the blankets up to her neck and gazed towards the bay window. She could see by the movements of the trees that it was windy outside. Leaves whirled through the air and the windows gave a rattle. She hopped out of bed and dressed as fast as she could. Her jeans slid down to her hips, so she had to fold them over at the waistband to keep them up. She cupped her breasts with her hands. Although small, to her relief they were still there.

She found her mother in a rickety old garage in the Hatherleys' garden, her head under the bonnet of the car. She was back in her overalls, her hair hanging untidily in wisps out of a grubby khaki turban.

Rusty suddenly realized how unhappy her mother must have been, for the difference in her manner was extraordinary: she looked positively radiant. Rusty strolled over to her. The air reeked of petrol and oil.

'Doesn't the smell put you off?' she said.

'No. I love it.'

'I like the smell of wood and paint,' said Rusty. 'I guess that's sort of the same thing.'

Rusty stared at the engine. She was still trying to figure out what it was that made her mother enjoy fiddling around with them so much. She thought of Aunt Hannah and her sculptures.

'It's a little bit like sculpture, isn't it? Only it moves and is made of metal and stuff.'

Her mother stood back and gazed at the arrangement of cylinders and wires. 'Yes,' she said, surprised. 'Some of these engines have a real beauty about them. I'd never thought of it like that. It *is* rather like a moving sculpture, I suppose.'

Aunt Hannah sculpted out of all sorts of materials – wood, clay, stone – but she'd never made anything out of metal. Maybe Rusty'd suggest it to her in her next letter.

'Aunt Hannah sells some of her sculptures,' said Rusty suddenly. 'Maybe you ought to fix broken-down cars and sell them too.'

Her mother burst out laughing.

'What's so funny?' said Rusty. 'I think it's a keen idea.'

'Well, yes, I suppose it is, but I'd need a garage, and to be honest I don't think anyone would buy a car if they knew that I'd fixed it.'

'Why not?'

'Because I'm a woman.'

'But people ask you to fix their cars here.'

'That's because they know me and I've built up a reputation.'

'So you could do it again.'

Peggy gave one of Rusty's plaits an affectionate tug.

'I'm serious,' said Rusty earnestly. 'Why is it everyone in this country always looks at all the things that might go wrong first, instead of starting something and then seeing what happens. Then if something goes wrong, you can figure it out a little bit at a time.'

Just then, Mrs Hatherley poked her head round the door.

'Hello, Rusty,' she said. 'I'm just off to feed the chickens. Harry's in the kitchen. He'll give you breakfast.'

'I can manage all right,' said Rusty.

'I'm afraid,' whispered her mother, when Mrs Hatherley was out of earshot, 'it wouldn't be fair to ask for milk.'

'It's O.K.,' Rusty whispered back. 'A glass of water will be just fine.'

She was about to leave when she stopped.

'Mother, did the G.I.s like tea?'

'No. As soon as they could, they had coffee supplies sent over here. And doughnuts.'

'Doughnuts!' said Rusty. 'What I wouldn't give for a doughnut!'

Harry met her at the kitchen door.

'Hello,' he said cheerily. 'I've been instructed to feed and water you.'

He stepped back and with a grand gesture ushered her into the kitchen. Rusty frowned when she caught sight of his hands. They were covered in clay.

'What are you doing?'

He pointed to several lumps of clay on the board by the sink. 'I'm trying to make soup bowls.'

He rinsed his hands hastily under the tap and wiped them on the seat of his shorts. He grabbed a frying-pan from a shelf, put it on the cooker, and proceeded to knife out some dripping from a bowl.

'It's O.K.,' protested Rusty. 'I can do it myself.'

'I've had my orders,' he said, cracking an egg into the pan. 'Cut yourself some bread and shut up.'

'Nobody lets me do anything,' she muttered, carving a chunk of bread from a loaf. She was just about to add, 'Don't they have *any* sliced bread in this country?' but stopped herself.

'Harry,' she said, as she handed him the bread, 'do the kids at your school hate the ones who have come back from America?'

He took the peculiar-shaped piece of bread and threw it into the frying-pan. 'No. In fact, we envy some of the things about them.'

'Like what?'

'The films and shows they've seen. That sort of thing.' He glanced at her out of the corner of his eye. 'It's just that sometimes they don't know what we're talking about.'

'Like what?'

'Well, if we talk about something that's happened during the War, they can't join in and they don't like it that they've missed out, and I suppose that makes them a bit miserable. But it's not our fault. Now,' he added, 'how do you want your egg? Sunnyside up or over easy?'

'Boy, how do you know that? I never heard anyone say that over here.'

'Most of the Americans are boarders, and sometimes I eat with them.'

'Sunnyside up,' said Rusty. 'Boy, you can really cook.'

'It's only fried egg on fried bread,' he said, sliding it from the pan on to a plate.

Rusty took the plate and sat at the table.

'This is really good.'

Harry returned to rolling the clay into a long worm. He coiled it around in circles, layer on layer to form a bowl shape.

'Where'd you learn to do that?'

'At school.'

Rusty started feeling jealous again. She found herself saying rather pompously, 'We don't have time for all that kind of thing at *my* school. We have *so* much studying to do.'

'Oh yes?' said Harry, unperturbed. 'I don't like studying. I don't mind reading about things after I've done them or if I'm looking up something for a reason, but I'd hate to have to learn lots of facts and dates off by heart.'

'Well, if you don't learn things by heart, you can't pass exams, can you?'

He shrugged. 'I'm not interested in passing exams. I

want to be a potter and be judged on what I can make.'

'A potter!' said Rusty incredulously. 'Well,' she continued, copying her mother, 'that's the sort of thing you can do for a hobby, *after* you've passed exams.'

To her annoyance, he laughed. 'Don't be so bloody silly,' he said.

She almost yelled out, 'That's an order mark!' How could he be so sure of himself? 'I bet your parents won't let you,' she stated.

'Why ever not?'

'Well,' she said smugly, 'maybe it's just that you can't take exams at your school. At *my* school we can take exams and go to college.'

'So what? We can do that at our school, too. You don't have to be so superior about it.'

'I am *not* being superior,' she exclaimed.

'Oh yes you are. In fact you're turning into a little prig.'

Rusty leapt to her feet. 'At least I'm not a pantywaist like you.'

'A what?'

'A pantywaist! A coward. If there was a war on, I'd volunteer for the army. I wouldn't be a, you know, pacifist like you and let other people do all the fighting and sit at home and do nothing.'

'Who says I'd do nothing?' said Harry loudly. 'If you must know, little Miss Bloody Know-It-All, I'd do something to keep people alive, like working on a farm and helping grow food, or be in an ambulance or bomb disposal squad.'

'I bet!' she said. 'You'd be too scared.'

'Yes, I probably would be scared, but I'd rather do that than wave flags and sing patriotic songs and then use that as an excuse to kill lots of people.'

'You're nuts!' she yelled.

'And you're a pompous ass!' he yelled back.

'Well, your ears are too darned big, if you want to know.'

'And so's your mouth.'

'Well . . . you can go to hell!'

And with that she stormed out of the kitchen.

It wasn't until she had reached Beatie's house and had rocked herself violently backwards and forwards for half an hour in the old car tyre that she began to cool down.

She hadn't meant to say all those dumb things. Everything just came out all wrong. It didn't when she was with Lance in their Cabin in the Woods. If she could smuggle back a saw and a couple more tools, and maybe even a paintbrush, in her grip, she could take them back with her and use them there. Then she could make it into a really good home and hiding place. Harry and Beth could just go lose themselves. She gave a triumphant smirk. Boy, if they knew about her Cabin in the Woods, *they'd* be the ones to be jealous. With that thought in mind, she leapt off the tyre and left it swinging wildly behind her.

24

'It's preposterous! Absolutely preposterous!'

Rusty was leaning over the heavy wooden banister eavesdropping. The outraged voice that was soaring from downstairs belonged to her grandmother. All Rusty's mother had managed to tell her was that she had been left Beatie's house. Her grandmother hadn't allowed her mother to get any further.

'The woman must have been deranged!' she stated.

It was Monday evening, Rusty's last night before returning to school. She and her mother had spent most of the day travelling back.

On Sunday, when her mother had returned to Beatie's, she had immediately started tinkering around with the Bomb. As soon as it had fired into life, she had driven them for miles along the narrow Devon lanes, and in the evening they had bought fish and chips and had driven out to a beach, where they had eaten them sitting on the running-board of the car, facing the sea.

On the way back, her mother had caught a red fox in her headlights. She slowed down so that it could escape, but it was mesmerized by the lights. Eventually she stopped the car and switched them off.

'Go on, foxy,' Rusty whispered. 'Go find yourself a nice safe hole somewhere. Say, why am I whispering?'

'I don't know,' replied her mother. 'I suppose it's because it's dark.'

She turned the lights on again. The fox had gone. The Bomb gave a loud bang and started to rumble.

'The dark doesn't make *her* whisper,' laughed Rusty.

They lurched forward.

Rusty sat back. The dials on the wooden dashboard lit up and blinked, making the car strangely cosy.

'You really like this "bomb", don't you?' said Rusty.

'Love her.'

'But she's so old!'

'There's nothing wrong in being old.'

'But how can you . . .?' She stopped.

'You're wondering why I love her so much?'

'Uh-huh.'

'Well, this is the first thing that I've ever paid for out of my own money, and also *I* made her work. So she's a sort of symbol, do you understand?'

'I think so. You mean, when you see her, it reminds you of what you achieved, that you didn't just dream it all up.'

'Exactly.'

'Yeah. I know what you mean. Me and Skeet helped Uncle Bruno build a rowboat last summer. When we put it into the water, I was so excited I could hardly hold the oars.'

'Yes, I felt something similar when I first drove this old girl,' said Peggy. 'A sort of butterfly-feeling inside.'

That morning, after their good time together the previous day, Rusty felt mean about sneaking the tools into her grip. She had tied an old pair of her mother's navy overalls firmly around them so that they wouldn't rattle, placed the bundle at the bottom of the grip, and packed the rest of her clothing on top.

Now the bundle was hidden at the bottom of her bedroom wardrobe. All she had to do was to persuade her mother to let her take an early train to Benwood House so that she could hide it before school started.

'I thought you'd be pleased,' she heard her mother

saying. 'You're always complaining that you find young children a bit of a strain. Charlie and Virginia can spend their summers there.'

'When's summer?' came her brother's high-pitched voice. 'Is it tomorrow?'

Rusty returned to her room.

Lying on the bed were four letters: one from Uncle Bruno and Aunt Hannah, one from Kathryn, one from Skeet and one from Janey.

She picked up the snapshots beside them and sat on the bed, her back resting against the high wooden rail. Most of them were of Kathryn with the summer stock company, looking calm and happy, but the snapshot she had looked at over and over again was the one of Uncle Bruno and Skeet standing barefoot, a huge fish dangling between them. There was Uncle Bruno, like a big bear, with his dark summer beard, his old floppy hat, check shirt, and pants cut to the knees. And beside him stood Skeet, all blond crewcut and freckles, his jeans rolled up, his white T-shirt filthy, and his eyes screwed up from looking at the sun. They were both grinning and pointing madly at the fish.

'Next summer,' she whispered, 'I won't be in some leaky house in Devon – I'm gonna be with you.'

The letters worried her, though. Uncle Bruno had mentioned that he and Aunt Hannah had sent on a trunk of hers to England with the help of a Navy friend of theirs three months ago and had she gotten it yet? Rusty didn't want them sending any of her stuff over; she wanted them to keep it all for when she came back.

Kathryn talked of rehearsals for a Christmas show at high school. She was taking real voice classes now in her spare time. Rusty remembered her saying in that quiet manner of hers, 'You know, you ought to work in the theatre. Maybe be a scene painter, or stage carpenter, or even a set designer.' It would never have occurred to

Kathryn not to try for something you really wanted to do. Uncle Bruno was always telling them that if you were lucky enough to have a dream, you ought to go for it hell for leather, and even if you didn't succeed or you changed your mind, you'd still have had some interesting experiences on the way.

But it was Skeet's and Janey's letters that worried her most of all. She felt that they were both growing away from her. Janey had been asked out to a football game by one of the boys in the high school. He was the son of a doctor. Janey's mom had bought her a camel coat to wear.

And her date had bought her a corsage, a huge single chrysanthemum, to wear on the coat. Rusty knew they cost at least fifty cents, sometimes even a dollar. He must really like Janey. It sounded serious. And Skeet mentioned that he had gone to a roller-skating party, and he'd lent Rusty's skates to a girl in his class. He hoped Rusty didn't mind.

'Virginia?'

Rusty hopped off the bed and opened the door.

Her mother was standing in the hall, holding Charlie in her arms; he was still attached to his teddy bear like a Siamese twin.

'I want you to keep your grandmother company.'

'You mean, I have to be alone with her?'

'You can tell her about your holiday. I'm going to give Charlie a bath and put him to bed. Then the three of us can have supper together.'

Rusty gave a resigned sigh and opened the door into the drawing room.

Her grandmother was sitting in her winged armchair. 'I suppose,' she said, after an awkward silence, 'you had better be seated.'

Rusty threw herself into the hard stuffed armchair opposite and gazed at the dark, ticking clock on the mantelpiece.

Her grandmother stared at Rusty's feet, which were tucked up underneath her. Rusty pulled them out and swung them to the ground.

'Well, Virginia,' her grandmother said sweetly. 'And how was your stay in Devon?'

'It was O.K.'

'What did you do there?'

'Well, Mother and I went out in the Bomb for a ride yesterday, and then –'

'The Bomb?'

'It's her car.'

'I see.' She paused. 'And where exactly did you go?'

'Oh, all over the place. Mother showed me where she and lots of other W.V.S. ladies had to evacuate hundreds of people so that the Americans could get ready for D-Day, and then we –'

'The Americans weren't the only ones fighting in the War, you know.'

'I didn't say they were,' said Rusty, bristling. 'Anyways, we bought some fish and chips and put vinegar and salt on it and ate it out by one of the beaches. It was –'

'You ate fish and chips?' said her grandmother slowly.

'Right.'

'On the beach?'

'Uh-huh. We sat on the running-board and –'

'You ate them out in the open?'

'Uh-huh. Out of newspapers. With our fingers.'

Mrs Dickinson Senior sat back and pursed her lips. 'I see.'

Thank goodness for that, thought Rusty. She didn't want to have to repeat the whole thing all over again.

Suddenly there was a loud knock at the front door.

'Oh dear,' said her grandmother, flustered. 'It's Mrs Grace's day off.'

'It's O.K.,' said Rusty, springing to her feet. 'I'll go answer it.'

As she walked through the hallway, she could hear splashing sounds coming from the bathroom and Charlie giggling.

She opened the door.

Outside stood a tall thin man in his forties, wearing the uniform of an army major. He was deeply bronzed, and his cropped hair and moustache were bleached almost white. Over his arm was a khaki raincoat. A large leather attaché case stood by his feet.

'Hi,' said Rusty. 'May I help you?'

He frowned for an instant and took a long hard look at her, from her brown-and-white saddle shoes, bobby socks and jeans that had been folded up to calf length, to her sloppy blue sweater, her cascade of long, flame-coloured hair, and the piercing green eyes.

'Virginia?' he said.

Rusty was startled. 'How'd you know that?'

'Don't you recognize me?' he said quietly.

She shook her head.

He looked so tired and bewildered that she felt sorry for him.

'I'm your father,' he said.

25

If it had been in the movies, her mother would have swept down the stairs in a beautiful gown, her hair waved, her face glowing; her father would have thrust Rusty aside and cried, 'Peggy!' and she would have replied 'Roger!'; they would have rushed into each other's arms and embraced against a background of violin music. Instead, Rusty gaped stupefied at the man, repeating, 'Father?'

Her grandmother rediscovered the use of her legs and came running into the hall, and her father gave his mother a polite peck on the cheek, while she clasped him to her bosom.

After recovering from the shock, Rusty ran up the stairs, yelling. Minutes later, her mother appeared on the landing, her face shining from the steam of the bathroom, her short hair damp and tousled. Charlie was in her arms, wrapped up in a towel, his hair sticking up wildly.

And no one moved.

Her father glanced quickly at her mother's trousers while she gazed down at him, stunned.

Eventually she walked down the stairs.

'I had no idea,' she began weakly. 'Why didn't you let me know you were coming?'

'I tried to,' he said. 'But the phone always seemed to be engaged.'

Mrs Dickinson Senior looked a little guilty. 'I'm sorry,' she said. 'I can't stand that thing ringing, so I sometimes just take it off the hook.'

Rusty noticed a flicker of anger pass across her mother's face and then it was gone.

'So,' he said abruptly. 'This is Charles.'

'Yes.' She smoothed his hair down. 'Charlie,' she murmured, 'this is your daddy.'

Charlie put his arms round Peggy's neck and buried his face in it.

Mr Dickinson placed his hands awkwardly behind his back.

'I'll put him to bed,' said Peggy. 'He'll catch cold in this towel.'

He gave a nod.

'And perhaps you could change into something a little more respectable,' said Mrs Dickinson Senior, lightly.

Peggy blushed. 'We've only just returned from Devon,' she explained. 'It was Virginia's half-term.'

'Roger,' gushed Rusty's grandmother suddenly, 'for goodness' sake, let me take your coat and cap, and come and sit in the drawing room. You'll find it just as you left it.'

Rusty followed on behind him.

'Yes,' he said on entering. 'It is.' He looked puzzled. 'I thought this was requisitioned.'

'It was, but I had everything put in storage, and luckily it survived the bombs. I managed to have it all moved back and arranged before Margaret and Virginia and Charles came back. Margaret didn't do a thing. I mean, she didn't have to do a thing. Sit down.'

As Rusty sat down in one of the armchairs, she heard her grandmother whisper, 'You've come back just in time, my dear. Your son needs a father's hand.' She leaned back and took a long hard look at him. 'You've changed so much,' she remarked.

'I expect we've all changed a little,' he said, and he glanced at Rusty. 'I hardly recognized Virginia.'

'Oh, you can call me Rusty. Everyone back home does.'

'My dear,' said her grandmother stiffly. 'You *are* back home.'

'I mean,' Rusty stammered, 'back in Connecticut.'

'Rusty?' he repeated.

'On account of my hair. Uncle Bruno said it reminded him of leaves in the fall.'

'That's Mr Omsk,' explained her grandmother.

'Well, if you don't mind, I shall continue to call you Virginia. After all, that is what we christened you.'

'O.K.' She leaned forward. 'I guess we're a little bit the same, really. I mean, we were both sent away from England. The tea's the worst thing here. I still haven't gotten used to it yet.'

'Well, actually, I wouldn't mind a cup right now.'

'Oh, Roger,' said his mother, 'how foolish of me. I'm afraid it's Mrs Grace's day off. I'll go and make a nice pot for us all.'

As she left the room, Rusty and her father stared awkwardly at each other.

'And how was your half-term?' he said.

'O.K. We went to Beatie's place.'

He nodded. 'And how is she? Your mother has told me quite a lot about her in her letters.'

'Oh,' said Rusty quietly. 'She died. We had to go hear the will read on Saturday.'

'I see. I'm sorry about that. Your mother sounded very fond of her.'

'Beatie was the tops.' Some instinct told her to steer clear of the subject of the will. 'I go back to school tomorrow morning,' she said. 'But maybe they'd let me have a week off – I mean, with you coming back and all.'

'If everyone did that, there'd be chaos.'

'I guess,' said Rusty, disappointed. He could at least have put up a fight, though. 'Anyway,' she added, 'I'll see you on Friday night.'

'Oh? What's happening on Friday?'

'I come back here for the weekend.'

'You come back here for the weekends?' he said slowly.

Just then her mother walked in. Her father sprang to his feet. Rusty knew that her mother was wearing her better clothes, but she suspected that her father did not. Above an old tweed skirt she wore a simple cream blouse and a grey cardigan that had been darned at the elbows and cuffs. She drew out a packet of cigarettes from her cardigan pocket and took one out.

'Do you have a light?' she asked.

'No. I'm afraid not.' He sat down again.

She walked over to the fire. There was a spill of rolled newspaper by the grate. She pushed it into the fire, lit the cigarette, and stood leaning against the mantelpiece.

'I didn't know you smoked, Margaret.' He tapped his fingers on his knee.

She nodded. 'Someone handed me one during a raid in Plymouth.'

The W.V.S. had helped collect half a street of mutilated bodies that night, and then one by one they had accompanied the surviving relatives and friends to the mortuary to comfort them as they identified what remained.

'I was as sick as a dog at first,' she said quickly, 'but after that I suppose I got used to it.'

'I didn't know you had cut your hair either,' he said.

'Well, yes. It was far more convenient.'

They heard the clatter of the tea-trolley in the hall. Peggy hastily placed her cigarette on the mantelpiece so that the lit end jutted out over the edge. 'Sit down, Mother,' she said. 'I'll bring it in.'

'Thank you. I was beginning to think I'd been forgotten.' And she gave a short laugh.

To Rusty's surprise, her grandmother sat down beside her father, almost as if she was a chaperone.

Peggy drew out two low tables and laid the cups and saucers out.

'I'll be mother,' said Mrs Dickinson Senior.

At first Rusty didn't understand, but then she realized

that 'being mother' meant that you were the one who poured out the tea.

Peggy picked up her cigarette from the mantelpiece and sat on the edge of the winged armchair, opposite Rusty. Rusty stared at her father. He looked so uncomfortable and out of place sitting on a sofa in his uniform. He sat, bolt upright, as stiff as if he had a poker up his back. If there were grades for good carriage, Ja⁚ey would have given him an A.

'I hear,' he said, turning to Peggy, 'that the woman whose house you were billeted in has just died.'

She turned swiftly. 'Yes,' she said.

'And what about the other woman who lived there?'

'She's moved into rented accommodation in Southampton with Susan. She married a G.I. She's waiting there to be posted out to America.' She drew on the cigarette. 'Actually, I've had some good news this weekend. She's expecting a baby.'

'Yes, well, that's hardly the thing to talk about over tea,' said Mrs Dickinson Senior, casting a swift glance in Rusty's direction.

Peggy ignored her. 'I'm glad for her. She's had enough unhappiness. Captain Flannagan is a kind man. Susan adores him.'

'We've all had to suffer unhappiness,' said Rusty's grandmother lightly, 'but we don't all run off with G.I.s to cure it.'

Rusty again saw the flicker of anger in her mother's eyes.

'You see,' Peggy explained, 'soon after she received a telegram informing her that her husband was Missing Believed Dead, her younger child was killed in an air-raid on Plymouth.'

'Yes,' went on Mrs Dickinson Senior relentlessly, 'I lost my husband in the First War, but I wouldn't have dreamt of remarrying.'

No one'd have you, thought Rusty.

'By the way, Roger,' said her grandmother, 'I saw Mr Bartholomew, and he told me to remind you that your old post is waiting for you and that you can take it up any time you like.'

'There's no rush, is there?' said Peggy. 'After all, Roger might want to start something fresh.'

'Nonsense,' said Mrs Dickinson Senior. 'Jobs are hard to find.'

'Mother does have a point,' he said, putting his cup clumsily back on the saucer.

And then Rusty's grandmother said something so staggering that Rusty almost fell out of the armchair.

'And we've just had some delightful news. This friend of Margaret's has left her the house in Devon. We can sell it and do some repairs on this house.'

Rusty and Peggy stared at her, absolutely speechless.

'Is this true?' said Rusty's father.

'What?' said Peggy, as if in a dream. 'Well, yes and no. Yes, she has left the house to me, and no, I won't be selling it.'

Her mother-in-law looked aghast. 'You don't intend to keep it?'

'Yes.'

'But how are you going to look after it?'

'Mother does have a point.'

'Odd weekends. The children's holidays. Who knows, we might want to move down there.'

'But Margaret, you can't possibly keep it,' said Mrs Dickinson Senior. She paused. 'I think you should at least put it in Roger's name.'

'I'm afraid I can't do that either.'

'But Margaret,' said her husband, 'you know how impractical you are. You wouldn't have a clue.'

'I have changed, you know. I'm not quite as useless as I used to be five years ago. And anyway, I'm afraid it's legally impossible. I'm not allowed to sell it for seventeen years, and it's a stipulation of the will that it remains in a woman's name.' Peggy threw her cigarette end into the fire. Crafty Beatie, she thought, she must have foreseen all this.

'It is rather odd, I must say,' said her husband.

'No, I don't think so,' said Peggy. 'Charlie loves it there. So do I. I suppose Beatie thought she'd like us at least to have the opportunity of spending our holidays there. I'm sure you'd like it, too. We could all go there in Virginia's Christmas holidays.'

'I was rather looking forward to spending Christmas here.'

'Of course you were,' put in his mother. 'I've never heard such nonsense.'

'I didn't mean Christmas Day. I meant in the New Year.'

'We'll see,' he said.

'More tea, Roger?' said his mother.

He nodded and pushed his cup and saucer in her direction.

The next morning, to Rusty's relief her mother agreed readily to letting her catch an earlier train. She seemed pleased that Rusty was eager to return to school, and relieved to get out of the house. For the first time she brought Charlie with her. It couldn't have been more perfect for, with Charlie for Peggy to look after, Rusty could easily insist on carrying the grip without arousing suspicion.

They were sitting on a platform bench a full ten minutes before the train drew in. Rusty was shocked by her mother's appearance: her face was ashen and she looked as though she had had no sleep.

'When is that man going away?' Charlie said suddenly. He was sitting with his teddy-bear on Peggy's lap.

'What man, darling?'

'You know,' he said, twisting himself around. 'The man with the moustache.'

'Oh, Charlie!' she exclaimed. 'You are a funniosity. I told you. He's your daddy.'

'Can't I have Uncle Harvey instead?'

'Of course not. Don't be silly.'

'I don't like that man.'

'You wait. You'll have lots of fun with him.'

'Why doesn't he smile?'

'I expect it's because he's very tired.'

'Oh.'

'Next weekend we'll all do something together,' she said. 'It'll be like being a real family again.'

'Grandmother too?' asked Rusty.

'I expect so.' But when Peggy saw Rusty's expression, she burst out laughing. 'Oh, Virginia,' she said, 'you're quite dreadful!'

'So's she.'

'Oh, stop it.' And she attempted to smother her laughter. Charlie started giggling too, though he wasn't quite sure what it was all about.

For a moment Rusty wished she could stay there with her mother and Charlie, and the three of them could just go off somewhere together but, before she could say anything, her train pulled into the station.

She stood up, kissed her mother, and then bent down and kissed Charlie on the cheek.

'Ugh!' he said, rubbing his face hastily, but Rusty could see he liked it. When she looked at her mother, she was surprised to see that she had turned quite red and there were tears in her eyes.

'I guess I better be going,' she muttered.

Her mother nodded. 'I'll see you on Friday.'

Rusty pulled open one of the train doors, slammed it

quickly, and leaned out of the window. The whistle blew and the train began to move away in a cloud of steam.

'So long!' she yelled.

Her mother laughed. 'So long!'

Charlie thrust his teddy-bear forward and made one of the paws go up and down.

'Monster,' she muttered warmly.

It was easy smuggling the tools into Benwood House. Immediately Rusty entered the school grounds, she sneaked around to the back, ran across the lacrosse pitches, threw the bundle of tools over the wall, and sprinted back towards the Fourth Form cloakroom of Butt House.

Gradually, the other girls started drifting into the cloakroom, chatting and laughing, while Rusty sat on one of the benches, her heart beating.

Within minutes a bell started to ring. It was time for assembly.

26

On Thursday night, Lance arrived over a quarter of an hour later than usual. Rusty had almost given up hope when he stumbled up the field, hot and breathless.

'Sorry,' he gasped. 'I had a bit of trouble getting out!' He glanced down at the sodden bundle in her arms. 'What's that?'

'Tools. I'll show you at the Cabin. I've got a whole bunch of stuff to tell you. My father came back and my mother got a house.' She took out her torch and began walking hurriedly into the woods, telling him all about her half-term as fast as she could.

At last they reached the slope with the three tall trees. As they slid down towards the old gate, Rusty gazed at the remains of the house.

'It's almost as if it's waiting for us,' she murmured, 'don't you think? Like an old friend.'

She pushed aside the gate and ran through the grass towards the exposed hallway. 'Hi there, Cabin!' she said.

'You're crazy,' commented Lance behind her.

'Well then, I hope I stay crazy. 'Cause it sure feels good.' She turned. 'Let's go get the oil-lamps.'

She strode across the hall and pushed open the cellar door. It gave a loud creak. They raced down the stairs and picked up a lamp each, took them back up to the Cabin, and placed them on the stone hearth in front of the fireplace.

'Just shine the flashlight on me so I can see what I'm doing,' said Rusty.

The knots on the bundle were too damp to undo. Rusty

took out her jack-knife, cut the string, and then unrolled the overalls. Inside lay a small axe, a saw, a large paint-brush, a small paintbrush, and an assortment of tools.

'Where on earth did you find these?' gasped Lance.

'Except for the axe and the paintbrushes, the tools were left to me in Beatie's will. There's a whole lot more, back at my mother's place.'

'Is Beatie the lady in Devon who died?'

Rusty nodded, and then suddenly felt very sad. Lance put his hand on her shoulder and gave her a gentle shake. 'Hey, cheer up,' he said. 'What are you going to do with it all?'

She shrugged. 'I don't know. First of all I'm going to cut us some wood for a fire.'

'What about matches?'

She unwrapped an old headscarf of her mother's. Inside lay a small cardboard box. 'I took them from the mantel-piece at my mother's place. I didn't think it was stealing. After all, no one'll be there to use them. I just hope the rain hasn't gotten to them.'

While Lance held the torch, Rusty lit a match.

'They're dry,' she whispered.

She lit the two lamps, sending a soft, flickering light around the room. Then she jumped up. 'Come on, let's go find some wood. It's beginning to feel like home already.'

They collected armfuls of leaves and twigs and branches, throwing them into a pile.

'Right,' said Rusty, 'now we have to sort them out into size. Little bitty thin ones at one end and the biggies at the other end.'

Using a stick of wood, Rusty raked the grate out. There was a bent shovel and a bucket by one of the alcoves. The bucket had a small hole in the bottom, but it'd do for the moment, thought Rusty, as she shovelled year-old ash into it. She picked up some of the thicker branches and began chopping them into smaller pieces.

Lance was mesmerized. 'Thank goodness I don't have to do that,' he said. 'At least we have firewood at school.'

'Then it should be a cinch,' said Rusty.

'Don't say that. It makes me feel even worse.'

'I'll do it like we do in Girl Scouts. Watch!' she said.

She placed all the leaves in a pile on top of the grate. Then she began to build a pyramid of wood on top of the leaves, using the tiniest twigs first and then going up in size.

'We'll leave the really big ones till after it's gotten good and hot,' she said, lighting a match. 'Now, keep your fingers crossed that it'll catch.'

She squatted down low and pushed a flame into the leaves. It took several minutes before the fire caught.

'I think the pyramid's falling,' whispered Lance as the wood began to hiss and move.

'I just hope it doesn't put it out,' she whispered back.

'Why are we whispering?'

'Search me.' She began to giggle.

After the two of them had been blowing into the base of the wood for a quarter of an hour, the fire burst into life.

'From now on,' said Rusty, 'we should always bring some wood in to dry. This is a little damp from last night's rain.' She tossed some branches into the fireplace. 'This is the life, eh?'

He nodded, grinning. 'All we need now,' he said, 'is some pork and baked beans and a guitar.'

'Come on,' she said. 'Let's bring up the rest of the stuff from the cellar.'

They dragged up the unbroken camp-bed and placed it in front of the fire, hanging the overalls and a blanket over it. The other blankets and pillows they placed on the floor.

'Boy, look at that steam!' exclaimed Rusty as great clouds came wafting up from the blanket.

'Next Tuesday I'll try and bring some things back with me too,' said Lance. 'I don't think my half-term is going to be as exciting as yours, though.'

'Well, mine wasn't exactly exciting,' she said. 'Just mixed up. You know, I didn't recognize my father at all. I mean I had a photograph of him, but in the photograph he was fatter and white, and his hair was dark and he didn't have a moustache. I mean, I didn't even recognize his voice! Did that happen to you?'

Lance looked down hastily at his feet. 'Well, I don't see too much of mine, actually.'

'Why not?'

'I told you. My parents aren't living together at the moment.'

'Are they divorced?'

His head shot up. 'Oh no!' he said, horrified. 'Nothing like that! It's just for the time being. He's working in Scotland, you see, and my mother didn't want to move there.' He'd got all serious-looking again. 'So anyway,' he stammered, 'I'll be staying with an aunt down on the south coast. By the sea.'

'I love the sea.'

He brightened up. 'Shall I bring you back some sea-weed?'

'Sure. We can hang it above the fireplace. Then it can be our Cabin in the Woods by the Sea.'

He grinned. 'By the way,' he said, 'there's something I've been meaning to tell you. This afternoon we had rugger practice.'

'How did you make out?'

He gave a thumbs-down sign.

'Nobody would pass the ball to me. I did manage to grab it once, but before I'd run a couple of feet, everyone was on top of me, calling me ... guess what.'

'Yank?'

He nodded.

'And it still hurts?'

'Yes. But I hurt all over anyway.'

'More beatings?'

'Yes. Because I'm so useless at fires and so slow. I go as fast as I can, but I feel so miserable that it makes me go slower.'

'I know it,' said Rusty. 'Sometimes when the morning bell rings, I feel so heavy inside that I can hardly move.'

'Trouble with me is, the more he beats me, the more miserable I feel and the slower I get.'

'Isn't it the end? I have that with lessons. The more I try in class, the more I ask questions or take an interest or be friendly, the more of a troublemaker they say I am.'

'But something really good happened to me today,' he added.

'Is that possible?' said Rusty wryly.

He smiled. 'It happened after the game. I was dragging myself off the pitch when some of the older boys who were watching started making comments about me. And I couldn't understand what they were saying. So I watched their mouths. And you're right. They hardly move their lips at all, the ones who talk that way. And I suddenly remembered you imitating them and I just started to laugh. And then I had a picture of all those marbles in their mouths and that made it worse and I couldn't stop. And I said, "I'm sorry, but I can't understand a single word you're saying. You're just going to have to move your mouths a bit when you speak to me, because us Yanks" – that nearly gave the game away, *us* Yanks – "we like to move our lips when we talk." And I just started laughing again. And a couple of the other chaps started laughing, too. And the ones with the tight mouths asked them what they were laughing at, and they pointed to me and said, "*Him!*" But the *best* thing was that the prefect I fag for had been watching this on the other side, and he came over and slapped me on the back and said, "We'll anglify you yet, Yank," and when he said *Yank* it didn't feel so horrid any more. It was O.K.!'

'And he's the one who beats you. Right?'

'He's the one who beats me the most.'

'So maybe he won't beat you any more.'

'If I don't light his fires properly he will.'

'O.K.,' she said, handing him a branch. 'From now on, you're in charge of this one. The next time we meet, you'll do it yourself.'

They turned the blankets and overalls over so that they would dry on the other side.

As Rusty stared into the fire, she remembered how she and her mother had sat in front of one, only a few nights back. She glanced at Lance who was gingerly placing a branch on the fire. She wanted to ask him how he got along with *his* mother, but he always looked so sad when she asked him about his family.

'It won't bite,' she said, when he jumped back quickly.

They blew out the lamps and, when the embers had almost died out, they opened the door of the Cabin and peered out.

'It's so cold,' moaned Rusty.

They stepped out and ran through the grass to the gate. 'So long, Cabin,' said Rusty over her shoulder.

'How long is your half-term?' she asked as they walked among the trees.

'From tomorrow until Tuesday morning.'

'When should we meet up? Wednesday?'

'I'd rather not. I have rugger on Thursday. I'd like to get a good night's sleep before that.'

'O.K. Thursday again. Then you can tell me how the practice went.'

Soon they were by the wall.

'Have a good half-term,' she whispered.

'I'll try.'

She had just begun to climb the wall when she stopped. 'Lance?'

'Yes.'

'Don't forget the seaweed.'

He smothered a laugh. 'O.K.'

'And don't laugh or we're in for it.'

He gave a loud snort, turned swiftly, and ran off in the direction of the field.

As Rusty began climbing up the scaffolding again, she found it more difficult, for the bars were so cold that they numbed her hands. She stuck her fingers in her mouth, and then warmed them under her armpits. Hauling herself up, she gritted her teeth as the wind bit into her cheeks and seeped into her ears.

It took her much longer than usual to undress and clean up her sneakers, for she could hardly move her fingers at all. She slipped in between the ice-cold sheets and lay there, rigid. Stiffly curled up, she drifted in and out of a fitful sleep.

She was woken by the sound of the rising bell. Outside, it was still dark. She watched as Judith Poole and the other girls stumbled around for their dressing gowns. She stretched across and took hold of hers. When the others had turned their backs, she pressed it to her face and took a long, hard sniff. She smiled. It smelled of wood-smoke.

27

The prefect left Rusty to walk down the driveway alone; she wanted to dash off to a lacrosse practice. Rusty, secretly relieved, promised not to tell on her.

Her mother was waiting for her at the school gates. As Rusty drew nearer, she was unnerved to see how pale and drawn her mother had become. She leaned forward to take Rusty's grip.

'It's O.K.,' said Rusty. 'I can manage.'

Her mother nodded weakly, and they crossed over the road to the bus-stop.

It wasn't until they were in the train that Peggy began talking. She was staring bleakly out of the window when she said, rather too lightly, 'How do you feel about not staying at school during the weekends? I mean,' she added, turning, 'do you think perhaps you would make friends more easily if you stayed?'

'Uh-uh.' She crossed her fingers in the pockets of her Beanie. 'I like coming back weekends. Why? Don't you want me to?'

'Of course I do. It's just that ...' She paused. 'Your father seems to think that you'd adjust to England more quickly if you remained for the whole term and we just saw you at half-terms and holidays. He's not accustomed to weekly boarding. He seems to think it's neither one thing nor the other.'

Rusty looked away. She felt choked. Boy, he'd only met her one evening.

'Doesn't he like me? I mean, did I do something wrong?'

'Of course you didn't. He only wants what's best for you.'

Her father was in his study when she arrived back. 'He is not to be disturbed,' said her grandmother.

Rusty hung up her hat and Beanie and took her grip up to her bedroom. She crept back down again, ran past the drawing room, knocked on the study door, and pushed it open.

Her father was sitting at a large, leather-topped desk covered with papers. He was wearing a dark-grey suit, but his bearing still seemed military. He glanced up quickly.

'Hi!' said Rusty. 'I thought I'd come and see you.'

She came in and closed the door firmly behind her. A small fire was glowing in the grate. She stood there, smiling sheepishly.

'How do you like the uniform? Awful, isn't it?'

He drew himself up. 'I did ask, Virginia, that I wasn't to be disturbed. I'll see you at dinner.' He gave a short wave of his hand indicating the door, and leaned over his papers again.

Rusty stepped towards the fire.

He looked up, staggered at her disobedience.

'It's O.K.,' she said. 'You go on. I'm just going to make up your fire a little.' And she picked up the tongs. 'I guess you do the same with coal as you do with wood.'

'Virginia, did you hear what I said?'

'Sure I did,' and she put some more coal on. 'I'm just making it a little more comfy for you. Now,' she said, turning around, 'do you want me to bring you in a cup of tea? I used to bring in Uncle Bruno a coffee when he was working, so I know how it is. Only he didn't do a lot of work at home. He tried to finish it at the office. He said he liked to forget about it as soon as he'd gotten back. But sometimes, when he was in the workshop, I'd go get him a nice cool beer, and he liked that.'

'Virginia, I asked you to leave.'

'I know it. But do you want me to come back with tea?'

'No. Leave the room. That is an order.'

Rusty gaped at him. 'An order? You sound like you're in the army.' She laughed. 'I guess you still are. Or are you?'

He sprang to his feet.

'O.K.,' said Rusty, backing towards the door. 'I didn't mean to bother you.' And with that she opened the door swiftly, only to find her grandmother hovering outside.

'I distinctly told you,' she snapped, 'not to disturb him.'

Supper was a polite affair. Rusty's father sat at the head of the table, her grandmother at one side, and Rusty and her mother opposite. Charlie was in bed. Most of the conversation took place between her father and grandmother, while her mother remained almost silent.

'And how is school, Virginia?' said her father.

'It's O.K.'

'Don't you feel you're missing something, not staying there at the weekends? When I was a boy, we used to get up to all sorts of japes then.'

'Uh-uh. I like coming back.'

Again, she crossed her fingers under the table.

'Well, I've decided to let you continue coming home for the time being, but if for any reason I feel it would be better for you to remain at school, arrangements will be made for you to do so.'

'Mother?' said Rusty, turning. 'Is that what you think?'

'I make the decisions in this house,' he said firmly.

Her grandmother gave a satisfied smile.

'You're kidding!' said Rusty. He sounded like something out of a Victorian melodrama.

'And that's another thing, Virginia. I would prefer it if slang was not used in the house.'

'What's wrong with slang?'

'I forbid it.'

'You *what*?'

Her grandmother's face turned almost purple. 'You see what I mean,' she said quietly.

Rusty felt her mother's hand on her arm.

'Come on, everyone,' she said. 'Let's not have an argument.'

But her father was glaring at her. 'Virginia, if you wish to continue coming back here each weekend, you had better learn the meaning of obedience.'

Before Rusty could answer back, her mother squeezed her so hard that Rusty held her breath instead. She picked up her fork and resumed eating.

'And, Virginia, we eat with a knife and fork at the same time in this country. I'm surprised that the school hasn't corrected you.'

Rusty ignored him.

'Virginia, did you hear what I said?'

She looked up. 'Yes, sir.'

'Right. That's enough. Go to your room!'

'What for? I haven't finished eating yet.'

He jerked his chair backwards and got to his feet. 'How dare you answer me back!'

'Why shouldn't I?'

Her grandmother gave a faint cry and held her napkin to her mouth.

'Virginia,' said her mother softly, 'do as your father says. You'll only make it worse for yourself.'

'But why am I being sent to my room? For eating the way I've been taught was correct for five years? Is that it?'

'Leave this room immediately!' bellowed her father.

Rusty flung her napkin on to the table and stalked out.

'I told you she was rebellious,' said Mrs Dickinson Senior. 'Margaret! What are you doing?'

'I'm going to have a word with her,' Peggy said, rising.

'You will do no such thing,' snapped her husband. 'Sit down.'

'No.'

'Margaret, that is an order.'

'Is it! How interesting.'

'Margaret!' said Mrs Dickinson Senior. 'Come back.'

But Peggy was halfway out of the room.

Mrs Dickinson Senior turned hastily to her son. 'You see what I've had to put up with!' she said.

Rusty hardly had time to sit on the bed when there was a knock at the door.

It was her mother. Rusty watched silently as she closed the door and came and leaned over the wooden footboard of the bed.

'Why did you have to go and say that?' she said.

'Say what?' said Rusty. She curled her legs up underneath herself. 'I don't go for all this "you must not answer me back" stuff. I mean, that's what dictators are like.'

'But why did you have to be sarcastic?'

'How was I sarcastic?'

'You didn't have to call him *sir*.'

'What! I wasn't being sarcastic – I was being respectful. We always used to call Uncle Bruno *sir* if we were getting told off.'

'Oh, I see,' said her mother, and she came and sat at the end of the bed.

'Only with Uncle Bruno, he'd tell us off and then we'd be miserable, and that'd make him miserable, so he'd either go take us out for a soda or start laughing.'

Her mother gave a sigh. 'I'm afraid he'll expect an apology from you.'

'For being respectful?'

'For answering back.'

'What's wrong with answering back? Aunt Hannah and Uncle Bruno never told us off for that.'

'You're not living with Uncle Bruno and Aunt Hannah now.'

Don't I know it, thought Rusty.

'Look,' said her mother. 'It's not going to be easy for us to live together again, but we've just got to muddle through somehow. We've all been away and had different experiences and we've got to . . .' She faltered '. . . try and be a family again. Your father hasn't even been here a week yet, and he's had a difficult enough time as it is with Charlie.'

'He's been getting the "treatment", right?'

Her mother nodded. 'It's been Uncle Harvey did this and Uncle Harvey said that and –'

'And all the rest! I guess me talking about Uncle Bruno must have made it even worse.'

'When did you do that?'

'In his study; you know, after Grandmother told me not to go in there.'

'Oh dear,' she said. 'That's his inner sanctum.'

'Don't go Latin on me. I have enough of that at school.'

'It means it's his holiest of holy places. No one must venture in there unless invited or on very serious business.'

'I asked if he'd like a cup of tea. That's serious business, isn't it?'

'Oh, Virginia!' she said, unable to suppress a smile.

They looked at each other.

'Mother,' Rusty said slowly, 'I *still* can't get used to being called Virginia. I know it's me, but it feels like I'm standing next to someone. Do you feel that when someone calls you Margaret?'

Her mother looked startled for a moment, and then nodded.

'Yes, I do a bit. It's almost as if I should be the way I was four years ago.'

'But that's how it is with me!' said Rusty. 'Like I should be a little kid.'

'But you are a "little kid".'

'Oh, Mother, I'm almost a teenager.'

'A what?'

'A teenager.'

'What on earth is a teenager?'

'Someone who's thir*teen*, or fourteen, or fifteen . . . Don't you call them that here?'

'I've never heard the expression.'

'Well, in the States we even have teen *magazines*. Anyway, how come all the people in Devon call you Peggy?'

'There were *three* Margarets in the W.V.S. when I joined, Margaret, Maggie and Meg. So I became Peggy and it caught on.' She stood up. 'Look, I'll try and smuggle up some bread and hot milk, but think about what I said, won't you?'

'About apologizing?'

'Yes.'

'O.K.'

As soon as the door was closed, Rusty drew out a small bundle of letters from under the mattress and pulled out the snapshot of Uncle Bruno and Skeet with the fish. She had always thought of Uncle Bruno as being her father. It must be awful for her real one to come back and find her and Charlie comparing him with someone else . . . Especially if the someone else was more fun.

At breakfast there was no sign of her father. Rusty was informed that he would only be eating with them at supper, so Charlie, who had his earlier, would not be eating with him at all. Rusty found this very odd.

It wasn't until after lunch that her grandmother said she had permission to go to his study. After she knocked at the door and entered, he gazed disapprovingly at her jeans and motioned her in.

'I believe you have something to say, Virginia.'

Rusty held her hands behind her back and crossed her fingers.

'Uh-huh.'

He looked puzzled. 'Does that mean yes or no?'

'It means yes. Uh-huh means yes. Uh-uh means no.'

He cleared his throat awkwardly and clasped his hands, resting them on the desk of scattered papers.

'Boy,' she said, 'have you got a lot of papers to sort out.'

He frowned.

'Oh yeah,' she said. 'I came to apologize for answering back.'

He drew himself up. 'You realize,' he said, 'that an apology means that you promise never to do it again, don't you?'

'I guess,' she said.

'Guessing is hardly enough.'

'What if you went nuts? I mean, I'm not saying you could go nuts. But what if you said, "Rusty, your hair is green and you have three legs"? Then I'd have to disagree, wouldn't I? I'd have to say, "No. My hair is not green and I only have two." Legs, I mean, not two hairs.'

Her father stared at her.

''Cause if I had two hairs I'd look bald and you wouldn't be able to see what colour they were anyway.' She swallowed. 'I remember once Uncle Bruno telling me about Spike Jones and the City Slickers, and one of 'em said to the other, "You've got thin hair," and he said, wait for it, "Well, who wants *fat* hair?"'' She paused. 'Get it?'

It was obvious that if her father did, he didn't think it amusing. If only he'd smile, just once.

As she stood there, she realized that she'd mentioned Uncle Bruno again.

'Your mother has suggested that we go out tomorrow

for a drive,' her father said. 'I have made arrangements to borrow a car for the day. I shall be picking it up this evening.' He looked down at her jeans. 'I shall expect you to be dressed appropriately.'

'That sounds neat. I mean the trip, not the –'

'Yes,' interrupted her father. 'I think that will do. I'll see you at dinner this evening. And by the way, your mother has explained the misunderstanding over "sir" Father or Daddy is quite sufficient.'

Rusty waited for an apology, but none came.

'And now, if you don't mind, I have rather a lot of work to do.'

On Sunday afternoon they all assembled in the hall in their Sunday best. Mr Dickinson gazed at Rusty's L. L. Bean coat and saddle shoes. 'Have you no English clothes?' he said.

'Only my school uniform and I don't want to wear that out. Especially when Mother gave up her coupons to pay for it.'

Peggy blushed. Underneath her heavy W.V.S. coat she wore the same tweed skirt and cardigan that she had changed into the night her husband had returned.

Mrs Dickinson Senior was decked out in navy blue. Navy-blue hat, navy-blue coat, gloves, shoes, and discreetly darned pale silk stockings. Her father, who wore a dark suit several sizes too big for him, carried a trenchcoat over his arm.

Charlie, who was holding on to his teddy-bear with fierce determination, was in flannel shorts, tie and an old green coat. His curly red hair, although flattened down with water, was already springing outward rebelliously.

Mr Dickinson led them out through the door and down the road, almost in formation. He looked so stern that Rusty had a fit of the giggles.

They turned a corner and stepped across the road to a

278

car that was the image of the Bomb, only somewhat newer. Mr Dickinson stood by the bonnet.

'Mother,' he said, 'you sit in the front. Margaret, at the back with the children.'

As they climbed into the car, Charlie exclaimed, 'Why are you getting in the back, Mummy?'

'Well, it'll be rather nice for us to be sitting together and looking out of the window, won't it?' she replied.

As soon as everyone was seated, her father started the engine. It gave a gentle rumble and moved forward.

They had hardly driven two miles when Charlie piped up, 'Mummy, why is that man driving?'

'Charlie,' whispered Peggy, 'that's your daddy.'

Over his shoulder Mr Dickinson stated quietly, 'Margaret, I have asked you to call him Charles. He's not a pleb, you know.'

'What's a pleb?' asked Rusty.

Peggy put her finger hastily to her lips.

'I don't like him,' said Charlie. 'When is he going away?'

'Charlie,' said his mother firmly, 'don't be unkind.'

'Margaret,' warned Mr Dickinson.

'I mean Charles,' she added quickly.

'Are we going to Beatie's?' Charlie wanted to know.

'No, darling, we're just going out to see the countryside.'

'Can I pick flowers?'

'I don't think there'll be many out now, but yes, if we see some, you can pick them.'

He gave a satisfied sigh and wriggled himself back into the seat.

Rusty gazed out of the window at all the bombed buildings, and for the first time she began to feel sympathy for the many people who had lost their homes and their loved ones. She remembered Harry's remark about the children who had been away in America, how they couldn't understand what he was talking about; for a moment she felt angry at her parents for sending her away. She had a sense that something very important had happened in England, and she knew she had missed it.

Gradually they left the buildings behind and emerged on to the open road. Charlie stood up, attempting to see the trees. Her mother sat him on her knee, while her father and grandmother chatted pleasantly, mostly about the weather and about people whom they knew from the past.

They stopped by a pretty little stone bridge that draped itself over a tiny hill. A stream gurgled underneath it. Her mother clasped Charlie tightly and held him over the wall so that he could see. Rusty stood beside them and rested her elbows on it.

Mrs Dickinson Senior remained seated in the car, while Rusty's father paced awkwardly up and down the lane.

'Look, Mummy,' yelled Charlie, pointing. 'A fish! I saw a fish!'

'Let's go for a walk,' said Peggy suddenly, and she lowered Charlie back on to the ground.

'And explore,' he said.

'Yes, explore.'

'Can I come too?' said Rusty.

'Of course you can.' She turned. 'Roger, we're going for a walk. Are you coming?'

He hesitated.

'And what shall *I* do here on my own?' said Mrs Dickinson Senior peevishly.

Rusty's father glanced at her and then cleared his throat.

'I'd better stay with Mother,' he said.

Peggy nodded, and the three of them began walking.

For no apparent reason, as soon as they were out of sight they started to run quite wildly. Charlie released his mother's hand, thrust his teddy bear into her arms, and began shrieking, his small arms pumping madly up and down as he jumped and kicked loose stones.

Rusty lifted him on to her back and galloped beside her mother, making whinnying noises like a horse.

Exhausted, they stopped at an old stile and leaned over it, catching their breaths. As the wind shook the hedges, Rusty was vaguely aware of Charlie singing, 'Ten Green Bottles' and getting all the numbers wrong.

'I suppose,' said her mother quietly, 'we'd better be getting back.'

'I guess so,' murmured Rusty.

By the time the car was in sight it had begun to rain and they were running again, only this time without the lightness they had possessed earlier.

They clattered over the bridge and across the lane, and dived, laughing, into the back-seat of the car.

'I'm glad to see someone has enjoyed themselves,' said Rusty's grandmother stiffly. 'You *were* rather a long time.'

'Party pooper,' muttered Rusty under her breath.

Her father climbed into the car and slammed the door. By now the sky had grown dark. The engine gave a splutter, followed by another splutter, followed immediately by silence.

Rusty glanced at her mother. She caught her eye and then turned swiftly away.

Her father attempted to start the car again, but with no result.

'I'm sorry, Mother,' he said. 'I'm afraid I shall just have to have a look at it.'

He jumped out of the car, pulled up the collar of his trenchcoat, and folded back the bonnet.

Outside, the rain began to beat heavily on the roof.

'Mummy,' said Charlie, 'why don't you mend it?'

Mrs Dickinson Senior turned around sharply. 'Don't talk nonsense, child. Your father is going to fix it.'

'But that's what mummies do,' he stated. 'They're the ones that fix cars.'

'Where on earth did you pick that idea up, Charles?'

Charlie was confused. He tugged at his mother's sleeve. 'Mummies do fix cars, don't they?'

'Some do,' she said awkwardly. 'Not all of them. Auntie Ivy doesn't, does she? And she's a mummy.'

Charlie thought for a moment, then sat back. 'Oh yes,' he said simply.

Within minutes he sat up again.

'But *you* do, don't you?'

She nodded.

'So why don't you mend this one?'

'Well, I expect Daddy would like to do it himself.'

'Is he really my daddy?'

'Yes, of course he is.'

'But Uncle Harvey said that my real daddy would play with me.'

'If you're nice to him, I expect he will. But you haven't been very nice, have you?'

'But I don't like him,' he said. 'So he can't be my real daddy, can he?'

Half an hour passed. Rusty could see that her mother was growing tense. She'd already smoked several cigarettes. Suddenly she stubbed out the one she was smoking and climbed out of the car.

'Margaret!' said Rusty's grandmother. 'What are you doing?'

Before Rusty could stop him, Charlie said, 'She's going to mend the car.'

Mrs Dickinson Senior turned around slowly and glared at him. 'Charles, if I hear one more word out of you, you will be going to bed early *and* without any tea.'

Very slowly, Rusty turned the handle under her window so that she could eavesdrop on what was going on outside.

Her mother was standing beside her father.

'It's all right, Margaret,' he said, irritated. 'Just be patient.'

'Let me have a look. I did a course in car mechanics with the W.V.S.'

'Yes, I'm sure you did, dear,' he said. 'I suppose they taught you how to put petrol in it and clean the wind-screen.'

Boy, thought Rusty. And she had been sent up to her room for sarcasm! *He* should be sent to the moon.

'No, Roger,' said her mother politely, 'but I know this type of car very well. You're probably used to army vehicles. At least let me have a look. It might only be water in the juice. It's quite common in these cars.'

'Margaret, I am quite capable of dealing with a car engine.'

'I know you are, Roger. But so am I.'

There was an awful silence.

Rusty drew herself away from the window. She could feel her heart pounding, only she couldn't figure out why. I mean, no one was shouting. No one was throwing their arms up in the air, or hitting the car with their fists. On the contrary, both of them were being as polite as anything.

Through the spattered windshield Rusty watched her mother peer under the bonnet. Her father stood back, his hands on his hip.

'All right, Margaret,' she heard him say. 'Have your little look, but then please leave me to deal with it.'

Rusty's mother threw off her coat, pushed up her sleeves, and then, very gracefully, she put one leg up on to the wing.

'Well, really!' exclaimed Mrs Dickinson Senior. 'What does she think she's doing?'

'She's mending the engine!' said Charlie, exasperated.

Just then, her mother gave a cry.

Rusty hurriedly rolled down her window and peered out. 'What is it?' she yelled.

'Same old problem,' Peggy said over her shoulder.

Rusty saw her look up and smile at her husband. Rusty couldn't see his expression, since he had his back to her, but, from her mother's hurried dive back into the engine, she imagined it wasn't too wonderful.

As she tinkered with the engine, her mother grew visibly more relaxed. Even when her father refused to fetch something from the boot, she appeared quite unperturbed, and went and fetched it herself.

Rusty noticed that although her father was great at giving orders, he was terrible at receiving them. Her mother had to ask him several times to turn the engine over and give the self-starter a push before, with very bad grace, he flung the door open and turned on the car light.

'What on earth is she up to, Roger?' said his mother. 'Really, you know how hopeless she is.'

Charlie sprang forward angrily. Rusty quickly grabbed his teddy and moved the legs up and down. 'Say, look at Teddy, Charlie. He's dancing.'

He swung around and sat down with a bump.

> *'I'm singing in the rain,'*

she sang,

> *'I'm singing in the rain.*
> *What a glorious feeling, I'm happy again.'*

And she threw the bear up in the air.

Suddenly the engine spluttered into life. Her mother gave a thumbs-up sign and began wiping her hands on a rag. Her father sank into the driver's seat and slammed the door.

Outside, her mother folded the bonnet back into place, snatched up her coat and the tools, and ran around to the boot. Inside the car, Charlie was jumping up and down excitedly.

'See? I told you. Mummies *always* mend cars.'

Peggy opened the door and stepped in.

'Ugh!' cried Charlie. 'You're wet!'

Her hair was dripping down her face in rivulets and her clothes were clinging to her in dark damp patches.

'Oh, Mother,' said Rusty.

She put a finger on her lips.

'Was it water in the juice again?' asked Charlie.

'That's right, darling. And a bit of grit.'

As soon as her mother had closed the door, her father turned off the light and the car moved forward. In the half-light, Rusty was acutely aware of the silence. Her grandmother was staring stiffly ahead, her father the same, while her mother gazed out of the window. Meanwhile, Charlie was making his teddy-bear sing and dance, only now it wasn't 'Singing in the Rain'.

> *'There's water in the juice,'*

he sang,

> *'There's water in the juice,*
> *Ee aye the addio, there's water in the juice.*
> *There's . . .'*

He stopped. 'I've forgotten it,' he said. 'What's the next line, Mummy?'

'I've forgotten too.'

He turned to look at Rusty.

'Uh, let me see,' she said.

> *'There's dirt inside the gas, there's dirt inside the gas,*
> *Ee aye the addio, there's dirt inside the gas.'*

'And then what?'

'I can't remember. Uh.

'*The jets are all fouled up,*'

she sang.

'Yes,' he cried. 'I like that one. *Fouled* up.'

'O.K. Ready, set, go!'

'*The jets are all fouled up,*'

they sang,

'*The jets are all fouled up,*
Ee aye the addio, the —'

'That will do,' thundered her father. 'I don't want to hear one more word from either of you for the rest of the journey!'

They fell silent.

Over his shoulder, Rusty noticed that he was gripping the wheel so tightly that his knuckles were white.

'Why can't we sing, Mummy?' said Charlie.

'Because Daddy has to concentrate on his driving and he can't drive if you make such a —'

'Margaret!' he roared. 'I am quite capable of driving a vehicle in any conditions. The reason is quite clear. It is because I say so. And that is that.'

'Come on, darling,' Peggy whispered. 'See how dark it is now. You lean back and close your eyes for a few minutes.'

Charlie wriggled back into the seat and drew his teddy close to him.

Peggy lit another cigarette. In the flicker of the match-flame, her hands shook.

28

Rusty attempted to explain to Lance how awful it was at her grandmother's and how her parents were like strangers with one another; but she soon gave up, because it upset him so much that he couldn't even look at her. And she remembered then that his own parents weren't living together.

As the weeks progressed, Rusty managed to smuggle odd bits and pieces – like her trapper cap and Windbreaker – back to the school, and lived for clear nights.

Lance began to grow more cheerful, but he tended to come, weather permitting, always on Tuesdays and Thursdays, so that sometimes Rusty visited the Cabin on her own. It took him some time to pick up the knack of making fires. It wasn't easy learning in the middle of the night when he was tired and it was freezing cold; but Rusty never gave up encouraging him, because doing so took her mind off her own troubles.

And Lance tutored her in Latin, although progress was slow, since the lessons couldn't start until the fire had been lit. Rusty still disliked the language, but it seemed to cheer Lance up. Unlike Rusty, he liked his Latin master, who was apparently so enthusiastic about his subject that Lance had grown to love it.

As November blew icily into December, Rusty lived in a strange, dark sort of tunnel. The girls continued to ignore her, the teachers continued to dislike her, and the weekends grew more nightmarish. Soon she grew so adept at daydreaming that she could turn off her surroundings and enter her own private cinema in seconds. Every day she looked anxiously out of the window at the sky. If it was the slightest bit overcast, her stomach shrank so much that it seemed to fold itself back to the base of her spine. Rain was her jailer.

One weekend she discovered, quite by accident, that her parents did not sleep in the same room, and it worried her. After all, Aunt Hannah and Uncle Bruno even slept in the same bed. When she and Skeet and Kathryn were little, they used to crawl into it with them at weekends and romp around on Uncle Bruno's knees.

Her mother grew distant and began to work again at the nearest W.V.S. centre and, although it was never said in Rusty's presence, she knew that her father and grandmother disapproved.

And Charlie began to throw tantrums. He reminded Rusty of a cat she knew, which hissed at you when you approached it, but, as soon as you stroked its chest, it became all soft and friendly again. But Rusty was prevented from hugging him. Her father said that he was a boy, not a baby, and that he'd have to learn to act like a man.

One evening she and Lance were sitting in the Cabin in the Woods, talking. At about 1 A.M. it had started to rain, so they couldn't leave. It was their last evening together before the Christmas holidays.

'Funny,' said Rusty, 'I usually hate the rain, but now that I'm here, I like it. Means I get to stay longer.'

'If it doesn't stop, we'll have to leave in it and get wet,' said Lance anxiously.

Rusty shrugged. 'Oh well.' And she threw another branch on to the fire. 'I wish we didn't have to have a vacation. It's so long, too. Over four weeks!' She groaned.

'I thought you hated school,' said Lance. He gave the fire a prod with a branch. 'Do you think you're getting used to it?'

'To school? Are you kidding?'

'Well, *I'll* be glad to get back to school.'

Rusty was astounded. 'Are you nuts?'

He shook his head. 'It's far better than tiptoeing around and being polite at my aunt's. At least at school you're not miserable on your own. There's plenty of other people there as miserable as you are.'

She pulled one of the old blankets around her shoulders, like an Indian squaw. 'It's *this* place I'll miss,' she said. 'I feel like it's my home now, don't you?'

He stared into the fire. 'I told you,' he said. 'School's my home, really.'

'But, Lance,' she said, leaning forward with intensity, 'if you come with me to America, Aunt Hannah and Uncle Bruno, they'd let you live with us, I'm sure they would.'

He glanced at her out of the corner of his eye. 'You're not really going to America, are you, though?'

'I certainly am,' said Rusty hotly.

'So why not now?'

'Because it's too darned cold, that's why. I'm going to wait till it gets warmer.'

'And if it doesn't?'

'I don't know. When I'm good and ready.'

He looked away.

'You don't believe me, do you?'

'I'm not sure.'

'You wait,' she said, huddling closer to the fire. 'As soon as I have some money, I'll get a train to Exeter, catch the Plymouth train, and then smuggle on board a ship.'

They fell silent. A large gust of wind howled through the trees outside.

'I wonder,' said Rusty quietly, 'I wonder what everyone back home is doing. I can't imagine Christmas without them. No Thanksgiving was bad enough. But no Christmas . . .' She lowered her head.

Lance turned away, embarrassed. Hastily, she brushed the tears aside.

It was past three o'clock when the rain stopped and they left the Cabin. By the time they had emerged from the woods, Rusty's sneakers were caked with mud, and although it was no longer raining, a mist-like drizzle spattered their faces and seeped into their dressing gowns. After she and Lance had wished each other a hurried Merry Christmas, Rusty pulled the flaps of her trapper cap down over her ears and began climbing the wall.

The lacrosse pitch squelched noisily under her feet. As soon as she reached the hard ground under the scaffolding, she scraped the mud from her sneakers and wiped them in the grass.

She stared up at the scaffolding, gripped one of the bars, and hauled herself up quickly. Her foot skidded along it. She stopped. Funny, she thought, less than two months earlier she was trying to throw herself off this scaffolding. Now she was struggling to stay on it.

By the time she managed to reach the dormitory window, she was damp all the way through to her pyjamas. She pulled off her sneakers and two pairs of socks and carried them, together with her uniform and sponge-bag, out of the dormitory and down the stairs to the washroom. She didn't dare turn on the light. Instead, she propped her torch on the small window-ledge above one of the sinks. Her teeth chattering, she stripped and hung her Windbreaker, cardigan, pyjamas and underwear over all three radiators. Shivering and naked, she washed, put on her uniform, minus her cardigan and socks which were slowly steaming. She undid her plaits, rubbed her hair vigorously with a towel, brushed and replaited it and then desperately began cleaning her sneakers with a wet handkerchief.

She was shocked to hear the morning bell ringing. She hurriedly pulled on her cardigan and a pair of socks, stepped into her sandals, grabbed the rest of her clothing and sneakers, and wrapped them in her dressing gown. Already she could hear footsteps coming down the stairs. She turned the light on, ran back to the windowsill, and flung her torch into her dressing-gown bundle. Then, as casually as she could, she picked up her sponge-bag and towel and sauntered towards the door, where she met Judith Poole and the three girls from her dormitory.

'Order mark,' growled Judith Poole sleepily. 'You know you're not supposed to get up before the bell rings.' She glanced up at Rusty's head. 'Have you washed your hair?'

'Uh-huh. It was getting itchy.'

'Oh, leave her,' said her friend, Reggie. 'If you give her any more order marks, the House'll do badly.'

'There is such a thing as honour,' snapped Judith. 'You know I don't like giving order marks.'

I bet, thought Rusty, sneaking quickly out of the door.

'But it's my duty to report any . . .'

Rusty was already out of earshot.

It was during assembly, when the form places were being announced, that Rusty learned to her surprise that she had come in tenth in her form. Second from the bottom. From all the comments made about her school-work, she had expected to be last. But her English was reasonably good, and by the end of the term she was beginning to pick up the mathematics and scrape through the history tests. What was even more surprising was that she was not the worst in the form when it came to Latin. Just the next to worst. That was thanks to Lance's testing her vocabulary and verb declensions. However, in French, geography, scripture and botany she was still hopeless.

She was so numbed with tiredness that it all passed over her head. All she was conscious of, as she sat there with the other girls, was her damp cardigan and socks clinging to her.

They stood up to sing the school song. When they had

291

finished, Rusty was amazed to see that some of the girls were quietly dabbing their eyes. Rusty gazed, stupefied, at them. Boy, they had actually been moved by the words of the song; about the glory and honour of the school and all that stuff. She shook her head. At least she had survived the first term. Now all she had to do was find a way of surviving the holidays.

As soon as Mrs Grace had opened the door of Rusty's father's house, Peggy sent her upstairs to wash her hands. On the way up, she leaned over the banisters and saw her mother go towards the study. She was carrying the envelope with Rusty's school report in it.

In the bathroom Rusty stared at her face in the mirror. It surprised her to see how much thinner she had become. She took a good look at her teeth. When Lower Four A had to visit a dentist, she was the only one who didn't have to have any fillings. When the dentist said she had teeth like a race horse, someone had commented, 'And the brains of one.' And Filly had actually said, 'Horses are jolly clever, if you want to know.' Rusty had been surprised. For a moment she thought Filly was sticking up for her. But she wasn't. She was sticking up for horses.

Rusty dreaded meeting her father. She had hardly finished having her tea when the summons came. Her grandmother strode in, poker-faced, and asked her to go and see him immediately.

When Rusty opened the study door, she found him standing with his back to the fire. 'Close the door,' he said.

She did so, and stood rather awkwardly in front of it.

'I hope,' he said angrily, 'you have some explanation for this.' And he waved the report.

'Uh-huh,' she began. 'See, back in America we don't start some subjects until high school. We sort of catch up later, I guess. And the history I studied was American history, and some of the spelling I learned was different.

For instance, in America we spell theatre with an *er*, here you spell it *re*, see. And some of the words have tw l's instead of one *l*, so it's confusing. I don't think I did too badly, though. I only came tenth, and one place from the bottom in Latin, and it's my first term.'

'Virginia,' he said quietly, 'I have yet to come to your academic achievements. What concerns me is your appalling behaviour. You seem to have a record number of marks.' He slammed the paper with his fist. 'Bad marks, order marks, punctuality marks, and even' – he paused as if to gain breath – 'a *discipline* mark!'

'Oh those,' said Rusty. 'They're on account of my accent.'

'Are you trying to tell me that you were given a *punctuality* mark because of your accent?'

Rusty nodded. 'Because of my accent, no one'd show me around, so I kept getting lost in the hallways, and that made me late.'

'And the *discipline* mark?'

'Oh, that's because I spoke to a boy. Do you believe it?'

'You spoke to a boy?' he said slowly.

'Uh-huh. See, he was sent to Vermont, where Grandma Fitz and Gramps live. That's Mr and Mrs Fitzgibbons. They're Aunt Hannah's mom and pop. And I hadn't met –'

'Virginia!' he roared. 'If I ever hear of you talking to or having anything to do with a boy, you will be confined to your room for your entire holiday period. Is that understood?'

Rusty stared at him aghast.

'The only males you will be allowed to associate with,' he continued, 'are myself and your brother.'

'But why?'

'Because I say so.'

'Big deal!'

re you speak to me in that manner! How dare

uldn't I? I think you're just about the meanest
r met.'

Go to your room this instant,' he said, stepping forward.

'My pleasure,' she shouted back.

She slammed the door behind her and stormed up the stairs. As she passed the bathroom door, her mother flung it open.

'Virginia,' she said, 'what's happening?'

'Father's sent me to my room. And that's where he'd probably like me to stay.' She whirled around to face her mother. 'I wish I'd never come back here. I wish I was with Aunt Hannah and Uncle Bruno.'

It was too late. The words had left her lips. Her mother looked devastated. She turned hastily away.

As Rusty hauled herself up the stairs, she felt horrible. She'd have given anything just to die there and then; just to go to sleep and never wake up.

She threw open her bedroom door and crawled into bed. She was too tired and too cold even to cry.

She was woken up by the bedside lamp being turned on. Her mother was standing by the bed with a cup of cocoa and two slices of bread and margarine. Rusty pushed herself up to a sitting position. The room was so cold that a great cloud of mist rose from her mouth. Her mother handed her the cocoa and sat quietly at the end of the bed.

Rusty peered at her over the mug.

'I'm awfully sorry about what I said,' she whispered. 'I was just so mad. He never lets me explain or anything . . .' Her voice trailed away.

'Drink that cocoa and eat up,' Peggy said.

Rusty slowly sipped the drink and ate her way through

what she realized was her supper. When she had finished, she pulled the blankets and eiderdown up to her neck.

'I'm sorry about the report, too,' she said. 'I'm trying awful hard, but sometimes it just doesn't go in.'

'Do you think,' said her mother hesitantly, 'that you'd get on better with your schoolwork if you stayed at school?'

'Oh no,' said Rusty quickly. 'I'm doing O.K. Even with Latin. *Amo, amas, amat, amamus, amatis, amant.* See? I love. You love. He, she, it loves.' She paused.

'Look,' said Peggy, 'try and be patient with your father. He's not used to being with children. It's all very strange to him.'

Why was it, thought Rusty, that she had to be patient with everyone? She had to be patient with Charlie, patient with her grandmother, lose her accent, and now be patient with her father. No one was patient with her.

'Mother,' she said slowly, 'I'm not going to apologize to him for answering back, because I don't think it's wrong.'

'Oh, Virginia.'

'I'm sorry.'

'Well, I'm afraid you're confined to your room until you do.'

'But that's blackmail! I mean, what am I going to do about Christmas shopping?' She paused. 'Oh well, since I don't have an allowance, I guess I couldn't buy anything anyway.'

Her mother stood up.

'I'll try and see if he'll compromise. But he's pretty displeased about your bad conduct at school, and your grandmother is quite horrified.'

'But, Mother, I got a whole bunch of marks just for saying "O.K."'

'And some, I suspect, for answering back?'

'A couple.'

Her mother looked embarrassed for a moment. 'Your

father also tells me that you received a discipline mark for talking to a boy.'

Rusty nodded.

'Why, exactly, did you speak to him?'

'He'd been sent to Vermont. He'd even gone skating on Lake Champlain, winters. It was an accident. I heard someone call him *Yank*. I thought it was me first of all, but then I saw this boy across the road, so I called out "Yank" too, and he turned around. I mean, he was from New England.'

'Well, I'd rather you didn't do it again,' she said gently. 'That behaviour is rather looked down on here. Do you understand?'

'No, I don't. What's wrong with talking to a boy?' She was about to add, 'He's my buddy,' but she swallowed the words down quickly.

'I know it's difficult, but if a girl is known as someone who associates with boys, she's not considered "nice". There'll be plenty of time for all that sort of thing when you've finished university.'

Rusty nodded dumbly. She was too staggered to speak.

Until Christmas Eve, Rusty stayed in her room except for breakfast and lunch. She was allowed a small electric heater, but it gave out little warmth, and she soon developed blisters on her legs from sitting too close to it. One day she cleared her dressing-table and spread out her stencilling equipment. At first she couldn't summon up any enthusiasm at all, but gradually, as she began making sketches and mixing the paints on an old plate, the colours seemed to cheer her up.

She dipped the squares of thick card that Grandma Fitz had given her into a solution of linseed oil and turpentine, dried them, drew designs on them, and carved them out with her special stencil knife. Once she had cut out the designs, she pressed the cards firmly on to the paper.

Using one flower-and-leaf design, she painted the leaves

green and the flowers with the mustard-yellow paint. One design was of a single round-headed flower, stem and leaves. She painted the flower crimson and the leaves and stem brown. In between the leaves she placed a tiny stencil of small-petalled flowers and painted them yellow.

She remembered the time when Grandma Fitz had taken her to visit some old houses in New Hampshire and Massachusetts. They had travelled hundreds of miles to see them, and each time they had walked into one of them Rusty had been astounded, for on the walls, curtains and bedspreads there had been an extraordinary array of different stencil designs. Because some of them had been painted as far back as the 1800s, the paint was a little faded, but Rusty could still see them as clear as clear. There were leaves and wild flowers, running vines, hearts, acorns, birds, pineapples, baskets and urns of flowers and fruit, weeping willow trees, men and women in horse-drawn carriages or in sleighs, and they were painted on lampshades and boxes, in the panels of doors and on furniture, in the richest and palest of reds, greens, Prussian blues, black, rust and ochre.

As she sat in her bleak bedroom, the memories of those trips with her American grandmother slowly flooded back; and as she started remembering some of the old traditional designs, she felt she was back in the Fitzes' home in Vermont, with everything spread out all over the long, cherry-red table, in front of a great roaring fire.

The night before Christmas Eve, Rusty's father granted her permission to go with her mother and Charlie to see the Christmas lights.

They took a train to London. Rusty was disappointed. Compared with the Christmas lights in America, the English ones were a washout. But Charlie was completely entranced by them.

'It's the first time he's seen Christmas lights,' explained her mother. 'He's been used to the blackout.'

Christmas Day was orderly and quiet. After a polite meal of chicken and vegetables, they all went into the drawing room, where a small Christmas tree stood in the corner. It was so unlike the noisy Vermont Christmases, where the tree was as high as the ceiling, and where endless gifts and candy and popcorn hung from the branches and filled half the floor space. As they sat down, and her father stood by the tree handing out the parcels, Rusty suddenly spotted a group of packages from America addressed to her.

'I paid a visit to Devon, the last week of your term,' explained her mother, 'just to check that the roof hadn't fallen in, and they were there, waiting for you. Mrs Hatherley thought we might be spending Christmas there, so she hadn't bothered to send them on.'

Mrs Dickinson Senior cleared her throat. 'I hope you'll open your family's presents first, Virginia,' she said stiffly.

Luckily the Omsks and Fitzes had sent Charlie presents too: a car that you wound up with a key, coloured pencils, and a large jigsaw puzzle made of wood.

From her father Rusty received writing paper and stamps for her thank-you letters, and from her grand-mother handkerchiefs. Her mother gave her a small hand-made doll.

'Thank you, Mother,' said Rusty, hiding her dismay. She knew it must have been hard getting a doll, but it made her feel like such a little child.

Eventually she opened the presents from America.

Jinkie had sent two pairs of elegant white bras and pants, Alice a warm tan-and-green-plaid shirt, Skeet a beautiful fishing fly, Janey a pair of bobby socks, and Kathryn the latest Nancy Drew mystery book.

From Grandma Fitz and Gramps she received a book called *Early American Stencilling on Walls and Furniture* by

Janet Waring. Together with the book were jars of paint, linseed oil, turpentine and spare cards. From Aunt Hannah there was a huge ochre-coloured sweater with a big *R* on it in a russet colour.

'It's a sloppy Joe!' she yelled.

The last parcel was from Uncle Bruno, and was so well wrapped that it took her a while to battle through all the cardboard. Inside was a record.

'Frank Sinatra!' she whispered.

'Thank goodness we don't have a gramophone,' said her grandmother.

'It's O.K.,' said Rusty. 'I know this one by heart. It's my favourite. That's why Uncle Bruno sent it. I can imagine it going round and round, and I'll hear the words and the tune and everything.'

Just then she noticed that Charlie was gazing up at her, entranced. He stared at her for a moment and then suddenly began pushing the car along the floor.

'Broom, broom!' he growled.

It was the final Friday before Rusty's return to school. Charlie had gone to bed, and Rusty was in the bathroom dipping several cards into a solution of linseed oil and turpentine to make them more durable. She lined the bath-tub with newspaper and pegged the cards on to a piece of string she had attached over it. She was just opening the door to leave when she heard her father's voice rising loudly from the drawing room.

'I've never heard anything so absurd!' he shouted. 'Go to university? What are you thinking of?'

Boy, thought Rusty, her father was on her side. He didn't want her to go to university, either. Maybe she could go to art school after all. She couldn't quite hear her mother. Words like 'independent', 'more security', 'women nowadays', came drifting up the stairs.

'And all this Latin is quite absurd.'

'But she needs it for university.'

'Quite. So if she doesn't do it, then the subject of her going need never rise again.'

Better and better, thought Rusty.

She slipped out on to the landing.

'At least let her continue these next two terms in the same form. It would be cruel to have her put in a B form now.'

'The B's?' gulped Rusty.

'After all,' continued her mother, 'you're the one who's worried about her being unsettled.'

As Rusty crept down the stairs, she heard her father say, 'And when she's finished at school, she'll do a good cookery course *and* if she's fortunate she'll make a good marriage.'

Rusty was stunned. She didn't want to do a cookery course either.

'Well, I want her to have a career,' said her mother.

'Margaret!' said her grandmother. 'What can you be thinking of?'

'You've done perfectly well without a career,' said her father.

'But I have enjoyed earning my own money.'

There was a pause.

'And when did you ever earn your own money?'

'In Devon. As a mechanic.'

'But I thought that was voluntary.'

'The work I did for the W.V.S. was, but I was paid for private work.'

'Yes. Well,' her father said at last, 'it's hardly the sort of thing to brag about.'

'Anyway, dear,' said Mrs Dickinson Senior, 'the War's behind us. We've all had to do strange things. Now we've got to get back to normal.'

Just then the telephone rang. Rusty dived back up to

the bathroom as Mrs Grace came shuffling into the hall to answer it.

Rusty kept the bathroom door slightly ajar.

'Peggy?' said Mrs Grace into the receiver. 'I'm sorry, but there's no Peggy here.'

The drawing-room door opened and Rusty's mother came into the hallway. 'It's all right, Mrs Grace,' she said. 'That's for me. Hello. Peggy here.'

Rusty opened the door a fraction wider.

'Ivy! How lovely to hear you. How are you?'

Rusty was about to close the door when she noticed the dismay on her mother's face.

'What!' she whispered. 'Are you sure?'

Rusty watched her push her hand through her hair.

'Yes ... Yes. But why didn't they let you know sooner? ... I see.'

Rusty knew something awful had happened, and she guessed that Ivy was pouring whatever it was out to her mother, for she hardly spoke.

'Now look,' she said at last. 'I'm going to catch a train down there tonight. No, no. I insist. I won't be able to stay long, I'm afraid. Just until tomorrow night. Virginia's just about to go back to school. But I'll come down again next week ... Oh, yes, she's settling in very well. Now don't worry about a thing. Yes. I'll be there as soon as I can.' She slammed the phone down and glanced at the drawing-room door. 'What a mess,' she murmured. 'What a bloody mess.'

Rusty was shocked. It was the first time she had heard her mother swear. She waited until Peggy had returned to the drawing room before slipping back out on to the landing. Downstairs it sounded as though all hell was let loose.

Within minutes, her mother was flying out of the door. Rusty sprinted up the stairs to her bedroom, hid her stencils in the drawers, and leapt on to the bed with a book. It wasn't long before her mother was knocking at the door.

'Come in,' she said nonchalantly.

Her mother stepped in quickly.

'What's wrong, Mother?'

'I'm going to Southampton tonight to see Ivy Flannagan. I've asked your grandmother and father to tell Charlie that I'll be back tomorrow evening. Remind him of that, won't you?'

'What should I say if he asks questions?'

'Say that Auntie Ivy is not very well and that I'm going to try and make her feel better.'

'Is it the baby?' she whispered.

Her mother shook her head. She looked agitated.

'Is she going to die, like Beatie?'

'No. It's nothing like that.' She leaned on the rail at the foot of the bed. 'She's just received a telegram from an Australian hospital. They say that her first husband is a patient there.'

'But I thought he was dead.'

'Apparently not. He was taken prisoner by the Japanese. When he was removed from the prison camp, he was hardly conscious, and for some reason he was taken to Australia.'

'But,' stammered Rusty, 'what about Captain Flannagan? I mean, they love each other, don't they?'

Her mother nodded. 'I'm afraid it's all a bit of a muddle.' She looked awkward for a moment. 'You will keep an eye on Charlie, won't you?'

'Sure I will.'

As soon as her mother closed the door, the gong sounded for supper. Rusty gave a loud groan and rolled off the bed.

'If a bomb fell, that darned gong would still be on time,' she muttered.

29

Rusty was washing Charlie's face when the gong sounded for breakfast. He wriggled and squirmed and pulled away from her.

'Look, Charlie,' she said. 'It's only for today that I'm doing it. Mother will be back tonight.'

'Why didn't she take me?' he asked crossly.

But Rusty could see that underneath his crankiness he was scared.

'You were asleep, see. And when the phone-call came, Mother had to run real fast to catch a train. But she said I should take good care of you. O.K.?'

He nodded miserably.

Again the gong sounded.

'Oh boy,' she whispered, doing up his sandals. She gave his hair a quick brush.

'Teddy too,' he demanded thrusting the bear forward.

She brushed him. 'There,' she said.

As they walked down the stairs, her father was standing in the hall looking at his watch.

'You're three and a half minutes late,' he stated.

'I'm not used to washing and dressing Charlie.'

'You should have allowed for that.'

And you should have helped, she thought.

'Don't let it happen again.'

Charlie scowled. Hastily, she manoeuvred him into the dining room, where Mrs Grace was hovering over the table.

'O.K., Charlie,' she said, pulling up a chair for Teddy. 'Better start breakfast, eh?'

He attempted to scowl at her.

'Ah, I saw a smile sneaking out,' she said, waving a finger at him. He shook his head and pressed his lips firmly together. 'Look, there it is, at the corners. It's just squeezing out.'

Charlie threw back his head and let out a gurgle of laughter.

The door opened and Rusty's grandmother walked in. She gazed disapprovingly at the shabby bear seated at the table. Charlie folded his arms and glared at her. He looked so fierce that it was all Rusty could do to keep a straight face.

'Ah,' said Mrs Dickinson Senior. 'So you've condescended to arrive.'

She took one look at Charlie's thunderous face and swept hurriedly back through the door, leaving Mrs Grace in charge.

After breakfast Rusty played downstairs with Charlie. He sat his bear beside him and, as he played, he talked to him. Poor Charlie, she thought. I guess with Susan gone, he doesn't have a buddy. And she couldn't imagine anyone being allowed to come home with him from his nursery school.

An hour after lunch Mrs Grace came to tell her that her grandmother wished to see her in the drawing room.

Rusty knocked on the door and pushed it open. Her grandmother was seated in her winged armchair. She was smiling.

'Sit down, Virginia,' she said gently. 'Mrs Smythe-Williams will be visiting us this afternoon and we'll be taking tea in here. I'd like you to join us.'

This was a change in tune. She usually wanted Rusty to disappear.

'Mrs Grace is baking us some scones.'

'Sounds swell,' she said. 'What about Charlie?'

'He can amuse himself for a little while. Mrs Grace will

look after him. Now, I'd like you to change out of those ...' and she waved her finger at Rusty's knees.

'Jeans,' said Rusty.

'Change into something pretty.'

As Rusty was about to leave, her grandmother added lightly, 'And take your time. I'd like Mrs Smythe-Williams to see what a young lady you've become.'

A compliment, too! thought Rusty. This was praise!

Upstairs in her bedroom she put on her cream blouse and flared tan-and-green skirt, her new bobby socks and sloppy Joe. She spat into a handkerchief and rubbed the whites of her saddle shoes vigorously, unplaited her hair and gave it a good brushing backwards and upwards, to give her scalp some exercise, as Janey would say. Her hair hung around her face and shoulders like a dark bushy cloud. She glanced down at her sloppy Joe. The *R* on it was the colour of her hair. She made a central parting and then tied it back with the green ribbons she had worn when she first arrived in England.

When she was satisfied, she made her way downstairs. To her surprise, her grandmother met her in the hall. Rusty twirled round in a circle.

'Oh,' said her grandmother, 'you look so much nicer in a skirt.'

Rusty headed for the dining room. Her grandmother looked startled.

'Where are you going?'

'I want to show Charlie how I look,' she said, and she opened the door.

Charlie was nowhere to be seen. Lying scattered on the floor were his jigsaw-puzzle pieces.

'Your father has taken him out for the afternoon. For a treat,' added Mrs Dickinson Senior quickly.

'Oh,' said Rusty. She felt disappointed. 'How come he didn't want me to go with him too?'

'Well,' said her grandmother lightly, 'I expect he'll do

something different with you. After all, boys and girls enjoy different activities, don't they?'

'I guess.'

She was just about to turn away when she noticed Charlie's teddy bear on the floor, and it struck her as odd, for, since they had left Devon, Charlie never went anywhere without it.

There was a tap at the front door. Her grandmother quickly beckoned Rusty into the drawing room, leaving Mrs Grace to answer it. Rusty still couldn't understand why her grandmother didn't go and answer it herself.

Eventually Mrs Grace opened the drawing-room door and announced the arrival of Mrs Smythe-Williams. Rusty stood up. It was the lady who had complained about Charlie, the one with the big nose.

She seemed surprised when she saw Rusty, but before she could say anything Rusty's grandmother motioned her to the sofa.

'I thought it would be rather nice if Virginia joined us this afternoon,' she said.

Mrs Smythe-Williams sat down. There was an awkward silence.

'And how is school?' she asked at last.

'It's O.K.'

'Have you had a nice Christmas holiday?'

'Swell,' she said, crossing her fingers in the folds of her skirt. The woman gazed down at it. For a moment Rusty wondered whether she'd noticed her fingers.

'They certainly use a lot of material for clothes in America,' she remarked.

'Yes,' said Rusty. 'Rationing over there isn't as tough as it is over here.'

'And how are you finding life in England now?'

'It's O.K. I'm getting used to it.'

'I expect you're glad to be back home.'

'Oh yeah. Sure.'

Mrs Smythe-Williams turned to her grandmother.

'She still uses American expressions, but I do detect an English accent creeping back.'

Mrs Dickinson Senior beamed. 'Oh yes, she'll soon be back to normal.'

'I expect she'll be glad to get back to school and be with all her friends again.'

'Yes,' gushed her grandmother. 'It's hard for a little girl to amuse herself in a house full of grown-ups. And how is Mrs Matthews?'

From then on, Rusty sat perched on the edge of the armchair while Mrs Smythe-Williams and her grandmother talked about a stream of people Rusty had never met.

'And where is Margaret?' asked Mrs Smythe-Williams.

'She's visiting a friend of hers who isn't very well.'

'Is she still helping with the W.V.S.?' she asked, lowering her voice.

Mrs Dickinson Senior nodded.

'But surely there can't be anything to do now.'

'She says that the Government has asked them to continue their work for the time being.'

There was a knock at the door and Mrs Grace wheeled in a tea-trolley.

'I really do marvel at the way you've managed to keep your china intact,' said Mrs Smythe-Williams.

Rusty's grandmother looked exultant. 'Why thank you, my dear.' She looked up at Mrs Grace. 'Thank you, Mrs Grace, we'll manage by ourselves.'

Mrs Dickinson Senior poured milk into the cups and the tea through a strainer.

'Virginia,' she said, holding up the small jug, 'would you be so kind as to fetch some more milk?'

'Sure.'

So slow was Mrs Grace that Rusty not only passed her

on the way to the kitchen but met her on the way back. She was just crossing the hall to the drawing room when she heard her grandmother say, 'Any woman who marries a G.I. deserves everything that's coming to her.'

Rusty froze, her cheeks burning. As she thrust open the drawing-room door, Mrs Dickinson Senior and her friend looked up hurriedly and smiled. Rusty was so angry that she avoided looking at them. She placed the jug on the trolley and sat down.

'Virginia,' said her grandmother brightly, 'would you like a scone?'

Rusty had hardly finished eating one when she heard the front door opening. Her father's voice came thundering from the hall.

'You will go to bed immediately!'

Rusty turned in her chair. She could hear sounds of sobbing. Suddenly the door was flung open and Charlie stumbled in.

Rusty sprang to her feet. 'Charlie!' she cried.

His head was like a small stubbled bullet. The only trace of his thick red hair was a gingery fuzz. He was taking in great gulps of air, his large eyes looking even larger because of his shaven head.

'Mummy,' he gasped. 'Want Mummy.'

Rusty knelt down and took hold of his hands. He pulled them away.

'Want Mummy.'

Mr Dickinson stood, rigid, in the doorway, his hands clenched.

'You are to go to bed immediately!'

'Was this the treat?' exclaimed Rusty.

'Virginia, you will hold your tongue.' He glared down at Charlie. 'He's made an absolute disgrace of himself. I actually had to hold him down forcibly so that the barber could cut his hair. At least he looks like a boy now.'

Charlie did not move.

'Charles!' he roared. 'This is your last chance. I'm going to the study to fetch my cane. If you are not in your bedroom by the time I return, you'll feel it across your backside.' And with that he stormed out of the room.

'Charlie,' said Rusty gently, 'come on. I'll take you.'

She tried to touch him, but he backed into the armchair, dazed. She turned to her grandmother, only to find her pouring out a cup of tea for her friend.

'Grandmother!' Rusty gasped. 'Aren't you going to do anything?'

'It's nothing to do with me,' she said politely. 'It's up to your father.'

Mrs Smythe-Williams began sipping the tea.

Rusty glanced at Charlie. There was a pool by his feet. 'Come on,' she whispered.

There was a loud slamming of a door and the sound of heavy footsteps approaching. Charlie started making strange gasping noises as if he had asthma. Rusty heard her father's heavy stride and turned to face him.

He stood at the doorway, a long thin cane in his hand.

'So you've deliberately disobeyed me!' he roared.

He strode towards the armchair where Charlie seemed fixed. The cane flew up. Rusty leapt and grabbed his arm. From then on it was all like a dream. She heard her grandmother and her friend gasp. She heard Charlie sobbing. She heard the cane. She felt it a couple of times across her head, and then it was on her arms and thighs. The next thing she knew, her father had suddenly left the room.

Her head and limbs still stinging, she took hold of Charlie's hand and led him out into the hall. At the foot of the stairs he hiccuped, 'Teddy!'

She tried to let go of his hand to retrieve the bear, but he clung tightly to her. They walked into the dining room and Rusty picked it up. As she handed it to him, she knew from the smell that he had filled his pants.

She carried him up to the bathroom and locked the door behind them. She didn't know where to start. She took off his shorts and underpants, piled them into a bucket, and filled it with hot water. Then she washed his bottom with a warm soapy flannel until he was clean.

She opened the bathroom door and peered out, then pulled Charlie out on to the landing and up the wide polished staircase to the next landing and up again to his bedroom.

For once he didn't wriggle or squirm. He simply held on to his teddy-bear and allowed her to put on his pyjamas and tuck him into bed.

Rusty pulled the chamber pot, which was under his bed, into view. She smoothed his forehead with her fingers. 'Tell you what,' she whispered. 'I'll make you as snug as a bug in a rug. O.K.?'

She raised each end of the pillow and tucked the sheets and blankets tightly underneath so that the raised pillow ends enclosed him. He smiled weakly.

'That's what Uncle Harvey does,' he said.

As soon as Rusty heard the knock at the front door, she sat up sharply in bed and looked at her watch. It was ten past nine. She hopped out of bed and eased the door open. There was silence, followed by a second knocking. Mrs Grace had already gone home. If someone didn't answer soon, Rusty would go down herself.

There were footsteps in the hall.

'Hello, Mother. Everything all right?'

'I think you had better come into the drawing room, Margaret.'

Rusty slipped out on to the landing and leaned over the banisters. She heard the door close and then, after a short while, open again. Her mother walked quickly across the hall towards the staircase. Rusty backed into her room and climbed into bed. Within minutes, her mother had walked past her room and into Charlie's room. Rusty heard her walk back along the landing and stop. She was outside her room now. The door opened slowly.

'Virginia?'

Rusty sat up and turned the bedside lamp on.

Her mother closed the door hurriedly and came over to the bed.

'What on earth has been going on? Your father says that Charlie was deliberately disobedient and your grandmother says you virtually attacked him. Your father's terribly upset because he hit you with a cane, and your grandmother says that you drove him to it. I can't seem to get any sense out of either of them.'

'He was going to hit Charlie with it and nobody did anything to stop him.'

'But I was told that Charlie had thrown the most terrible tantrums and had kicked and bitten your father and had refused to go to bed.'

'I didn't see him do that,' Rusty said. 'Maybe he did that at the barber's. I don't know. I didn't even know he'd taken him. They must have planned it all out.'

'Virginia, what are you talking about?'

'Grandmother sent me upstairs to change. She told me to take my time. It was so I'd be out of the way. When I came down, she told me Father had taken him out for a treat. She didn't say anything about him going to the barber's.'

Her mother looked shaken. She glanced up swiftly.

'If Charlie refused to obey your father, it does put him in a very difficult position.'

'But he was in an awful state. Crying for you and . . . I tried to take him up myself, but –'

'Perhaps a cane is a little harsh,' she said, 'but if he's disobedient . . .'

'But he couldn't move.'

'You mean he wouldn't.'

'No. He was like the red fox,' she said desperately. 'You know, the one that was caught in your headlights.'

Her mother sat down at the end of the bed.

'He dirtied his pants, too,' Rusty added quickly.

Her mother took a battered cigarette packet out of her cardigan pocket. She took out the remaining half of a cigarette and lit it.

For a while the two of them sat there saying nothing. Rusty could see that her mother was thinking.

'How is Ivy?' she whispered.

Her mother blew out a cloud of smoke.

'Upset.'

'Will she still be going to America?'

'She doesn't know what to do. She has to get in touch with her husband's family and the family in America. You see,' she said, turning, 'she's not even Mrs Flannagan any more. Because her husband is still alive, her marriage to Captain Flannagan doesn't count. She's back to being Mrs Woods.'

'But what about the baby?'

Her mother stood up. 'I don't know.' She paused. 'Now look, Virginia, this isn't your problem. And remember, this is between you and me. All right?'

'I won't tell a soul,' said Rusty, kneeling up. 'Cross my heart and hope to die.'

'You'll be back at school on Monday. You just concentrate on that. It'll all get sorted out in time.'

'O.K.'

Peggy was about to open the door when Rusty said, 'Mother, Grandmother said that anyone who married a G.I. deserves all that's coming to her. What did she mean? Jinkie's husband is a G.I., and he's really nice.'

Her mother stiffened. 'Did she now?' she muttered. Then without another word she opened the door and left.

Rusty had hardly sunk back into the pillows when there

was the almighty crash of a door slamming. It startled her. She shot out of bed, opened the door, and ran barefoot back on to the landing. She crouched by the banisters.

They were shouting now.

'I'm sick of Uncle Harvey this and Uncle Harvey that,' said a loud voice. 'I'm his father.'

'I know that, Roger, but you never give him a chance. You hardly spend any time with him at all. How can you expect him to treat you like a father if you don't make an effort to get to know him?'

'And what am I supposed to do with him?' he bellowed. 'Play chess? I mean, you can hardly have a conversation with him.'

'You can play with him.'

'Oh, really, Margaret. I haven't the time to play.'

'You never have. In fact, I don't think you know how.'

'I am an adult,' he snapped.

'Roger, you've got to spend more time with him – otherwise the situation is going to grow worse. You're expecting him to be some stiff-upper-lipped young Englishman. Well, he's not. He's only four years old.'

'And tied to his mother's apron-strings!'

'And you're not, I suppose!'

Rusty held her breath. There was a long silence.

After some time, she heard her grandmother say something about her mother needing another child. Rusty crept down to the next landing. 'When he's seven and away at boarding school, you'll have so much time on your hands,' her grandmother was saying.

'Charlie is not going to boarding school.'

Her father gave an artificial laugh. 'Oh, really?' he said. 'Have you taken on the role of father now?'

'Don't talk nonsense,' said her grandmother. 'Of course he's going to boarding school.'

'He is not.'

Oh yes, thought Rusty bitterly, it was O.K. for *her* to be sent away, but not Charlie.

'I'm sad enough as it is that I've spent so little time with Virginia. Ideally, I'd like her to be at a day school, but as long as we live here and have to creep around on tiptoe –'

'Margaret!'

'I'd rather she at least has the chance of some company of her own age *and* the chance to catch up with her education.'

'So you'd rather Charles stay a namby-pamby. A little sissy, is that it?'

'I'd rather be around to see him grow up.'

'It's out of the question. Of course he's going to boarding school. It'll make a man out of him. You should have seen the fuss he made in the barber's. I was ashamed of him. The sooner he has some male company, the better.'

'He had more male company in Devon than he does here.'

'Oh yes,' said her father. 'The beloved Uncle Harvey.'

'It seems,' said her grandmother insinuatingly, 'that this Harvey spent rather more time than was necessary with you.'

'And what do you mean by that?'

'Your conscience will tell you that, my dear.'

Rusty sat back, stunned. So that was it! Harvey and her mother must have been going out together! That's why her mother had turned so red when Rusty had asked her all those questions about him. She felt sick. It was as though someone had stuck a knife into her middle and was twisting it around. She crept back up to her room.

She had been lying in bed for only a few minutes when she heard the doorknob moving. In the half-light she saw a small figure clutching a teddy bear.

'Virginia,' Charlie whispered.

'Uh-huh.'

She heard him gasping, those strange gulping sounds that sounded as if he had asthma or a bad dose of the hiccups.

'Teddy's a bit frightened.'

'Is he? Maybe you should close the door and bring him over.'

He shut it quietly and padded over to the bed. 'He's a bit sad, too.'

'What do you think would make him feel good again?' she asked.

'I 'spect he'd feel better if he got into bed with you.'

'O.K.'

He handed the bear to her and she tucked it in beside her.

'Don't you think he'll be lonesome without you?' she asked quietly.

'I 'spect so.'

'Maybe if you got in too . . .'

He nodded, hauled himself up on to the bed, and snuggled down under the blankets. Gradually he pushed the teddy bear aside and moved in closer to her. She could feel him shaking.

'Virginia?' he whispered.

'Uh-huh.'

He began to cry. 'I want to go home.'

She pulled him close to her and stroked his stubbly head with her fingers.

'Yeah,' she murmured, holding him as tightly as she could. 'Me too.'

30

Rusty sat next to her mother on the station platform and picked at the skin along the side of her fingernails. The letter from her father, requesting that she stay at Benwood House at weekends, lay sealed in her blazer pocket. Even as she tried to make some sense of the weekend, her grandmother's remark kept thundering repeatedly inside her head. She pressed her nails deep into the flesh of her hands.

Her mother was staring vacantly into the distance.

'Mother,' she blurted out quickly, 'did you go out on dates with Harvey?'

Her mother looked up, startled. 'Pardon?'

'I said, did you go out on dates with Harvey?'

'We spent some time together.'

'Without Charlie? Just the two of you?'

She nodded.

Rusty turned away. 'Did you go to dances? Stuff like that?'

'Yes.'

'How could you do that when Father was away fighting?'

Her mother gazed wearily at her.

'I did nothing to be ashamed of,' she said. 'We kept each other company, that's all. He was a good friend.'

'Did you like him?'

'I liked him very much.'

But did you love him? she wanted to say, but she couldn't bring herself to ask it.

A train was approaching the station. Rusty stood and picked up her grip.

Soon her mother was beside her.

'Virginia,' she said quietly, 'about the weekends. I think it's for the best. Until we sort things out at home.'

Rusty refused to look at her.

'It's all your fault. You shouldn't have made friends with that man,' she said bitterly.

Before her mother could speak, Rusty whipped open a door, leapt into the train, and slammed it behind her.

Uniformed girls pushed by her in the corridor, giggling and shouting. Rusty ignored them and walked past the compartments without stopping. 'Hey, watch where you're going!' exclaimed one of the older girls, as Rusty shoved her way past.

Eventually she found a quiet corner, pushed her grip up by the wall, and sat on it, her head in her hands. She hated her mother. She hated her father. She hated her grandmother. She hated school. She hated England. She hated everybody and everything.

She opened her grip and took a look at the clothes and stencils, and the stencilling equipment she had hidden under her pyjamas. Next to her jeans, plaid shirt, Windbreaker and trapper cap lay the half-dozen stamped envelopes her mother had given her.

'We're only allowed to write Sundays,' Rusty had reminded her.

'I know.' And she had handed her some money. 'This is your pocket money for the term. You'll need to give it to Matron.'

The money was in the inside pocket of her blazer.

Rusty didn't remember much about the journey or the rest of the day. As the girls drifted into their various cliques, she continued to rage inside. She moved automatically up to Matron to collect her sheets and towels, and back to the dormitory to unpack her trunk. She slipped her other clothes under the mattress and hid the stencils and stencilling equipment behind the chest of drawers.

If anyone spoke to her, she snapped angrily at them and was surprised to find that they scuttled away.

It wasn't until she was lying in bed in the dark that she remembered the envelope.

By Friday morning Rusty had still not touched the envelope containing her father's letter. All through lessons she waited to be summoned to the Headmistress's study. Her parents were bound to have contacted Miss Bembridge by now, she thought, for they would probably be wondering why she hadn't been in touch with them. But nothing happened. Everything seemed to continue as normal.

When the afternoon lessons began, Rusty's heart was pounding so fast she thought she would be sick. She stared with fixed concentration at her books and ticked off the minutes in her notebook. Prep was almost unbearable. She knew she should give the envelope to someone, but she couldn't seem to form the words or move in the right direction.

As usual, she was granted permission to take her grip up to the dormitory, and as usual she placed her pyjamas, dressing gown and sponge-bag in it, adding underneath them the clothes, stencils and stencilling equipment she had smuggled in.

Downstairs, the same prefect stood in bored fashion by the arched entrance to the hallway of the wing that formed Butt House. Rusty changed into her outdoor shoes in the Fourth Form cloakroom, pulled on her rubber galoshes over them, and slipped into her Beanie, hat and scarf.

The prefect walked through the door with her. They had hardly turned the corner when the prefect said, 'Look, you'll be all right on your own again, won't you?'

Rusty nodded. She didn't dare open her mouth.

Without looking back, she walked around to the front of the school, down the drive to the large wrought-iron gates. She lifted up the heavy latch, swung it open, and, in case anyone was watching said, rather feebly, 'Hello, Mother, how nice to see you,' and closed the gate.

As soon as she was hidden behind the wall, she ran along the pavement to the corner, jumped over the ditch, and scrambled through the trees. A car swept by, its headlights sending a wide arc across the road.

She pulled her grip over a bush and flattened herself against the wall.

She moved cautiously along the wall to the next corner and peered around. Ahead of her lay the woods.

'O.K.,' she murmured. 'Here goes.'

It took her longer than usual to reach the tall trees at the top of the tiny slope, for she had to make countless detours.

Once inside the Cabin, she lit one of the lamps and placed it on the stone platform in front of the fire. It was then that she remembered the letter. She undid her Beanie, pulled out the crumpled envelope from her blazer pocket, and propped it up on the mantelpiece.

She cleared the grate and got a fire going. It seemed strange to be doing such a familiar action in such unfamiliar clothes. She had been used to being in the Cabin dressed in pyjamas, with her cardigan and dressing gown on top. It felt out of place somehow to be in her uniform. She spread out one of the blankets and sat cross-legged on a pillow, staring into the fire and adding wood.

The school thought she had gone home. Her parents thought she was at school. She had a whole weekend to herself: two days to make the Cabin as homey as she could.

As soon as the flames were roaring up the chimney, Rusty blew out the lamp. She warmed her pyjamas and dressing gown in front of the fire, hung up her uniform on the hook at the back of the door, and got into her nightclothes. She wrapped the blankets around her like a caterpillar in a cocoon, rolled herself on to the camp-bed, and lay huddled on top of it, watching the fire.

She was woken by the light coming in through the windows. She sat up quickly. A great cloud rose from her lips. It was freezing. It was the first time she had seen the Cabin in daylight. Cobwebs hung from the corners, and dust and grime covered the faded white walls. She pushed herself out of the roll of blankets, put on her jeans, plaid shirt, cardigan, Windbreaker and sneakers, and pulled on her mother's overalls. As she buttoned them up, she could still smell the oil on them. She rolled up the trouser bottoms and sleeves and went out to explore.

All around her, sticking out of the mounds of bricks, plaster and timber, were various abandoned objects.

Having located the kitchen, she scrabbled among the debris and found a large oval wooden tub, a bucket, a rickety old step-ladder, various pieces of torn material, the head of a broom, and a cracked mirror.

She turned the tap on. It gave a rumble and shuddered. Dark-brown liquid oozed out. Eventually it flowed more easily and became almost clear.

Rusty knew it would be dark by four o'clock, and she wanted to get as much done as possible.

She sliced the twigs off a long thin branch and wedged it into the hole in the head of the broom. Her stomach gave a hungry gurgle. Ignoring it, she cleared the Cabin out, unhooked the curtains, and left them to soak in the bucket.

Then she attacked every room like a whirlwind, shoving the broom into every corner and crevice, sweeping the walls and floor.

As soon as she had finished, she dragged up one of the large cans of paint from the cellar and prised the lid off. The paint was so thick that she had to hold a stick with two hands and grip the can between her feet before she was able to stir it into creaminess.

By the time she had painted the ceiling, walls and two alcoves with the two paintbrushes she had smuggled back from Beatie's, it was already getting dark. She washed the brushes under the tap, pulled the camp-bed and blankets back into the Cabin, and began to lay a fire.

The next day she painted the door and windowframes.

Having no soap, she squeezed and rinsed the curtains repeatedly until the water was clear, and hung them soaking from the branches of the surrounding trees, smoothing the material so that when they dried they would have no creases in them.

Then came the part she had been waiting for: the stencilling.

She knew that it would be difficult to keep the paint at a steady consistency. If it was too watery, it would dribble over the card and down the wall; if it was too thick, it would stick out oddly in congealed lumps.

A sharp pain stabbed at her stomach. She stood for a moment until it had passed. It was just another hunger cramp.

She peeled off several strips of the faded wallpaper from upstairs and began slowly and methodically to try out her mixed colours. Back at the Omsks', Aunt Hannah used to spend hours encouraging her to do colour exercises. Sometimes she had got so bored and impatient with that, but, as Aunt Hannah said, everything has its own grammar. The more words you knew, the more you could express yourself, and colours were a little bit like that. And when Rusty had mixed something up to the exact colour that she wanted, and had danced up and down in the studio, Aunt Hannah would grin and say, 'Atta girl,' and all that endless dabbling around made some kind of sense.

She was glad that the paint on the walls wasn't such a stark white. There was the slightest touch of yellow in it, making it more buttermilk in colour.

Rusty stood on the ladder in the far corner opposite the windows, and stencilled flowers and leaves in barn red, ochre and green, climbing down and stippling the stubby stencil brushes on the old wallpaper if they dripped too much, and then climbing back up and doing a balancing act, with the stencil card in one hand and the brush in the other.

She moved the step-ladder around the room and did the same in the other corners; but where the alcoves were, she made the design level with the mantelpiece because she had an idea of putting shelves there. Once she had painted the corners, she returned to the far wall, the one with no windows, door or fireplace, and gradually stencilled a trail of vine leaves that dipped and arched all the way to the design in the next corner. Then she returned to the beginning of the trail of vines and very carefully placed another stencil card over it, painting in yellow daisy-shaped flowers so that they nestled among the leaves. By the time she had reached the second corner with the yellow daisies, it was already mid-afternoon.

She climbed down the step-ladder and stood back to look at her work, thrusting her hands into her mother's baggy overalls. For the first time in months, she felt like her old self again.

Outside, the curtains were completely dry, but so cold to the touch that Rusty wondered at first if they were still a little damp. She hung them back up at the windows.

'Boy!' she yelled. 'They're the same dark green as the vines!' And she danced like a lunatic on the wooden floor.

She tore in and out of the Cabin, dragging in as much wood and leaves and dry wallpaper as possible, in an effort to beat the darkness. Under the rubble she found three broken kitchen chairs. She hauled them into the Cabin.

Two of them had their backs broken and legs missing. The one with a back had only two legs. She took a torch outside and found two more legs. With a lot of sawing and banging, she made two stools by hammering a leg into each vacant hole and sawing off the broken backs completely.

It was later, while she was sitting on one of her home-made stools, turning bricks and planks of wood over to help them dry out in front of the fire, that she began to realize the seriousness of what she had done.

She decided that she must plan her return trip to school carefully. She wrote a letter to her parents, telling them how she was getting along in maths and English, and added that she hadn't received many order marks that week. She didn't tell them how lonely she still felt and how, for no apparent reason, she had started snapping at everyone, or how she hated them both for hating each other.

The next morning she rose early, hammered in a nail above the mantelpiece, and hung the cracked mirror up over the fireplace. In spite of the bitter cold, she stood outside by the tap and washed, and cleaned her teeth. Her fingernails had traces of paint around and beneath them, so she had to rub the skin violently and use a small nail to push out the paint from underneath.

She ran quickly into the Cabin, stood in front of the mirror, and brushed her hair firmly, plaiting it and adding the regulation green ribbons at the bottom. Once she had her uniform on, no one, she thought, would ever suspect that she hadn't been with her parents that weekend. She pulled on her galoshes over her walking shoes, put on her hat, Beanie and scarf, and stood in the doorway for a moment, to take a last look at the room. She closed the door, stepped over a pile of bricks, and walked into the grass.

Once she reached the ditch next to the road, she leapt over it and skidded on to the pavement. To her right was the bus-stop, and a little farther ahead a pillarbox. She ran along the pavement and put her hand inside her pocket for her letter to her parents. It was then that she remembered the one her father had written! She had left the envelope propped up on the mantelpiece.

She posted her own letter and walked back swiftly to the bus-stop. She needed time to think. If anyone spotted her, she could always pretend that she'd just hopped off a bus.

There was nothing she could do about it now. She'd have to wait until her next visit to the Cabin. As yet, she still didn't know if she had been discovered. If she had, she would know, the moment she stepped through the school gates.

No one said a word. She stood in assembly and filed out with the others to the classroom and was, as usual, ignored. No one came to the classroom with a summons for her to see the Headmistress; no one said she smelled of paint or dust; and no one, as usual, asked her what she had been doing all weekend. She slept deeply that night.

On Thursday night, as arranged, Lance was waiting for her on the other side of the wall. They grinned at each other. It was all Rusty could do to keep herself from hugging him.

'Hiya, Yank,' she whispered.

'Hiya, Creeper.'

'Boy,' she said, as they headed for the woods, 'have I got a surprise for you.'

She thought he would admire her for staying there over the weekend. She thought he would be impressed. Instead he grew quiet.

'What are you going to do?' he said, when they reached the slope that led to the gate.

'How do you mean?'

'About the letter from your father? I mean, they're bound to find out sooner or later.'

She shrugged and pushed the gate open.

'I don't know. I thought I'd hand it over tomorrow, but then if the letter's dated inside, it'll give the game away.'

'You realize,' he said, 'that if you're caught, you could be expelled, and then . . .'

He fell silent and they went on walking through the grass.

'And then my life would be over?' she muttered. 'Is that what you're saying?'

'I was thinking of mine, actually,' he said bashfully. 'If they find out that I've been meeting you here, I might be expelled, too.'

Rusty stopped. 'I hadn't thought of that. Look,' she said, turning around, 'if I *do* get caught, I won't squeal on you. I promise. O.K.?'

He nodded and followed her over a small pile of bricks that lay in front of the hallway.

'Now,' she said, 'you stay here. I want it to be a surprise.'

She stepped into the Cabin with her torch and lit the two lamps.

'O.K.,' she yelled. 'You can come in now.'

The door opened slowly and Lance peered in. He stared around at the walls, his eyes and mouth growing wider and wider.

'I say,' he exclaimed.

'Come in. Come in.'

He closed the door behind him.

'Whaddaya think?' she said, doing a James Cagney impersonation.

'It's frightfully good!' he said. He gazed at the designs. 'How on earth did you do it?'

'They're stencils. Traditional American. I'm going to paint the panelling in the doors too, and around the windows. That is, unless you have some other ideas. After all, it is your Cabin too.'

'I wouldn't know where to start.'

They stood awkwardly for a moment.

'Let's get a fire going,' she said. 'I want to begin sawing up those planks.'

'Oh Lord. I'm hopeless at all that stuff.'

326

'It's O.K. I'll do it. But if you can hold the planks steady, it'll make it easier.'

While Lance dealt with the fire, Rusty laid a plank across the two stools. Then, a pencil in her mouth, she went over to one of the alcoves, measured the width of it with a piece of string, laid it across the plank, and made a mark.

'What are you doing?' asked Lance over his shoulder.

'I'm going to make shelves.'

'Aren't you taking all this a bit seriously?'

'Nope. For the first time in months I'm having some fun.'

'But what on earth do you want shelves for?'

'It'll make it more like a real home. You wait and see.'

He frowned and then lit the pile of dry leaves and torn wallpaper under his pyramid of wood.

'You know,' said Rusty, noticing, 'you've really got the knack now. When we go back to America, you'll be able to have your own cookouts.'

He sat on the fireplace step and stared at her. 'You're mad,' he said.

'If I wasn't, I think I'd go crazy.'

He shook his head.

'Here,' she said. 'Hold this steady for me.'

He leaned on one end of the plank and Rusty started sawing.

Between pauses to throw branches on the fire, Rusty sawed while Lance talked. Behind them the branches hissed in the fireplace.

Rusty asked Lance about his holiday, but he veered away from the subject. He just said he was glad to be back at school, but there was one good thing that had happened in the vacation. 'After Christmas, I ran every day,' he said.

'You ran?'

'Yes. It was an excuse to get out of my aunt's house,

and also I wanted to get really fit so that when I came back I'd surprise them all.'

Rusty stopped sawing for a moment. 'Where'd you run?'

'Down to the beach and along the pavement beside it.'

'I'd love to do something like that. Only I'd like to roller-skate or go take a bike out. Did it make you feel good?'

He nodded.

'Sometimes, I wish I was a boy. I'm not allowed out on my own hardly at all. If I want to mail a letter I practically have to have written permission from the King!'

'But that's not the best part,' he said, butting in. 'This afternoon we had rugger. Hardly anyone could catch me, once I had the ball. I just ran and ran. One time I almost ran the full length of the field. I was so excited that I just swerved around the other chaps, leapt out of the way, and nearly scored a try.'

'That's swell.' And she began sawing vigorously again.

'The opposing team started calling me Yank. But it's completely different now. I quite like being called it.'

'I'm not called Creeper any more. I'm not called anything. I'm invisible.'

The end of the piece of wood she was sawing fell to the ground with a clatter.

By the time they left the Cabin, Rusty had ten 'shelves' sawn.

'Can you come tomorrow night?' she asked.

'Tomorrow's Friday.' He looked worried for a moment. 'You're not going to stay here for the weekend again, are you? It's awfully risky.'

'I don't know. I might.'

'Anyway, I can't come. You see, because I did so well this afternoon, I've been asked if I'd like to join in some trials for the reserve team for my House.'

She could see he was overjoyed.

'That's terrific. See, I told you you'd make it.'

He grinned.

'So when we can we meet?' she said. 'Saturday?'

'I'd rather it was *after* the weekend.'

'O.K. How about Monday?'

'All right.'

She pulled some money out of her dressing-gown pocket. 'Could you buy me some sandpaper when you go into town?'

'I don't know,' he said slowly. 'We have to go in a foursome. The others might get suspicious if they saw me buying it.'

'Well, take the money anyway. If you can't buy it, you can give it back to me.'

'I'd rather you gave it to me afterwards. Our pockets are checked. We have to hand over all our pocket money to Matron at the beginning of term and then have it ticked off as we collect bits of it. Don't they do that at your school?'

'Uh-huh. But they don't know I have it. Remember, they still think I'm a weekly boarder.'

On Friday after prep, Rusty walked – as casually as her beating heart would allow – up to the dormitory to pack her grip. Outside it was pouring with rain. The prefect was waiting for her downstairs, gazing dismally out through the arched doorway.

'You don't have to come with me,' said Rusty. 'I'll be all right by myself.'

'Are you sure?' said the prefect, brightening.

Rusty nodded and walked out around the corner along the side of the school building to the front. Ahead of her, at the foot of the long drive, stood the large towering gates. The night was as black as black. She wanted desperately to run, just in case somebody suddenly yelled out, 'Virginia Dickinson, come back here immediately!' But she went on steadily, her feet splashing forward, opened the gate, and closed it swiftly behind her. She took a backward glance at the four-winged building that she hated so much. Shafts of light seeped out through drawn curtains as the rain swept across it.

She turned quickly and ran alongside the wall, over the ditch, and through the trees.

By the time she had reached the Cabin, the rain seemed to have soaked into her bones, making her fingers shake and her teeth chatter, like someone doing a clog dance inside her mouth.

The rain turned into hail. She watched the tiny icy balls bounce viciously against the windows while she laid the fire.

Once the fire had gathered strength, she picked up the bricks and placed them at each side of one of the alcoves, laying a cut plank on top. It fit beautifully. On top of the plank, at the sides, she piled up more bricks and laid another plank across them. When she had constructed five shelves on each side, she sat on a stool in the middle of the Cabin and surveyed her work.

'This is getting to be more like a real home every day,' she whispered.

She wrapped the blankets around herself and lay down on the camp-bed. Her plaits were still damp. She lifted them up so that they draped over the top of the pillow . . . anything to avoid them trailing down her neck.

In the morning she hunted through the rubble for any objects she could put on the shelves. She remembered Kathryn saying that what made a stage-set look real were all the little details like ornaments, books on the shelves, pictures on the walls.

She scrabbled around, picking up any book she could find. They were all damp. Upstairs there were three faded paintings of rural scenes. The glass in the frames was cracked and broken, but there was a rusty chain at the back of each, so they could still be hung up.

She was just pulling away some wood from a high mound of rubble when several of the bricks and lumps of plaster slid aside, revealing a table. She pushed the debris off it and hauled it out. It was split off at one end and two of the legs were missing but, on examining it carefully and finding the legs, she felt hopeful that she could attach them back on.

She dragged it across to the Cabin and after a lot of manoeuvring finally managed to pull it through the doorway.

For the rest of the day she worked away at the table. She rescrewed the legs on, replaced some of the bent nails, and strengthened the top. Then, after measuring it, she sawed off the ends so that they matched up. Even after a good wash, the wood was grey and rather dismal-looking. A good lick of paint would change that, though.

That evening she dried as many books as possible in front of the fire, knocked all the glass out of the pictures, and hung them up on the walls. Occasionally she had the most terrific bouts of hunger and cold, but keeping busy kept both feelings at bay.

That night she slept in a happy exhausted stupor. Inside her Cabin she felt untouched by the world outside. She felt safe and she didn't hurt any more.

On Sunday she placed the dried books on the shelves, put her carpentry tools and stencil equipment on a special shelf of their own, and under the two bottom shelves stacked as much chopped wood as would fill the space from the floor up. The rest of the wood she put in the wooden tub.

After she had painted vine leaves and birds in the panels of the door, she wrote another letter to her parents. The one from her father still lay propped up on the mantelpiece. She couldn't bring herself to touch it now.

The following morning she cleaned herself up and headed for the woods. It had started raining again. She just hoped she wouldn't appear too muddy. She posted her letter and walked back through the school gates. Since she hadn't eaten since Friday, she felt a little light-headed, but she was beginning to grow used to being hungry. It was when she bent down to remove her galoshes that she felt dizzy. She sat down quickly on the cloakroom bench, and the feeling passed.

In assembly, when she still hadn't been publicly hauled up by the Headmistress, she felt both relieved and worried. She'd been away two weekends, yet nothing had happened. She was almost disappointed. It meant that nobody cared about her or missed her at all. Still, maybe she was on a winning streak and could go on like this until half-term.

At midnight, she met Lance by the wall. He was beside himself with excitement.

'I'm in one of the reserve teams for my House,' he cried.

Rusty immediately began walking into the woods.

'Did you get the sandpaper?' she said abruptly.

'What? Oh. Well, I managed to get hold of a couple of pieces from the woodwork room. I didn't go into town after all. You see, one of the chaps in my House who's already in a team had heard how fast I was on Thursday, and he asked if I'd like to go for a run with him and do some practice in passing. So I jumped at the chance.'

Rusty stared ahead. She just wanted to reach the Cabin. Then she'd feel all right.

'Aren't you pleased that I'm in the reserves?'

She glanced at him. 'Sure I am. I guess I'm a little cold. That's all.'

She *was* pleased that he had got into the reserves. But it was the way he talked about it that unnerved her, that and his mention of the other boy.

They came to the tall trees by the slope and slid down.

'Oh, by the way,' he said, as they walked through the gate, 'you know the prefect I fag for?'

'Uh-huh.'

'Well, yesterday he actually *praised* me for the way I lit his fire! I mean, he actually praised me!'

'Does he ever thank you?' she said over her shoulder.

'Pardon?'

'It doesn't matter.' And she strode on ahead.

'He's really rather decent,' went on Lance. 'I think I'm awfully lucky to be his fag, really.'

Rusty felt such a heel. She resented his enthusiasm for school people and school activities, and yet he had been so miserable when they first met. She ought to feel happy for him.

'I want to surprise you again,' she said. 'Wait there.'

As soon as he stepped inside, she could see by his face that he was staggered. She leaned against the chimney breast with an artificial swagger, one leg crooked nonchalantly across the other.

He stared at the alcoves, the pictures on the walls, the neat piles of chopped wood, and then spotted the wooden table.

'I found it under all that junk outside,' she said. 'It was broken but I fixed it. Look at the panels on the door.'

He closed the door and gazed at them admiringly.

'I wish you could see it all in the daylight. Then you could see the colours right.'

He turned around slowly. He was frowning.

'Don't you like it?'

'Oh yes,' he said.

'So what's wrong?'

'You stayed another weekend.'

'I told you I might. Look, don't worry. It's a cinch.'

He drew out the two pieces of sandpaper. 'I'm sorry,' he said, 'it's not much. What did you want it for?'

'I was going to sand the edges of the shelves. They look nice like that. Well, never mind. This'll probably be enough for the table.' She looked at him. 'Who's going to do the fire?'

'I will.'

'O.K.'

She started sanding the sawn ends of the table. She was acutely aware that Lance wasn't talking very much, but she was too scared to ask him why. It was only when he had got the fire going that he came over and watched her.

'See what a difference it makes?' she said lightly. 'It comes up all nice and smooth.' She began to round off the sharp corners. Eventually she could stand it no longer. 'O.K.,' she said. 'What's wrong?'

He leaned on the table and traced his fingernail along the wood.

'Well,' he said, 'you know how much I want to do well in rugger?'

'Yes, though I don't know why it's such a big deal.'

'I told you. It's the only way I can be noticed. I mean, once I've done something for the House or the School, I'm bound to make friends.' He paused. 'Anyway, there's this boy I went running with on Saturday. He came and watched me play in the afternoon, and he was jolly impressed.'

'So?'

'So I don't think I'll be able to come here so often, because I'll be joining him for practices, which means I'll really need to get a good sleep at nights.'

Rusty looked away. She felt choked.

'I'll still come on Thursdays.'

She threw a pillow on the floor and sat down in front of the fire. Lance came and sat beside her.

'I really like it here,' he said. 'I think you've made it look splendid.'

'So how come you don't want to visit any more? I thought we were buddies.'

'I'll still be coming.'

'I guess.' And she picked up a branch from the wooden tub and threw it on to the fire.

It was a dismal evening. Rusty felt Lance slipping away from her like Janey and Skeet and Beth, and she felt helpless to do anything about it. The two of them sat there quietly, making small talk until the fire had died down.

On Wednesday, Rusty received another letter from her mother. It was all about something funny that Charlie had said, and how pleased she was that Rusty's schoolwork was progressing well. And she talked about how hard her father was working at the office and how she thought it might be a nice idea for them all to spend the Easter holiday in Devon. It wasn't until the postscript that she mentioned her father's letter. It said:

P.S. We still haven't received a reply from Miss Bembridge. We realize that she must be very busy, and we assume that it's because you've settled in well as a full-time boarder that she perhaps hasn't felt the need to contact us yet. Could you ask her to get in touch with me, preferably by letter, as I'm never quite sure when your grandmother has taken the phone off the hook. It would just make me feel more at ease. I'd like to call her myself, but your father seems to think I'm making a fuss over nothing.

Rusty folded it up and shoved it into her blazer pocket. She desperately wanted to have a quiet think but, before she knew it, a bell had rung. Thinking was out of the question. From now on her every hour was accounted for.

That night she lay awake until the dawn, and it was a struggle to stay awake in the classes the following day. The teachers, thinking she was stupid, made the usual sarcastic comments about her to the other girls, but she was completely oblivious to them. All she cared about was whether the sky remained clear.

It was the Bull who sent her to Matron. She had asked her to stand up, as it was obvious she hadn't heard the question she had been asked. Rusty had hardly dragged herself to her feet when she woke up on the floor and found that the side of her forehead was bleeding. The next thing she knew, two extremely strong arms were hauling her up into a sitting position and pushing her head firmly between her knees.

Orders were being snapped out to other girls to help lift her back into the chair.

'Now, my girl,' Miss Bullivant roared, 'you are to go *straight* to Matron.'

'I feel O.K. now,' she mumbled. 'Guess I must have got up too fast.'

'I'll pretend I didn't hear a certain word,' the Bull snapped.

When Rusty looked up, she actually saw a twinkle in her eye. Boy, she looked almost nice.

'Thank you, Miss Bullivant.'

'Right,' she bellowed. 'Off you go to the San. And stand up *slowly*.'

San? Oh yes, that was the infirmary.

'Yes, Miss Bullivant.'

'Now go on with you, girl!'

Rusty moved hazily from the classroom and down the corridors towards the San. She had arranged to meet Lance that evening, and it wasn't raining. She couldn't be put in the San tonight. She just couldn't.

Matron looked as thin and grim as ever. She sat behind a sparse desk in a cold, well-scrubbed room and glared at her.

'And what can I do for you?' she said accusingly.

'Miss Bullivant sent me. I passed out in class.'

'I assume you mean you *fainted*.'

'Yes, ma'am. And I guess I must have caught my head on the corner of someone's desk. But it's only a scratch.'

Matron rose and took a cursory glance at it.

'So you fainted?' she said. 'Sounds like constipation to me.'

Rusty gulped. That'd be another dose of Number 9! Boy, she hated that stuff; but if she didn't take it, she might have to stay in the San.

She watched Matron pull the muddy-coloured bottle out of a cupboard.

That day she picked up five order marks for running in the corridors en route to the lavatory, plus a sixth for yelling in exasperation, 'I have the runs!'

At midnight, even as she climbed down the scaffolding, she had to stop at intervals, every time a pain shot through her empty insides, and wait until it had passed.

The fact that Lance wasn't by the wall to meet her only heightened her irritation. After fifteen minutes of waiting she headed on through the woods to the Cabin and set to laying a fire. She felt so cold that she ached.

While she was warming herself, she heard someone moving through the grass. She stiffened. The door opened and in walked Lance. He closed it hurriedly behind him, and pulled up a stool by the fire.

'Sorry I'm late. I had a bit of trouble getting out.'

He opened his hands to the flames. He looked awkward, secretive. For a while neither of them spoke.

'How did the rugger go?' she asked.

'Actually it went splendidly. Vernon-Jones thinks that if I carry on the way I'm going, I've a good chance of getting into the team next year.'

'Who's this Vernon-Jones?'

'He's the chap I was telling you about. The one I've started running with.'

Rusty stared into the fire. 'Next year?' she murmured. 'So you really won't be coming back to America with me?'

'I never said I would,' he remarked quietly.

She snatched up a couple of pieces of wood from the tub and hurled them into the fire.

'Look,' he said. 'Why don't you just make the best of things? I'm sure you'll make friends at your school soon.'

Rusty whirled around and glared at him. 'I suppose now that they've started getting friendly, you don't want us to be buddies any more. That it?'

He blushed. 'Not exactly. Only it is getting rather dangerous.'

'O.K.,' she snapped. 'Are you trying to tell me you don't want to come here any more?'

He clasped his hands together tightly and looked down at the floor.

'You've done an awful lot to help me,' he muttered. 'And I'm really grateful. I mean, what with the fires and cheering me up when I was miserable.'

'Uh-huh. And?'

'It's just that I'd hate it if any of the other chaps found out about me meeting you here.'

'In case they tell? And you get a beating?'

'No, I could face that. But . . .' He hesitated. 'It's because you're a girl.'

Rusty looked at him quickly. 'But we're not doing anything mushy. We're not dating or . . .'

'No. It's not that. You see, if they thought I had a friend who was a girl, they wouldn't think much of me. They'd laugh at me or think I was stupid or a bit of a namby-pamby. I wouldn't have a hope of getting in a team then.'

A namby-pamby? Where had she heard that word before? She had a vague memory of crouching down by some stairs, eavesdropping. And then she remembered. It was what her father had called Charlie.

'So a namby-pamby is a boy who likes girls, is that it?'

'No. It's being wet, you know, oversensitive. Cowardly. Like a girl. Empty-headed, soppy, that sort of thing.'

338

Rusty sprang angrily to her feet. 'You really take the cake!'

Lance looked almost alarmed. 'I don't think that way about you, but the other chaps will.'

'You make girls sound like creatures from outer space.'

'Well, I don't mean to. But boys *are* more adventurous and strong, you know. I mean, that's what *they* think.' He turned and pointed to the walls. 'I mean, look at all this nice stencilling you've done. Boys are no good at that sort of thing. They have to be tough,' he stammered. 'I mean, girls are good at making places homey, like . . .'

Rusty stared at him in amazement. 'What the heck's happening to you? You get into a reserve team and suddenly everything's different. Last semester you hated those "chaps", now they're "rather decent". If you want to know something,' she said, waving at the walls, 'it was *men* who used to do stencilling and make houses pretty inside. They had their own stencil cards and equipment, and they used to ride on horseback all over the place, miles and miles, and then stay at someone's place, paint their walls and furniture, even the floors, and then they'd move on again. So you're talking through your hat. You can make a place homey *and* be strong too, *and* be brainy. Boy,' she said, shaking her head. 'You are the dumbest thing out. What about the pioneers? They had to make a home in the middle of nowhere, with wild animals around them, stuff like that.'

'Well, there's no such things as pioneers now,' he said pompously.

'There certainly is. I'm one.'

'Don't be an ass. You know it's all pretend.'

'You sure have changed your tune!'

He leapt to his feet. 'It's all your fault that I can't come here again. You've made it too risky.'

'Well, those "friends" of yours'd be right about you. You *are* a pantywaist, or a namby-pamby, or whatever you call it. But not because you've been with a girl. It's because you're afraid of what *they'll* think. You're afraid to be different. You sound just like the girls at my school, cooing and spilling goo over a game. You just have to do what the darned Romans do. No wonder you like Latin!'

Lance turned on his heel, flung open the door, and slammed it behind him. Rusty felt devastated. She hadn't meant to say such hurtful things.

She sank down on the stool and buried her head in her hands.

The effects of the Number 9 treatment lingered into the next day. As soon as she had swallowed down some breakfast, she began running for the lavatory again.

As the lessons dragged slowly on, Rusty kept her eye on the door, waiting once again to be discovered. She had history in the afternoon and found, to her alarm, that the Bull kept staring at her.

'Virginia Dickinson,' she roared, 'come up here.'

Rusty hauled herself forward.

'Stand there in front of me,' Miss Bullivant said. 'I want to take a good look at you.'

She peered at Rusty from her head to her feet and back up again.

'You eating?' she snapped.

'Yes, Miss Bullivant.'

'Well, you look too thin, if you ask me. Far too thin.'

'Must have been the Number 9 Matron gave me.'

At that the class giggled. Rusty was amazed. It was the first time she had ever made any girl laugh at a joke of hers.

She was halfway down the aisle when Miss Bullivant called out to her again. 'Feed you at home all right, do they?'

Rusty turned around. She could feel her face growing hot. 'Yes, Miss Bullivant.'

The teacher gave a grunt and returned to the Monmouth Rebellion.

The classes were over and Rusty sat in the large room where the fourth-year prep was taken. She propped her head up with her hand. She was still smarting inside from the quarrel with Lance. She felt he had somehow betrayed her.

Eventually the bell rang and she gathered up her books. When she came out into the corridor, she found the prefect who was normally in charge of her on Friday evenings waiting for her.

'I'm sorry,' said Rusty. 'Am I late?'

'No. I'm early. Look,' she said, 'do you mind if I don't see you off again?'

'No. Of course not.'

As soon as Rusty was around the corner, she leaned against a wall out of sheer relief. Then, as usual, she took her grip up to the dormitory, packed, and walked out of the arched doorway to another weekend of freedom.

That weekend she did nothing but paint. The only can of paint that was still usable was dark green. She painted the table and the two makeshift stools and, while they were drying, stencilled a design of leaves and flowers in the centre of the main wall. It was a little lopsided, but it was the best she could do.

She placed a pineapple design on the centre of the table, using the ochre for the pineapple and dark brick red for the leaves at the top of it. Grandma Fitz said that the pineapple was a symbol of hospitality. She could pretend to have visitors for meals. Even as she thought of that, her stomach gave an insistent gurgle.

On Sunday afternoon she sat by the fire, just gazing around at the colours. She wished she could share it with someone. She boiled some water in the saucepan over the fire and, when it had cooled, drank it.

The next morning she posted her letter to her parents and went back into school.

She stood with the others as they recited their way through a series of prayers, sang a hymn about fighting the good fight, and then sat down for the sermon from the Headmistress.

'And now,' said Miss Bembridge after several announcements had been made, 'I have some rather good news for you all. Today I will be sending off letters to your respective parents informing them that half-term will be two days longer than planned. The reason for this extension is that a team of workmen will be coming to the school to remove the scaffolding.'

32

She knew it was risky running away during the week because by breakfast she would already be missed, but she judged that she didn't have any choice. She was all right for money, for she still had the pocket money that she should have handed over to Matron, plus her fare back for the return journey at half-term in case her mother couldn't meet her. She had no idea what time the trains started running. She just hoped that it was before anyone would notice her absence.

For the last time she laid and lit a fire in the Cabin. As the flames leapt and flickered up the chimney, she gazed at the walls, drinking in all the colourful designs. It wasn't just *her* in the Cabin, it was bits of everyone else, too. The stencilling was Grandma Fitz, the colours were Aunt Hannah, the smattering of basic carpentry was Uncle Bruno and Gramps, the books and knick-knacks on the shelves were Kathryn, the chopped-up wood was her and Skeet and Janey and all the gang on Sunday nights in the winter; and in the midst of it all were the carpentry tools that Beatie had left her, and the overalls and headscarf belonging to her mother.

She changed into her jeans, plaid shirt, school cardigan, Windbreaker and sneakers, lowering the turn-ups of her jeans so that they hid her regulation school socks. She'd have given anything to have had her Beanie and a bag of some sort, but there was no way she could have smuggled them up to the dormitory from the cloakroom without being caught. They weren't even allowed to take a book upstairs.

She stuffed her screwdriver, gimlet and pliers into one of her Windbreaker pockets, and her stencil brushes, knife and torch into the other. They were the only tools small enough to fit in. She put on her trapper cap and took a last look at the Cabin. It broke her heart to leave it, together with the rest of the carpentry tools, but once she had got back to the Omsks, she'd work and save up for some others. She closed the door firmly behind her and headed for the woods.

There was no one at the station but her. The ticket man eyed her suspiciously through the grille as she asked for Exeter and pushed the money through.

'Bit young to be travelling on yer own, aren't you? 'Ow old are you?'

'Fourteen,' she lied. 'Going on fifteen.' After all, she was as tall as the Fifth-formers. No reason why she shouldn't get away with it.

'American, aren't you?'

She nodded.

He frowned. ''Aven't I seen you 'ere before?'

'No. I'm always being mistaken for other people. I guess it's 'cause I have such a regular sort of face.'

He grunted. 'You being met at the other end?'

'Sure I am.'

He shook his head and muttered, 'I don't know. Parents nowadays. Ain't even light yet. Wouldn't 'appen in my time. These Americans. Still, s'pose they know what they're doin'.'

Rusty took the ticket and the change as calmly as she was able. Lack of sleep and sheer tension made her rigid with cold. She stood on the windy platform and stamped her feet in an effort to prevent her toes from numbing up, and pulled down the flaps on her cap to protect her ears.

All the time, as she waited, she was expecting the ticket

man to suddenly roar out, 'Say, I know what you are. You're a runaway!'

At long last a train appeared in the distance. As it crawled slowly towards the platform, she willed it to speed up. As soon as it had stopped, she flung open a door. It was as cold inside the train as out. There was no heat on at all. The train was empty. She ran down the corridor and chose a compartment.

Even when the train started moving, she still didn't feel safe. If the school had been alerted, they might have already contacted the railway station. It was a slow train. It stopped at every single tiny station, and each time it stopped it seemed to be for ever.

Eventually she reached the station where she and her mother had had the tea and buns. She hopped out and began waiting for the connection to Exeter. To her horror, it was announced that there was a delay of two hours. The handful of people on the platform took the news with resignation. Rusty grew colder and more anxious as the minutes ticked by.

When the train had arrived and everyone had piled in, and it finally moved out of the station after waiting there a full quarter of an hour, Rusty began to relax. Again she had a compartment all to herself.

She stared out of the grubby window at bombed streets and stations and towns, interspersed with stretches of muddy or drenched green fields, and began to think about the Omsks.

She had loved being called 'one of them Omsk kids', but she remembered how Skeet and Kathryn, Alice and Jinkie called Aunt Hannah and Uncle Bruno Mom and Pop, and how, when she accidentally called them that too, they would gently remind her that her real mom and pop were missing her and loved her, and that although they loved her as if she was their own daughter, she had to remember that someone else did too.

She began to wonder if perhaps they'd want her back after all. Without her they'd be a real family again.

Although they felt like her real parents, they weren't, and they never could be. As she swallowed her tears, she saw everyone in Connecticut drifting away from her. Skeet was roller-skating with a girl who was using her roller-skates, and Janey was dating someone and had probably made new friends. As she sat in the cold bumpy train, she felt that no one would want to be friends with her ever again.

By the time the train had arrived at Exeter and she had stumbled out on to the platform, she had decided that the Omsks, like her parents, wouldn't want her living with them.

She handed in her ticket and wandered out of the station. The next train to Plymouth would be a while yet, so she decided to take a walk.

As she made her way down a side street, she noticed two W.V.S. vans parked outside a building. She froze.

Suddenly it was August, and she was sitting beside her mother in the large furniture-van, and it was the first time they had been together in five years; and she knew then that she just had to have a talk with her, explain everything.

She looked around for a phone booth and saw one standing, dark and solitary, in front of a flat landscape of rubble. She stepped inside and fumbled in her pockets for pennies, reading the instructions about button A and button B. She was trembling so much, she had to keep taking deep breaths so she could think straight. She lifted the receiver and dialled the operator. Eventually a woman answered, and Rusty gave her mother's last name and address.

Finally, the operator was speaking to her again. Rusty put her money into the slot.

'You're through now,' said the woman.

Rusty was astounded. 'What do you mean, I'm through? I can't be. I haven't even started talking yet.'

'I'm sorry?' began the woman, but Rusty slammed the phone down.

'Typical *English* phone,' she yelled, and she pushed open the door in a rage.

She had hardly walked a few yards when she heard the sound of money tinkling behind her. She turned in time to see a small, shabbily dressed boy pressing button B in the phone booth and collecting the money *she* had just put into it. And then it suddenly dawned on her. Of course! With English phones, when they said you were through, it meant that you were *connected*. The boy looked up quickly and ran as fast as he could in the opposite direction. It was the last straw.

'Right,' she muttered, and she stalked back towards Exeter station.

She had just enough for a ticket to Plymouth. This time the train was smaller. She remembered now, it was one of the kind that had no corridor. Instead, the compartments had a door at each end. She found an empty one, sat down, and leaned her head against the window. She caught a glimpse of her reflection in the glass. She'd grown used to being pale, but she wasn't prepared for the two dark grooves etched below her eyes.

Just as the train began to move, the door was flung open. Rusty jumped and her heart started thumping. But it was only a plumpish woman in her fifties with a basket of shopping. She returned to gazing out of the window.

It wasn't till the train pulled out of the next station that she realized that the woman was staring at her. Suddenly, the train was running alongside the estuary, where the boats and birds sat bobbing on the water and those beautiful little houses stood on the hill opposite. And then, within minutes, there was the sea, large and tranquil, lying right alongside her. And for once she wanted to slow down. She loved this crazy train and the tiny railway line and the pinky-brown cliffs.

Just then the woman leaned forward.

''Scuse me,' she drawled, 'but I'm sure I knows a relation of yours.'

Rusty looked at her, startled.

'I can see yer not English, though. American, are you?'

Rusty nodded. She was growing used to not giving explanations.

'Funny,' the woman said, puzzled. 'What's yer name?'

'Guinivere,' Rusty blurted out.

'Guinivere what?' said the woman.

As they drew out of the next station, Rusty saw a torn advertisement on the wall. 'Virol,' she said. 'Guinivere Virol.'

The woman caught sight of the handle of Rusty's screwdriver, which was sticking out of her pocket. Rusty casually pushed it back in.

'That's a funny name,' the woman said.

'I guess,' said Rusty as brightly as she could.

'Bit young to be on yer own, ain't you?'

'I'm being met at the other end.'

'Oh. Where's that, then?'

'Plymouth. My aunt lives there.'

'Oh. Where'bouts?'

'I don't know. It's my first visit, see.'

'Well I never,' said the woman. 'You looks the spittin' image of a W.V.S. driver I used to see round 'ere.'

Rusty could feel her cheeks growing hot. She looked hastily out of the window.

The woman got off at Newton Abbot, leaving Rusty alone again. Relieved, she leaned back and closed her eyes.

The train gave a violent jolt. Rusty glanced out of the window, flung open the door, and stepped out on to the platform. As the train drew out of the station, she realized that she had got off too soon. It was the station she had arrived at when she had first come to England.

'Oh boy,' she said, hitting her head with her hand, 'what a goop!'

Strangely enough, though, she felt quite pleased to see the old place again. It was already afternoon. Maybe it was good she had got off here, after all. She could go sleep at Beatie's and then set off early for Plymouth the following day.

As she walked through the station gate, she remembered how she and her mother had been greeted by a rather anxious W.V.S. woman; how her mother had gone off to fix the van and how angry Rusty had been; how she had disapproved of her mother's messy hands and shabby appearance. Boy, she must have been unbearable.

Her thoughts were interrupted by a gentle tap on the shoulder. She jumped guiltily. It was a woman in railway uniform.

'Ticket, please,' she said, smiling.

'Oh yeah. Sure.' And she drew it out.

'This is for Plymouth,' the woman said.

'Can I use it from here tomorrow?'

''Fraid not.' Then, seeing Rusty's face, she added, 'Bring it anyway. I'll see what I can do.'

As Rusty took it back and walked away, the woman gazed after her, puzzled. 'Hey!' she yelled. 'Send me regards to yer mother.'

Rusty nodded and hurried on.

As soon as she was out of the station, she took a right turn and went on walking until she reached the tiny dirt road where Mrs Hatherley had dropped her and her mother off in November. She walked briskly past the tiny lodge-house at the entrance to the Estate, and within minutes she was looking down a grassy slope on her right to the river. The sun was out, and dotted about on the grass were snowdrops and primroses. She slowed down, afraid of reaching Beth's school too soon and being seen.

Suddenly there was a light shower of rain. She ran part of the way down the slope and stood for a while under a tree for shelter. As soon as it was over, the sun came out. She climbed up the slope again, and there across the sky was a rainbow.

Rusty stood there, mesmerized. Was it possible to fall in love with a place, when first of all you had disliked it? She hadn't thought all that much of Devon when she had first arrived. It had seemed small and tame and claustrophobic. It lacked the grandeur of Vermont and the intensity of the Connecticut climate, but now it seemed so beautiful and it smelled so rich. She stayed there, staring at the rainbow for some time, before returning to the sheltering tree. When the dusk had begun to fall, she stepped out from underneath it and climbed up the slope and back on to the path.

By the time she reached the cluster of school buildings, it was dark. No one would be able to see her if she was careful.

Rusty ran up the slope along the outside, and headed for the building at the end. From inside there came a loud animal noise, followed by a burst of laughter. She flung herself against the wall. The windows were too high up for her to be able to see in, but she realized that there were children in the hall rehearsing a play. The characters in the play had strange, foreign-sounding names like Chonga, Tonga, Wonga, Tala and Mela. There were two clowns called Sneezer and Boozer, the crew of a ship called the *Mary Jane*, a monkey, a snake, an ostrich, a baby elephant, a mother elephant and a crocodile.

Rusty squatted down beside the wall and shoved her hands deep into her pockets. She edged along the wall to where the ground fell away to a lower level. Still keeping to the outside of the buildings, she crept cautiously to a set of windows and peered in.

It was a workshop. Half a dozen boys and girls were making things out of wood. A boy in the corner was making a lampstand. A girl was making a small bookcase, and another girl was hammering a nail into an orange crate. Rusty sprinted quickly past the window and peered in so that she could see into the other side of the workshop. There, in a corner, a group of children were making scenery. Two boys were busy building flats while two other girls and a boy were painting them. There wasn't a uniform to be seen. They were all wearing old sweaters, and skirts or shorts. A man strolled over towards them and they began talking casually with him. He seemed really interested in what they were doing – but what was even more astonishing was that they called him by his first name!

Quickly, she drew herself away from the window. Looking quickly from side to side, she sprinted as fast as she could over the courtyard to the inside wall on the opposite side.

She could hear children talking and someone playing gramophone records. She edged her way along until she came to a window. Inside a small room, two girls and a boy were having a serious discussion and sharing some home-made fudge. One of the girls rewound the gramophone and turned the record over. It was a single room with one bed in it, a shelf for books, a table and chair, and all sorts of pictures stuck up on the walls. Rusty crouched down and crept past. The next room was a single, too. A boy was lying on the bed reading. She was puzzled. Maybe they didn't have dormitories at this school. In the next bedroom, four children were sitting on the floor playing a very hectic card game.

Hearing a sound behind her, Rusty ran swiftly to the end of the courtyard and pushed open a door. She was immediately surrounded by a cacophony of sound: singing, a violin, viola, cello, flute, recorder and drum, coming from various rooms inside. She ran across a hallway, flung open another door, and fled outside. Again she had a feeling that she had been seen, but she didn't dare look behind her. She leapt down the slope and ran across the field towards the farm. Although her side hurt, she staggered on past the farm and turned up a sodden dirt track.

The ground grew softer and muddier as she ran, and her feet were sucked into it, dragging her back. As soon as she reached the gate, she hauled herself over it and stumbled crazily up the wet slope towards the woods.

Once there, she leaned against a tree-trunk, gasping. A twig broke. She swung round and stared into the darkness. She took her torch out and turned it on, but there was no one there.

As she staggered on through the woods, the sky grew darker. Eventually she heard the sound of the river, and she knew that that meant she was near the bridge by Staverton Bridge station. She pushed on, her feet and ankles becoming encased in mud. The sound of the river was louder now. At last she stepped out on to the road. Ahead of her was the bridge.

As soon as she had crossed over it, she began running again, putting as much distance between her and the railway station as possible. Gradually the sky grew blacker till she really couldn't see her hand in front of her face. She turned on her torch and half walked, half ran, hoping that a car wouldn't suddenly appear from around a corner and hit her.

It took her an hour before she reached the Hatherleys' house. As soon as she saw the lights from their windows, she turned her torch off and pushed herself up against the hedge. A dog barked loudly from inside.

'Darn it!' she muttered.

With one dash, she fled past the driveway. She was too tired to stop now. Her legs had taken over, and they simply went on placing her feet one in front of the other.

She felt so relieved when she saw the opening in the hedge and the dirt lane. Ahead of her, creaking in the wind, was the long, battered wooden gate that led into the front garden of Beatie's house.

The Bomb was still standing there, looking abandoned. She staggered over the grass to the front door. It was locked.

Around the back, she found the conservatory door was open. She fell in and closed it quickly behind her. As soon as she entered, she discovered that there was still no electricity. She shone her torch through the kitchen and hall, and opened the living-room door.

The room was bare, except for the blankets she and her mother had used, which were folded up by the fireplace. She swung the light to an object in the corner by the bay window. It was a trunk with several foreign labels stuck to it. She flashed the torch's light over the surface. The trunk had been to Spain and Scotland and to places she had never even heard of, but it was definitely the one that Aunt Hannah and Uncle Bruno had mentioned in their letters.

She began sawing her way through the rope with her jack-knife. After much grunting and pushing, she prised open two large clips and lifted the lid.

She stared, amazed, at the American newspapers, magazines and comics. She'd forgotten how colourful and thick they were. She was about to read a strip cartoon when she remembered that there were things packed underneath. She pushed them aside and let out a gasp.

At the top was the round, multicoloured rag rug she had made one winter. She pulled it from the trunk and spread it out on the floor. There were a hundred memories in that rug. There were whole episodes of *The Lone Ranger*,

353

Sky King, Superman and *Captain Midnight*. And Jack Armstrong the All-American Boy with his B-17 Flying Fortress and his Uncle Jim. And Molly McGee saying, after *another* wardrobe of stuff had come crashing on top her, 'T'ain't funny, McGee.'

And then at weekends the Starlit Balloon, when the dance bands played *Your Hit Parade* and the Sunday night Jack Benny shows and the thriller, *The Shadow*. It all seemed like something she'd dreamed up. But there was the rag rug on the floor, so it must have been real.

Next in the trunk was the log-cabin patchwork quilt Grandma Fitz had made her. She laid it across her knees. Each large square was made up so that the tiny centre square was an ochre colour. Surrounding it in rectangular strips were reds and oranges. That represented the fire. Gradually the strips became darker, till the ones at the edge were black. That was supposed to be the glow around the fire becoming more shadowy. She loved it. It made her think of sitting in the dark by a log fire.

As she pulled out various sweaters and dresses, she gave a loud whoop. There were two of her thick woollen snow-suits, her sunsuits with the matching blouses, shorts and wrap-around skirts, and a large framed photograph of Frank Sinatra. There were her warm L. L. Bean boots and flannel shirts, and her red boxing-glove-shaped mittens with the fleecy lining. It was then that she discovered her books and comics underneath.

'*My Friend Flicka*!' she whispered. 'And *The Yearling*!' She'd wept buckets over that.

There were horsey books, Nancy Drew mystery books, *Bambi* and *Lassie Come Home* and the Terhune books – all dog stories like *Treve* and *Wolf*, *The Way of a Dog* and *Crazy Quilt*.

'A collie down is a collie never beaten,' she stated. 'Oh no! I don't believe it!'

It was *Lochinvar Luck*, the Terhune book that her Girl

Scout troop had given her when she'd been sick. On the front it had a picture of a collie standing on a cliff top, and in the background was a fiery sky and tall green fir trees in a valley. Between the pages was a tiny card, with flowers in a basket on one side, and underneath 'Best Wishes for a Speedy Recovery' were lots of tiny signatures that filled both sides of the card.

There were also several Ernest Thompson Seton books all about coyotes and wolves and bears, including some of the ones she used to borrow from Gramps' library in Vermont.

'*Old Silver Grizzle*,' she muttered. '*Lives of the Hunted, Wild Animals I Have Known, The Biography of a Silver Fox.*' She gave a yell. '*The Bobbsey Twins!*'

She flicked open a book about a church mouse. 'Ah, here it is:

> '*Snap, whack, bang,*
> *Goes the snap-rat bang,*
> *Goes snap bang,*
> *Goes whack bang,*
> *Fuss, fuss, fuss!*'

She used to love Uncle Bruno reading that out loud.

And there were lots of other books in the trunk, books she'd loved when small, like the two Thornton W. Burgess books, *Old Mother West Wind* and *The Adventures of Peter Cottontail*, and, joy of joys, *Ferdinand the Bull*, who loved to sit under a tree and smell the flowers, rather than go into a bull-ring.

'Charlie will just love him,' she whispered.

She lowered the book. What was she talking about? She was leaving Charlie behind.

She put it aside as a familiar sound filled the room. 'Oh my gosh,' she murmured. 'Rain!' And she ran for the door with her torch.

'Now just hold your horses,' she shouted as she stumbled weakly up the stairs with a bucket and bowl.

As soon as she had dumped them under the drips, she draped herself over the banisters and slid down. It took an enormous effort to muster up enough energy to carry the next armful of containers up the stairs. Once she had laid them out, she collapsed on the landing and sat with her back against the railings, her legs outstretched. As the rain continued to hammer on the roof, Rusty sat, exhausted and cold, listening to the different-sounding drips. She remembered the last time she had been up there, how she had seen her mother laugh out loud for the first time and how they had sung 'Ten Green Bottles'.

And as she sat there, she realized, in spite of the fact that she still didn't know an awful lot about her mother, that she had grown to love her and that she didn't want to leave her again. And as she sobbed in the dark, under the leaking ceiling, among all the drips and plops, she told herself she was sure pioneers must cry sometimes.

By the time she had stopped crying, she had made up her mind that she would find a way of returning to Benwood House the following day. She dragged herself down the stairs to the living room, pulled her patchwork quilt over to the fireplace where the blankets were folded, lay on the floor and dragged them over her. She didn't even take off her cap or her muddy sneakers. She was just so cold, she couldn't move.

She dreamed that she could smell wood-smoke, and that when she woke up, Mrs Hatherley, Beth and Harry were building up a large fire in the grate, and warming bricks in front of it. Then she dreamed that they were removing her sneakers and socks, wrapping pieces of flannel around the bricks, and placing them by her feet and body. And as she lay there, with the warmth of the bricks soaking into her, she saw Beth and Harry sitting in front of the fire with old blankets around their shoulders; and once, when she opened her eyes, Harry turned round and smiled, and she knew he didn't think she was a pompous ass any more, and she sank back into the warmth, strangely contented.

33

Peggy stared silently at the hastily painted cream walls. She was hardly aware of the other people standing in the room. She was too stunned. She took in the yellow and barn-red flower designs, the different-coloured greens in the leaves and the vines that trailed along the walls, the bird designs in the panelled door and around the two windows. She noticed her daughter's dressing gown and pyjamas flung over the camp-bed, next to Peggy's own overalls and scarf, and the carpentry tools arranged neatly on one of the shelves next to the stencils.

On the dark-green table with its central pineapple design stood an oil-lamp. A few small flowers and tendrils were stencilled down the table legs and on the two matching stools. Another lamp stood on the step in front of the fireplace. Leaning against it was an unopened envelope addressed to Miss Bembridge, but it was the note above which caught her attention. It was a piece of torn wallpaper that had been stuck on to the nail from which the mirror hung. On it in scrawled handwriting it read:

Dear Lance,
They're taking away the scaffolding so I'm running away. I'm going back home. I'm sorry I was mad at you. I hope you get into the team.

Love Rusty.

She glanced at the thirteen-year-old boy in the scarlet-and-grey uniform, and she felt sorry for him. He looked so small and pale among the adults who surrounded him.

His Housemaster had his arm around his shoulder. He looked like a kindly man.

Miss Paxton, Rusty's Housemistress, stood next to a policeman who was in the process of taking down information. 'And where do you think she's heading, sonny?' he asked.

'I promised I wouldn't say,' Lance muttered. He looked hastily at his Housemaster. 'We didn't do anything wrong, sir. Except . . .' He faltered.

'Yes?' said the police quietly.

'I stole some sandpaper from the woodwork room.'

'Anything else?' said the policeman.

Lance shook his head. 'I'm sorry I took it, sir,' he said to the teacher. 'She did try and give me money so that I could buy it, but I couldn't get it because I didn't go into town.'

'What did my daughter want sandpaper for?' said Peggy shakily.

'She mended this table. One of the ends was broken, too, so she sawed off both ends to make it even. She wanted to sand it, and round the corners, before painting it.'

'My daughter mended and painted this table?'

He nodded. 'And the stools. She painted the walls and did the stencilling and fixed the shelves up and dried out the books and . . .' He paused. 'She called it her Cabin in the Woods.'

Peggy was shattered. She had had no idea that her daughter was so talented. She had honestly believed that she was doing the best for her by making her give up art and gymnastics, in order to take extra Latin, French and maths, for she saw university as the only alternative to the cooking course her husband had planned for her. It horrified her to realize that she had behaved in the same way towards her daughter as her parents, mother-in-law and husband had behaved towards herself. So many people all expecting her to be what she wasn't, all attempting to prevent her from doing what she wanted, as if the act of her wanting anything was a selfish crime. Even now, the little work she did for the W.V.S. was disapproved of. Instead, she was expected to sit at home and receive people.

'She taught me how to make fires,' Lance mumbled, 'so I wouldn't get the cane so often. I helped her a bit with her Latin. It was a sort of swap. She said her Latin mistress hated her, and she *had* to catch up with Latin because –'

'That's not true,' interrupted Miss Paxton hurriedly.

Lance blushed. It was obvious that he hadn't realized who she was.

'The girl was just insolent. Believe me, I tried my best with her. You can see by all this,' she said, indicating the Cabin, 'what a deceitful, uncontrollable creature she is.'

Peggy ignored her. She gazed intently at Lance. 'Was she *very* unhappy?'

He nodded.

'And you?'

He nodded again. 'It's my fault really,' he began. 'I told her I wasn't coming here again and we had a quarrel. I'd made friends with someone else.' He turned to the Housemaster. 'Will I be expelled?'

'That's for the Headmaster to decide.'

'Please, sir, I don't mind being caned, but please . . .'

'I'll put in a good word for you,' he said gently. 'But you must tell the police where you think she might have gone.'

Just then the sound of someone running very fast through the grass and across the hallway made them all turn sharply.

The door was flung open, and there stood a red-faced prefect. 'She's come back,' she panted. 'She's at school. She's with a Mrs Hatherley.'

Peggy stifled a cry. 'Oh, thank heaven,' she whispered.

They were a strange crowd walking through the woods.

Lance took the lead, as he knew the trail signs that Rusty had laid, and it was a better route. His Housemaster strode firmly by his side. The policeman, the prefect, Peggy and Miss Paxton followed. The latter two did not even look at each other but stared silently ahead, both angry for different reasons.

When they reached the school wall, the policeman turned to the Housemaster.

'I don't believe we need trouble you any more, sir. I think it might be wiser to take the boy back to school. We'll be in touch.'

The Housemaster nodded. 'Come along, Brownlow,' he said.

Lance looked up at Peggy. 'Will you tell Rusty something for me?' he asked.

'Of course I will.'

'Will you tell her I didn't mean all those things I said about girls?'

Peggy nodded.

Lance turned, his head bowed, and he and the Housemaster set off down the sloping field.

As soon as they were approaching the school gates, Peggy had a strong desire to run towards the building, just to catch a glimpse of her daughter. For a moment she remembered her, aged seven, a timid child bound for America, a small suitcase in her hand and a label on her overcoat. And she remembered, too, the anguish she had felt as the tiny girl had joined the other children and then turned back to wave; how she had been unable to say, 'Goodbye, Virginia'; how the words had stuck in a lump at the back of her throat, for it was as though her heart was breaking into a thousand tiny pieces and she didn't want her daughter to know. She just wanted her to be safe.

Now, as she walked slowly up the school drive, a harsh

gust of wind blew suddenly across the grounds, so that the group staggered a little from the shock of it.

Peggy noticed the scaffolding. 'Miss Paxton,' she said quietly, 'how far up are the windows to the dormitories?'

'Virginia's dormitory is at the back of the building,' Miss Paxton replied evasively.

'But how far up is it?'

'Second set of windows down from the roof.'

Peggy gazed up. It was a terrific height. And to think her daughter must have climbed up and down it, in the dark, in her night attire, night after night. She realized even more acutely how desperate Rusty must have been to have taken such a risk. At times she must have frozen on that scaffolding.

They approached the arched front entrance to the school. In the panelled hall she could see two figures seated on chairs. She strode quickly towards them and gazed down at her daughter. She was shocked. Virginia had lost at least ten pounds in weight.

Rusty stared at her trapper cap, which she was twisting in her hands.

'She was at your place,' said Mrs Hatherley. 'I didn't force her here. She had already decided to come back.'

'But why didn't you phone? I've been at my wits' end.'

'She was in a terrible state last night. I've never seen anyone so cold. I thought I'd wait until she'd had a good night's sleep and let her tell me her side of things before phoning. I phoned several times this morning, but the line was engaged.'

'My mother-in-law,' muttered Peggy.

'So we came here to straighten things up at school.'

The policeman cleared his throat. Peggy had quite forgotten there were other people present.

'I won't say anything to the young lady, ma'am,' he began. 'Looks like she's learnt her lesson. Looks like she could do with a good meal and all.'

362

Miss Paxton pursed her lips. 'I'll have a talk with Miss Bembridge,' she stated, and with that she and the prefect walked up the stairway.

Peggy knelt down in front of Rusty and took hold of her hands. They were icy. She squeezed them.

'Why didn't you tell me how unhappy you were?'

'Because you looked unhappy, too,' Rusty whispered. She glanced up quickly. 'I'm awful sorry,' she blurted out. 'Everything just happened one on top of the other, and when they said they were going to take the scaffolding away, I knew I wouldn't ever be able to go to the . . .' She stopped.

'The Cabin in the Woods?'

Rusty looked surprised. 'How do you know about that?'

'Lance told me.'

'Lance?! But how? I mean . . . I never squealed on him. Did he squeal on me?'

'You left a note for him, remember? All the police had to do was to make inquiries at the boys' schools around here for someone called Lance. It didn't take them long to find him.'

'But how did they find the Cabin?'

'Soon after you were reported missing, the police began searching the area. They came across the bombed house fairly quickly, and inside was your note.'

'Mother,' she said frantically, 'will Lance get expelled?'

'I shouldn't think so. His Housemaster seemed awfully kind. I think he'll stand by him.'

'I did try,' Rusty murmured, 'but every time I was friendly with someone or got interested in class, it all turned out wrong.'

Peggy smiled sympathetically. She turned to Mrs Hatherley. 'Ruth?'

'Don't say anything. Beth and Harry are holding the fort. We're more than pleased to help out.'

'Do you want to stay overnight? I can put you up.'

She shook her head. 'If you don't mind, I'll be gettin' on back.'

Just then the prefect came down the stairs. 'Mrs Dickinson,' she said, 'Miss Bembridge would like to see you and Virginia upstairs.'

Rusty hauled herself to her feet. 'Thanks for everything, Mrs Hatherley.'

Ruth Hatherley gave a dismissive wave.

'I suppose we'd better go and face the music,' said Peggy.

Rusty nodded, and together they followed the prefect up the stairs.

It was all over very swiftly. There was nothing her mother could say that would change Miss Bembridge's mind. Rusty was to be expelled. She listened silently as the Headmistress described her as quick-tempered, wild, deceitful, a bad member of the community, but, more than that, a thoroughly bad influence. Expressions like 'boy-mad' and 'a threat to decent young girls' came thundering across her desk. Rusty couldn't believe she was describing her. She knew that she had done wrong, and she was sorry, but she was quite prepared to turn over a new leaf.

And then, amazed, she watched her mother grow angry. 'It was quite obvious that my daughter was unhappy. Just look at her,' she said. 'She's underweight and thoroughly ill. Surely her Housemistress or a teacher must have seen that something was wrong?'

'I believe,' butted in the Headmistress, 'that all is not as it should be at home, Mrs Dickinson. I have been having a long and interesting conversation with both your husband and your mother-in-law.' She paused. 'I think it's a case of like mother, like daughter.'

'And what do you mean by that?'

Miss Bembridge glanced aside at Rusty. 'There are

certain subjects I prefer not to discuss in front of a child. Although I suspect, since this escapade with the boy, she is probably a child no longer.'

'I don't understand,' said Rusty. 'What does she mean?'

Her mother took her hand and squeezed it.

'She looks quite the young innocent, doesn't she?' commented Miss Bembridge.

Peggy rose angrily to her feet. 'Is that all you have to say?'

Miss Bembridge sat stonily erect, her hands clasped. 'No. I suggest that if you wish to correct your daughter's behaviour, it would be in her best interests if she were put into a convent school. A strict one. Your husband agrees with me.'

'Thank you,' said Peggy stiffly. 'I presume, unlike her former principals, that you won't be writing anything favourable in her school report.'

'I think that rather unlikely.' She stared at Rusty, her face white with suppressed anger. 'Never, in all my years at Benwood House,' she said hoarsely, 'has a girl disgraced herself and the school in such a despicable manner.' She stood up. 'Matron will send on your daughter's trunk. Meanwhile I would appreciate it if your daughter would collect as many of her belongings as possible.' She glanced disdainfully at Rusty's attire. 'I would also appreciate it if she left the school grounds in the Benwood House uniform. A prefect will be outside to escort her to the dormitory.' And with that she indicated with a curt nod that they should leave.

It was the same prefect who had shown Rusty around as a new girl on her first day. 'Hi,' said Rusty quietly.

'Hello,' the girl answered, her face reddening. 'I've been told to take you to the dormitory.'

Rusty followed her up the stairs, dazed. It felt odd walking through the drab brown corridors in her jeans and sneakers, like walking into church in a bathing suit. They walked on quickly, neither of them speaking.

In the dormitory, while Rusty changed her clothes, she realized, as the baggy green gymslip hung from her shoulders, that this was the last time she would ever put on the Benwood House uniform. She remembered all the coupons her mother had saved so she could buy it, and she felt guilty. She put the tie under her collar and knotted it.

'Is it straight?' she asked.

The prefect looked startled. 'Yes,' she stammered. She stood yards away, as if Rusty had some infectious disease.

While Rusty stuffed her grip with clothing, the prefect hovered awkwardly in the background, until suddenly she blurted out, 'Are you going to have a baby?'

Rusty whirled round and stared at her.

'I mean,' the girl added, red-faced, 'did you, you know, do anything with that boy?'

'No. We were just friends,' said Rusty. 'He was evacuated to the town where my American grandparents live.'

'But didn't you, you know, *do* anything?' the prefect continued. 'I mean, you can tell me.'

'What do you want to know?'

'Well, it's going around the school that you actually spent whole nights with him' – she swallowed – 'in your pyjamas. Is that true?'

'Sometimes.'

'Well, doesn't that mean,' she whispered, 'that you're going to have a baby?'

'You don't get a baby just by talking with a boy in your pyjamas,' said Rusty.

'Don't you?'

'Don't you know?'

The girl shook her head.

'Look, can't you ask someone to explain it all, or get a

book or something? I don't feel like going into it right now. O.K.?'

Rusty froze for an instant, realizing what she'd said. 'I can say O.K. for as long as I like now, I guess. Well, until they send me somewhere else.' She gave a weary sigh. 'Let's go.' And she picked up her grip and headed towards the door without a backward glance.

Her mother was sitting on a chair in the hall at the foot of the staircase. Seeing Rusty, she rose quickly and they stepped outside into a bitter February afternoon. As they walked down the school drive, Peggy gazed silently into the distance. Rusty wished her mother would speak to her. She figured she must be awful disappointed with her and very ashamed.

'Mother,' she began.

'Yes?' Peggy said, still gazing ahead.

'You know me and Lance? Well, we never did anything mushy. We weren't going steady or anything. Honest.'

'I know.'

'I had no friends at school, see. I was lonely. I just wanted a buddy, that's all.'

Her mother stopped and put her arm around Rusty's shoulders. Rusty slipped her arm around her waist.

'Mother?'

'Yes.'

'I'm awful sorry about what I said about Harvey. I guess . . .' She hesitated. 'Were you lonely too?'

Her mother gave her a light squeeze. 'Dreadfully.'

They both quickened their step. Once clear of the gates, Peggy suddenly gave a relieved smile.

'And do you know something?' she said. 'I don't regret a single minute of our friendship.' And she gave one of Rusty's plaits an affectionate tug. 'He made me laugh.'

They resumed walking, Rusty running to keep up with her.

'But what about me?' she blurted out. 'Aren't you mad at me? Aren't you ashamed of me? I mean, my life is ruined now, and . . .' She paused. 'Mother? What are you doing?'

Her mother had hitched up her skirt and jumped over the ditch, towards the bushes.

'I'm going back for your carpentry tools.'

'Oh, Mother!' Rusty said, breaking into a smile.

But she could get no further. She was too happy to speak.

'Come on,' Peggy said. 'You'll have to come with me. I need you to show me the way.'

34

Rusty sat on the window-seat in what used to be Beatie's bedroom and gazed out at the garden and river. It was a morning in May. She leaned back in the alcove and hugged her knees, drinking in the sunlight that flooded through the windows. She had loved this room ever since she had first seen it. Now it was her very own.

She hadn't had time to do much to it yet, but even just removing the blackout curtains and that revolting dark wallpaper had made an immediate difference. She and her mother had filled in the holes in the walls and had sanded them all down, and her mother had offered to help paint them, once she was able to get hold of some pale distemper. And then Rusty could stencil away to her heart's content.

In the centre of the room was a dark wooden bed with her patchwork quilt on it, and on the wooden floor her rag rug. The room had – what would Aunt Hannah say? Potential. That was it.

She wished her father had come to live in the house too, but her mother explained to her how he wanted things to be just the way they were before 1940 and, as she said, she couldn't start pretending she was the same person as she had been six years ago. That was something Rusty understood. It would be like her parents wanting her to be a seven-year-old when instead she was almost a teenager. But all the same, she did feel sorry for him, for in spite of his anger she reckoned he was missing something. Every day, Rusty was discovering that her mother was really a lot of fun. She was just a little shy, that was all.

It was now two months since Rusty had been expelled. She was at last beginning to put on weight again, so that her jeans hung from the waist instead of baggily from her hips.

After her return to her father's house the atmosphere had been so taut she had hardly dared to breathe. More fights followed, interspersed with periods of polite and uncomfortable silence, and her grandmother insisted that she remain either out of sight or constantly guarded. Again, she was treated as if she had some contagious disease. She had learnt very quickly that expulsion had brought shame on the family, and there was talk of sending her away as soon as possible to a convent boarding school. Her mother had simply said no, she was to go to a day school; but her grandmother and father stated that no day school would accept her, that she was marked for life, and that they'd just have to be very grateful if they could find a strict convent school that would be willing to take her on.

And so it went on, until one day, when her mother was out with Charlie, her father had called her to his study and had informed her that he and her mother were going to separate and that she could either choose to go to Devon with her and Charlie, or stay with him. And even as Rusty stood there, stunned, she saw the hurt in his eyes.

'But if I stay with you,' she had said, 'you'll send me away again.'

And he had said yes, he would, so that she would have another chance.

He hadn't even waited for her to reply. He said that he could see what her answer was, and that she had better realize that he would 'cut them off without a penny'.

And Rusty had said, 'But why don't you come to Devon, too?'

It was out of the question, of course.

Once back in Devon, though, the sadness wore off a bit. She was still surprised by the lush greenness of the place and the soft air. But it had been her visit to the school on the Estate that had made the real difference.

She had been staggered when her mother informed her that she had made inquiries about her becoming a pupil there, and that the Head would like to meet them both.

Rusty dreaded the meeting, for her mother had already told him of her expulsion. She had been totally unprepared for the short, balding man in his fifties with the spotty bow-tie and old jacket. She had watched him light up his pipe, and had liked him instantly. When he spoke to her, he encouraged her to speak, and he listened as if he really wanted to know about her. The other teachers she met were like that, too.

When she and her mother finally left the school, knowing that she had been accepted, they caught each other beaming and had burst out laughing.

'It wasn't as bad as I thought,' Peggy had said.

'It wasn't for me, either,' added Rusty.

And now here it was. Her first day. It would have been nice if she'd been with Beth in the Senior Section, but since she knew she would be spending the summer term in Harry's group in the Middle School before transferring with him in the autumn, she had started to spend more time with him. Beth was always up at the school farm anyway, helping out. Mrs Hatherley said jokingly that she thought Beth would be quite happy to stay there as a boarder.

Peggy yelled up the stairs. She still called her Virginia, but Rusty was getting used to having two names.

She flung open the door and nearly tumbled over a bucket on the landing. She glanced at the cracked ceiling. Her mother had actually started getting the wheels in motion for having the roof fixed. The only snag was lack of money. She guessed that all her mother's savings were going towards paying her and Charlie's school fees.

She leapt down the stairs and went flying out through the front door. Charlie was sitting in the back-seat of the Bomb, bouncing impatiently up and down. His hair had grown back so that he looked like a little boy again, not like a convict out on parole. He leaned over the front seat and beeped the horn. 'O.K., O.K.,' said Rusty, breaking into a run. 'Boy,' she said, sliding in next to her mother, 'I've never seen anyone so eager to get to school.'

Charlie started singing a made-up song with a tune that changed constantly and went something like 'Going to see the rabbits and the mice, and the mice and the rabbits, and the rabbits and the mice'.

'What's he talking about?' asked Rusty.

The engine gave a bang before subsiding into a loud rumble.

'Pets' Corner!' yelled her mother.

'I'm going to a *proper* school now,' said Charlie, standing up and leaning on the seat.

'We won't be going to any school,' said Peggy, 'if you don't sit down. I can't see through the back window.'

Charlie sat down with a bump. 'Can you see now?' he said.

'Wonderfully.'

She backed the rattling machine out of the garden and on to the dirt road. Rusty sat back and rattled with it.

'I'm a wibbly wobbly wibble,' sang Charlie. 'I'm a wobbly wibbly wobble.'

At last the car bumped out on to the small road and they were on their way.

Rusty still couldn't help feeling nervous. That Headmaster and the other teachers had seemed so friendly that she began to wonder if she had dreamt it all. Maybe they had been nice to her because her mother was around, and, as soon as she'd left her there, they'd all start picking on her.

'I'll see if I can get hold of a second-hand bicycle,' said her mother. 'Then you'll be able to come back home independently.'

'That'd be swell,' said Rusty eagerly. 'I like your English bicycles.' She swallowed. 'Sorry. I mean *our* English bikes.'

'Don't worry,' said Peggy. 'I think you'll always be half American.'

Rusty leaned back and stared out of the window.

'I wonder if I'll feel all English, or all American, ever,' she murmured.

'Do you want to?'

'I don't know. Do you think you can belong to two countries?'

'Perhaps. Sometimes it's an advantage. You can stand in one and look back at the other from a distance. See things more clearly.'

'Is that what happened to you when you came to live out here?'

Her mother nodded.

'How come Father didn't, then, when he went away?'

'I don't know. Perhaps it's because that house is all he's ever known.'

'Too bad it wasn't bombed.'

'Yes,' said her mother sadly. 'I must admit that thought had entered my head.'

Just then Charlie piped up, 'Are there going to be any more bombs, Mummy?'

'No. The War's over now.'

'Are we nearly there?'

'Almost.'

'Do you think,' whispered Rusty, 'Father will come here, I mean, you know, on vacation?'

'I doubt it.' She reached over and squeezed Rusty's

knee. 'But I expect you'll be able to go and stay there sometimes.'

Rusty made a face.

'It won't be so bad,' said Peggy. 'Give it time.'

'I guess. At least I'll know I'll be coming back here.'

Her mother smiled.

As soon as they had reached the Estate buildings, Peggy turned down the lane that ran opposite the archway.

Rusty could feel her stomach fluttering. 'Do I still have to take Latin?' she asked.

'That's up to you.'

Rusty swivelled round in her seat.

'I really do get to choose what I study?'

'Yes.'

'Crumbs!'

Peggy burst out laughing.

'What's so funny?'

'You. That's the first time I've heard you say *crumbs*.'

Rusty grinned. 'I guess I picked that up off Harry.'

'Yes. Plus a few riper words, I've noticed.'

She had hardly stopped the car when Charlie scrambled out of the door and started running.

'We're almost there, aren't we?' said Rusty quietly.

Her mother nodded.

While Charlie raced on ahead, she and her mother sauntered at a more leisurely pace. Rusty noticed that her mother was looking thoughtful.

She stopped and placed her hand on Rusty's shoulder. 'You know,' she said, 'there'll still be restrictions here. I mean, rationing will go on, the food won't be as good and plentiful as it is in America, materials of all kinds are in desperately short supply, and you'll have to start all over again trying to make friends.'

'I know it.'

They approached a long grey building. The top half of the house was constructed of planks of wood that

374

overlapped one another. The bottom half of the house was grey stone.

'Clapboard!' exclaimed Rusty, pointing at the wood. 'Like in New England.'

'Yes. You'll probably find the odd American influence around,' explained her mother. 'The couple who bought the Estate and started the school – one of them was American. And your Headmaster used to be head of a school in America, I believe.'

Eventually they saw her school. It was a large house that stood opposite the three boarding houses. Rusty loved the shape of it. The walls went all in and out and, high up, a row of small sheltered windows lay tucked under the eaves of the roof. Suddenly she caught sight of a boy in an old shirt, shorts and sandals. There was no mistaking who he was. No one else she knew had ears that big. She waved.

By now she was conscious of other children running around chattering and laughing, and she began to feel extraordinarily shy. As she and her mother stood awkwardly on the path and two ten-year-olds hurtled by them on roller skates, Rusty stuffed her hands into her Windbreaker pockets.

Harry strolled over towards them.

'Hi,' she said.

He grinned and gave an exaggerated bow. 'I'm your escort.'

'How do you mean?'

'I'm going to show you around. Make you feel at home. That sort of thing.'

Rusty had hardly opened her mouth to speak when a strange rattling sound caused her to turn. She gave a gasp, for there moving towards them was the most peculiar-looking car she had ever seen: it had no roof at all; the front was squarish in shape, while the back tailed to a point like the end of a boat, with long wooden panels of varnished teak. There were two curved windscreens in the front and another, longer one for whoever sat in the back. The large wheels with their narrow tyres had big spokes in them. Two horns protruded from below the radiator, and a thermometer stuck up at the top. It had no doors, and the square bonnet was held down by a leather strap. Seated happily behind the wheel was the Headmaster. As the car slowed to a stop, it gave a few little *putt-putt* sounds from a large curved exhaust pipe at the back. The Headmaster gave Rusty and her mother a wave and then climbed out.

'Hello,' he said warmly. 'Thought I'd come and see you as it's your first day.'

'You mean,' said Rusty, hardly able to keep from laughing at the car, 'you mean you came specially to see me?'

He nodded and took a pipe out of his jacket pocket. Within seconds, two small girls had coming running up. One flung her arms around him.

The Headmaster said nothing out of the ordinary to Rusty, yet he made her feel very welcome. He seemed happy to see her and pleased that she'd come to the school, and he didn't put on an act that he was doing her some great favour that she had to be eternally grateful to him for, having been expelled from her other school.

Harry tapped her on the shoulder.

'I'll give you a quick look at a couple of the classrooms and the library,' he said, 'and then we can go down to the river. I'll show you the Pet Shed and the farm, and then introduce you to the rest of the teachers and your tutor later on.'

They strode around towards the back of the house. Out of the corner of her eye Rusty noticed a couple of children staring at her. She wanted to say, 'Hi,' but after two terms of getting a bad response at her other school, she found herself ignoring them.

They peered into a sunny classroom at the corner.

Three children were leaning casually on a long wooden table, where a tall slim woman appeared to be having a conversation with them. She looked up and waved.

'Hello, Rusty,' she said.

'I'm just showing her around,' said Harry.

Rusty drew herself shyly away from the window and walked hurriedly on. Harry soon caught up with her.

'How did she know my nickname?' she said.

'I told her.' He looked concerned for a moment. 'I mean, that is what you like being called, isn't it?'

Rusty nodded.

Harry took her along sunny corridors and up the stairs to the library, which was shabby but so warm and homey. Wooden shelves filled with books went all the way up to the ceiling, and the sun cascaded into it. The long woven curtains hung in ribbons, and the carpet wasn't just threadbare, it had holes in it. One boy was sitting in an armchair, his bare legs hanging over one arm. So absorbed was he in the book he was reading that he didn't even look up when they walked in.

Rusty and Harry peered out of the large windows at the sloping green fields flecked with buttercups and daisies.

'You know,' she murmured, 'I could just spend all day looking out of the window here. It's so pretty.'

They strolled down the stairs and stepped outside while Harry told her about the hour of useful work that everyone had to do before classes. 'It can be whatever you like,' he said. 'It can be on the school farm or in the gardens, or log carrying or sweeping, or you can help mend the books. We learn bookbinding here as well as printing.'

'Do I have to do that now?'

'No, not on your first day.'

As they turned the corner of the house, Rusty let out a groan. 'Oh no!' she cried.

The bonnet of the Headmaster's car was now folded

back, and he and her mother were leaning over it, deep in discussion.

'He's mad about old cars,' said Harry.

'And my mother's nuts about engines.'

Her mother looked up. 'I thought I heard your voice,' she said. 'Guess what? I've been offered a job on the Estate.'

'You're kidding!' yelled Rusty. 'Doing what?'

'As a mechanic. They need someone to help out with maintenance here.'

Rusty shook her head in disbelief. Her mother laughed, and she and the Head returned to engine gazing.

'I'll show you the woods,' said Harry. 'We've got a hut there. I'll show you Folly Island too.'

Rusty grabbed his arm. 'Say,' she breathed, 'I just realized. If my mother has a job here on the Estate, then that means she won't have to pay fees, doesn't it? Like your parents?'

'Yes, that's right.'

'That means I can stay here. Period. Zowee!'

They broke into a run. Two boys were standing by the path. 'Hello, Harry,' they said.

Harry joined them. Rusty stood by his side.

'Hi,' she said quietly.

'Hello!' said one of the boys. 'Are you American?'

'I was evacuated out there.'

'Have you only just come back?'

'Oh no. I went to another school first.' She felt her face growing hot.

'I like your jeans,' said the other boy.

'Me too,' added his friend. 'They're American, aren't they?'

Just then a girl passed by. She was barefoot and wore a loose green frock. Her blonde hair stuck out wildly. Rusty glanced at her. The girl stared back. Her intense blue eyes were far from friendly. She scowled. 'What's so bloody special about American jeans?' she snapped. 'Bloody America.'

Rusty felt her mouth drying up. 'I didn't say they were special.'

'Oh no,' said the girl. 'You wouldn't. I suppose you're used to them.'

'Come on, Rusty,' said Harry.

He seemed so cheerful, as if the blonde girl had said nothing more than 'Nice weather we're having, isn't it?'

Rusty walked numbly beside him towards a small opening in the trees, aware only of the ground becoming less grassy, more earthy and more blurred.

Harry slid down a small slope. Rusty stumbled after him. The other two boys had gone on ahead.

Harry touched her gently on the arm. 'Don't mind her,' he whispered. 'She didn't mean it. She had a letter a few days ago from her parents. They're getting divorced, and ever since, she's just been picking on everyone.'

Rusty looked at him, startled. 'Wait there a minute,' she said, and she turned and sprinted up the slope.

The girl was walking away in the other direction.

'Hey!' yelled Rusty. 'Hey, you!'

The girl whirled around. 'What do you bloody well want?'

'We're all bloody going down to the bloody woods to bloody Folly Island. Why don't you bloody well come too?'

The girl gazed hastily down at the ground. Rusty could see that the sides of her mouth were twitching. She gave a nonchalant shrug and, against her will, her face collapsed into a smile.

'All right,' she said, and she ambled towards Rusty.

Harry was still waiting for them below. He grinned up at them. As they slid together down the slope to join him, Rusty put her arm around the girl's shoulder.

'My name's Rusty,' she said. 'What's yours?'

It all started with a Scarecrow.

Puffin is seventy years old.
Sounds ancient, doesn't it? But Puffin has never been
so lively. We're always on the lookout for the next big
idea, which is how it began all those years ago.

Penguin Books was a big idea from the mind of
a man called Allen Lane, who in 1935 invented
the quality paperback and changed the world.
**And from great Penguins, great Puffins grew,
changing the face of children's books forever.**

The first four Puffin Picture Books were hatched in 1940 and the
first Puffin story book featured a man with broomstick arms called
Worzel Gummidge. In 1967 Kaye Webb, Puffin Editor, started the
Puffin Club, promising to **'make children into readers'**.
She kept that promise and over 200,000 children became
devoted Puffineers through their quarterly instalments of
Puffin Post, which is now back for a new generation.

Many years from now, we hope you'll look back and
remember Puffin with a smile. **No matter what your age
or what you're into, there's a Puffin for everyone.**
The possibilities are endless, but one thing is for sure:
whether it's a picture book or a paperback, a sticker book
or a hardback, **if it's got that little Puffin
on it – it's bound to be good.**